JAG IN SPACE

A JUST DETERMINATION

JAG IN SPACE

SPACE

A JUST DETERMINATION

JACK CAMPBELL

WRITING AS JOHN G. HEMRY

TITAN BOOKS

JAG IN SPACE: A JUST DETERMINATION
Print edition ISBN: 9780857689405
E-book edition ISBN: 9780857689597

Published by Titan Books
A division of Titan Publishing Group Ltd
144 Southwark St, London SE1 0UP

First edition: February 2012
10 9 8 7 6 5 4 3 2 1

This is a work of fiction. Names, characters, places and incidents either are the products of the author's imagination or are used fictitiously, and any resemblance to actual persons, living or dead, business establishments, events, or locales is entirely coincidental. The publisher does not have any control over and does not assume any responsibility for author or third-party websites or their content.

The right of John G. Hemry to be identified as the author of this work has been asserted by him in accordance with the Copyright, Designs and Patents Act of 1988.

Visit our website: **www.titanbooks.com**

What did you think of this book? We love to hear from our readers. Please email us at: readerfeedback@titanemail.com, or write to us at the above address.

To receive advance information, news, competitions, and exclusive offers online, please sign up for the Titan newsletter on our website: **www.titanbooks.com**

A CIP catalogue record for this title is available from the British Library.

Printed and bound in Great Britain by CPI Group UK Ltd.

To Dianne, Douglas and Robert.
Sister and brothers, good times and bad.
Thanks.

For S,
as always.

"These rules are intended to provide for the just determination of every proceeding relating to trial by court-martial."

RULE 102
RULES FOR COURTS-MARTIAL
MANUAL FOR COURTS-MARTIAL, UNITED STATES

1

ENSIGN PAUL C. SINCLAIR, USN

Upon completion instruction and when directed detach Duty Under Instruction; proceed port in which USS *Michaelson* (CLE(S)-3) may be, upon arrival report Commanding Officer for duty.

For perhaps the thousandth time since receiving them, Paul Sinclair reread his orders. Not for the first time, he thought how strange it was that one ship could be so many things. In the bland official wording of his orders, USS *Michaelson* was simply a destination for a newly commissioned officer. To the transportation personnel who had read those orders and arranged his arrival here at Franklin Naval Station, the *Michaelson* had been a moving target which Paul had to intercept at some point along the ship's travels.

But in an order of battle, such as the one Paul had consulted as soon as his orders arrived, the *Michaelson* would be identified as the third ship in the Maury Class of Long Endurance Cruisers (Space). Armed with the latest weaponry, carrying over two hundred sailors and officers, armored against the hazards of space and whatever threats might be posed by other humans in the nothingness between planets.

No, Paul corrected himself, not just *Michaelson*. United States Ship *Michaelson*. A commissioned warship, part of the United States Navy and legally a small piece of the United States, floating free of the world that had birthed her.

Paul looked up and across the gap of metal flooring which was all that now separated him from the open rectangle marking the quarterdeck of the *Michaelson*. If the ship had been in dry dock, inside a huge pressurized hall, then Paul could have seen all of her smooth, elongated football shape in a glance. The apparent streamlining had nothing to do with speed but rather the need to hide military vessels from all the instruments that could detect reflections from angles, corners and flat surfaces. However, now *Michaelson* floated in open space, connected to the naval base at this one point, the rest of her invisible behind the heavy bulkheads which protected the base from empty space.

Up close, here and now, the small visible portion of the ship loomed as both the most wonderful and the most frightening thing Paul had ever seen. *Four and a half years since I held up my hand and swore the oath of service. Four years at the Academy. Six months at various specialty schools. It all comes down to this. I'm supposed to be prepared for anything. Hah. Right now I'm too nervous to think straight.*

"Sir?" Paul fought down an impulse to jerk in surprise at the question, instead turning with careful deliberation to see a mildly curious senior chief petty officer standing nearby. "Do you need something on the *Michaelson*?"

"Uh… no. I mean, yes." The senior chief's expression became a little more questioning. "That is, I'm supposed to report aboard her. She's my new ship."

"Well, that's good for you, sir. She's my ship, too. Ready to go aboard?"

"Uh, thanks, ch— senior chief." Paul, wincing inside at almost addressing a senior chief as if he were a regular chief petty officer, grasped his small allowance of luggage firmly and followed in the senior chief's wake as he strode across the short distance. It never occurred to him not to follow. Chief petty officers didn't technically run the universe, but long-standing rumor held that heaven's CPOs did all the real work that kept the universe from falling apart.

Closing on the quarterdeck, he could see another ensign standing watch there along with a junior petty officer. The ensign carried a long, archaic brass telescope cradled under one arm, a sign of her status as officer of the deck. Paul came to rigid attention at the foot of the ship's entryway, turning to face the aft end of the *Michaelson*, and rendered his best salute to the national flag invisible in its compartment near the *Michaelson*'s stern. Turning again, he faced the other ensign and saluted once more. "Request permission to come aboard."

The other officer returned the salute casually. "Granted."

The senior chief repeated the ritual, then nodded toward Paul. "Got you some fresh meat here, Ms. Denaldo."

The ensign brightened, while the petty officer looked on warily. "A new body? Great." She thrust out a hand. "Kris Denaldo. Welcome aboard."

Paul shook the offered hand. "Thanks. Paul Sinclair."

Denaldo bent over to take an obvious look at the US Naval Academy ring on Paul's hand. "Aha. A ring knocker, eh?"

"Yeah. You?"

Denaldo grinned. "Notre Dame."

"You don't look Irish."

"So me sainted mother always said. Senior chief, my messenger is off escorting a contractor. Do you mind running Mr. Sinclair aft and handing him over to Mr. Sykes?"

"No problem, Ms. Denaldo. Oh, yeah, here's them ribbons you needed." The senior chief dropped a couple of small rectangles of colored silk into Ensign Denaldo's waiting hand while she smiled with delight. Paul tried to glance at the ribbons unobtrusively. Every ribbon an officer or sailor wore on their left breast represented an award or a medal. The awards they'd received gave a thumbnail glance at their achievements and career to date, and Paul couldn't help wanting to know something of what his new shipmate Ensign Denaldo had done so far. "National Defense Medal and Space Service Deployment ribbons," the senior chief continued. "That's what you needed, right?"

"Senior chief, you're a wonder. Nobody can get these two ribbons up here. How'd you find some?"

"Geez, Ms. Denaldo, if I told you, I'd have to kill you." The chief smiled broadly at his own joke, then beckoned to Paul. "You ready, Mr. Sinclair?" At Paul's nod, the senior chief led the way through a hatch into the ship's interior.

Instantly, it felt different. Outside (if you could call the inside of a space station *outside*) had been metal and recycled air, and the interior of the *Michaelson* was more metal and more used and re-used air. But everything felt tighter. The passageway they were in was barely wide enough for two people to pass. Overhead and on either side, cables, ducts and pipes ran off in both directions, every item labeled with cryptic codes indicating its function. Paul found himself hunching together for fear of hitting his head or arms against something or someone, feeling as if as much people and equipment had been crammed inside the hull as physics would permit. Paul suspected that might be literally true, especially after the senior chief popped open a smaller hatch and peered inside a space not much larger than an average Earth-side bedroom. "Mr. Sykes?"

A tall, lanky commander with a studiously relaxed expression looked up, waving a cup in their direction. On one lapel he wore the silver oak leaf of his rank and on the other lapel the multiple-oak-leaf insignia of the Supply Corps. "At your service, senior chief. What brings you to my lounge?"

The senior chief grinned, edging back to let Paul squeeze forward and into the room. "This here's Ensign Sinclair reporting aboard. Mr. Sinclair, that there's Commander Sykes, ship's supply officer." Paul nodded, trying not to let his uncertainty show as he tried to fix names to faces. "And this here's the wardroom, actually. You can almost always find Mr. Sykes relaxing here with some coffee."

"Not always," Sykes denied. "Sometimes I'm drinking tea. Thanks, senior chief." The senior chief sketched a half-salute and left, making the small space feel even smaller as he closed the hatch behind him. "Have a seat, Mr. Sinclair." Sykes waved grandly toward one of the other chairs grouped around the rectangular metal table. "Don't worry about strapping in. That's only required while we're underway."

Paul glanced at the chair as he sat, noticing harness straps lying at the ready. "The ship maneuvers during meals?"

"Not if we can help it. Or, rather, not if the line officers actually driving the *Merry Mike* can help it." Sykes smiled again, this time conspiratorially. "Being a limited duty supply specialist, I'm just a passenger of sorts."

Paul smiled back. Sykes' rank as commander probably put him on par with the other department heads and the ship's executive officer, but those others were all line officers, a term derived from the days when such officers commanded sail-powered warships which exchanged broadsides in the line of battle with other warships. Unlike the line officers, Sykes' status as a limited duty officer meant he exercised no authority over the actual operations of the ship. Even if the executive officer (another commander, if Paul remembered right) hadn't occupied a superior position in the command hierarchy of the ship compared to a department head, she still would've been senior to Sykes on operational matters. For that matter, line officer Ensign Paul Sinclair would also be senior to Commander Sykes for operational purposes (a daunting prospect Paul tried not to dwell on) even though Sykes was his superior officer otherwise.

Paul let his gaze wander around the small room. A slightly stylized painting of the *Michaelson* in near-Earth orbit was fastened to one wall. Another held the small opening through which meals could be passed to the officers from the tiny food prep area beyond. On the third... Paul blinked, looking again as if his eyes had betrayed him. "A skull and crossbones? Why is there a pirate flag in here?"

Sykes followed Paul's look, then chuckled. "Why is it here? Because neither the executive officer nor the captain has yet seen it and ordered it taken down. Some of your fellow junior officers stuck it up this morning."

"Why?"

"Why? Ah, there you're getting into 'line' issues. Operational stuff.

You'll have to ask a fellow ship driver." Sykes rubbed his forehead, momentarily serious as he frowned in thought. "Well, welcome aboard and all that. You'll eat, um, second shift."

"Second shift?"

"That's right." Sykes looked around the wardroom himself, then shrugged. "This space can't hold every officer at once. Well, it can if they're hanging off all four bulkheads and the overhead, but not for a nice sit-down meal like the captain prefers. So, you get second shift."

Paul nodded, repeating *second shift* in his mind several times to ensure it wasn't forgotten.

"Have you heard much about food in the space fleet?"

Paul shook his head.

"Good. Try not to look at it or taste it, and you'll do fine."

Paul hesitated, then nodded again.

"I imagine you want a bunk someplace?"

"Uh, yes, sir."

"Well, my young friend, you are in luck. It just so happens I have a vacancy. Come along, Ensign Sinclair." Paul hastily scooped up his bag, following the supply officer out the hatch and down a short passageway, ducking as he passed through other hatches and trying to hug the bulkhead to his right as an occasional crew member squeezed past going in the other direction. Sykes finally halted before a hatch with three nameplates already stuck on it. "Welcome, Mr. Sinclair, to the starboard ensign locker."

"Ensign locker?" Paul looked on with foreboding as Sykes rapped sharply on the bulkhead, then opened the hatch.

A bedraggled lieutenant junior grade glanced up from a tiny desk and raised one hand to wave two fingers in greeting. "What's up, Suppo?"

"Got you another roomie. Meet Ensign Sinclair."

"Ah, fer... Okay. I guess we won't be able to stretch out in here anymore."

"Too much luxury spoils the young. Everybody happy? Wonderful. I'm off to attend to my many and exhausting duties. He's yours, Mr. Meadows."

"Thanks, Suppo. I'll take him from here."

Sykes nodded and left as Paul carefully maneuvered himself and his bag into the ensign locker. The JG stuck out his hand as Paul dropped his bag. "Welcome to a tiny corner of hell. And I do mean tiny. I'm Carl Meadows."

"Hi. I'm Paul. Paul Sinclair." Paul looked around, taking in the three bunks stacked against one of the bulkheads, the four small desk and locker units ranked two-by-two on either side, and a fourth bunk wedged between the top of one set of locker units and the overhead. "I guess it's a good thing I packed light."

"A very good thing. You get the top bunk."

Paul glanced upward, noting the power cables and ductwork overhead, which reduced the clearance above the top bunk to something less than the three feet of space the other bunks enjoyed. "Lucky me."

"You're junior ensign, my lad. Get used to the short end of the stick." Meadows grinned to take the sting from his words. "Ship designers pack everything they can inside the volume of the hull. It makes for tight quarters. I hope you didn't believe all those movies that showed space crews living in individual luxury apartment suites."

"The ones with soaring ceilings and lots of floor space?" Paul laughed. "Heck, I've never lived that good back on Earth. I didn't expect it up here, in living quarters provided by the government."

"A wise expectation. For an ensign."

Paul laughed again, then surveyed the small amount of personal storage space and shook his head. "If this is an ensign locker, why is a JG living here?"

"Because I've not yet achieved the exalted rank of full lieutenant, after which I can aspire to a two-person stateroom which is about half the size of this place. That's supposed to be better. But it beats living in one of the ensign lockers. Your two other roomies are also men, by the way. I hope that doesn't disappoint you. Aside from me, you get to share quarters with Ensign Sam Yarrow, and Lieutenant Junior Grade Bill Door. Don't expect to see much of Bill. He's the computer systems officer. Basically, Bill lives in the mainframe compartment. If you and he end up on opposite watch schedules, you may never see him except for rare sightings when he actually sleeps in his bunk. We send Bill emails occasionally to make sure he's still with us." Carl pointed out the hatch. "As for our female counterparts, the port ensign locker is where the babes live."

"Babes? The female junior officers get called babes?"

"Sometimes. In private. If they're in a good mood. And even then only among the other junior officers," Meadows cautioned, "not around anybody ranked lieutenant commander and above, and never, not ever in front of the enlisted."

"So, what do the, uh, babes call us? Sometimes, in private, among junior officers, that is."

"Studs."

Paul unsuccessfully tried to smother a laugh. "First time I've ever had that nickname."

"Me, too. Enjoy it while you can. I have a suspicion the stud nickname is at least slightly facetious, though. I'm gunnery and fire control officer, by the way. Have you got any idea what your primary duty will be?"

"My detailer said I'd be assistant combat information center officer."

Meadows raised one eyebrow. "And you believed him?"

"No, not really. When do I find out for sure what my job will be?"

"When you meet the executive officer." Meadows canted his head in a direction Paul guessed to indicate forward and to port. "Commander Herdez. If she tells you that you'll be ACICO, then you'll be ACICO."

"What's she like?"

"She's the XO. She works our butts off. Then she works us some more. But Herdez knows what she's doing. The XO's a very sharp officer. And, trust me on this, when you screw up you'll find out just how sharp she can be." Carl grinned. "You'll note I said 'when you screw up', not 'if.' I've been the ensign route, and the best you can say for it is that it's a learning experience."

"Yeah." Paul sagged into one of the free chairs. "I'm really looking forward to it."

"Don't worry. From the dawn of time, naval officers have gone through the ensign stage, and most have later gone on to lead happy, productive lives."

"Most have?"

"Let's not talk about the others. You may meet some of them," Carl added enigmatically. "A word of warning, though. We're heading out real soon for a long cruise. We get underway in four days for a week of shakedown in the local operating area. Then another week back here to fix whatever breaks during the shakedown, and after that, we're heading out into the big, empty black for a long time. All of which means you won't have much luxury for learning the ropes onboard the Merry Mike. Hit the deck running, and keep your eyes and ears open."

Paul fought down a wave of apprehension. "Thanks. I guess everybody calls her the Merry Mike?"

"JOs do."

"Commander Sykes did, too."

"Oh, well. Suppo's a special case. I wouldn't use the name around the captain or the XO."

"I was starting to guess that. It seems to be said sort of... sarcastically."

Meadows pretended shock, then laughed. "She's a warship, not a fun ship! You know what we say after putting in twelve hours on the job? 'Great, we only had to work a half-day!' Mostly, it's more like twenty hours a day of work and watch-standing under what you might call demanding supervision."

"Huh." Paul bit his lip. "So the XO is tough. What about the other senior officers? The department heads? What are they like?"

"Uh-uh," Meadows demurred. "You make your own mind up on them. I don't want to predispose you."

"But—"

"Uh-uh."

"Okay." Paul glanced forlornly around the tiny stateroom. *My new home. For months at a stretch, with people I don't know yet who I may not like and who may not like me, working my tail off the whole time. Why did I ever volunteer for this?* "You said we'll be going out on a long cruise? Has the mission been announced?"

Carl grinned, one thumb idly rubbing the silver bar of his collar rank insignia. "Our mission? Arrrhhh, we be pirates, lad!"

"Huh?"

"We're—" Meadows stopped speaking at a rap on the bulkhead, followed by the hatch opening. An enlisted sailor looked in, silently handed him a folded cloth, then left. Meadows unfurled the cloth, revealing the pirate flag Carl had seen in the wardroom. "Ah. It appears one of our humor-challenged seniors finally saw this."

"Suppo told me they'd take it down."

"Yeah, that's what I figured. But, what the hell. Why pirates? That's an open secret. We'll be on sovereignty patrol. Enforcing the US claim on a very large volume of very empty space containing very valuable transit routes and the occasional very valuable rock."

Paul nodded. "Yeah. I know about the sovereignty bit. We need to enforce our claim of control or it won't have any legal standing."

"Meaning what? That's a real question. We're all a little vague on the reasons for what we're doing. Not that that's so unusual."

"Well..." Paul paused to order his thoughts. "You can't just claim something and then leave it. If you claim you own something, but then let other people use it without hindrance for a while, then eventually your claim won't be regarded as having legal standing anymore. You have to enforce your claim in some meaningful way. You know, it's like if you have a trademark on some word but let everybody use it all the time and never complain. After a while the word is legally in public domain and you can't enforce the trademark anymore. That's really simplified, and I'm sure a lawyer could poke all kinds of holes in what I said, but that's the general idea."

"Interesting." Meadows raised both eyebrows. "You know legal stuff, huh?"

"Sort of. I had a one-month gap in my orders, so they packed me off to a ship's legal officer course. I guess you could say I now know enough to be dangerous."

"Lucky you. Then you also know what 'enforcing' our claim means?"

"In theory..."

"In practice." Meadows smiled, this time without real humor. "Like you said, we can't let other ships just cruise through our space, can we? But we're not at war with anybody, not officially anyway, so we can't officially blow them away, if that should be necessary."

"Blow them away?" Paul stared. "You mean we'll be authorized to shoot at other ships?"

"That's the scuttlebutt. How we can get away with that when we're not at war with anybody, I don't know, but then I'm just a dumb JG."

"That's better than being a dumb ensign. Our orders really say that?"

Meadows shrugged. "That's the scuttlebutt," he repeated. "You'll see the actual orders when the rest of us do. For now, I better get you to see the XO. You don't want *her* thinking she's being dissed. No, sirree. Follow me."

Meadows went out the hatch, expertly ducking to avoid banging his head, and led the way through a maze of passageways in which Paul had already lost his bearings. His head brushed objects overhead twice, causing Paul to hunch even lower and envy the casual way Meadows ducked and twisted to avoid hitting things. A female ensign came around a corner, flattening herself against the bulkhead as Paul and Carl passed. "Hey, babe," Carl offered.

"Hey, yourself. New stud?"

"Yeah." Carl indicated the female ensign. "Jen Shen. Paul Sinclair."

"Charmed."

"Likewise."

Carl pointed a thumb down, where the aft portion of the ship lay. "Jen's the auxiliary machinery officer. She's not bad, for a snipe."

Jen bared her teeth. "That reminds me. I may need to have the ventilation in your stateroom taken off line. Maybe for several hours."

"Oh, God, please, no—"

"Just joking." She looked Paul over appraisingly. "Is Carl giving you the ten cent tour?" Paul nodded. "Did he warn you about Smilin' Sam, yet?"

"Smilin'... ?"

"Sam Yarrow," Carl amplified. "The bull ensign." The official nickname indicated Yarrow was the senior ensign onboard. "Don't call him Smilin' Sam to his face."

"But keep your eye on him," Jen added. "He's a snake."

"Now, Jen—"

"Don't 'now' me, mister. Paul, if Sam tries to pat you on the back don't let him unless you've got armor strapped on between your shoulder blades. Otherwise, you're likely to find a knife there." She smiled with mock sweetness at Carl. "But that's just *my* opinion. See ya. I got work to do, unlike some underemployed combat systems types."

Meadows shook his head, smiling wryly, as Shen hustled down the passageway. "Jen's got attitude to spare."

"I can tell. She seems squared away, though."

"Oh yeah, real squared away. You can trust Jen, on official business or on personal stuff."

"Thanks. So she's right about Yarrow?"

Carl hesitated before answering. "I don't want to predispose you—"

"Come on."

"Okay. The bull ensign's supposed to look out for the other ensigns, right? Sam Yarrow mainly looks out for Sam Yarrow. That's all I'll say. Now, onward. The XO awaits."

They went around another corner, ducking where cables and ducts came too far down from the overhead, until Carl stopped before a hatch with Herdez stenciled on it. He rapped twice, waited for an acknowledgement, then opened the hatch and waved Paul forward. "New officer reporting aboard, XO."

"Thank you, Mr. Meadows." Herdez rose from her chair just enough to shake Paul's hand. "Please wait outside while I speak with Ensign..."

"Sinclair, ma'am."

"Sinclair. Welcome aboard the USS *Michaelson*." Herdez sank back into her chair, gestured Paul to the stateroom's other seat, then held out her hand. "Your service record, please."

"Yes, ma'am." Paul hastily popped the data cartridge containing his service record out of his wallet and handed it over. As Herdez loaded the record into her terminal, reading it intently, Paul tried to surreptitiously study her and his surroundings. Herdez had a build that was slim, but even through her uniform seemed hard. She scanned her terminal with a stern expression which seemed habitual, radiating an aura of cool competence. Paul found himself hoping he never screwed up in her presence, yet simultaneously certain such an event was only a matter of time. Her stateroom, perhaps half the size of Paul's new shared quarters, was almost devoid of personal decoration except for one bulkhead which held a small collection of medallions and pictures, obviously memorabilia from Commander Herdez' earlier assignments.

"Impressed?"

Paul froze at the dryly phrased question, looking to see Commander Herdez gazing directly at him once again.

She pointed toward the memorabilia. "My 'Love Me' wall, Mr. Sinclair. Eighteen years of naval service are represented there. Perhaps you'll have such a wall someday, should you succeed in this profession." She paused, as if expecting a reply.

"I hope to, ma'am."

Herdez twisted one corner of her mouth in a brief smile. "Hope counts for far less than performance, Mr. Sinclair. Do well, and success will follow." She indicated the screen of her terminal. "You ranked two hundred and tenth from the top of your Academy class. Not bad. Could you have done better?"

Paul took a moment before answering. *Boy, that's a loaded question. Either 'yes' or 'no' could get me in trouble. I'd best just be honest.* "Yes, ma'am, I could have ranked higher."

"Why didn't you?"

"Because I didn't try as hard as I could have the first couple of years. I had some growing up to do."

"That's not unusual in a young person, though not all of them actually manage to mature. What about the last two years?"

"The last two years I elected to take a few courses that ate up a lot of my study time but earned only passable grades."

Herdez pondered Paul's statement for a moment. "Why did you elect to take those courses, then?"

"They were subjects I thought I ought to know, ma'am."

"I see." Herdez glanced back at the record, then at Paul. "But you could have received better grades in other courses you could have taken instead?"

"Oh, yes, ma'am. No question. I already had a good handle on the stuff in those courses." The answer popped out without Paul's thinking, leaving him wondering if the reply had sounded vain or thoughtless.

"Hmmm. You certainly demonstrated academic skills, regardless. Why did you volunteer for duty on the *Michaelson*, Mr. Sinclair?"

Paul swallowed to give himself time to consider the question, electing again for the truth. "They said they needed somebody in this assignment."

"They?"

"The, uh, detailers, ma'am."

Herdez seemed amused by the reply. "Well, Mr. Sinclair, you seem to be devoted to neither puffing up your resume nor to demanding ticket-punching assignments. That bodes well for you. I see you've also attended the ship's legal officer course."

"Yes, ma'am, but—"

"That's fortunate. The *Michaelson* needs a trained legal officer. You'll be assigned ship's legal officer as a collateral duty, effective now."

"Uh... yes, ma'am."

"As far as your primary duty, you'll be assistant combat information center officer."

"Thank you, ma'am."

"The last postal officer just departed the ship. You'll have that collateral duty as well." She looked questioningly at Paul.

"Yes, ma'am."

"And we need to get a better handle on security issues. You'll be assistant security manager."

"Thank you, ma'am."

"You'll be expected to pursue your open space warfare officer qualifications. I like to personally track the progress of our junior

25

officers in meeting those qualifications."

"Yes, ma'am." Paul tried not to flinch outwardly, thinking of the huge amount of material he would be required to master to earn those qualifications.

"Ship's office will assign you an inport and underway duty section. Do you have a stateroom?"

"Yes, ma'am, Commander Sykes—"

"Good. Have you met any of the other officers, yet?"

"Just Commander Sykes, Lieutenant Junior Grade Meadows and Ensign Shen."

"Good. You'll meet the rest of the wardroom soon enough."

"Yes, ma'am."

"Mr. Meadows can escort you around for the rest of your check-in procedure. While he is doing so, please inform Mr. Meadows that he'll regret it if I see that little flag of his again."

"Yes, ma'am."

"Welcome aboard, Mr. Sinclair. This is a challenging and demanding assignment. Give it your best."

"Thank you, ma'am. Yes, ma'am."

Commander Herdez rose slightly again, offered her hand once more, then waved Paul out.

Carl awaited him in the passageway outside. "How'd it go?"

Paul shivered. "Wow."

"Yeah. The XO's hell-on-wheels, isn't she?"

"She told me to tell you that you'd regret it if she saw that pirate flag again."

"Ouch." Meadows winced exaggeratedly. "It just fell into a black hole. Lost to the sight of humanity for eternity. How many jobs did you pick up?"

"My primary is ACICO, like my orders said, and I got, uh, three collateral duties. I think."

"Only three? She must like you."

"You're kidding."

"Nope. You meet Kris Denaldo, yet?"

"Yes. She's the officer of the deck, right?"

"Yeah. She picked up four collateral duties. And she's the assistant electronics officer." Meadows grinned. "Kris don't sleep much."

"I thought nobody slept much."

"They don't, but some sleep a little less than others." With one extended hand, Meadows indicated a route forward. "Well, shipmate, let's get you checked in with everybody else."

The next few hours were a blur for Paul. Names and faces went by, most disappearing from memory almost as soon as they did from sight. A blasé petty officer in ship's office downloaded a copy of Paul's service record and uploaded him a copy of the Ship's Organization and Regulations Manual. "Happy leisure reading, sir," the petty officer wished without any visible trace of irony. A pay clerk adjusted her database to reflect Paul's existence and newly qualified status for space hardship pay. A harried lieutenant arguing with a civilian contractor took a moment to flash a smile at Paul and welcome him to her duty section. A commander eyed Paul suspiciously, then plugged his name into the underway watch bill.

Then there was Commander Garcia, operations department head, and therefore immediate superior in the chain of command to both the Combat Information Center Officer and the Assistant. Garcia, squat and stolid, glowered at Paul even as he grimaced a brief smile of welcome. "You work for me, Sinclair. Is that clear?"

"Yes, sir."

"Legal officer. Who said you should do that job?"

Paul had already stiffened his posture in response to Garcia's attitude, and now spoke with equal stiffness. "Commander Herdez, sir."

Garcia glowered again, obviously wishing to say more, then just shook his head. "Don't screw up, Sinclair. This isn't some Academy game. You've got a lot to learn. Screw up, and I'll dump your ass into vacuum."

"Yes, sir." Behind Garcia, Paul could see Meadows making a face. "I'll do my best, sir."

"I hope so." Garcia turned toward Meadows. "See if you can locate Tweed and introduce these two." Then he stalked off.

Paul glanced at Meadows. "Who's Tweed?"

"Lieutenant Jan Tweed."

"Garcia doesn't like her?"

"Garcia doesn't like anybody." Meadows waved Paul forward again. "Technically, Jan Tweed'll be your immediate superior, so try to get along."

"Is that hard?" A headache, which had been building throughout the last few hours, began throbbing with renewed strength.

"Uh..."

"Carl, don't let me hit a mine."

Meadows grinned. "Good analogy. Jan Tweed is an okay person, she just don't do much. That can be real aggravating if you're depending on her. Copy?"

"So that's why the *Michaelson* needed an Assistant in CIC?"

"That's one reason. See, Garcia told me to 'try' to locate Tweed because sometimes she's real hard to find. Especially when she's needed. Like if she's supposed to relieve you on watch? Don't count on her showing up on time."

Paul's headache flared a little worse. *Great. Somebody I can't count on, and she's the person I'll have to work most closely with. Well, maybe she won't be that bad. Maybe she's just got a bad reputation. I hope.* "I guess I should try to find her."

"Yeah. Let's check a few places. After we finish this check-off list of yours."

"Who's left?"

Carl chuckled. "Dazed and confused, huh? Think about it, Paul. Who haven't you seen yet?"

"Umm... oh. The captain."

"Right-o. So let's go see your new lord and master."

The captain's cabin was located not far from the bridge of the *Michaelson*. Carl paused before the hatch, indicating the letters spelling out P. C. Wakeman on it, then rapped and waited. At the sound of a gruff "Enter," Carl swung the hatch open and gestured Paul inward.

Captain Wakeman, sitting before his desk in a stateroom that appeared slightly larger than that occupied by Commander Herdez, squinted at Paul as if examining an unwelcome pest. "Yes?"

Paul came to attention and rendered his best salute. "Ensign Paul Sinclair, reporting for duty, sir."

"Oh. Hmmm." Wakeman fiddled with his desk terminal for a few moments, scowling. "Your record's supposed to be in here. Why isn't your record in here? You checked in with ship's office, didn't you?"

"Yes, sir."

"Well, they didn't put your record in here." Wakeman glowered at Paul, then with an apparent effort relaxed his face into a semblance of camaraderie. "But we'll take care of that later. Welcome aboard, Mr....uh..."

"Sinclair, sir. Paul Sinclair."

"Yes. Of course. Ah, Academy? Good. Good." Brief smiles flickered across the captain's face, coming and going in a manner which suggested nervous twitches. "Well, let me tell you, this is a great opportunity for you. Outstanding. Lots of visibility. Chances to excel. But you have to be a team player. Are you a team player, Mr.... ?"

"Sinclair, sir. Yes, sir."

"Sinclair. Right. The team. That's important. And you know who the captain of your team is?"

"Uh... you, sir."

Wakeman nodded vigorously. "Right. Right. And you, you're a blocker. And a tackle. You tackle problems before they become problems. You block bad attitudes and bad morale. Because you're a team player."

"Yes, sir."

"Visibility. Yes." Wakeman relaxed slightly, leaning back and gazing upward. "Opportunity. That's good. Opportunity to succeed." He sat silent for a long moment, lost in a reverie, while Paul waited and tried not to show any sign of impatience until Wakeman abruptly focused his attention back on Paul. "Well. Welcome aboard."

It took Paul a few seconds, until Captain Wakeman frowned in displeasure, to realize he'd been dismissed. Paul hastily saluted again. "Thank you, sir." He closed the hatch carefully as he exited, afraid he might bang it shut and draw the captain's wrath, then saw Meadows eyeing him. "Is he always like that?"

"Cap'n Pete? Oh, yeah." For the first time since Paul had met him, Meadows let his feelings for another officer show. "He talk to you about visibility?" Paul nodded. "Being on his team?" Another nod. "Be careful, Paul. Just try to watch your step."

"But what—?"

"I don't know. He's the captain. That's all there is to it. Come on, let's see if we can run down Jan Tweed for you." Half an hour later, after several frustrating attempts to locate Lieutenant Tweed, Carl was called away to handle something pertaining to the ship's weaponry. Paul, left to his own resources, wandered through the ship, repeatedly losing his way and encountering officers and enlisted who eyed him with curiosity. He was standing before a large hatch with No Entry—Authorized Personnel Only stenciled on it in large letters when a familiar voice interrupted him. "Mr. Sinclair?"

Paul turned, seeing the senior chief who'd first brought him onboard. The joy of seeing even that small familiarity caused a wave of relief to wash through him. "Yes, senior chief. How's it going?"

"Could be worse, sir. I been looking for you, but you've been moving around a lot." The senior chief eased back, indicating his companion. "First Class Master-at-Arms Ivan Sharpe, Mr. Sinclair. Being as you're the new legal officer, I knew you two should get together."

"Thanks, senior chief." Paul extended his hand even as the master-at-arms did the same. "Pleased to meet you, Petty Officer Sharpe."

Sharpe looked Paul over carefully while he shook Paul's hand. "Looking forward to working with you, sir."

The senior chief leaned forward, commanding attention immediately. "Sheriff Sharpe's a good petty officer, Mr. Sinclair. You can count on him. I gotta go handle some work, now."

"Thanks again, senior chief," Paul called after his retreating back, then faced Sharpe again. "Sheriff?"

Sharpe spread his hands, grinning fiercely. "A man's got to have his handle, sir. And I am sheriff of this here town."

"What's that make the legal officer? The town judge?"

Sheriff Sharpe shook his head. "Commander Herdez is judge and jury around here, Mr. Sinclair."

"Judge *and* jury? Then where's the captain come in?"

"The captain?" Sharpe kept his expression carefully noncommittal. "The captain is God, sir."

2

Paul opened his eyes, staring blearily upward through the darkness at the dim images of ducts which seemed only inches from his nose. The shrill whine of the bosun's pipe echoed through the ship's intercom, its trilling notes gradually dying out. A moment later, a voice rapidly recited the words that officially began every day on every ship. "Reveille, reveille. All hands turn to and trice up. The smoking lamp is lit."

Paul lay still, unwilling to rise. *There isn't any smoking lamp. There hasn't been a smoking lamp for who knows how long, and even if there were a smoking lamp, people, haven't been allowed to smoke on ships for who knows how long. But every day we say we light the lamp in the morning and put it out at night. The Navy. Centuries of tradition unmarred by progress.*

A groan from somewhere in the ensign locker announced one of his roommates rolling out of his bunk. A moment later, a desk light flickered to life, bringing more groans from the other occupants of the stateroom. "Put it out, man."

"Sorry. Got to see if they fixed the port power distribution net last night. Hey, who had the mid-watch last night?"

Paul closed his eyes again even as he answered. "I did." The mid-watch ran from midnight to 0400 in the morning, leaving little room for sleep on either side of it. Paul had spent most of the watch trying to stay awake, a task made slightly easier by the need to keep from dropping the long glass, the telescope which had to be carried by the officer of the deck.

"Did any contractors come onboard?"

"Uh, no. A couple left, but no new ones came on."

"Damn! They don't give us enough technicians because they claim outside contractors can do the work, then they don't give us contractors! Damn!" The hatch swung open, then slammed shut as Ensign Sam Yarrow stormed out. Paul looked blankly at the closed hatch, trying to remember Yarrow's face. They'd crossed paths repeatedly in the last couple of days, but only for moments at a time, and every event somehow merged into the haze of too much happening too fast. He still didn't have any real personal impression of the fellow ensign he'd been warned against.

A heavy double-rap sounded, then the hatch swung open again and Commander Garcia stuck his head inside. "Sinclair!"

Paul hastily rolled out of his bunk, barely avoiding whacking his head on a support bracket, and stood facing his department head, still blinking against the light and hoping his guilt at being caught in his bunk didn't show. "Sir."

"Where's Tweed?"

"Lieutenant Tweed? I... I don't know, sir." *And how the hell am I supposed to know right now? It's not like I'm sleeping with her. And if I was, I'd really be in trouble.*

"Find her! Find her and then the two of you find me! Understand?"

"Yes, sir."

The hatch crashed shut, leaving the stateroom dim once more. Carl Meadows yawned. "Have a nice day, sir," he advised the hatch, then rolled out of his own bunk. "Hey, Paul. Welcome aboard."

"You already told me that, uh..." When? Had it only been the day before yesterday?

"Two days ago. Time flies when you're having fun."

"In that case, time must be approaching light speed right now."

"Yeah." Carl yawned again, scratched himself, then checked his scheduler. "Don't worry, though. It gets worse."

Paul sighed, then hurriedly dressed and shaved before heading out in search of Lieutenant Tweed. Several minutes into his search, he came face to face with Master-at-Arms Sharpe. "Good morning, Mr. Sinclair," the Sheriff announced cheerfully.

"If you say so."

"Don't forget, sir. XO's screening at ten hundred."

"Uh..." *How can I forget something I didn't know? I've got to remember to read the plan of the day as soon as I get up.* "Ten hundred?"

"Right." Sheriff Sharpe smiled. "That's ten A.M., sir."

Paul couldn't help smiling back at the audacity of the statement. "I know that. They did teach me to tell military time."

"Can't take anything for granted with a new ensign, sir. See you at the XO's stateroom at ten hundred."

"Sure. Say, have you seen Lieutenant Tweed anywhere?"

Sharpe paused, then used his thumb to point forward. "She might be in the classified materials vault."

"She might be, huh? Thanks, Sheriff." Paul hurried along, vaguely recalling that the "vault" containing the most sensitive classified material on the ship was located next to the ship's combat information center. After asking a passing sailor for directions, he found the door and rapped softly. Getting no response, he rapped again, harder.

"Wait." The lock on the hatch cycled open, then a lieutenant with a slim face and a guarded expression gazed out. "Oh. Paul, right? Whatever it is will have to wait. I'm doing an inventory."

Paul nodded in apparent agreement, even though he could see Tweed blinking sleep from her eyes. "Commander Garcia said he needed to see us both. At once."

"He did?" Tweed looked around as if seeking an escape route, then shrugged. "Okay. Let's go."

Garcia's temper didn't seem to have improved in the brief period since Paul had last seen him. Their department head glared at Paul and Lieutenant Tweed, then shoved a portable reader at them. "Where's the pre-ex for the simulated tracking drill this morning?"

Paul stared at the reader while dread grew in him. A pre-exercise message laid out coordination procedures for drills involving more than one ship. Most of the information was canned, Paul already knew, and simply had to be spelled out again, but every exercise required a pre-ex message to every unit involved. "I... I..." Lieutenant Tweed was frowning in thought, then looking sidelong at Paul with a worried expression. *She told me to take care of it. I remember now. Oh, geez.* Commander Garcia's eyes were fixed on him, hard and angry. Paul swallowed, then spoke in a voice he knew sounded thin. "I was supposed to take care of it, sir."

"You were *supposed* to take care of it. Why didn't you?"

"I intended doing it today, sir—"

"The exercise is today! Didn't you review the exercise material as soon as you got told to take care of the pre-ex?"

"No, sir. I... didn't."

Garcia's face reddened. Paul's department head looked as if he were barely restraining himself, then shook his head like an angry bull. "You'd better not screw up like this again, Sinclair. Now, I personally will have to coordinate all this on the fly. Do you think I'm happy about that, Sinclair?"

"No, sir."

"Were you planning on leaving the ship this evening, Sinclair?"

Michaelson was due to get underway in the morning. Paul had already been invited out to a bar crawl with the other junior officers, but now he shook his head, knowing what his answer had to be. "No, sir."

"Good. At least you got *that* right." Garcia stomped away, leaving Paul and Jan Tweed alone.

Lieutenant Tweed tried to smile sympathetically. "It happens to everybody."

Paul held back a bitter reply, angry with her for not warning him the message had been a short-fuse item, but also knowing it had been his own fault he hadn't checked on it before postponing action. *And at least she didn't blame me for it right off. I guess Carl was right. You can't count on her, but Tweed won't mess me over deliberately.* "Yeah. First time for everything. I'm sure it won't be the last. Should I try to help the commander with fixing this up?"

"Uh-uh. Bad idea. Garcia will cool down while he works, unless you're there to remind him you screwed up." Tweed checked her watch and smiled briefly again. "Hey. Breakfast time. Coming?"

"No, thanks. I'm not too hungry right now."

"Suit yourself."

Paul wandered down the passageway, his eyes fixed on the deck, feeling angry at his own failure but still resentful of Commander

Garcia. *It's my fault, but it's also not like that guy is providing any real guidance or support for me. What's that they say about officers on ships? They eat their young. I guess that's true.*

A body blocked his progress, causing Paul to look up into the sympathetic face of Ensign Sam Yarrow. "Hey, Paul, I heard Garcia did a number on you."

"Yeah."

"Too bad." Yarrow placed a friendly hand on Paul's shoulder. "Garcia's a real hard-ass, isn't he?"

"Sure seems to be."

"He riding you hard?"

"Real hard."

"Damn shame. I bet you didn't deserve getting chewed out, did you?"

"Well, uh..." Paul let his words trail off, suddenly wary of Yarrow's apparent concern. "I don't know. I made a mistake."

"A big mistake or a little one? You've got to have a chance to learn. Right?"

"Uh, right. Look, I've got some other stuff to handle. See you later."

"Sure thing."

Paul spent the next few hours working through his to-do list, making sure nothing else would miss being done on time, then hustled to be outside the XO's stateroom prior to ten hundred. Sheriff Sharpe was already waiting, along with the familiar senior chief, who grinned in greeting. "Howdy, Mr. Sinclair."

"Hi, senior chief. What's your name anyway?"

The grin widened. "Senior Chief Kowalski, sir. Leading chief on the *Michaelson*. That's why I'm here for XO's screening."

"Right." Paul nodded absently, trying to dredge up his memories of the XO screenings he'd attended during his limited fleet experience. Most violations of military rules and regulations weren't handled by courts-martial, but by non-judicial punishment. NJP had its own rules and limitations, and allowed a commanding officer to deal with the great majority of breaches of good order and discipline in a quick and effective manner. But not every offense technically referred for NJP needed to be handled even in that fashion, which led to the XO's screening, where the executive officer reviewed each case and decided whether it should go on up to the captain or could be disposed of without taking that step.

Two more chiefs arrived, each with a sailor in tow, then Sheriff Sharpe rapped on the XO's hatch and received permission to enter. Paul, Senior Chief Kowalski, and Sharpe crowded into the stateroom, Paul following the others' example by flattening himself against one bulkhead to leave a small space clear in the center. Commander Herdez nodded in general greeting, then pointed toward the hatch. "Let's start with Alvarez."

Sharpe leaned out, signaling to one sailor, who entered along with her chief. Alvarez stood at what could technically be called attention, though she somehow imbued the stance with an air of insubordination. "Attention!" Sharpe snapped, then stepped back as Alvarez tightened her stance marginally.

Herdez scanned her reader, her face as hard as the metal deck, then looked up at Alvarez. "Seaman Alvarez, you are charged with two violations of the Uniform Code of Military Justice. Article 86, failure to go to an appointed place of duty, and Article 91, insubordinate conduct toward a petty officer. Chief Thomas."

The chief petty officer accompanying Alvarez wedged herself slightly forward.

"What happened?"

"During morning muster, Seaman Alvarez was not present, ma'am. She had still not appeared at the completion of muster, so I went down to the berthing compartment and found her in her rack. I ordered her to get up immediately and, instead of complying, Seaman Alvarez made a number of obscene remarks directed at me."

Commander Herdez' face somehow seemed to harden even further. "It seems to me that Seaman Alvarez should also be charged under Article 91 with disobeying an order from a petty officer. Is that correct?"

Chief Thomas chewed her lip for a moment before answering. "Seaman Alvarez did get up and proceed with her duties after I, uh, motivated her, ma'am."

"Hmmm." Herdez shifted her gaze back to Alvarez. "Seaman Alvarez, what do you have to say?"

Alvarez displayed an apparently insincere mix of regret and earnestness as she spoke. "I was sick, ma'am. Real sick. I could hardly move at all. I tried to tell Chief Thomas, but she wouldn't listen. So I got up anyway, but it was real hard. But it wasn't my fault, ma'am."

"Real sick?" Herdez looked back at Chief Thomas. "Did you send Seaman Alvarez to sick bay?"

"I did, ma'am. The doc reported Alvarez had a bad hangover, that was all."

"A hangover."

Alvarez spoke again, licking her lips nervously. "I didn't drink that much the night before, ma'am. Just a little. It was some bad booze. Real bad. Or somebody slipped me a Mickey. You know, to rob me or somethin', but I got back to the ship anyway. The doc wouldn't listen, though."

Herdez shook her head slowly, her eyes fixed on Alvarez. "Neither will I, because your story is not very believable. Sick bay would have spotted any traces of drugs in your system from a Mickey, but you refused such a test. Why?"

"I, uh, they coulda taken my word—"

"They also could have detected other drugs, perhaps. But I can't charge you with offenses I only believe you committed." Herdez looked toward Sheriff Sharpe. "This case is referred to captain's mast. Dismissed."

Alvarez, her head down so no one could read her expression, followed Chief Thomas out. Commander Herdez nodded to Sharpe. "Next."

Sharpe leaned out the hatch. "Seaman Franco."

Franco entered with his chief, then stood at rigid attention, almost quivering with nervousness. Herdez favored him with a stern look, then checked her reader. "Seaman Franco, you are charged with violating Article 86, failure to go to an appointed place of duty. Chief Blucher?"

Chief Blucher tilted his head toward Franco. "Seaman Franco, he didn't show up for morning muster yesterday. He got back to the ship maybe a half hour late, after liberty had expired."

"What do have to say, Seaman Franco?"

Franco twitched, his face rigid. "Ma'am, I... uh... didn't... realize the time."

"What were you doing that made you so unaware of your duties on the ship, Seaman Franco?"

"I... uh... ma'am... um... a friend..."

The corner of Herdez' mouth twitched. "Chief Blucher, can you shed any light on this?"

"Yes, ma'am. I believe Seaman Franco has a new girlfriend ashore."

"Ah. Your first girlfriend, Seaman Franco?"

Franco nodded once, his face rigid, worried eyes fixed on the far bulkhead. "Yes, ma'am. Uh, I mean, first real girlfriend."

"I see. And you were engaged in some activities with this girlfriend which caused you to be late returning to the ship?"

"I... I'm sorry, ma'am. I really didn't realize..."

Herdez turned to Chief Blucher again. "What sort of sailor is Seaman Franco?"

"He's a good sailor, ma'am. Hard worker."

"Has he been in trouble before?"

"No, ma'am."

"Very well." Herdez fixed a stern gaze in Franco. "Then I believe this can be handled without referring the case to the captain. Chief Blucher, ensure Seaman Franco understands the consequences of failing to attend to his duties because of... social activities. As for you, Seaman Franco, it's not hard to balance your social life with your professional responsibilities as long as you think with the upper part of your spine instead of the lower part of it. I don't want to see you here again. Is that understood?"

"Yes, ma'am. Th-thank you, ma'am."

"Dismissed."

Franco and Blucher trooped out, while Senior Chief Kowalski rubbed his face to conceal a smile. "Thanks, commander."

Commander Herdez kept her own face solemn. "No thanks needed, senior chief. Franco is a good sailor, but more than one good sailor has wandered astray. Putting the fear of God in him at this point should ensure he stays on track. Alvarez, on the other hand... senior chief, I want you to be thinking about ways to get her transferred off this ship if necessary."

Kowalski nodded. "Okay, ma'am. She's a bad egg. But the shore establishment don't like it when we dump bad sailors on them."

"Since the shore establishment sends them to us in the first place, I don't see where they have cause to complain. See to it, senior chief. Thank you, Petty Officer Sharpe. Mr. Sinclair, I'll need to see you tomorrow afternoon."

"Yes, ma'am." Paul went cold inside, imagining his foul-up with Commander Garcia had attracted even worse attention than he had imagined.

Herdez weighed Paul with her eyes, making him feel as if she were looking through him. "It's a legal issue, Mr. Sinclair. Thank you."

Paul followed the others out of the stateroom. "Sheriff, you got a minute?"

"Certainly, sir." Sharpe seemed to be in good humor.

"I guess you enjoyed that little act with Franco."

"That I did, sir. But it wasn't no act. The XO meant what she said." Sharpe inclined his head to indicate Commander Herdez' stateroom. "If you don't mind my saying so, sir, that was a good leadership lesson in there."

"I'd already figured that out, Sheriff. But tell me something. How much trouble do we have with sailors?"

Sharpe grinned. "They're sailors, bless 'em. They get drunk, they get in fights with girlfriends and boyfriends and bartenders and cops and other sailors, they get home late, they say or do something stupid. It happens."

"I know that much. What I was wondering was, do they get in much trouble when we're underway? I mean, are XO's screening and captain's mast going to demand a lot of my time once we're underway?"

"Oh." Sheriff Sharpe grimaced. "Look at it this way, sir. You're gonna go out on a long patrol. You're stuck in a metal box for months. No liberty. No booze. What're they gonna do to you if you mouth off or steal a little food or try to jury-rig a still so you can get drunk? You can fine them, but what's less money mean when there's no place to spend it? You can bust them a paygrade, but so what? You wake up in the same little box of a berthing compartment, eat the same rotten food, and do the same job. Even if we stick 'em in the brig, that's just a private room. And bread and water? That's better than half the meals they serve on the mess decks. So, I guess your answer is, yeah, we get a lot of work underway. The good sailors don't act too much different, though even they know any punishment don't mean much compared to six months stuck inside this can, but the bad actors figure it's open season for the first few months. Once we hit the halfway point, they start cleaning up their acts. Ain't nobody wants to be on confinement when we get home. No, sir. But up 'til then, it's gonna be busy, Mr. Sinclair."

Paul blew out air in a long sigh. "Thanks, Sheriff. I guess I'll be seeing a whole lot of you."

"That's because you're a lucky man, sir." Sharpe chuckled, then brought his right hand up in a salute. "By your leave, sir?"

Paul returned the salute, unable to fight down a smile of his own at the exaggerated military courtesy. "Go away, Sheriff."

"Thank you, sir!"

Paul was still smiling when he reached his stateroom, but the smile faded as soon as he saw the message from Commander Garcia demanding his immediate presence in the combat information center. Paul hastened to CIC, finding the compartment jammed with enlisted operations specialists and Lieutenant Jan Tweed, as well as Garcia.

"Where the hell have you been?" Garcia barked the question without taking his eyes off the tracking screen.

"Attending XO's screening, sir."

This time Garcia took a moment to glare directly at Paul. "Why?"

"Commander Herdez requested—"

"You're needed in here. Get to work."

"Yes, sir." Paul glanced hopelessly toward Tweed, who was slouched in a corner.

Tweed beckoned him over with a small gesture, then indicated two enlisted sailors operating a console nearby. "Hang around there, Paul," she advised in a whisper. "Just watch and learn."

Paul stole a glance toward Garcia. "But he said for me to get to work."

"This is work. Learning is work. Keep your eyes and ears open. That's the best way to avoid mistakes."

"Shouldn't I do anything?"

"If Garcia wants you to do something, he'll tell you. Until then, just stay out of his way."

Paul nodded, positioning himself near the enlisted. *Great. My department head issues vague orders to do something while he runs this drill personally, and my division officer tells me to do nothing while she tries to hide in a corner. Well, I won't be happy doing nothing for long, but Tweed's right that I need to learn a lot about operations in here.*

Paul had toured combat information centers before, he'd taken courses on what happened in a CIC, and had even experienced a few CIC simulator runs during training. A CIC did exactly what its name said, collecting all available information to support combat decisions and carry out combat actions ordered by the ship's captain. Every sensor funneled readings and detections to this compartment. Every communications circuit was monitored here, either by humans or computers listening for keywords. Intelligence reports came here, their data and estimates added to the welter of information. Skilled personnel evaluated what they saw, monitoring displays that hopefully gave a ship's commanding officer everything needed to make critical decisions, decisions that might literally involve life and death. If those decisions dictated that weapons were to be employed, someone in this compartment might well fire those weapons.

Despite his training, Paul found being part of a real CIC to be daunting. *Funny how much different it is to actually be expected to participate in a real CIC compared to some simulator drill. I'm actually part of this. What part, I'm not sure, yet.* He glanced over at Tweed, hunched in her corner. *The CIC officer is supposed to be running all this, making sure all the enlisted specialists are doing their jobs well and making sure the information displayed for the captain is clear and accurate. Everything seems to be running great. Is Tweed being smart by letting capable enlisted do their jobs, or is she just giving them free rein because she doesn't want to supervise them?* Paul took a long look at Commander Garcia, hunched over a terminal and snarling commands. *Or has Garcia effectively taken over Tweed's job and left her nothing to supervise, regardless of how she feels?* The last possibility was particularly worrisome. Despite his misgivings, Paul had no doubt he could learn to carry out a CIC officer's responsibilities. But he also knew he wouldn't have much chance of ever doing that if Commander Garcia insisted on personally running the show.

He watched and he listened, feeling a growing sense of reassurance at the ease with which the enlisted specialists handled their jobs, increasingly deciding that Tweed's passivity was a combined result of two of the factors he'd earlier considered: Garcia's involvement and confidence in her personnel. She wasn't being allowed to run things, but she didn't have to run things. The path of least resistance ran naturally right to the corner Tweed occupied.

Gradually, the commands issued and information displayed began to make sense. He had to think in three dimensions rather than the two-dimensional movement of surface ships on Earth, and radically change his perception of distances and speeds involved, but the basic process of detection, localizing and tracking wasn't really different from that used on the waterborne ships Paul had trained on.

The two enlisted at the console directly before Paul were responsible for evaluating sensor detections. For the most part, they spent the drill trying not to look bored as detections popped up in what was obviously a predictable sequence. Paul watched them with increasing frustration, wanting to ask specific questions but unable to interrupt the drill being run by Garcia.

Garcia finally stood, slapping a few control buttons, swung a narrow-eyed gaze around the compartment, then left without a word. The sailors visibly relaxed and began bantering among themselves. Paul looked for Tweed, but she was already heading out the other hatch. *I guess the exercise is over.* "Excuse me," he asked the two enlisted specialists at his console, "could you guys give me a run-down on this gear?"

The senior of the two petty officers smiled obligingly, but shook her head. "I'm sorry, sir. We've got to power it down for some scheduled maintenance. Maybe some other time?"

"Sure. Thanks." Feeling once more like excess baggage, Paul made his way out of the compartment as well, then stood for a moment in the passageway, uncertain. *Okay, so I'm going to have to learn a lot of this job on my own. I can do that. And the first thing I'm going to do now is learn enough of the ship's organization manual to avoid any more unnecessary screw-ups.*

Paul took his bearings. He'd figured out a few paths through the ship to different destinations, and didn't want to risk veering off his route and getting lost again within the maze of decks and passageways.

With increasing confidence in his knowledge of the way, Paul made his way back to the ensign locker, feeling a small measure of relief that none of his roommates were present. Carl Meadows wouldn't have been bad company, but Paul still wasn't sure how sympathetic he'd be to the travails of another junior officer. And he was still wary of Sam Yarrow.

Paul sat down, called up the ship's manual to check on procedures, then flinched as the hatch to the ensign locker boomed open. Ensign Jen Shen entered, her face dark, and punched the nearest locker hard enough for the metal to bow in temporarily. Waiting a moment, Shen slammed another blow at the locker, then dropped into the nearest chair and glared at Paul. "Idiots. Stupid, brainless, butt-kissing idiots."

"You appear to be a little upset."

"Just a little. I've got a piece of gear called a reverse osmosis device. It makes the water we recycle fit to drink. I've actually got three, but if only two work then eventually we run low on water and everybody gets real unhappy. Ask me how many working reverse osmosis devices I have."

"Something tells me the answer isn't three."

"It's not. Oh, I can make the piece of junk work in fits and starts by tweaking stuff and threatening it, but effectively it's broke. But can we report that? Maybe get a new one before we deploy? Heck, no, Ensign Shen! Because we can't deploy with only two working osmosis devices. We gotta have three! And heaven forbid we should upset anyone by telling them we only have two, because that might cause our deployment date to slip and the fleet staff would have a hissy fit."

Paul knew he shouldn't say it, but he did. "Two out of three ain't ba—" He ducked as Shen threw the closest available object at him. "I'm really sorry. That sucks. It doesn't make sense, either. I mean, what happens if one of the two working osmosis devices goes down hard?"

"We head home and pray we make it on time. Like I said, it's stupid." Shen buried her head in her hands. "But you have to get used to it. It's all about looking good. And not looking bad. Admitting something is broke looks bad. So everybody pretends everything is fine." Paul sat silent, at a loss for words, until she raised her head again to regard him. "Speaking of looking bad, I'm surprised you were in any mood to joke."

"You mean that exercise message I messed up? I can't believe how many people have heard about that. I'm not happy, but I've got to learn from it and move on. Right?"

She stared at him for a moment. "Do you want to know what I just overheard Ensign Sam Yarrow discussing with Commander Garcia?" Paul felt his blood chill, but nodded anyway. "Something along the lines of 'I can't believe Ensign Sinclair thinks you're a hard-ass who's riding him too hard.' Did you say that?"

"No! He did!"

"Yarrow?"

"Yes, Yarrow! He came up and talked all sympathetic and asked me if I thought Garcia was a hard-ass and stuff, and all I did was kinda agree."

"Uh-huh." Shen hid her face again. "Sorry, Paul. I warned you."

"That slimy bastard! He actually put words in my mouth!"

"Uh-huh. How's the back feel?"

"Like I had ten inches of cold steel between my shoulder blades. I'll kill him! I can't believe he would do something like that."

"Usually, the victim doesn't know. I just happened to blow past and Yarrow didn't see me until too late. I could tell from the look on his face that he knew I'd tell you. Want some advice?"

Paul sat brooding for a long moment. "I guess I'd be an idiot to say no, and I already know your opinion of idiots."

Shen grinned. "That you do. My advice is, pretend it never happened. Keep Smilin' Sam at arm's length but don't ever let on you found out. That'll get him real nervous, wondering what *you're* up to. Maybe it'll make him nervous enough to lay off you."

"Is that what you do? Keep Yarrow nervous by not letting on what you're doing?"

"Me? Hell, no. I told Yarrow if he messed with me again I'd stuff him down the solid waste disposal chute. He's probably still playing games behind my back, but at least he's being cautious about it. You're a little more low key than I am, though, if I read you right."

"Yeah. I think so." *Just about everybody's more low key than Jen Shen, if I read her right.* "Okay. I'll take your advice. And thanks. What about Garcia? He must be ready to toss me out the nearest airlock."

"Probably. But he won't, because assaulting a subordinate would look real bad on his record. The best way to handle Garcia is to do the best job you can. If you do good, he'll lay off you. Nothing else will satisfy him except knowing you're not going to make him look bad."

"There's that phrase again. 'Looking bad.' Jen, I don't get it."

"What's not to get?"

Paul waved a hand around to encompass the entire ship. "There seems to be such a mix of people on this ship. I figured the space branch would be, you know, sort of the best and the brightest."

She laughed sharply. "Boy, and I thought I was young! You want the run-down, Paul? There's basically three kinds of people up here. You represent one of them. You volunteered for duty in space. You're idealistic, hard-charging, ready to conquer the universe for humanity."

"I'm not that—"

"Hey, I'm using you as an archetype. When you're a symbol of something you can't quibble over details." Jen leaned back, gazing wistfully out the hatch. "I used to be like that. Now... I don't know. The second type up here are the Carl Meadows of the Navy. They're just out to survive. Keep a low profile, get the job done, don't sweat anything that doesn't need sweating."

"Carl's a real decent guy."

"I didn't say he wasn't. What I said was he'll never make admiral. Carl knows that. He's not going to kill himself chasing a goal he wouldn't really want if he got there. Look around. He's not the only officer in the wardroom like that."

"You mean like Commander Sykes, too?"

"Oh, yeah. Suppo's the king of the slackers. If I ever convert to that religion entirely, he's the guy I'll worship." She sighed. "Then there's the third group, the unjustly exiled. In their eyes, anyway. They got stuck out here, far from all the plum jobs that just about guarantee promotion, far from all the admirals looking for adoring protégés, far from everything. The only way people hear about what you've done in space is if you screw up big time. And I mean big time." Jen flashed a smile. "Messing up an exercise message doesn't make the grade. So these exiles work their butts off, or make their subordinates work their butts off, in hopes they'll grab the golden ring and return home with glory, medals and promotion opportunities galore. In sum, they wanta look good. Problem is, they're not that good to begin with. Which is why they got exiled in the first place."

"I see. That makes a lot of sense. Garcia's an exile, isn't he?" Jen nodded. "And so's the captain."

"Oh, yeah. Cap'n Pete would sell his mother for a ticket back to fleet staff, where he could impress the admiral with his social banter and devotion to the admiral's well-being."

Paul smiled ruefully. "I believe it. But what about the XO? She doesn't seem to fit any of those groups."

Jen frowned. "No. She's sort of an idealist, but not in the 'future of humanity in space' sense. For Herdez, it's the Navy. That's what she believes in. She doesn't give a damn what happens to her. She's here because they told her the ship needed a good XO. Don't ask me how I know that. But, fair warning, Paul, she supports the captain. That's the Navy rule. Don't think because Cap'n Pete is doing something stupid that Herdez will step in and try to stop it. She's the XO, he's the captain. That sets the rules of the universe as far as she's concerned."

"Thanks. Warning duly noted." Paul let his face momentarily sag, once again overwhelmed. "Man, if I had any idea what I was getting into..."

Shen grinned again. "Don't let it get to you. Endure. Find some hobby to keep the insanity and the big black outside at bay."

"What's your hobby?"

"I punch lockers."

Paul smiled back. "I'm glad I'm not a locker." He looked over at his, suddenly concerned again. "I hope I packed everything right." In the morning the *Michaelson* would be maneuvering, and any object not properly fastened down would become a victim of physics.

"I'll check it for you," Shen offered. She popped his locker, eyeing his gear, her face intent, transformed instantly into an experienced professional. "Looks good to me. If anything, you overdid some of the tie downs. But better that than underdoing them." Shen stepped back, glancing questioningly at Paul. "No pictures?"

"Uh, no. No girlfriend."

"Too bad. Or maybe good. Shipboard life is hell on relationships, if you haven't already figured that out."

"I'd guessed. No time for them, right?"

"Right. And if you found any time, you'd be halfway to nowhere when it showed up. You can't even phone home because the distances are so huge light-speed lag makes conversations a pain in the neck, and most of the time you can't send messages either because the ship's trying to keep emissions to a minimum so no one can detect us."

Paul nodded wearily. "So good luck maintaining a relationship with someone off the ship. And I know what regulations say about relationships among crewmembers."

Jen nodded quickly back. "Right again. Don't even *think* about that. If you fall in love, or lust, with someone else on this ship then keep it to yourself until you're walking off the ship for the last time enroute to your next assignment. Then you can share your emotions or whatever with the object of your affections to your heart's content. But don't try it while you're both still assigned to this ship. The XO's not amused when she finds out about that sort of thing."

"Has it been a big problem on the ship?"

Jen shrugged. "A big problem? No. But it happens. We had a couple of enlisted who got busted and fined, one of them subsequently being transferred to the US Navy's equivalent of Siberia. Then there was a lieutenant some time back who couldn't keep his hands off a seaman in his division."

Paul stared in disbelief. "In his division? He messed around with an enlisted sailor in his chain of command? How could he be that stupid? And unprofessional?"

"If you'd ever met the guy, you'd know how he could be that stupid and unprofessional. Of course, if you wanted to meet him now, you'd have to visit the brig where he's serving hard time. Like I said, Herdez doesn't tolerate anything that threatens the chain of command. If you've got a roving eye, try to park it while you're onboard."

Paul laughed. "Jen, to be perfectly honest, one of the few faults I can't lay claim to is a roving eye."

"Not a Don Juan, huh?"

"Nope."

"Good for you. That'll make life onboard easier for you. And if you really need some photos for your locker, you could do what Yarrow does. He's got pictures of his sports car posted."

"You're kidding."

"Take a look when you get a chance." Ensign Shen clapped Paul on the shoulder. "I have to get back to pleading with my bosses for sanity to prevail. Vainly pleading, no doubt, but I have to try so I can scream 'I told you so' with my dying breath. Hang in there, Paul."

"Thanks, Jen."

"You're feeling lost and overwhelmed, right?"

"Does it show?" The thought alarmed Paul, already worried over his performance onboard the ship so far.

But Jen shook her head. "No. You're doing a good enough job of projecting confidence. But it wasn't all that long ago that I was new to the ship. I remember. Boy, do I remember. A lot of things don't get easier, but that part does. Trust me."

"I sure hope you're right. Are you going out with the others tonight?"

"I wish. I've got duty, and even if I didn't I'd be fussing over that damned osmosis device. You?"

"Nope. I'm sort of voluntarily confined to the ship while I reflect on the error of my ways."

"A wise man. See you around. Maybe we can catch a flick after dinner." She smiled again. "My treat."

"I thought movies in the ship's entertainment system were free."

"They are." Laughing, Ensign Shen headed out into the passageway.

3

Paul sat, rechecking his seat harness and hoping his nervousness wasn't apparent to every other person on the *Michaelson*'s bridge. He couldn't decide whether his assignment as junior officer of the deck while the *Michaelson* got underway had been the result of malice or chance, but as he scanned the displays around him Paul was acutely aware that a major screw-up right now could cause extensive damage and cost lives. Not that it seemed likely he would be given such a responsibility right off the bat. However, Paul's discovery of the assignment when he read the underway watch bill had done nothing for his peace of mind. Nor had learning who would be supervising him in that assignment.

He looked over at Lieutenant Tweed, occupying the officer of the deck position, outwardly calm as she ran down checklists. Outwardly calm, but Paul thought he detected tension in her movements. On either side of the bridge, the captain and XO sat in elevated chairs, surveying all the activity around them.

Paul reviewed his own checklist for the third time, then studied the maneuvering display. This close in to the station, it displayed a representation of the *Michaelson* in her berth along with details of Franklin Station itself. The station resembled a huge disc with a hollow center. That disc, Paul knew from his brief stay on-station, held everything from living quarters and administrative offices to repair facilities and bars. Above and below the disc were the dry-docks and berths for the ships the station existed to serve. The whole arrangement rotated just fast enough to generate a feeling of normal gravity in the mid-sections of the disc. When ships berthed at docks along the top or bottom of the disc, facing bow in toward the center and stern out, they joined in that rotation and gained the same feeling of gravity along the same axis that their main drives would accelerate in space. It was all extremely simple, except the part about actually berthing to the station and then leaving it without slamming into anything.

Tweed looked over at Paul, smiled thinly with her lips sealed shut, then made a small thumbs-up gesture. Turning, she faced Captain Wakeman. "Captain, all departments report they are ready for getting underway. We have received clearance from station control to get underway."

Wakeman peered around the bridge, as if suspicious of her report, then nodded. "Very well. Get the ship underway."

"Aye, aye, sir." Tweed focused intently on her display. On ships that sailed water, the bridge sat high and forward, a place from which the conning officer could see and safely direct activity. On space ships, the bridge sat nestled deep within the hull, as safe from external threat as human measures could render it, every view of the outside provided by remote monitors. "All hands, prepare to get underway. Seal quarterdeck access and retract brow."

"Seal quarterdeck and retract brow, aye," the petty officer of the watch echoed in a routine designed to ensure he had heard the order correctly. "Quarterdeck sealed. Station has retracted brow. All seals confirmed tight."

"Take in lines two, three, and four."

"Take in lines two, three, and four, aye." On the outside of the station, grapples released their grip on some of the lines holding the *Michaelson* tightly to the station. As the lines were released, they were reeled in under constant pressure to prevent them from whipping about and damaging the hull. "Lines two, three, and four secure."

"Port thrusters all ahead one-third." Despite the breaking of some of the physical bonds to the station, the ship's mass conformed to Isaac Newton's old laws, one of which said mass kept doing whatever it had been doing until something else affected it. Without the thrusters, the *Michaelson* would have stayed drifting near the station. "Let out lines one and five."

"Port thrusters all ahead one-third, aye," the helmsman echoed.

"Let out lines one and five, aye," the petty officer added.

Under the push of the thrusters, the *Michaelson*'s mass began moving away from the station, the two lines still tethering her paying out slowly as she did so. Centrifugal force inherited from the rotating station began edging the ship outward and to the side as well, putting extra demands on the computers controlling the tension in the lines. They had to maintain just enough pressure to keep the lines taut, but not enough to pull on either the *Michaelson* or the station. Paul watched, feeling the many tons of mass that made up the *Michaelson* slowly gathering momentum, knowing that a wrong application of thrust or a misguided tightening of a line might bring the ship inexorably back into contact with the station.

Tweed waited, watching her displays, the XO watching her, and

Captain Wakeman watching his own monitors. "Stand by to let go all lines. Let go all lines."

"Let go all lines, aye. All lines let go."

Behind Paul, the bosun's pipe sounded. "Underway! Shift colors!" Where a surface ship would have lowered its bow and stern flags and raised one from the main mast, the bosun on the *Michaelson* simply punched a key on his console, changing her self-broadcast identity code to indicate the ship was no longer tethered to another object with a fixed orbit.

Lieutenant Tweed nodded stiffly, still watching her display, where the separation between ship and station grew steadily as the *Michaelson* swung out and ahead. Paul could see a fine sheen of sweat on her upper lip. "Port thrusters all ahead two-thirds. Main drive all ahead one-third."

"Port thrusters all ahead two-thirds, aye. Main drive all ahead one-third, aye."

Paul felt a kick in his back as the *Michaelson*'s powerful main drive kicked in, shoving the ship forward even as the maneuvering thrusters pushed her farther away from the station. On his display, the ship's projected course now formed a beautiful arc leading away from the station.

Tweed watched as the display showed the ship's actual path rising to match the projected path set by the station traffic monitors. Just before the two paths merged she called out more commands. "Secure port thrusters. Main drive all ahead two-thirds."

"Port thrusters secure, aye, main drive all ahead two-thirds, aye."

Tweed looked back to where the quartermaster sat. "Recommendation?"

"I recommend course two three zero degrees absolute, up fifteen degrees, ma'am. That will take us toward the center of our assigned operating area."

Tweed looked toward the captain, who nodded brusquely. "Very well," she acknowledged. "Helm, bring us to course two three zero degrees absolute, up fifteen degrees. Captain, request permission to secure from getting underway."

"Permission granted."

Tweed gestured to the petty officer of the watch, who triggered the ship's intercom. "All hands, secure from getting underway. The ship remains in maneuvering status. All hands exercise caution in moving about."

USS *Michaelson* shuddered as the helm orders caused thrusters around her hull to fire, killing drift in one direction, then bringing her bow around to the desired course. Paul watched the process unfold on his display like a piece of fine art, the current course track once again sliding gently into perfect alignment with the desired course.

"The captain has left the bridge." Startled by the petty officer's announcement, Paul looked around, suddenly realizing he had been paying attention to nothing but the track display. *That's dumb. Even I should know better. I have to stay aware of everything going on while I'm on the watch.*

The XO unbuckled herself as well, moving carefully against the force provided by *Michaelson*'s main drives. "Good job, Ms. Tweed."

"Thank you, ma'am." Tweed watched Herdez leave the bridge, then sighed heavily, leaning back against the acceleration. "God. It's over."

Paul eyed her with surprise. "You handled that real well."

"It surprises people. I know."

"That's not—"

"Yes, it was. Don't worry about it. I understand. I'm just glad it's over." Tweed wiped her lower face with one hand, smearing the sweat, and breathed deeply several times.

Paul watched her, unable to match what he'd already seen of Jan Tweed with the way she'd handled getting the *Michaelson* underway. "Were you really that worried?"

She cocked one eye at Paul, then snorted a brief laugh. "Paul, I was scared out of my mind. I always am."

"But you did it real well, ma'am. It was like... like, a piece of art."

"Thanks. The key is to feel the ship. Don't just look at the displays. Feel how she's moving. Some of these clods just try to jerk her around and end up burning enough reaction mass to get us to Jupiter and back." Tweed looked annoyed. "My name's Jan. Any lieutenant who needs to be formal with other junior officers needs an ego-ectomy."

"Aye, aye, Jan."

"Good. How about you take the conn now?" Paul felt his guts twist, then nodded. Having the conn meant he would be responsible for giving commands controlling the *Michaelson*'s course and speed. Even with Lieutenant Tweed sitting nearby, and even with experienced sailors at the controls, it was a huge responsibility. Yet it was also a responsibility he should shoulder as soon as possible. *You only learn to drive ships by driving ships.*

Tweed turned slightly, speaking loudly enough that her voice carried across the bridge. "This is Lieutenant Tweed. Ensign Sinclair has the conn."

"This is Ensign Sinclair," Paul stated as steadily as he could, trying to match Tweed's tone. "I have the conn." The petty officer of the watch and the helm watchstander nodded in acknowledgement.

Tweed grinned. "Scared?" she whispered.

"Terrified."

"Good. Stay scared. People who relax end up having collisions. Just keep on eye on the contacts being tracked. The equipment is supposed to let us know if anything is on a collision or near-miss track relative to us, but it isn't smart to trust that entirely. Keep an eye on the tracks and be ready to react if any act funny." She called up data on her screen. "See this? That's our track through the operating area. Here's how we're coming in. Looks like there's a couple of other ships out there, but they've got their beacons on and are well clear of us."

"Right. Beacons."

Tweed watched Paul intently. "You know why beacons are important, Paul? Why we need to know if they're on or off on us or other ships?"

"Well, they make it easier to see the ships, right?"

"You might say that. *Michaelson* and other warships are designed to be as environmentally passive as possible. That means they're real hard to see. Visually, infrared, radar, whatever. What happens when you're walking around things you can't see?"

"You trip over them."

"Yeah. Every second you're standing watch up here, you have to think about other ships tripping over us because they can't see us, or us hitting someone we didn't see until too late." She grinned nervously. "I hate it. Really."

"I can see why." Paul's mind briefly looked ahead, to endless hours worrying about unseen objects in the *Michaelson*'s path, then he shut down the vision. *If I think about that too much, it'll scare me to death.* "Jan? Can I ask something personal?"

"Depends. Ask and I'll let you know if I want to answer."

"You handled getting us underway just fine. Right now, you feel like you're in charge. Really capable. But, well, I don't know how to say this—"

"I've got a reputation as someone who can't be trusted and shirks responsibility. Is that it?"

"I didn't—"

"You don't have to." Tweed slumped a bit, staring glumly at her displays. "I'm not a bad officer, Paul. I'm not going to foul up anything big or hurt a fellow officer. But I miss little stuff. Here and there. It adds up. And when I miss little stuff I get chewed out, and I don't like that. So I hide. Don't look like that. I know that's what people say. It's true. I will be the happiest human in history when I leave this ship. Until then, I'm just trying not to screw up any big things. Okay?"

"Okay."

"Enough on that. Here's another tip on something that's gotten me into trouble more than once." Tweed grinned in obvious self-mockery. "Distance in space is weird. You feel like it takes forever to get anywhere, but then you find yourself someplace a lot quicker than you expected. And you're not ready for getting there because your mind is in long-distance-nothing-happening coast mode. How far are we from the operating area?"

"Uh..." Paul checked his scan frantically, surprised when he saw the projected arrival time had already shrunk appreciably. "Closer than I thought."

"We move fast up here. Earth instincts are totally out of whack with the distances and the speeds. So get as much ready as you can, as soon as you can, *before* you're actually at the objective. Go ahead and work up the maneuver needed to match us onto our planned track once we get to the OPAREA."

"Okay." Paul brought up his display, concentrating on the 3-D picture. The maneuvers needed were easily calculated, just calling for plugging in the amount of thrust you wanted to use from both the maneuvering thrusters and the main drive. Then the answer popped up as a time to turn and activate the drives. "How's this?"

Tweed looked the solution over, then nodded. "Looks okay to me."

"Do we need to call the captain for this?"

"Not necessarily. Scheduled maneuver. But I will. Or I'll let you do it. I don't like talking to him all that much." Tweed grinned nervously again. "Just also be sure to give the petty officer of the watch a five minute heads-up so he can broadcast a warning to all hands that the ship will be maneuvering."

"Right. Five minutes' warning." They sat silently for a while, watching the paths of the *Michaelson* and other contacts, natural objects and manmade, curving around through the navigational displays. Part of Tweed's warning to be prepared in advance came back to Paul, so he called up the standing orders and reviewed the part explaining how the captain wanted calls to him to be handled. *Short, quick, detailed, complete. How can something be all those things at once?* Paul thought about his sole encounter with Captain Wakeman to date, then looked over where Lieutenant Tweed sat studying her displays with the demeanor of someone walking through a minefield. *So many ways to mess up. So many opportunities to mess up. It's easy to see how Jan Tweed ended up this way. But if I let it get to me I'll end up like her.*

"Paul."

Sinclair tried not to jerk in guilty surprise as Jan spoke right on the heels of his last thought. "Yes?"

"We're coming up on that course change."

"We are?" Paul checked his display, appalled to see less than ten minutes remained until the optimum time for the maneuver. "Okay. Okay."

"Relax. I'm here. The petty officer at the helm knows his job. There's no other ships detected within a thousand kilometers. You can't screw up too bad. Ready to call the captain?"

Paul hesitated, wishing Tweed would take on that responsibility, then nodded. He mentally ran through the wording of his statement again, then keyed the circuit to the captain's cabin. "Captain Wakeman. Bridge."

After a brief pause, a clipped answer came. "Yes."

"Sir, this is the junior officer of the deck. We are, that is, the *Michaelson* is approaching—"

"Briefly. Spit it out."

Paul swallowed. "We are coming up on a course change in six minutes, captain."

"Why?"

"To enter our operating area and merge with our track, sir."

"Very well."

The circuit clicked dead. Paul fought down a wave of annoyance, glancing over at Jan, who shrugged in reply. "Bosun mate of the watch?"

"Yes, sir."

"Notify the crew that we will be maneuvering in five minutes."

"Aye, aye, sir." The bosun mate keyed the intercom, calling out the warning throughout the ship.

Paul waited, watching the minutes and seconds count down. At zero, he called out commands in a voice he thought a little too loud, a little too strident. "Helm, maneuvering thrusters at one-third power.

Bring us to course one eight zero degrees absolute, up ten degrees. Maintain main drive at all-ahead one-third."

"Maneuvering thrusters at one-third, aye. Coming to course one eight zero degrees absolute, up ten degrees." *Michaelson* shuddered again as the thrusters pushed her onto a new vector, her mass slowly responding to the pressure. Paul watched with a sense of pleasure as the ship swung onto the projected course vector he'd calculated.

"Captain's on the bridge!"

Paul looked around frantically as Captain Wakeman hopped into his chair and fastened his harness, then looked over at him and Tweed. "Let's get going!" Wakeman commanded. "Thrusters on full! Main drive ahead two-thirds!"

Paul glanced at Tweed, who quickly signaled him to comply. Hastily checking the display again to ensure the maneuver wouldn't cause immediate problems with other contacts in the area, Paul called out the commands. "Thrusters on full. Main drive ahead two-thirds." The helm echoed the command, then the *Michaelson* jumped under the multiplied force of her drives. Inertia and acceleration tugged at Paul, making him thankful for his tight harness, as the ship yawed into a tighter, faster turn. The hull groaned, complaining of the strain on its structure. Paul scanned his display, watching the ship's projected track swinging far off the planned course through the OPAREA and trying to understand the reason for the captain's orders.

Wakeman leaned back, grinning happily even though his face reflected the stress of the maneuvers. "This is more like it! Looking good, people! Now, where are we going? What are we doing?"

For the first time in his life, Paul felt his jaw actually drop in amazement as he stared at Wakeman. *He has no idea where we're going or why and he kicked the ship around like that?*

Tweed signaled him again, a resigned expression on her face, speaking softly. "I'll take it, Paul." Then, in a louder voice she called to the bridge. "This is Lieutenant Tweed. I have the conn. Captain, we are enroute our planned track through the OPAREA..."

Paul felt his attention straying from Tweed's words, still stunned that a cruiser had been jerked around for no discernible reason. He watched the subsequent maneuvers, as Tweed nursed the *Michaelson* back onto the track the ship had been intended to take. Captain Wakeman looked increasingly bored, then abruptly popped out of his chair and headed for the hatch.

"The captain has left the bridge!"

Paul looked over at Tweed, sure his face still showed his emotions. "Why'd he do that? What was the point?"

Tweed looked like she'd eaten something bitter yet familiar. "He told us. 'Looking good.' Pushing the ship through that high-speed turn set off alerts on every ship in the area, and back at the station where they're still tracking us. He was showing off."

"That's it?"

"That's it. Get used to it."

The watch crawled to its end without further event. Carl Meadows was Paul's relief, listening to the turn-over with jaded stoicism and checking the list of scheduled events for his watch. "Okay. I got it."

"Thanks. On the bridge, this is Mr. Sinclair. Mr. Meadows has the watch."

"This is Mr. Meadows. I have the watch and the conn. See ya, Paul."

He left the bridge, moving with caution under the unfamiliar conditions of being underway. The push of the *Michaelson*'s main drive provided an illusion of gravity, but not normal gravity. Paul fought down a quiver in his arms and legs brought on by relief and tension, still grasping a handhold just outside the bridge as Jan Tweed came through. "Uh, thanks, Jan."

"Don't mention it. You going to lunch?"

"I don't think my stomach can handle it."

"Oh, yeah. Don't worry, you'll get your space legs in a while. Remember, we've also got the second dog watch." Paul nodded numbly, recalling that the watches around the evening meal were 'dogged' in half so both watch sections could eat. "Be sure to eat dinner early if you're up for it by then."

"Thanks." Paul made his way to his ensign locker, trying not to notice the amusement his shaky progress and strained expression brought out in the crew he passed. He made it to his bunk, lay down, and stared at the already familiar pipes, wires and ducts running just above his nose.

At some point, he must have fallen asleep. The bang of the hatch opening startled Paul awake. "Hey, Sinclair. You in here?"

"Yeah, Sam." He'd followed Jen's advice, not letting on he knew about the trick Sam Yarrow had pulled on him. It had seemed to make Yarrow nervous in a manner Paul found gratifying.

"The XO said to remind you she wanted to see you."

"Right now?"

"I guess. What's up?"

"I don't know." The honest answer seemed to annoy Yarrow, bringing another spurt of satisfaction to Paul. He rolled out of his rack, very cautiously, and made his way to the XO's stateroom. "Commander? You wanted to see me?"

Herdez seemed unfazed by the effects of being underway. Except for the straps holding her to her seat, they might still have been moored to Franklin Station. "Take a seat, Mr. Sinclair. Be sure to strap in."

"Yes, ma'am."

Herdez passed over a data cartridge. "I want you to take a look at this and give an evaluation. It's our patrol orders and rules of engagement. They're still not for general distribution, so share that card with no one."

"Ma'am?" Paul was sure his face reflected his bafflement. *I'm an ensign who can barely find his way around the ship, and she's asking me for an evaluation of operational orders?*

Herdez almost smiled at Paul's reaction. Almost. "I don't need an operational assessment, Mr. Sinclair. I want a legal assessment. These orders require us to do certain things in certain ways. I want to know how you would interpret them in legal terms based on the training you've received in that area."

"Yes, ma'am." Paul hesitated, turning the data cartridge in his hand. "Am I looking for anything in particular, XO?"

"Anything you don't understand, anything you can't pin down, anything that might need interpreting. Understand? If we're being sent out under orders crafted in legalese, I want to know what they might mean to someone who was seeing them for the first time. Thank you."

"Yes, ma'am." Sensing he'd been dismissed, Paul left the stateroom, pausing in the passageway to once again examine the data cartridge. *She didn't say so, but the XO doesn't seem to trust these orders. What's in them that's got her worried? And if someone as good as the XO is worried, maybe I ought to be scared to death.* Paul headed back to his stateroom, thankful he'd brought all his notes from the legal course.

"Sinclair!"

Paul stopped in his tracks at Commander Garcia's hail. "Yes, sir?"

"Where the hell is Lieutenant Tweed?"

I've got a feeling I'm going to get incredibly tired of hearing that question. "I don't know, sir."

"Find out. No, never mind. Get your division's training records and meet me in the Operations office."

"Yes, sir." *Training records? Oh, man, I've hardly glanced at those.* Paul glanced at the data cartridge. *I could use this as an excuse. Tell Garcia the XO needs me to do this right away... but then Garcia might ask the XO. And doing that would set me down Jan Tweed's road right off the bat. I can't start out hiding. She didn't even start out that way, I bet.* He stowed the cartridge in one pocket, pondering his next step.

"Make way." Kris Denaldo shot Paul a curious glance as he edged to the side of the passageway to let her past. "I've hardly seen you since you came aboard."

"It's been a busy few days, Kris."

"I bet. You're still trying to figure out which way is up, right? Jen told me to help keep an eye on you. Need anything?"

Paul nodded, thinking as he did so that Bull Ensign Sam Yarrow should have been the one telling other junior officers to help out the new guy. "Yes, but nothing you can help with. Garcia wants to see my division's training records."

"And... ?"

"Well, I haven't even looked at those, yet."

"Oh. You ought to. It's a good way to learn your enlisted sailors' names and abilities."

Paul bit back a sarcastic reply. *That's good advice, even though there's about a hundred things I ought to do within the next couple of days.* "I will, but

Garcia wants to see the records now, and I'm not even sure where they are."

"Then just ask... never mind."

"What?"

Kris Denaldo looked embarrassed. "I was going to say you should just ask your division officer, but that's Jan Tweed, so..."

"So I may not even be able to find her. What else can I do?"

Kris shrugged. "Get ahold of your chief."

"My chief?"

"Your senior enlisted. That's Chief Imari, right? I've heard she's a good chief, so she should be able to help you if anyone can."

Paul brightened. *I've been thinking I'm alone in this job, but I do have people I can count on to at least show me the way. People like my chief, and people like some of my fellow junior officers.* "Thanks, Kris. That's great advice."

She was already moving away from him, continuing on down the passageway. "No problem. Gotta run. See you around."

Locating Chief Imari didn't prove to be hard, as she was in the combat information center working at one of the terminals.

"Divisional training records? No problem, Mr. Sinclair." Imari tapped in a couple of commands, popped out a data cartridge, then stood. "Let's go."

"Uh, chief, Commander Garcia said he wanted to see me."

"Did he say he didn't want to see me, too?"

"No."

"Then let's go, sir."

When they reached the nearby Operations office, Commander Garcia glanced from Sinclair to Imari with a sour expression, snatched the proffered cartridge from Imari's hand, then scanned the data rapidly. "Sinclair, has Seaman Frost completed all the requirements for damage control training?"

Out of the corner of his eye, Paul saw Chief Imari incline her head in a surreptitious nod. "Yes, sir."

"Hmmm. What about Petty Officer Kaji? Is she done with her passive tracking qualifications?"

This time Chief Imari twitched her head ever-so-slightly to one side and back. "No, sir."

"She should have finished that training by now. Will she have it done by the time we return to the station?"

Another nod. "Yes, sir."

"Hmmm." Commander Garcia swiveled to view Chief Imari and Paul squarely. "These look okay. Keep on it, Sinclair."

"Yes, sir."

"Did you need something, chief?"

"No, sir. As the divisional training assistant, I figured I should accompany Mr. Sinclair."

Garcia looked from Imari to Sinclair, then pulled out the data cartridge and pointedly returned it to Paul before pivoting back to face his terminal. "That's all."

Paul nodded to the back of Garcia's head and followed Imari out and back to CIC. "Chief, you saved my butt in there."

"No, sir. I did my job, part of which is to help young naval officers through their learning process."

Paul grinned. "Thanks. But I ought to take over maintaining these training records. I'm being paid to do it, after all."

"Mr. Sinclair, how many jobs do you have right now?"

"Ummm, five."

"Yes, sir. So if I handle part of one of them, you got to figure the Navy is still getting its money's worth, right?"

"That's true, but—"

"But nothing, sir. I'm the division's training assistant. That's official. There ain't anything wrong with me keeping these records up."

"Commander Garcia told *me* to do it."

"Yes, sir. And good officers don't try to handle every task they're responsible for themselves, do they? They delegate them." Imari reached and took the data cartridge from Paul. "Just like you're delegating this particular job to me. With all due respect, sir, you probably don't have the time to maintain these records right."

"Chief, I can't argue with that. But I do want to go over those records with you and be familiar with them."

"That's good, sir. Want to do it now?"

"Yes, I—" Paul stopped, remembering the data cartridge he'd received from Commander Herdez. "I want to, chief, but there's something the XO told me to take a look at."

"The XO?" Chief Imari looked slightly disconcerted. "She's giving you tasking directly?"

"No, chief, not like that." If the executive officer had been directly giving Paul orders on what to do within his division officer's job, instead of routing such instructions through Commander Garcia, it would have been a gross breach of the chain of command and poor leadership as well. "It's something to do with my collateral duty as ship's legal officer."

"Oh." Imari didn't try to hide her relief. "That's okay, sir. You take care of the XO's stuff and we'll get together on the training records later."

"Thanks again, chief. Hey, *is* Kaji going to get those passive tracking quals done?"

"Yes, sir. We had a little conversation about that and I think she's real motivated now."

Paul kept a straight face with some effort. "Sounds good. Later, chief."

Since his ensign locker was both empty and likely to be the best place for any degree of privacy, Paul loaded the XO's data cartridge into the terminal at his desk and began carefully picking his way through the convoluted official wording. The early sections were essentially boilerplate, standard wording with slight modifications to fit the exact circumstances of the *Michaelson*'s upcoming patrol.

Then he reached the section on operating instructions, and began bogging down. "USS *Michaelson* is to conduct a thorough patrol of the US space sovereignty zone, ensuring through her actions that all violations are countered in such a fashion that US sovereignty is unchallenged." *What does that mean exactly? A challenge to sovereignty can be as subtle as somebody sticking their toe into our claimed area of space. But these orders say we have to counter every violation. If the captain lets a single incident go unchallenged, we wouldn't be carrying out our orders. But "countered in such a fashion that US sovereignty is unchallenged" implies that we've got to really hammer anyone trying anything. Or does it? The lawyers who taught me this legal stuff could have taken a phrase like that and made it mean anything.*

Paul read on, a headache growing as he tried to nail down meanings in phrases which seemed to grow increasingly vague. "Actions are to be tailored to reflect requirements of the operational situation as well as tactical considerations... swift and effective response to emerging opportunities is expected... care should be exercised in avoiding unnecessarily provocative situations... nothing in these orders should be construed as limiting the captain's ability to respond appropriately to any situation."

The rules of engagement proved even more twisted than the operating instructions. "USS *Michaelson* shall ensure that any violations of US space sovereignty are countered with all appropriate and necessary actions." *"Shall" means the captain has to do it, but do what? "Appropriate" and "necessary" are both situational words. What one person thinks is appropriate in a certain case, someone else might declare inappropriate. So the captain has to do something, but they won't tell him what he can or should do. It's up to him to figure it out. Wait.* "USS *Michaelson* should refrain from any and all action(s) likely to generate activity resulting in adverse consequences for national policy objectives." *So we "shall" do everything "appropriate" but "shouldn't" do anything inappropriate, I guess.*

On one level, the instructions made sense. After all, captains of ships, by long tradition and legal precedent, were given great powers and expected to exercise a tremendous amount of discretion in using those powers. For Earth-bound or near-orbit operations, that old rule no longer really applied thanks to virtually instant communications networks which gave higher authority the ability to monitor and direct any action by a captain. But out in deeper space, the light-speed limit on communications meant that long periods could still elapse between the need for a decision and whatever direction came back from home. Captains had to be trusted to make decisions without precise instructions.

But these orders are still too vague. There's no upper or lower limit on them. "Appropriate and necessary"? That could be nothing. That could be opening fire and destroying another ship. Or anything in between.

Paul read on. "The safety and security of USS *Michaelson* shall be safeguarded against hostile activity by taking all actions required in accordance with the tactical and operational environment." *How does that "shall" rank compared to the "shall" that directs the* Michaelson *do whatever it takes to prevent US sovereignty from being challenged? What if someone after the fact decides certain actions taken were or weren't "required"? Heck, it says "all actions required." "All"? We could be nailed if they think we didn't do one thing that someone could judge "required."*

He skipped down a ways, suddenly eager to see the accompanying intelligence assessment. "Aggressive challenges to our sovereign claimed areas may materialize... foreign forces encountered may be operating under unknown rules of engagement... composition or nature of foreign spacecraft likely to be encountered remains unknown... possible hostile action cannot be ruled out but cannot be predicted at this time... unconventional threats remain possible... warning of hostile action may not be timely..."

Paul rubbed his forehead, closing his eyes but still seeing in his mind the words of the orders he'd been reading. *So, if my assessment of the legal meaning of these orders is right, we're being ordered to do everything we should do, but nothing we shouldn't do, against an unknown level and degree of threat, and do all that without making anybody mad that the US doesn't want to make mad.* He thought of Captain Wakeman, happily hurling his ship through extreme maneuvers in the hope it might impress anyone who might be watching, without much thought to where the ship was actually going and planning on doing. *And the paragon of good judgment and careful analysis who is supposed to decide what's "appropriate," "necessary," and "required" in every circumstance is Cap'n Pete Wakeman. Good grief.*

Paul began writing a report to the XO, working through it word by word to avoid implying anything about his opinion of Wakeman's judgment or ability to execute the orders. *Just lay out the contradictions I see, and the areas in which guidance is vague enough to create potential problems. The XO doesn't need me telling her how to operate a ship. And I've got a feeling that if anybody on this ship can read between the lines and see trouble ahead, it's Herdez.* He wasn't thrilled with the end result, but couldn't think how to improve upon it, so he sent it to the XO's inbox and hoped it would at least come close to meeting her standards.

4

Lieutenant Jan Tweed slowly reached forward, gently tapping a few controls on her watch station console. In the dim lighting of the bridge, the gentle radiance of the illuminated control panels seemed to glow like small candles behind colored glass. On the screen displaying an image of the outside, nothing could be seen but endless dark spotted with countless stars, each bright and hard as a diamond. Somehow that vision of emptiness sucked the warmth from the bridge, leaving Paul shivering slightly, even though he knew the temperature inside the ship was comfortable for both humans and their machines.

The ship's night had been in effect for hours now, with reddened, minimal internal lighting which helped keep human sleep cycles on track. When sunrise officially arrived in a few more hours, the internal lights would brighten to mimic daylight on Earth. But for now, darkness ruled both inside and outside the ship, as did a quiet aimed at aiding the sleep of those crew members fortunate enough not to be on watch.

One month out of Franklin Station, weeks away from routes frequented by humans (though *frequented* often meant little in the vast spaces of the solar system) the *Michaelson* proceeded on a patrol marked so far by isolation and emptiness. Paul glanced at the time as Tweed worked at the casual pace of someone who knew they had hours of boredom yet to endure. The mid-watch had started at midnight, ship's time, even though Paul had actually been on the bridge a half-hour earlier for turn-over with the officer he was relieving on watch. It would run until four in the morning, or 0400 on the twenty-four hour military clocks. Paul's thoughts idly wandered back to the days when he'd called that time 4 A.M., back before the Academy had rearranged the way he thought about time and a lot of other things. Back then, the eerie quiet of a world where almost everyone and everything else was asleep had been foreign to him. Now, the low lighting, the hushed silence aboard the *Michaelson* and the cold-beyond-cold outside the ship's hull combined to leave him chilled and subdued.

Tweed leaned back again. From the speaker near her position, odd sounds began issuing. Something like whale song, veering wordlessly up and down the scale, snatches of almost-words growing to near-audibility then fading away, bursts of random static that somehow seemed to form patterns just beyond his grasp, and beneath it all a low hiss of background noise.

Paul shivered again. "What *is* that?"

"Space ghosts." Tweed's lips quirked in a smile that was only half-humorous. "That's what they're called, anyway. You lower the noise filters for your radio receiver and expand the frequency reception band. Then you hear them."

A long, low moan whispered across the circuit. "Jeez. That's weird. I guess it's actually really weak signals, Earth-origin and like that, too weak and distorted to be understood? And background radiation and stuff like that?"

"Technically, yeah. A physicist can give you a full run-down of the likely origin of every sound you hear. But... if you listen to it, out here, you hear other stuff. Stuff that doesn't seem to fit technical models." A sound like a whisper, seemingly just a fraction too quiet to be understood, echoed softly, then vanished into a series of static bursts that almost sounded like Morse code, but weren't. "That's why they're nicknamed space ghosts. If you listen long enough, you start to hear things. Long-lost ships calling for help, maybe. Aliens sending messages, maybe threats or maybe greetings. Other stuff." Jan Tweed half-smiled again. "I served with a warrant officer once who swore that one night he heard his name called, clear as a bell, by an old shipmate. A shipmate who'd been dead several years."

Paul fought down another shiver. "He was probably just messing with you. You know warrants. They love to play games with the minds of junior officers."

"Maybe."

"Mr. Sinclair?" Paul turned as his name was called. Petty Officer Juniro, the quartermaster of the watch, was nodding solemnly. Usually, the quartermaster and the bosun mate of the watch sat in the rear of the bridge, conversing among themselves in a social world separate from that of the officers until professional duties required communication. "Sir, there's stuff out here that doesn't belong in any technical manual. That's a fact, sir." The bosun nodded as well, her face somber. "You heard of the Titan Expedition, right?"

"The Titan Expedition? Which one?"

"The second, sir. Where they lost those people?"

"Oh, yeah. An ice quake, wasn't it?" He glanced at Tweed for confirmation. "They'd landed on what they thought was a stable section of the ice sheet covering that moon of Saturn, but then the sheet started breaking apart and throwing out plates of ice that could have sliced through the ship, so the lander had to do an emergency lift-off to avoid being destroyed. Several members of the exploration team didn't make it back in time."

"Right, sir. And then the fourth expedition."

"The fourth? That had two landers, if I remember right. That's about all I know of that one."

Juniro nodded, his eyes intent. "Right, sir," he repeated. "The third expedition, that one went somewhere else on Titan, but the fourth came back to near where the second one had landed. And it had two landers. Well, they hadn't been down long, the first ship's night in fact, when the watch standers on the first lander spotted some people moving on the surface." Paul raised his eyebrows to indicate interest as Juniro continued. "They was surprised, you see, 'cause there wasn't supposed to be anybody out exploring just then. But they spotted these suits moving. After they saw the first couple of them they tracked back and spotted the others coming up out of a cleft in the ice. Then they watched 'em, six of 'em, walk up to the second lander and walk up the access ladder and into the airlock."

Paul glanced at Tweed, then back at the quartermaster. "So?"

"So, like I said, sir, there wasn't supposed to be anybody on the surface just then. The watch notified the expedition commander and he called the second lander and demanded to know who the hell had sent a party out. And the second lander says 'Nobody.' They said they hadn't sent anyone onto the surface. So then the commander asks 'em who just came aboard the lander and they said 'Nobody.' And sure enough, the auto-logs for the second lander didn't show anybody coming in through the airlock. But the three watch standers on the first lander, three of 'em, sir, all swore they'd seen six suits walk to that lander and climb aboard."

Juniro paused, looking from Paul to Lieutenant Tweed to the bosun. "That's when they remembered the second lander had been the same lander used in the second expedition. The one that left those crew members behind, sir." Juniro paused again. "And there'd been six of 'em, sir. Six crew left behind to be swallowed by the ice. Well, the instruments all said nothing had happened, but the watch standers on the first lander, they knew what they'd seen. Those six crew members, they'd finally made it back to their lander."

Silence stretched, before Paul became aware he was holding his breath and inhaled deeply. He glanced at Tweed, who was frowning at the deck, then at the two enlisted. The quartermaster and the bosun nodded at each other, apparently sharing in a knowledge born not of physics but of years riding the deck plates, no trace of covert mirth on their faces. A long, undulating rhythm of static rolled out of Tweed's speaker, ending in a brief shriek which seemed to choke off abruptly. Outside, the stars glittered coldly.

Carl Meadows chuckled softly. "Juniro's a bull artist, Paul. He can spin a great sea-story, but don't buy any bridges from him."

"So that stuff about the fourth Titan expedition isn't true?"

Carl shrugged. "I've no idea. Could be."

"The logs from the expedition—"

"Wouldn't prove anything. If the incident wasn't there, you could argue the commander ordered them not to log it, or that the logs had been censored afterward."

Paul frowned. "I thought logs couldn't be altered once they were recorded."

"Oh, hell, Paul. Maybe *I* ought to try to sell you a bridge. Of course they can alter logs. They're just electronic data. I don't care what safeguards officially exist, I'll guarantee you there's ways to get around them. Stuff happens that no one wants to be in logs, right? So you change history a little. Click, click, click. Never happened. All is right with the world."

Paul laughed. "Okay. So I'm naïve. I'm an ensign."

"You've been one for a few months, now." Meadows grinned. "You've got to start learning sometime."

"Yes, sir, Lieutenant Junior Grade Meadows, sir. So what do you, personally, think? Is that Titan stuff just a ghost story?"

Meadows pursed his lips, then shrugged again. "Hell if I know. Sometimes that stuff is easy to believe. Other times it sounds like nonsense. On the bridge, on the mid-watch, in the middle of nowhere, it plays real. But tell it in a bar on Franklin Station and you'd probably find yourself laughed out of Earth orbit."

"Then you're an agnostic on space ghosts?"

Carl grinned again. "Human spirits can seem a long ways away out here, but it's too damn cold and empty to be comfortable with atheism. Call me a space ghost pragmatist."

"Aye, aye, sir."

"Hey, Sinclair!" Paul winced slightly as Ensign Sam Yarrow stuck his head in the stateroom. Turning, he saw Yarrow standing in the hatch to the ensign locker and smiling at him with apparent commiseration. "I just wanted to give you a heads-up. Commander

Garcia was checking how his junior officers were doing on their open space warfare officer qualifications." Paul barely kept from wincing again. With everything else demanding his time, he hadn't even looked at his OSWO qualification requirements in over a week. "He wasn't too happy. Sorry to be the bearer of bad news."

Yeah, I bet. I also bet you were the one who got him thinking he should check on my OSWO quals, after you'd gotten a bunch of your own OSWO stuff signed off. Outwardly, Paul just nodded. "Thanks."

"No problem. Just—"

"Coming through. Make way," Kris Denaldo barked, elbowing Yarrow to one side. Ignoring Yarrow's glower, she focused on Meadows. "Carl. You promised to check off some of my OSWO qualifications. I've got maybe half an hour before all hell breaks loose again. You free?"

"Free enough." Carl gestured to Paul. "And, by sheer coincidence, Paul here is also ready to get some of his OSWO stuff signed off. Right?"

"Uh..."

"Right. Come on." Meadows and Sinclair crowded out past Yarrow, then Denaldo flattened herself against the bulkhead to let Meadows take the lead as he headed for the compartments near the outer hull.

Paul steamed silently until Kris tapped his shoulder. "What's up?"

"Oh, our supportive bull ensign just screwed me again. I suppose he's screwed you plenty of times, too."

"He'd like to." She laughed as Paul reacted to the double-meaning. "Not that he has a hamster's chance in hard vacuum of getting his wish. But as for the sort of screwing you're talking about, don't let it get to you. Life's too short. Days are too short."

"How do you keep going, Kris? Every time I see you, you're in motion."

"My mind's always five minutes behind the rest of me. By the time I realize I'm exhausted, I'm already past that point and doing something else."

Carl Meadows stopped at an access hatch leading toward the outer hull, keying the monitor next to it. "Lieutenant Meadows, Ensign Denaldo and Ensign Sinclair accessing maintenance trunk B-205-E."

An engineering watch stander responded, his voice tinged with boredom at the routine. "Purpose of access, sir?"

"Officer qualification review."

"Anticipated duration?"

"Fifteen minutes."

"Permission granted to access maintenance trunk B-205-E, Lieutenant Meadows. Notify the damage control watch upon exiting the space."

"Affirmative." Carl cracked the hatch, its squarish dimensions betraying the constricted nature of the maintenance trunk it guarded, then waved Kris Denaldo through. "Ladies first. Paul, you follow me." Paul fought down a tinge of claustrophobia as he watched the other two swing inside a tunnel-like access trunk with sides measuring only about a meter wide. As if sensing Paul's misgivings, or perhaps remembering his own experiences, Carl grinned back at Paul as he swung in. "We're lucky, you know. If they didn't have to make these things wide enough for someone in a full protective suit to squeeze through they'd be a lot narrower."

"Lucky us." Paul followed cautiously as the small party moved several meters along the trunk before Carl called a halt.

"Okay." Carl Meadows pointed to the outer surface of the trunk they were in. A pattern was visible there, of hexagons joined at every side and repeating as far as could be seen. "Ensign Denaldo, what are we looking at?"

"The water-blanket."

"That's its nickname. The official nomenclature is... ?"

"Sorry. That's the Ship's Inner Hull Thermal Absorption Barrier System. Mark Four."

"Mod?"

Denaldo twisted to look back at Carl, her expression exasperated. "Why do I need to know the mod? This is a, uh, Mod Two. But that doesn't matter, because the only difference between the different models is superficial."

"Who told you that?"

"Jen."

Carl nodded. "Jen's right, but you're wrong. Why do you have to know the mod number? Because your qualification standards say you have to know the mod number. And that means when you go up for a screening board they'll ask you the mod number."

"So I have to know it not because it's important but because I'm going to be asked anyway?"

"Exactly. Sometimes it is important to know the mod number, so they make you know it all the time. Okay, here we have a Mark Four Mod Two Ship's Inner Hull Thermal Absorption Barrier System. What's it do?"

"What it says." Kris waved her hand at the hexagonal honeycomb. "Every one of those hexagons outlines a cell filled with water and interconnected to every hexagon next to it. That water barrier forms the inner hull of the ship, and absorbs all the heat generated by the crew and equipment."

"What else does it absorb? Paul?"

Paul swallowed, thinking through his answer before replying. "It also absorbs any incoming heat or radiation striking the outer hull. That protects the crew from radiation, and our reflected heat signature is reduced to a minimum, making the ship harder for anyone to spot against the background of space."

"Right. Why do we use water for that?"

"Because water is the best heat sink in the known universe?"

Carl nodded. "Right again. It also stops radiation pretty darn good, and using it as a barrier gives us a place to store water we need for the ship and crew anyway. But what happens to the heat this stuff absorbs? Kris?"

"It gets circulated by pumps, with higher-temperature water cycled toward the main machinery room. Once it gets hot enough there, they run it through a low-pressure tube—"

"Which is actually named?"

"A Venturi tube. Increases velocity and reduces pressure. The hot water flashes to steam, and the steam gets shunted to counter-rotating turbines which supply some of our electrical power. We convert our own waste heat into another source of energy we can use."

"And recycling everything out here is a real good idea. Unfortunately, as Ensign Shen will tell you, those turbines like to break down just when you need them the most, and if one goes down you have to take down its partner as well. Paul, why do we need counter-rotating turbines?"

"Because if we just had a turbine going in one direction its torque would force the ship to rotate."

"Uh-huh. And what happens if something knocks a hole in the

inner hull? How many water cells do we lose?"

Paul hesitated, then spotted Kris Denaldo waving her hand at him, one index finger extended. *Oh, yeah. I know this. Thanks, Kris.* "One. Seals activate automatically on all six sides to isolate a cell if there's a pressure drop."

"And why is having a shield of water armor real useful in combat?"

"Because the water flashes to vapor when it gets hit. That dissipates the energy of the hit on the ship as well as anything could."

"Excellent. What a fine crop of ensigns we have these days." Carl, pretending to ignore the rude responses of Paul and Kris to his sarcasm, hauled out his personal data link and tapped in some information. "Congratulations. You two have just signed off some of your damage control and engineering OSWO qualifications."

"Thanks, Carl." Kris gestured down the way they'd come. "Can we egress the exit now? I've got things to see and people to do." Moments later, they were out of the access trunk, Paul luxuriating in the suddenly expansive-seeming confines of the corridor, and Kris Denaldo was swinging rapidly away. "See you guys around," she called, before vanishing around a corner.

Paul shook his head. "Does she ever slow down?"

"Not that I've ever seen." Carl sighed audibly. "That babe is too damn driven. No off switch and her main drive is battle-shorted on full speed ahead. She's going to run into a brick wall someday and fly into lots of little pieces."

"Can't anybody get her to slack off before then?"

"They've tried. I've tried. The only one who might be able to work it is the XO. She could stop a good-sized moon in its tracks just by glaring, I think, but so far she's letting Kris run. I guess Herdez wants her to set her own limits instead of having them imposed."

"I hadn't thought of that." Paul suddenly found himself yawning hugely. "Sorry. I had the mid-watch. I think I got about four hours' sleep last night."

"Well, there's your problem, ensign. You aren't getting enough done because you're spending too much time in your bunk." Carl grinned, then sobered. "Seriously, though. I know there seems to be four times too much to do every day, because there *is* four times too much to do every day, but if you'd take a bit of advice from an elderly lieutenant junior grade you'd set aside enough time each week to get two or three OSWO qualification standards signed off. It may seem to be adding another complication, but by keeping your department head happy it's actually simplifying your life no end."

"Thanks, Carl. I appreciate the advice." Paul's own data link chose that moment to chime urgently. He checked the display, reading carefully since he didn't trust himself to scan text after so little sleep. "MA1 Sharpe is asking me to meet him at my stateroom."

"Well, it's not high noon, so I guess the Sheriff doesn't mean you ill. It's sort of odd he's paging you, though. That doesn't happen too often, enlisted paging officers."

"It doesn't?" Paul felt a chill run down his back. "Something tells me I better find the Sheriff fast."

"Good idea."

Paul emulated Kris Denaldo, swinging through the corridor far faster than he'd have dared a few weeks before. Rounding a corner, he saw Master-at-Arms Sharpe floating at parade-rest next to the ensign locker. "What's up?" Paul demanded as he braked so swiftly that Sharpe flinched from a possible collision.

"I was just on my way to captain's mast, sir. Which is scheduled to occur real soon, now."

"Captain's mast." Paul closed his eyes momentarily, then opened them to check the time. "I've still got five minutes to get there."

"Yes, sir. And you really wouldn't want to miss captain's mast, sir."

"No, I wouldn't." *Wakeman would rip my head off if I wasn't there on time.* "Thanks for looking out for me, Sheriff."

"My pleasure, sir."

Sharpe smiled broadly as he turned to go, which for some reason exasperated Paul's overstrung and overtired nerves. "Sheriff, why the hell are you always so damn cheerful?" Paul demanded as he followed Sharpe down the corridor.

Ivan Sharpe looked back over his shoulder for a moment, grinning wider. "Because I get to work with fine, young officers such as yourself every day, sir."

"You know where you can stick that reply, Petty Officer Sharpe." Sharpe's grin didn't waver. "Yes, sir."

The passageway outside the cramped space officially designated the crew's mess was crowded with personnel. Those awaiting their turn before the captain weren't hard to spot from their expressions and body language, which ranged all the way from sullen defiance in some cases to the sort of look you'd see on a deer caught in headlights in others. Every sailor awaiting mast had at least two companions as escorts, their division officer and their leading petty officer. Paul hesitated a moment, amazed at the number of sailors who'd been able to get into enough trouble to face the captain even though they were a million miles from anywhere, then followed the Sheriff into the mess.

Senior Chief Kowalski was already there, nodding casually to Sharpe in greeting, then sketching a half-salute to Paul. "Top o' the morning, Mr. Sinclair."

"Good morning, senior chief. Where do I stand?"

"You mean float?" Kowalski gestured along the bulkhead. "You and me hang here, sir. The captain's gonna be up there, the witnesses and division officers and such on the bulkhead opposite you and me, and the accused right in the middle."

"Sounds like fun." Paul positioned himself carefully. A careless choice might leave him without nearby leverage to quickly halt any drifting his body might attempt, and Paul had no intention of letting his feet float between the captain and a mast case.

Kowalski nodded to Sharpe again. "MA1 Sharpe, please notify the captain we are in readiness for mast."

"On my way, senior chief."

It left a few minutes for Paul to look around, feeling awkward. *This is my first real captain's mast. Funny. They call it that because the captain used to stand in front of the ship's mast while he rendered judgment. Up here the ships don't even have radar masts, but we still call it that.* He tried to focus on his all-too-brief legal training and experience. *Okay. This isn't really a legal proceeding. Captain's mast is non-judicial punishment. That means no rules of evidence or right to a lawyer or things like that. Heck, why do they even need me here?* Somehow, he knew better than to ask that question.

Sharpe leaned into the mess just far enough to yell, "Attention on deck!" Paul and Senior Chief Kowalski stiffened in place, holding the posture as Captain Wakeman pulled himself into the mess. Wakeman took his position, peered at Paul as if uncertain as to his identity, then waved one hand. "At ease. First case."

"Aye, aye, sir." Sharpe leaned back into the passageway. "Petty Officer Arroyo."

Arroyo entered, visibly nervous, his uniform immaculate.

Commander Sykes followed, somehow managing to appear to lean against the bulkhead even in zero g, along with his assistant Lieutenant Junior Grade Bristol and Chief Petty Officer Mangala. "Petty Officer Arroyo?" Captain Wakeman made a question of the name, squinting at the charge sheet displayed before him. "You are charged with violating Article 108 of the Uniform Code. That's Loss, Damage, Destruction, or Wrongful Disposition of Military Property of the United States." Wakeman's expression hardened and his chin jutted out. "That's a very serious offense, Petty Officer Arroyo." Looking back to the charge sheet, Wakeman read out loud. "In that Petty Officer Third Class Arroyo, on or about 1 September, 2098, did wrongfully dispose of military property of the United States by consuming same—" Wakeman glanced up and around the small room. "Consuming? Just what government property are we talking about?"

Commander Sykes cleared his throat. "A package of frozen peaches, sir."

"A package of frozen peaches?" Wakeman glared suspiciously at Arroyo. "You ate a package of frozen peaches? Do you know how much people look forward to having a few slices of peaches out here? And you ate a whole package?"

Petty Officer Arroyo gulped audibly before speaking. "Captain, I didn't eat any peaches. I swear. I told Chief Mangala when he signed for the shipment that it seemed short, but he didn't—"

"Chief Mangala?" Wakeman pivoted to focus on the chief.

Mangala shook his head with deliberate slowness. "No, sir. Captain, I been keeping my eye on Arroyo here. Guys like him always slip up sooner or later. When I ran inventory on those peaches and came up short, I knew who done it."

"Did Arroyo tell you the shipment seemed short before you signed for it?"

"I don't remember nothing like that, captain."

Commander Sykes cleared his throat again, drawing the captain's attention. "Sir, Petty Officer Arroyo is an excellent sailor with a good record. I would suggest this is a case of misunderstanding or miscommunication."

"You don't think he ate the peaches?"

"No, sir."

"What about you, Lieutenant Bristol?"

Bristol spoke with such care he seemed to be forming each word as a separate sentence. "I agree with Commander Sykes, sir."

"Hmmm." Wakeman looked from Arroyo to the charge sheet and back again. "Your officers seem to think a lot of you, but your immediate supervisor doesn't. How do you account for that, Petty Officer Arroyo?"

Arroyo made to shake his own head, then stiffened as he remembered to maintain himself at attention. "I don't know, sir. Chief Mangala just doesn't seem to like me. I do my best, but he's never satisfied."

"Hah." Wakeman's glance swept across Commander Sykes and Lieutenant Bristol. "Let me tell you something, Petty Officer Arroyo. There's not a thing, not a single thing, wrong with demanding good performance from your subordinates. Some people seem to be afraid to do that. But a good supervisor," here his gaze flicked to Chief Mangala, "knows what matters is trust. Trust and good performance."

Commander Sykes spoke again, his voice even. "Captain, I believe this incident has been blown seriously out of proportion and would be best dealt with within my own department. There is no need for non-judicial punishment of Petty Officer Arroyo."

"If you believe that, then why is he here in front of me?" Wakeman pointed his index finger at Arroyo. "Why is that?"

Sykes took a deep breath. "Chief Mangala insisted on charges being brought before this venue."

"Well, that couldn't have been an easy thing. But stealing peaches... that's bad."

"Captain, I'm convinced Petty Officer Arroyo did not steal any peaches."

"Then you believe Chief Mangala is lying?"

"No, sir. I believe he is mistaken."

"Hah. Okay, then. Anything else? Petty Officer Arroyo, this is a bad thing. Very bad. I don't find you persuasive. You should devote more effort to satisfying your chief here. I hereby reduce you in rate to E3 and fine you half-a-month's pay for two months. You decide whether those peaches were worth that much! Dismissed."

Arroyo, looking stricken, exited, followed by Chief Mangala. Commander Sykes left last, looking daggers at Mangala's back. As Arroyo passed Sharpe, the Master-at-Arms helped him along with a firm hand on one arm and a nod of encouragement. Sharpe turned back to face the room, his eyes meeting Paul's but betraying no emotion. Paul shifted his eyes enough to see Senior Chief Kowalski's face and caught the same expressionless gaze. Paul wasn't certain what he'd just witnessed, but whatever it was, nobody but Captain Wakeman and Chief Mangala seemed happy with the outcome.

"Next case," Wakeman stated gruffly. A slow parade of seamen and junior petty officers followed, each linked to violations of the Uniform Code of Military Justice ranging from Article 86 (Absent

Without Leave), through Article 112 (Wrongful Use, Possession, etc. of Controlled Substances), all the way to Article 134 (the General Article). The captain interrogated each sailor, asked that sailor's superiors for their views, and then rendered judgments. He glanced toward Paul a couple of times, but never spoke to him or asked him questions. As time passed, Paul became aware of a growing crowd in the corridor as crew members gathered awaiting their noon meal, which couldn't be served until the captain's mast was completed. More than once, Sheriff Sharpe made threatening gestures to silence the crowd.

"Last one, captain," Sharpe finally announced.

"Good. About time. What's wrong with the middle management on this ship? I shouldn't have to... never mind. Bring 'em in and let's get this over with."

Sharpe leaned back into the corridor. "Seaman Alvarez."

Alvarez came in, slightly better turned out than she'd been for XO's screening, adopting a posture as close to attention as could be achieved in zero g. Her division officer, Lieutenant Sindh, took up position opposite Paul and nodded to him in brief recognition. Chief Thomas came last, standing next to Sindh. As Sharpe's eyes rested on Alvarez, his face momentarily displayed dislike and contempt before settling back into formal lines.

Captain Wakeman scanned the document before him, frowning, then looked up at Alvarez and spoke quickly as if rushing through the procedure. "Seaman Alvarez. You're charged with being absent from a place of duty and insubordination toward a superior petty officer. Articles 86 and 91. What do you have to say for yourself?"

Alvarez licked her lips before speaking in a slightly pleading voice. "Captain, sir, I should have made it to formation on time and I shouldn't have mouthed off to Chief Thomas. I made some mistakes, sir. But, like I told the chief, I think somebody slipped something into my drink the night before. It wasn't no normal hang-over. No, sir. I tried to get up and get to formation, but I couldn't. I really tried, sir."

Paul, his eyes on Alvarez, caught a glimpse of Chief Thomas and Lieutenant Sindh rolling their eyes toward the ceiling in mutual reaction to Alvarez's contrite statement.

Captain Wakeman frowned again, looked down at the charging document, then back at Alvarez. "Then you're saying you did it but it wasn't your fault? Is that it?"

"Yes, sir, captain. I mean, I guess it was my fault I wasn't more careful where I drank. But I didn't ever mean to break no regulations, sir."

Wakeman looked over at Chief Thomas. "What exactly did Seaman Alvarez say to you that prompted this insubordination charge?"

Chief Thomas cleared her throat, then pointed her jaw toward Alvarez. "She told me to go to hell, sir. I told her to get up to morning formation, and she told me to go to hell."

"Hmmm." Wakeman shifted his gaze to Lieutenant Sindh. "How about you? What kind of sailor is Seaman Alvarez?"

Lieutenant Sindh spoke softly but firmly. "Seaman Alvarez is a difficult individual. She requires almost constant supervision and direction. Her appearance and military bearing are usually marginal. I do not consider her an asset to my division."

Wakeman blinked, then focused back on Seaman Alvarez. "You don't have a good record. Your supervisors don't think much of you. What do you have to say to that?"

Alvarez slumped slightly, as if feeling overwhelmed. "Captain, sir,

I really want to be a good sailor. I'm trying. I am."

Captain Wakeman blinked a few more times. "Seaman Alvarez, I hate seeing a potentially good sailor go to waste. I think with a little more inspired supervision you might come around." He turned slightly to face Lieutenant Sindh and Chief Thomas, wagging one finger at them. "Seaman Alvarez is an opportunity to display your abilities as managers. I want to see what you can do with her." Wakeman faced Alvarez again. "Ten days' extra duty. Forfeiture of one-half month's pay, suspended for six months pending good behavior."

"That's all? Sir?" Lieutenant Sindh blurted out, than snapped her mouth shut.

"That's right. That's all. Dismissed." Without waiting for Alvarez, Sindh and Thomas to depart, Wakeman plucked up his data link and headed out the hatch so quickly that Sharpe barely had time to yell "Attention on deck!"

Paul found himself relaxing after holding a tense posture he hadn't been aware of. In the center of the room, Alvarez had also relaxed, a smug expression spreading across her face.

"Alvarez." Chief Thomas, her face as hard as the metal bulkhead, spoke the one word, drawing the seaman's gaze, then crooked her finger in a come-with-me gesture. Alvarez's expression shaded quickly from smug to alarmed and then defiant as she followed the chief out of the mess.

"Mr. Sinclair." Senior Chief Kowalski said his own brief farewell then was gone. Paul followed Lieutenant Sindh out silently, judging it unwise to speak to her given the rigidity of her neck muscles. As he cleared the mess, crew members began rushing in, clamoring for their meal.

"Sheriff?" MA1 Sharpe turned at Paul's call, holding himself against the bulkhead as crew members pushed by into the mess. "Thanks again for making sure I made it to captain's mast on time."

Sharpe snorted, plainly out of sorts. "Glad you enjoyed it, sir."

"Uh, yeah. What was that bit with Arroyo, anyway?"

"Sir, with all due respect, I don't want to talk about it. Perhaps you ought to ask Commander Sykes."

Yeah, I should. I also ought to have more sense than to ask a petty officer to comment on something the captain did. "I saw Chief Thomas take Seaman Alvarez with her."

"That's right, sir. The captain told Chief Thomas to see what she could do with Seaman Alvarez, didn't he? Me, I'd love to see what I could do with Seaman Alvarez. I'd probably start by feeding her piece by piece through the solid waste recycler, then I'd dump the end result out the nearest airlock."

"I take it you're glad you're not Chief Thomas."

"Sir, if I may say so in confidence, right now Chief Thomas is so pissed off she's probably trying to pound a hole through the hull with her head. And if she succeeds, she'll plug that hole with Seaman Alvarez's worthless butt. Sir."

Paul exhaled heavily. "Then she won't get off as easy as it seems?"

"Not if Chief Thomas and Lieutenant Sindh can help it."

"Good. Just one more question, Sheriff."

"Is that a promise, sir?"

"Yeah. Why the hell was I there? The captain barely looked at me, and he certainly never asked me for any legal advice."

Sharpe obviously couldn't help smiling at the question. "Mr. Sinclair, do you have a car back on Earth?"

"Yeah."

"Have you got a jack in the trunk?"

"Of course I do."

"Just in case you need it to change a flat tire, right? But even if you never have a flat and never need that jack, you've always got it handy in the trunk of your car. Just in case you ever do need it."

Paul managed a small laugh. "That puts my role in perspective, Sheriff. Thanks for the ego boost."

"My pleasure, sir."

Paul headed back toward officers' country. He'd become aware that his own stomach was growling with hunger, but he had fifteen minutes before his shift was served in the wardroom. That meant he could grab about ten minutes of sleep before then.

5

"Hey, Paul." Lieutenant Mike Bristol hauled himself into the wardroom seat next to Paul, fastening the lap belt with the ease of long practice. "Got a minute?"

"Sure." The assistant supply officer and Paul hadn't crossed paths too frequently so far, but everything Paul had heard about him was good. The same went for Commander Sykes, of course. Steve Sykes and Mike Bristol had even earned praise from the prickly Jen Shen. *A lot of supply types don't understand operational needs,* she'd told Paul. *You're dying because you need a spare, and they won't open the supply office because it'd interfere with the Supply Department badminton tournament or something like that. But Sykes and Bristol are good pork chops.* Paul resolved, for the umpteenth time, to find out why supply officers had been given the nickname pork chops instead of that of some other food-derived term. Given the fact that Mike Bristol was Jewish, calling him a pork chop seemed not only odd but also slightly blasphemous.

Bristol inclined his head toward where Commander Sykes occupied his habitual place at the other end of the wardroom table.

"The boss and I weren't too happy with what happened to Arroyo."

"Yeah. I gathered that. Sorry."

"Well, you're the ship's legal officer. Is there anything we can do about it? I mean, any recourse or appeal or something like that?"

Paul made a helpless gesture. "Technically, yes."

"Technically?"

"I just looked it up myself because I was curious. The Uniform Code of Military Justice says any individual is allowed to appeal an action of their commanding officer."

"Really? Who does the appeal go to?"

Paul smiled thinly. "The commanding officer's immediate superior."

Bristol absorbed the information, then laughed sharply. "That'd be the commodore. So Arroyo would have to ask the commodore to overturn an action of one of his captains?"

"Right."

"What are the odds of that happening?"

"You've been in the Navy longer than me. What do you think?"

Bristol shook his head. "I think Arroyo would be better off praying for an angel to shower the ship with packets of peaches, because that's probably more likely to happen."

Paul nodded. "I'm afraid so. The lawyers who taught my course said it wasn't too common. Mind you, if the captain had done something clearly outside his authority, something like exceeding the limits of punishment he can impose under the UCMJ by ordering Arroyo to hard labor or a bad conduct discharge, then the commodore would have to overrule him. Other than that, you're really spitting into the wind to even try."

Bristol shook his head again. "That's nuts. I mean, I understand why the process exists. There's no courts out here and you need a way to impose discipline. But I can't imagine what civilians would do if somebody told them they had to live with something like NJP."

Paul spread his hands. "You're right. It has a reason. A good reason. But you're also right that civilians wouldn't stand for it. Can you imagine any civil court putting up with Article 134?"

"Which one's that?"

"The General Article. Basically, it says that if anybody does anything you think is bad, even if it's not specifically cited as illegal in all the other punitive articles, you can just charge them under Article 134. It sort of allows you to make up the law to suit your needs. Within reason, of course."

"Wild." Bristol looked around conspiratorially. "So if I said bad things about the government and the captain happened to like whichever political party was in power, he could charge me with violating Article 134?"

"Uh, no, because saying anything derogatory about the president or Congress is illegal under Article 88, Contempt Toward Officials."

"I can't say anything bad about the president, even if I don't like him or her? What happened to freedom of speech?"

"You're in the military. You, uh, forfeit certain rights as a result."

Commander Sykes laughed briefly. "Welcome to the land of the free, Lieutenant Bristol."

"Of course," Paul added, "if you did something like, say, abuse of a public animal, then you'd be charged under Article 134."

"Abuse of a public animal?"

"Yeah. That's a specific offense listed under Article 134."

"What does that... no, I don't think I want that question answered. So there's nothing legal-wise we can do about Arroyo?"

"No. Not in any practical sense. Unless the captain changes his mind."

"Fat chance. Okay, that's what I figured, but I also figured it didn't hurt to ask."

Paul nodded in agreement. "If I could help, I would. Is there anything you guys can do for Arroyo?"

Commander Sykes replied before Bristol could, his relaxed tone at odds with his words. "I'm afraid all we can do is bend every effort toward getting Arroyo promoted back to petty officer as soon as possible. Outstanding fitness reports, commendations, that sort of thing. Oh, don't look disapproving, young Sinclair. We won't be giving Arroyo anything he doesn't deserve. The man is an excellent sailor."

"Chief Mangala doesn't think so."

"Ah. Chief Mangala." Commander Sykes took a slow drink of coffee. "He's allowed a personal dislike of a subordinate to translate into effectively framing that subordinate for a crime that likely never occurred. And he undercut my own authority to do it. I am not easily aroused to anger, but that chief has crossed the line."

"What can you do to a chief? I thought they were pretty much bullet-proof."

"No one is bullet-proof, lad. Chief Mangala's error is in believing as you do. But I have friends in certain offices back home, offices where orders are written. I will guarantee you now that the moment we arrive back at Franklin Station, Chief Mangala will find orders awaiting him, orders which will transfer him immediately to an assignment so unpleasant as to make service on this ship seem a lost paradise."

Paul grinned. "I didn't think any assignment could do that."

"Ah, 'where ignorance is bliss.' Get on my bad side, Mr. Sinclair, and you'll find out how wrong you are." Sykes smiled as he spoke to rob his words of any real threat.

Mike Bristol perked up unexpectedly. "Say, speaking of getting back, you work in Operations, Paul. Any truth to the rumor we might head home early?"

"None that I know of."

Sykes chuckled. "I've been on a number of extended deployments such as this, Mike. On every one, the rumors of being ordered to return early begin within a couple of weeks of departure. Those rumors have never proven to be anything but wishful thinking."

"Too bad." Bristol rubbed his chin, staring at the painting of the *Michaelson* on the far bulkhead. "What would it take to get us home early, anyway? Some international crisis?"

"I don't know," Paul confessed. "I haven't seen anything in the intelligence summaries that seems out of the normal. Trade disputes, low-level fighting in a half-dozen places around the world, all the usual stuff."

"Any ships anywhere near? I understand we're supposed to keep other ships out of this area, unless they get permission to go through it first."

"That's right. So far, though, everyone going through has made at least a gesture at asking permission, and most of those have been near the boundaries of the area we're patrolling. But the solar system's geometry is changing, so that might change also."

"Huh?" Bristol cocked a skeptical eyebrow. "The solar system is changing?"

"Its geometry. You know, everything's rotating about the sun in different orbits at different speeds. To get from, say, Earth to Mars requires different paths at different times of the year."

"And I thought logistics was complicated. What if a ship belonging to some foreign power does try to come through without our permission? What'll we do?"

Paul scratched his head. "To be perfectly honest, Lieutenant—"

"Mike."

"Okay. To be perfectly honest, Mike, what we do is up to the captain."

"We don't have orders?"

"We do." Paul frowned, remember the convoluted wording and evasive language of their orders. "But they pretty much leave it up to the captain's judgment as to what to do."

Bristol's jaw sagged for a moment. "Just like non-judicial punishment, huh?"

"Yeah, effectively. Just like that."

"Oh, great. I guess I better hope that doesn't happen. And I better forget about us getting back ahead of schedule."

"It's probably just as well," Paul offered. "I'd imagine if they needed us home early it'd be because something really bad had happened. I'm not so sure that'd be a good thing."

Commander Sykes took another drink, then sighed. "From the mouths of babes. As you say, Mr. Sinclair, getting home early would only be worth it if it didn't involve getting into a situation even worse than boring figurative holes through some of the more vacant space in the solar system. Be careful what you wish for, gentlemen. There's always a worse alternative."

Bristol grinned. "As Chief Mangala will discover."

"Ah, yes. Chief Mangala. Beware the wrath of pork chops." Sykes settled back in his chair, even though the gesture was meaningless in zero g, a small smile playing on his lips.

Half a day later, in the same wardroom, the Arroyo/Mangala affair assumed trivial significance to Paul as he and Kris Denaldo watched a friend in agony. Carl Meadows was shaking his head continuously, as if hoping he could deny a fact out of existence, his voice strained as he spoke. "Oh my God."

Paul reached out a hand toward Carl's shoulder, then drew it back, uncertain how to react. "What happened?"

"Petty Officer Davidas. He's dead."

"What? How?"

"We don't know. It just happened. He was working on one of the pulse lasers. It had been de-energized and tagged out. I saw the physical tag placed and watched the virtual tag placed on the automated systems controls. But the thing got energized somehow while he was lying across it."

"Holy Jesus." Kris Denaldo crossed herself in reflexive fashion. "He couldn't have stood a chance."

"No. Fried instantly. Never knew what hit him, I'm sure." Meadows buried his head in his hands. "Oh, God."

"Lieutenant Meadows." Commander Herdez hung in the hatchway. "I have appointed Commander Garcia to conduct an investigation of Petty Officer Davidas' death. Ensure he receives full cooperation from everyone in your division."

Meadows raised his head. "Yes, ma'am."

Her gaze shifted to Paul. "Ensign Sinclair. Provide Commander Garcia with any legal or other support he needs."

"Yes, ma'am." *Oh, great. Garcia already hates every second I spend on legal duties, and now I have to work directly with him on legal stuff.* Paul glanced over at Carl Meadows' drawn expression. *What right do I have to worry about that? A guy just died. I can be such a jerk sometimes.* "Carl, I better check with Commander Garcia right away. If there's anything you need..."

"Yeah."

Paul detoured to his stateroom first, calling up his copy of the Manual of the Judge Advocate General to refresh his knowledge on investigations. *Okay. Death of military personnel falls under the Command Investigation category. Garcia doesn't need to be sworn in in order to run the investigation. He only needs a preponderance of evidence... except if he decides Davidas or somebody else caused the accident deliberately. Hope that doesn't come up. It's prohibited to make any determination as to whether the death was in the line of duty.*

Garcia answered Paul's knock with a gruff grunt, then glowered at him as Paul stammered out his mission. "I don't need an ensign's help to do my job. Everything is spelled out in the manual, right?"

"Yes, sir. Chapter II of the JAGMAN. There's a sample report format at the end of the chapter."

"I've already looked at that. Do I need to swear anybody in when I take statements from them?"

"No, sir. Swearing in is not required for a command-level accident investigation. You can swear somebody in if you want to, though. The oath you use is in Chapter II."

"How long do I have to finish this?"

"A death investigation is supposed to be completed within twenty days, sir."

"Good. I won't need nearly that much time." Garcia focused on his own screen again, his face reddening with familiar anger.

It took Paul a moment to realize the anger wasn't directed at him. *Is he really that upset over the death of Davidas? It can't possibly make him look bad. Just when I thought I had Garcia pegged, he turns out to care about something besides his own reputation.* Paul stood awkwardly, wanting to leave but unable to do so until dismissed. "Sir, is there anything I can assist you with?"

Garcia's eyes locked back on Paul and held there for a long moment. "Yes, as a matter of fact, Sinclair. As long as you're standing there, go down to sickbay and make sure the doc knows what he's supposed to put in his report."

"Yes, sir." Paul left, steeling himself for the visit to sickbay and praying whatever remained of Petty Officer Davidas wouldn't be visible.

The ship's doctor nodded wearily at Paul's arrival. "Yes, I know. You people need an autopsy of sorts. I'm not a forensic pathologist, you know. I work on the living. That's by choice. But I should be able to tell you what killed the man. It's pretty obvious. I don't suppose you want to see for yourself?"

"No! No, sir." Paul swallowed hastily, his stomach suddenly feeling just as it had when he first encountered zero gravity. "There's a format you're supposed to follow. Do you... ?"

"Probably, but let me see." The doctor scanned the form for a moment, then nodded and made a notation in his own data link. "Okay. I'll use that form. Am I supposed to fill out all these areas?"

"As many as possible, sir. The report needs to rule out possible contributing factors to the accident."

The doctor snorted derisively. "I guarantee he didn't die from a drug overdose. Or alcohol poisoning. But I still need to test for drugs or alcohol?"

"Yes, sir. Not that anyone thinks those were a factor, but we have to rule it out."

"The body tissues have suffered extensive trauma. Serious

oxidation from the energy that hit him. I might not be able to get a good test."

Paul swallowed again. "You just have to try, sir. If... if there's no way to make a determination, we'll have to work with what evidence is available."

"Fine. I'll do my best." The doctor let his gaze wander toward a sealed storage bin. "Not that my best could have helped that poor bastard. I work on the living."

"Yes, sir."

"Do you have any idea yet how this happened? Aren't there some sort of precautions taken to ensure equipment isn't energized when someone is working on it?"

Paul glanced at the doctor, surprised by the question. *But then, how would he know about electrical safety procedures? That isn't what he does.* "Yes, sir. They use tags. There's an actual physical tag put on the circuit where it's switched off, saying don't turn it on because someone is working on it, and there's a virtual tag saying the same thing that's placed in the electrical distribution system software to prevent anyone from remotely activating the circuit."

"Why didn't they use these tags?"

"They did, sir. At least, that's what everyone involved is saying. Maybe someone overrode the virtual tag, or pulled the physical tag off the circuit. If so, we'll find out."

"I see." The doctor scowled at his table surface. "Then you can punish whoever was responsible. That won't help Petty Officer Davidas, you know."

"No, sir, it won't. But punishment isn't the primary reason for the investigation. Finding out what went wrong is most important. So we can try to make sure it never happens again to any other sailor."

The doctor nodded, his scowl fading. "Good. I'm glad to hear that. Sometimes you line officers seem obsessed with punishment, with trying to brow-beat the rest of the world into your model of accountability for any mistakes. If the goal of this investigation is to save lives, then it's a very good thing."

"Thank you, sir."

"Thank you?" The doctor looked at Paul skeptically. "Did I say something about you personally?"

"I'm a line officer, sir. For better or worse. And I'm assisting in the investigation, which means I have a personal involvement there, too."

"Line officers." The doctor shook his head. "You all think you're Atlas, carrying the world around on your shoulders. If you stopped for a moment, if you made a small mistake, the world wouldn't crash and break, you know."

Paul looked away. The burden of his chosen profession suddenly felt very heavy. "With all due respect, sir, it did for Petty Officer Davidas." He only hoped it hadn't been due to a small mistake on the part of Carl Meadows.

Garcia handled the investigation with what could only be described as ruthless efficiency. Carl came back shaken from his interview, but refused to complain. "He asked me tough questions. That's exactly what he should be doing."

Kris leaned close to him. "Questions about what?"

"Stuff I expected, really. He asked me to describe everything I did relating to the accident. Whether I personally saw the virtual tag-out activated and tested. Whether I tugged on the physical tag-out to make sure it wouldn't fall off."

"I thought they found the physical tag still in place."

"They did. Garcia's making sure it didn't drift off and then somebody put it back after the accident."

"Why, that—"

"No." Carl held up a hand. "He's not being a bastard. He has to check that, rule it out. I know that tag was on firmly. But if Garcia doesn't prove that to everybody's satisfaction then he wouldn't be doing me any favors. Right, Paul?"

Paul nodded. "Right. Garcia has to check out every possible angle and ensure he knows what really went wrong. If Carl's innocent of wrongdoing, he'll prove that."

Kris glared at him. "*If?*"

Paul's head suddenly felt cold and empty. "I said *if?* Carl, I'm sorry, I didn't—"

"That's okay. It's easy to make a mistake." Carl fell silent as the implications of his own words sank in, then smiled bitterly. "Looks like a lot of people are saying dumb things today."

Paul shook his head, angrier at himself than he'd ever been. "No. What I said wasn't dumb. It was stupid. You've told us you followed procedures and did everything by the book, just like you told Garcia. I'm really, really sorry."

Carl nodded, and Kris Denaldo lost her own anger. "Just make sure you don't make that kind of slip of the lip when you're talking to Garcia, Paul. Tell me something, though. What kind of standard is Garcia using to judge Carl? Is the fact Carl followed procedure good enough?"

"It should be. But the standard is a guy called ORP-man."

"ORP-man? Is that some kind of weird super-hero?"

Paul managed to smile. "No. ORP stands for *ordinary, reasonable* and *prudent*. An accident investigation is supposed to look at what an ordinary, reasonable and prudent man or woman would have done. You don't have to be perfect. But just sticking to procedure isn't good enough if a reasonable person would have noticed a problem and done something about it."

"ORP-man. That sounds so stupid."

"Yeah. But it kind of makes sense. I mean, isn't that the standard you'd want to be judged by?"

Kris frowned. "I don't know. It depends on who's doing the judging, and what their definition of ordinary, reasonable and prudent happens to be. Doesn't it?"

"Well..." Paul frowned as well. "I guess that's right. But, Carl, you're careful. You're smart. You'll pass that test."

Carl twitched a smile. "I sure hope so. Like I said, I told Garcia everything I did. All the procedures I followed. But I didn't tell him something else, because I couldn't."

Paul stared. "What? What didn't you tell him?"

"Anything I didn't do because I didn't think to do it and still haven't realized I should have done. Any procedure I should have followed but didn't know I should follow. And that might be what killed Davidas."

Kris leaned forward again, her anger this time directed at Carl. "You did not kill Petty Officer Davidas. You are not that big of a screw-up, Mr. Meadows."

"I'm glad you think so. I hope you're right."

"Jen told me she'd trust you with her life. Would Jen Shen say that if she didn't mean it?"

"No."

"You've still got a division to lead, Carl. This investigation will clear you. Until then, keep your head clear. I've got a watch to stand right now." Kris pulled herself from her seat, gesturing to Paul to follow. As soon as they'd left, she pointed back to the ensign locker where they'd left Carl. "I've got ten thousand things to do, as usual. But you keep an eye on him, Paul. You're living in the same compartment. If you think he's losing it, you make sure Jen and I know."

"I don't think he'll lose it, Kris. He's depressed, but that's understandable."

"Yes, it is. I just want to make sure it doesn't go beyond understandable depression. Okay?"

"Okay." Kris headed rapidly down the passageway. Paul watched her until she swung around a corner. "Carl? I've got some work to do in the operations spaces."

"So do it."

"Are you going to be okay?"

"Yeah. See you at lunch."

Paul followed in Kris Denaldo's wake, but he hadn't gotten far when he heard his name called.

"Paul." He turned, seeing Lieutenant Sindh in the door to her stateroom. "How's Carl holding up?"

Paul didn't know Sindh all that well, but he'd never heard anything bad about her, and she was on Jen Shen's list of good people. "Not too well. You can tell he's torn up inside."

"Losing a sailor isn't easy. Wondering if you're guilty of somehow causing that death is harder. Paul, I'm what you might call a lay minister. Not Carl's religion, but the role of ministering is fairly universal. Tell Carl for me that if he needs to talk, I'm available."

"I will. Thanks."

Around the next turn he met Jen Shen. "Hey, Paul. How's Carl?"

"Could be better."

"What's funny about that question?"

"Funny?" Paul hadn't realized he'd quirked a brief smile. "Nothing. It's just that Lieutenant Sindh asked me the same thing a few seconds ago. Are you a lay minister, too?"

"Me? I don't think so. But if you think Carl needs somebody's shoulder to cry on, let me know."

Paul nodded, this time smiling gratefully. "I think he does need that, but I don't think he's ready to do it."

"Men. Why you refuse to deal with emotions, I don't know. How's Garcia's investigation coming? Any idea?"

"Not a thing."

"You're supposed to be his assistant."

"No, I'm supposed to be assisting him. When he needs it. I've asked. He hasn't needed it."

Jen came close, peering into Paul's eyes. "If you heard they were going to railroad Carl, you'd tell us, wouldn't you? You'd tell him?"

Paul didn't have to wonder if his shock at the question showed. "How can you even ask that? I haven't heard anything that'd justify railroading Carl, and if I knew they were trying I'd do everything in my power to derail it."

Jen grinned as she eased away again. "I kinda thought that. I just wanted to hear it from you."

He glared at her. "How could you even wonder about that?"

"You're a nice guy, Paul. Sometimes nice guys have a problem with standing up to jerks."

"I don't."

"Hey." Jen came close enough again to squeeze his arm. "Sorry."

Paul tamped down his temper. *I guess it wasn't all that unreasonable a question. And what right do I have to get bent out of shape while Carl's going through this investigation?* "That's okay. But I don't let people walk all over me, or all over my friends."

She nodded. "You already said that. Look—"

Her next words were cut off by the shrill of the bosun's pipe over the ship's general announcing system. "Attention all hands. Use of fresh water is restricted to essential purposes only until further notice. Ensign Shen, your presence is requested in the after auxiliary machinery room."

Jen slapped the palm of her hand against her forehead. "Crap."

Paul eyed her with concern. "What happened?"

"What happened is one of my two working osmosis filters must have broken again. Damn. I've got to get down there and try to nursemaid the blinking piece of junk back into shape. Listen, I think you, me and Carl are all off watch after dinner tonight. If I've managed to get this filter mess cleaned up by then, I'll stop by your ensign locker. If you think Carl needs to vent, we'll squeeze it out of him together."

"Thanks. Even if he doesn't want to vent, I'm sure he'll be happy for the company. Smilin' Sam gets harder to put up with every day."

"Yeah. Too bad he wasn't the one who got fried on that laser." Jen grimaced at Paul's expression as she started on her way aft. "I know, I know. I shouldn't have said that. Bad Jen. Bad girl. Later, Paul."

"Later. Good luck."

One of the advantages of investigating an accident on an underway ship was that every witness was easy to find, and with the threat of Commander Herdez' displeasure looming behind Commander Garcia's demands, those witnesses produced their statements in short order. Paul heard that Garcia had also been insisting on reviewing all electrical system records and had caused numerous simulations to be run on possible accident scenarios. Jen Shen had been uncharacteristically supportive of Garcia's push to conclude his investigation as quickly as possible. "I don't like not being able to trust equipment. If that laser's capable of zapping anyone else working on it, we need to know yesterday." But Garcia's findings and conclusions, if any, remained a mystery for another twenty-four hours.

"Ensign Sinclair, your presence is requested in the executive officer's stateroom."

Paul jerked with surprise at the announcement. He'd just left the bridge ten minutes earlier after standing the afternoon watch. Carl, looking like he'd slept even less than usual in the last few days, had relieved him for the two-hour-long first dog watch. They hadn't said a word about the accident or the investigation, even though waiting for the results of the investigation was obviously an agony for Carl. Perhaps now that agony would end. Paul only prayed the announcement didn't portend the beginning of another agony.

When he arrived at her stateroom, Herdez held out a data cartridge. "Commander Garcia has completed his investigation into the death of Petty Officer Davidas." Nothing in the XO's voice or expression betrayed the results of that investigation. "Review it to ensure it complies with the requirements of the Judge Advocate General's Manual. I'd like it back as soon as possible."

Paul took the cartridge gingerly. "Yes, ma'am."

"The results of the investigation have not yet been approved by the captain. Do not share them with anyone."

"Yes, ma'am."

Paul hastened back to his stateroom and plugged in the cartridge, then read rapidly. *I'll skim it first for conclusions and then go back to check all the details against the JAGMAN. Where... where... there. No finding of fault.*

All parties followed proper procedures. Unavoidable accident. Recommendations to prevent reoccurrence. Whew.

Feeling a weight lifted from his spirit, Paul went back to the beginning of the report and began carefully comparing it to the examples he had and the instructions in the Judge Advocate General's Manual. So engrossed was he that he didn't look up when someone entered, only gradually becoming aware of someone else in the stateroom. "Carl? Your watch is over? Has it been two hours?"

"Yeah. It was on my end, anyway. What's so interesting?"

Paul hesitated, watching as Carl frowned at his reaction, then gazed worriedly at the display. "It's Garcia's investigation. He's finished. Herdez gave it to me to review for compliance with legal requirements. The captain hasn't approved the results yet so I'm not supposed to tell anyone about them."

"Oh." Carl looked away, the tension in his body obvious.

Hell. I'm not going to do this to him. "Carl. The report has no finding of fault. It says everybody did what they were supposed to do. The accident was unavoidable using correct procedures."

"How'd Garcia say it happened?"

Paul indicated the display. "The virtual circuit tag-out on the system fell through the cracks when the system techs had to do an emergency reboot and the system failed to carry through the temporary file. The physical tag-out didn't work because one of the switches in that junction failed, and the system automatically did a cascading power redistribution that required it to activate that circuit. With the virtual tag-out gone, the system didn't know it wasn't supposed to do that."

"Sounds sort of stupid to let a system reset switches like that in a non-emergency situation."

"That's what Garcia said. It was a one-in-a-million combination of events, but it could happen again. He recommends system software be altered to prohibit that kind of stuff without a human review of the action except during an emergency."

Carl Meadows stared somberly at his desk, then nodded briefly. "Okay. Thanks."

"I thought you might be a little happier to hear that news."

"I am. Really. It's just..." Meadows stared at his hands. "A sailor died, Paul. A Mark One Mod Zero human being ceased to exist... and it's nobody's fault. Nobody did anything wrong. Nobody caused it directly. Just an accident. Blast it, shouldn't there have to be a reason when somebody dies?"

"Carl, you need to talk to a chaplain about that. The meaning and purpose of life is way beyond my pay grade."

"Yeah. Not that the *Merry Mike* rated having a chaplain along on this little pleasure cruise, and I won't spill my guts to any virtual padre on the ship's computer systems."

"Don't forget Lieutenant Sindh's offer."

"I haven't. She's a decent person. Maybe I'll take her up on it, now." Carl rubbed his face wearily. "Damn, I wish I could get drunk."

"Drinking never solved anything."

"So says the youthful ensign. I'm not looking to solve anything, Paul, I just need something that'll help me unwind for one night." Meadows smiled crookedly. "Mind you, if I started taking that route to oblivion every night, you'd be right. You ever think about dying in combat, Paul?"

"Uh, sometimes."

"I know, we're not at war. Officially, anyway. Odds are if anything lethal happens to you or me it'll be an accident. But accidents just happen. You don't deliberately walk into them. Combat's deliberate, putting your life on the line while you think about it. Can you handle that?"

Paul hesitated before replying. "I hope so."

"An honest man. Diogenes, where are you? I hope so, too. I was thinking that if this accident was going to happen, then thank God that Davidas didn't have a chance to know it was coming. Thanks for letting me know what Garcia found out, shipmate. If you're done with that report, you'd best get it back to Commander Herdez before she finds out you've been talking to anybody about it."

"Right." Paul paused as he started to eject the data cartridge. "Hang in there, Carl."

"Hey, I lost a guy. It happens in this line of work. I'll get over it. Mostly."

"It wasn't your fault. You did everything you should." Paul pointed to his display. "That's official, now. You know Garcia wouldn't have cut you any slack."

"Yeah. I do know that. And it really does mean a lot to know I didn't make it happen by some careless act on my part. But I think it's going to take a while to work through me. You know?"

"I think so. Don't forget Jen's offered her shoulder if you need it."

"Now that's an attractive offer. Me leaning on Jen's shoulder. What do you think Smilin' Sam would do if he came in here and found me draped over Jen?"

Paul smiled at the vision. "His brain would probably explode."

Carl grinned as well, a trace of his old humor finally surfacing. "That might be worth what Herdez would do to me afterward. But, no, better not. I might like it too much."

"Watching Sam's brain explode?"

119

"No. Being draped over Jen." Carl raised his eyebrows at Paul's expression. "What? You've never thought about it?"

"I don't... I mean... I try not to..."

"They can't nail you for thinking, Paul. Not yet, anyway. Just don't tell Jen."

"There's nothing to tell Jen!"

"Oh, come on. How about Kris?"

"No!"

"Ah hah. Lieutenant Sindh? Lieutenant Tweed?"

"Carl, you——" Paul stopped, staring at Meadows. "You're riding me for fun. You're joking. You do feel better."

"Yeah. I do. Thanks for cluing me in on that report. It takes a real weight off me to know I didn't cause it, and apparently couldn't have prevented it. I imagine I'll spend the rest of my life wishing there'd been something I could have done anyway, but now I know that's just wishful thinking. Between you looking out for me on the investigation and the babes mothering me, I've been well taken care of. You're all good people."

"So are you, Carl."

Paul made his way back to the XO's stateroom and offered her the data cartridge. "As near as I can determine, ma'am, Commander Garcia's investigation complies with all the requirements of the Judge Advocate General's Manual."

"Thank you, Mr. Sinclair." Commander Herdez took the offered cartridge, then looked sharply at Paul. "You seem to be happy, Mr. Sinclair."

Uh oh. I let my good mood at how Carl felt show. But I wasn't supposed to tell him. Better be careful what I say. "Yes, ma'am. I'm, um, happy at Commander Garcia's conclusions."

"Did you think Lieutenant Junior Grade Meadows would be found at fault?"

"No, ma'am. But... I did fear that might happen."

Herdez turned back to her work. "Reserve your fears for events whose outcomes you can influence, Mr. Sinclair. Had Mr. Meadows failed in his duties, our duty would have been to call him to account. I will agree that would have compounded the tragedy of Petty Officer Davidas' loss, but it would have been necessary. To do otherwise would have betrayed Petty Officer Davidas' sacrifice."

"Yes, ma'am."

"Thank you, Mr. Sinclair."

Paul left, pondering the XO's words. *Duty means we do stuff we may hate doing. I've always known that in the abstract, but this would have been very real and very personal. Suppose Carl had been at fault? Would I have been willing to pursue that? Or would I have taken the easy way out and tried to cover up that fault? I'm glad I didn't have to find out.*

He went back to the stateroom, finding Carl had left, and laid down for a few moments, gazing at the tangle of conduits and wires not far from his nose whose patterns were becoming so familiar he had started to name the shapes he could imagine within them. Despite everything else his mind could fasten on, Paul found himself unable to shake Carl's earlier ribbing about Jen Shen. *Why'd it bother me when Carl joked about making out with Jen? Get a grip. Jen's never shown that kind of interest in me, and was the first person to warn me against onboard relationships. Yeah, I like her, but that's not the same thing as imagining some sort of involvement, and she's never shown any sign of doing more than liking me. Jen'd probably say I was an idiot if she knew I was even spending this much time thinking about it. Then she'd keep me at arm's length for the rest of her time onboard. Life's hard enough right now. Don't drive away*

one of the people who's making it bearable by giving in to ridiculous fantasies.
He rolled out of his bunk, strapped into his chair, and began going
over his OSWO qualifications. The drudgery of that should keep
him focused on reality.

Within a few hours, Captain Wakeman approved Commander
Garcia's investigation and forwarded it to fleet staff. Under normal
circumstances, the *Michaelson* wasn't supposed to send even the brief
transmission needed to shoot a compressed file of the report back
to Franklin Station, because even that short transmission surely
betrayed her general location to anyone watching carefully. But the
death of a sailor wasn't normal circumstances.

A few days passed, then the reply came. Investigation results approved
by Commander, United States Naval Space Forces. Recommendations
forwarded to appropriate authorities for action. Instructions for the
disposition of the remains of Petty Officer Davidas.

Paul checked his appearance carefully. Service dress uniforms
designed to hang naturally in gravity tended to get bunched up
and absurd-looking in zero g, and this was one occasion where he
wanted to ensure he looked as good as possible. Fortunately, before
leaving Earth he'd been advised to attach Velcro liberally beneath
the uniform blouse and trousers. The black armband around one
sleeve of his uniform blouse, just snug enough to stay in place and
weighing almost nothing, felt unnaturally heavy and tight.

"Do I look okay?" Carl Meadows appeared pale against the Navy
blue of his uniform, his relief at the results of the investigation
overshadowed at the moment by the ceremony they were about to
attend.

"Yeah, Carl, you look good. Ready?"

"Yeah. This doesn't seem right without swords."

"I know." On Earth, such a solemn occasion would require full dress uniforms with swords, their gilt pommels swathed in black. But even the tradition-obsessed Navy wouldn't allow officers to bring swords into space. Too much extraneous mass to haul around, and too many sharp points capable of causing damage to delicate components packed inside spacecraft hulls.

The quarterdeck area never felt large. With the burial party assembled in it, and with everyone trying to leave at least a small gap between themselves and the body tube holding the remains of Petty Officer Davidas, it felt tight enough to induce claustrophobia. Paul squeezed in next to Kris Denaldo, who smiled briefly in wordless greeting before turning a somber gaze back on the body tube. Carl moved farther forward, close to the body tube, where he joined the enlisted members of the burial party.

"Attention on deck." Everyone stiffened to the best of their ability as Captain Wakeman and Commander Herdez wedged themselves into the crowd. Wakeman, looking decidedly uncomfortable, muttered "at ease" and gestured toward Herdez.

The XO cleared her throat. "We are here to commit the mortal remains of Petty Officer Michael Davidas to the depths of space. His family has indicated their desire that he be cremated within the Sun's own fires. Upon completion of this service, his body tube will be fired on a trajectory which will, in the course of time, bring it to that end." She consulted her data link, then began reciting the Burial Service. As the words came out, Herdez' voice softened and took on a lilting cadence, drawing surprised glances from most of the officers and enlisted present. Ending, Herdez put away her data link. "Now, I invite you to join me in the Navy Hymn." She began singing, also softly, as the others on the quarterdeck joined in raggedly.

Eternal Father, strong to save,
Whose arm hath bound the restless wave,
Who bidd'st the mighty ocean deep
Its own appointed limits keep;
Oh, hear us when we cry to Thee,
For those in peril on the sea!

Eternal Father, King of birth,
Who didst create the heaven and earth,
And bid the planets and the sun
Their own appointed orbits run;
O hear us when we seek thy grace
From those who soar through outer space.

The singing tapered off, then Commander Herdez looked around the quarterdeck at those present. "The Navy Hymn was originally written in the 1860s. The verse speaking of those in space was added in the 1960s. Sailors have always faced peril, and not always come home. But Petty Officer Davidas is part of an endless line of explorers and seafarers stretching back for untold centuries. Now he has gone to join them, and their ranks are surely brightened by that." Herdez nodded to a bosun mate who placed his left hand on the controls of a portable stereo. "Hand salute."

Everyone somehow managed to find the room to swing their arms up and hold their best salutes.

The bosun hit the Play control on his stereo, and the slow, mournful notes of Taps echoed softly through the quarterdeck until the last, long measure trailed off into silence.

"Two."

Everyone dropped their salutes.

"That is all. Thank you for coming."

"Wait a minute." The beginnings of movement halted as Captain Wakeman finally spoke again. "I wanted to pass on some good news on this solemn occasion." A nervous smile flickered across his face. "As some of you know, we've been watching a South Asian Alliance ship for some time. He's been hugging the edge of our area, but he's just taken the plunge and he's coming right through without requesting permission. We're going to intercept that ship! Who knows, we may even have to seize it. It's a great opportunity, and, well, let's get after him!" Wakeman ducked out the hatch, leaving silence behind him.

Paul watched Commander Herdez' face as she eyed the captain's departure, her expression revealing no emotion.

After a brief pause, Herdez glanced around once again. "Dismissed."

Paul held himself in place, waiting for a few moments while others tried to wedge themselves through the hatches instead of fighting the crowd himself. His gaze settled on the body tube and the four sailors standing beside it along with Carl Meadows, ready to transport it to the launch tube from which it would be fired into space. *Another ship, coming through this area and apparently deliberately defying the US claim to this part of space. Does it know we're here? We might have been detected when we sent in the investigation report.* Rumors of Q-ships came back to haunt him. *Is it armed, a warship in disguise, maybe planning to surprise us and take us out before we can defend ourselves? Are we going to be in a shooting engagement before all is said and done?* He watched the body tube, wondering if it would be merely the first of many he'd see on this trip. Wakeman's enthusiasm seemed not only inappropriate, but also thoughtless. *I need to take another look at our orders.*

6

The other ship stood out easily against the backdrop of space, but then most objects did. Like all warships, the USS *Michaelson* carried a wide variety of eyes with which to scan the heavens for items of interest. Some were devoted to watching for natural objects that might pose a hazard to the *Michaelson* herself by blundering through the same location in space at the same time as the ship. Others watched for human artifacts, which could generate hazards of a different nature.

"Space is cold." Jan Tweed pointed at the read-out beneath the symbol representing the intruding ship. "Look how much hotter that ship is than the temperature of space around it. It's like seeing a campfire in the distance."

"Do we have any visual yet?" Paul leaned closer to the display as if that could somehow resolve details on the distant ship better.

"Just background occlusion." As objects moved through space they might not be directly visible themselves, but their movement could be spotted by watching them block the view of stars behind them.

"Nothing detailed."

"Strong temperature variation and background occlusion. Then it's not a warship."

Jan shrugged. "Or it is a warship, and he's turned off his can't-see-me system and is broadcasting vented waste heat instead of recycling it."

"I guess that could be true, couldn't it?" Paul glanced upward, as if he could somehow see the sophisticated system which made the *Michaelson* and other warships so hard to spot. Almost the entire outer hull was covered with micro-lenses interspersed with video displays. Anything a lens saw on one side of the ship was looped 180 degrees to the opposite side of the ship and displayed on a screen. With all the lenses and screens working, all you saw when you looked at the *Michaelson* was whatever the lenses on the opposite side were seeing, just as if the ship weren't there at all blocking the view. Effectively, the *Michaelson* bent light around her and remained invisible inside her cocoon. It wasn't a perfect system because small gaps existed in the lens/screen array, but you had to get pretty close to spot those gaps. With waste heat disposal minimized and directed out along an empty vector away from the ship, neither visual nor infra-red sensors had much chance of seeing the *Michaelson* from a distance.

"Yup." Tweed eyed him dubiously. "Did you read the intelligence assessment on Q-ships?"

"Yeah. 'Insufficient evidence exists to either prove or disprove the existence of Q-ship type combatants, so caution is advised when approaching other ships.'" Paul quoted. "That's a lot of help."

"Sir?" Paul turned at the question, seeing both enlisted watch standers eyeing him and Lieutenant Tweed. "Sir, we've heard these Q-ship things mentioned a lot. What are they?"

Jan made a deferring gesture to Paul, who ordered his thoughts before speaking. "The basic idea's been around a long time. You make a warship look like an innocent merchant ship, and when your prey gets close enough you drop the disguise and open fire."

"I saw a video where pirates did that," the bosun mate of the watch offered. "Way back when, with sailing ships and stuff. How come they call 'em Q-ships?"

"Because that's what the Brits called them during World War One. They had a serious problem with enemy submarines attacking their merchant ships, so they made these ships they called Q-ships as sort of a secret name. If a submarine approached on the surface to sink what it thought was a helpless merchant, the Q-ship would try to surprise and sink the sub."

"That's a nasty trick. So that guy we're heading to intercept might be that kind of trap?"

"It's... possible. There's no proof any Q-ships actually exist in space."

"Ships go missing," the quartermaster of the watch insisted. "Just gone."

Lieutenant Tweed smiled indulgently. "Accidents. Unfortunately, they happen."

"Well, maybe, ma'am." Plainly unconvinced, the quartermaster exchanged glances with the bosun mate, then the two enlisted watch standers launched into a whispered discussion of the pirate video one had seen.

"I don't think you convinced them," Paul muttered.

Jan smiled crookedly. "I know a little bit about fear, Paul. I don't like that we don't know more about this other ship, I don't like the way he's heading straight into our area so brazenly, and I don't like all the rumors about covert warships."

"A lot of rumors are just garbage. Totally wrong."

"How many rumors do you have to bet your life on them being garbage?"

"Not a lot." Paul tagged the ship's symbol and read the associated data as it scrolled by. "They think it's a South Asian Alliance ship?"

"That's what they think."

"The South Asians have been pretty aggressive lately, back on Earth."

"I read the same intelligence reports you did, Paul. If you're trying to reassure me, you're doing a lousy job."

"Do you think he knows we're here? If our transmission of the death investigation report betrayed our general location, why would he have decided to make a dash inside our sovereign claimed area?"

"You said the SASALs have been aggressive lately. Maybe knowing we're here is why that ship decided to come in. The timing's about right, anyway."

"But, why…?" *That's what a Q-ship would do, wouldn't it? If it was looking for a victim to come running up to it. But it's also what any other ship trying to challenge our sovereign claim would do. If we didn't react to the incursion when we had a ship nearby, it would make a stronger case that we hadn't enforced our claim.* "I really don't like this. I hope we handle this intercept real carefully."

"Why don't you let the captain know that?" She smiled briefly to rob the words of offense, then rushed to change the subject. "You ready for the zone inspection?"

"The zone inspection?" Paul rubbed his eyes. "I've hardly thought about it. With everything going on…" His voice trailed off as he caught the look on Jan's face. "The XO's just going to check our spaces, right? She's going to walk through and see how clean and well maintained they are. I'm sure Chief Imari—"

"Have you talked to Chief Imari about it?"

"Uh... I think I did."

"Paul, the XO is death on zone inspections. You better make sure the spaces you have responsibility for look good." She checked the time. "Not that you'll have much chance to fix them if they're not. The inspection is half an hour after we get off watch. Maybe you ought to give Chief Imari a call?"

"Yeah. Maybe." *But I've been doing so much extra work for Herdez on this legal stuff, and that's one of the reasons I didn't remember to do more preparations for this inspection. Surely the XO will take that into account. Still, I guess I better check with Chief Imari anyway.* Paul was reaching for the comm pad when their watch reliefs arrived. It wasn't until he was leaving the bridge that he remembered the aborted call to Chief Imari.

As it turned out, Paul wasn't able to locate Chief Imari before having to join Commander Garcia and Commander Herdez, who were ready to begin the inspection. "Where's Lieutenant Tweed?" Garcia barked, a question which now tended to instantly generate a headache in Paul. Fortunately, Jan Tweed rushed up a moment later, apologizing for being last in a swift, low voice and looking away rather than face Garcia and the XO directly. Breathing a silent prayer, Paul followed the others as the inspection party trooped through the Operations Department spaces assigned to the Operations Specialist Division.

For the most part, Herdez remained silent as they went through Tweed's spaces, occasionally checking a detail up close or nodding in brief approval over some well-maintained equipment. A gleaming knife-edge on an emergency hatch actually drew a few words of praise.

"Mr. Sinclair." Paul winced inside at the XO's tone as she pointed at a similar but tarnished edge in one of his spaces. "Unacceptable." His guts got tighter as they proceeded and Herdez issued head-shakes and frowns over discrepancies in cleanliness and maintenance.

At the end of the excursion, Herdez faced the others. "Good job, Lieutenant Tweed. Ensign Sinclair, your spaces need considerable work. I will conduct another inspection of them at fourteen hundred tomorrow. I expect them to meet standards by then." With a nod to Commander Garcia, she turned and headed away.

Garcia, his face darkening more with each passing second, waited until the XO turned a corner before rounding on Paul. "What the hell excuse do you have for not properly preparing for that inspection?"

A million possible answers flooded through Paul's mind, even though he knew only one answer would not only keep him from being verbally ripped apart but also be true. "I have no excuse, sir."

Garcia glowered, raising both hands in a threatening gesture he converted to a single finger not far from Paul's nose. "You will make sure your spaces are ready for the XO's reinspection tomorrow. There will be no discrepancies. Is that understood?"

"Yes, sir."

"If you ever fail a zone inspection in my department again, I will make sure you wish you'd never been born. Is that understood?"

"Yes, sir."

Garcia seemed to be on the verge of saying more, but choked off whatever it might have been then left, somehow managing to stomp even in zero g.

Paul took a deep breath, shuddering slightly. "Damn."

Jan Tweed, her head slightly lowered, was looking at him out of the corner of her eye. "You made Garcia look bad, Paul."

"I know. The cardinal sin. Dammit, I thought Chief Imari would take care of the spaces!"

"Paul, Chief Imari isn't your servant. She's got plenty of her own responsibilities. If you never indicated to her that you placed a priority on making sure your spaces were ready, why should she worry about it?"

"But—"

"But nothing. You can't put any of your jobs on automatic and expect Chief Imari, or any other enlisted, to do them for you. You have to show an interest and be involved." Tweed shook her head, her face reflecting past miseries. "Believe me."

"I do."

"This hurts worse, you know."

"What hurts worse?"

"The times you get chewed out and you really deserve it. They hurt a lot more than a chewing out you don't deserve."

"I won't argue with that. Thanks, Jan." *It's funny. Most people on the ship think of Jan Tweed as a failed officer, just putting in her time until she gets out of the Navy and can find a place to hide forever from the Commander Garcias of the world. But she just gave me a constructive leadership lesson, and chewed me out in a way I didn't even recognize as being chewed out until this instant. She could be ten times the leader Garcia is. Or I guess she could've been that someday, if she hadn't screwed up too much too early and been ridden too hard as a result.*

Chief Imari, when eventually found, expressed contrition for the state of the spaces and walked through them with Paul, noting specific items to be corrected no later than noon tomorrow. "Chief, I'll do another walk-through with you at noon, and if we spot anything that's been missed we'll have some time left to correct it."

"Good idea, Mr. Sinclair. Sorry again. We should have done this walk-through before the inspection."

"Right. Next time I'll make sure we do." He headed back toward officers' country, praying he wouldn't encounter Sam Yarrow, who surely had already heard of the inspection's disastrous outcome and would just as surely express mock sympathy while prying for any word or action he could use to dig Paul's hole a little deeper. Instead, he almost collided with Jen Shen.

She took one look at his face, then grabbed his arm. "This looks bad. Come and talk."

"Jen, I don't really—"

"Yes, you do. Whatever happened, we've all been there, Paul." A few moments later he was sitting in the port ensign locker, Jen hovering nearby and Kris Denaldo handling e-paperwork while keeping one ear tuned to the conversation. "What happened?"

Paul described the inspection, his lack of preparation, and its outcome. "Herdez went over those spaces like a Marine drill sergeant. She didn't cut me any slack at all."

"What'd you expect?"

"Well, hell, Jen. I've been busting my butt on stuff she assigned me to do. I thought, well..."

"You expected Herdez to give you some special treatment because you'd been doing extra work for her."

Paul flinched. "I guess that's right. Pretty dumb, huh?"

"Very dumb, even for an ensign."

"Thanks. But doesn't Herdez, well, owe me something for all that extra work? She must think I'm doing a decent job of it."

Jen laughed. "Oh, I remember when I was as young and innocent as you are now."

Kris Denaldo's eyebrows shot up. "Innocent? You?"

"I don't need any comments from you, Saint Denaldo. Okay, think carefully, Paul. We're talking about Commander Herdez here. If she likes the work you're doing, what does she do?"

Paul took a moment to think through the question, then grimaced. "She gives you more work."

"And harder work. Because that's how the XO thinks. She thinks that's a cool reward system. The more Commander Herdez likes you, the more work she gives you." Jen pointed toward Kris. "Case in point. Miss Perpetual Motion here. Look at her work-load. Commander Herdez must love her."

Kris Denaldo sighed. "I think it's gone beyond love. If I get any more duties assigned I'll assume she wants to marry me."

Jen chuckled, then swung down to hover at Kris' feet. "Oh, Ensign Denaldo, will you make me the happiest XO in the world and be my aide? All I can promise you is twenty-eight hours of work in every twenty-four-hour period."

"Really?" Denaldo squealed like an infatuated teenager. "Oh, commander! I don't know what to say!"

"Try 'Aye, aye, ma'am.'" Jen glanced at Paul as he started laughing. "Somebody's feeling better."

"You two are insane."

"So? It helps us cope with the wonderful lives we lead." Jen came back to perch near Paul, peering into his eyes. "Okay, so what have we learned?"

"Not to expect any favors from Commander Herdez."

"Because... ?"

"She figures riding me like an overloaded pack mule going straight up a mountain *is* doing me a favor."

"Very good. Kris, you got about an hour free anytime soon?"

"Uh, let's see." Denaldo checked her data link, then looked skeptically at Jen Shen. "How about half an hour? Forty-five minutes? That's it. Tops."

"Okay. Forty-five minutes it is. Paul, we've both been through this drill. You need those spaces to be immaculate tomorrow but you have to concentrate on the right kind of immaculate. Kris and I will do a run-through of your spaces and try to spot the problems the XO will fixate on so you can focus on fixing them."

"Jen. Kris. That's a real big favor. I can't ask—"

"You didn't," Denaldo pointed out. "We volunteered. Well, Jen volunteered both of us, but the principle's the same. You'd do the same for us, right?"

"In a heartbeat."

"Right. All for one and all that crap. Now will you please get out of here so I can get some work done?"

"Sure. Thanks. Jen, if there's ever anything..."

"Ask me that next time we're in port and I can't afford to buy any more drinks."

"You're on."

"Careful," Kris warned sotto voice, "or Smilin' Sam Yarrow will start spreading rumors about you two."

Jen grinned nastily even as she shoved Paul out the hatch. "I doubt it. Ever since I threatened to break his arm unless he moved his hand real quick, Yarrow's invested too much time spreading rumors I'm a lesbian. Paul, we'll run you down after we've done our spot-check."

Paul's guts still seemed like they'd never unknot, but he felt a lot better nonetheless. *Live and learn. I just wish the learning could be a little less painful.*

* * *

"How'd the reinspection go?" Jan asked as Paul assumed the watch and slid into his chair.

"Good enough, I guess. The XO said it was 'acceptable' and Garcia didn't rip my head off."

"You can't ask for much more from a day, can you?" She grinned in an uncharacteristic display of happiness, then rubbed her hands. "Plus we get to fire off a burn on this watch. How long's it been since the *Merry Mike* maneuvered?"

"I can't even remember." Most of the time they coasted. Every time the ship maneuvered, changing course and/or speed, it threw out signs that someone watching for ships could see. They could localize the *Michaelson* from such signs, though the longer the *Michaelson* remained silent after such maneuvers the greater the uncertainty such watchers would have of her current position. However, in order to intercept the intruder ship, they'd have to maneuver now. Paul checked his display, calling up the maneuvering information. Digits were counting off in one corner, showing the time remaining until the ship's thrusters pivoted her to a new heading and her main drives pushed her a little faster in the right direction. "Sweet."

"And simple. Mind if I take it?"

"Be my guest." Jan hadn't had to ask, since as officer of the deck she could assume any function of Paul's she wanted, but he appreciated that she didn't take advantage of that. Besides, the entire firing sequence of both maneuvering thrusters and main drive would be orchestrated by the ship's computers after they were given the go-ahead by the human watch standers. Pushing that single button would be a minor thrill, but one he was willing to let Jan Tweed experience.

Oddly enough, the pending maneuver made the first portion of the watch drag as they waited. At one hour prior to the maneuver Jan Tweed beckoned to the bosun mate of the watch, who raised his archaic pipe to his lips and shrilled out the ancient naval call to attention before making an announcement on the all-hands circuit. "All hands prepare for maneuvering in one hour. Secure all objects and materials. Undertake no task which cannot be completed prior to maneuvering." The message was repeated at the half-hour and quarter-hour points.

Five minutes prior, as the bosun was issuing his latest warning, Captain Wakeman entered the bridge. "Captain's on the bridge!"

Lieutenant Tweed saluted and indicated the main maneuvering display. "We are ready to execute our course and speed change, captain."

"Right. Uh, how long?"

"In five minutes, sir."

"No, no, no. How long will the maneuvering last?"

Jan flushed. "Ten minutes, sir. As indicated on the display."

Captain Wakeman glanced at the indicated data, his face sour, as Commander Herdez arrived on the bridge. "XO, has this maneuvering solution been double-checked?"

Herdez didn't hesitate. "Yes, sir. Three times." She looked at Tweed. "I believe the watch has run a fourth check."

"That's correct, ma'am."

"Hmmm." Wakeman settled into his chair, fumbling with the straps. "Can this watch team handle it? Shouldn't we have our varsity up here?"

Paul felt himself flushing this time at Wakeman's casual public questioning of his competence, but Herdez shook her head. "This is a capable watch team, captain. I'm certain they will execute the maneuver without any problem."

"All right. Let's get on with it, then."

Tweed signaled the bosun to issue the final advance warning at the one-minute point, while Paul maliciously wondered if Captain Wakeman would mess with this maneuver in the hope of impressing unseen watchers. *I can't believe he asked that question about us being able to handle it right in front of us. What a jerk.*

Jan looked at him a moment after the thought and quirked a smile, causing Paul a sudden worry that he might have spoken his last thought out loud. But she simply pointed to the timer, where the final seconds were counting down. "It's not much fun when the maneuvering computer handles everything, is it?" she murmured. With a final glance to either side at the captain and the XO, Tweed firmly pushed the approve button as the count hit zero.

Stresses jerked Paul against his straps as the maneuvering thrusters pushed the *Michaelson*'s bow around to a new heading, then rolled the ship slightly to accommodate the human desire to align themselves heads-up within the solar system. A tiny object went flying past Paul as the force of the thrusters generated a partial equivalent to gravity. Without thinking, he flung out one hand and more through luck than design managed to snag the debris. He glanced at it, apparently a data chip misplaced during routine maintenance, then looked to see if anyone else had noticed and found the XO's eyes on him. *It figures she'd have seen it. I don't think Herdez misses anything.* He braced himself for a withering look, but instead the XO actually seemed amused.

The thrusters cut off, then shoved from the opposite side, slowing the *Michaelson*'s bow with just enough force to halt the momentum of thousands of tons of mass and make the bow stop on the desired heading. A moment of silence and anticipation, then the main drives cut in, shoving everyone back in their chairs. Paul strained to pull in deep breaths even as the bosun whooped, "Yeee-hah!" After months of little or no gravity, the two g's of acceleration felt awful, but also exhilarating.

Now they were watching the time count down again. Paul's gaze switched between the digits showing burn-time remaining and the maneuvering display on which the marker representing the *Michaelson* and her course slid steadily onto the desired vector. The main drive cut off, and a few moments later the actual and desired vectors joined as one. Paul swallowed hard and gritted his teeth as his inner ears and stomach protested the many and varied changes in gravity conditions as well as the sudden return to zero g.

Lieutenant Tweed pivoted in her chair to face the captain. "Maneuvering completed successfully, captain. The *Michaelson* is on course for intercept."

"Hmmm. Very well." Wakeman unstrapped himself, then moved away unsteadily.

"Captain's left the bridge!"

"Thank you, bosun," Herdez replied. "And next time we maneuver, try to restrain your enthusiasm."

"Aye, aye, ma'am."

"Good job, Lieutenant Tweed." Herdez left even as Jan acknowledged the praise.

Tweed rubbed her neck. "Ahhh. So much for excitement." She noticed Paul staring intently at the maneuvering display. "What's up?"

"I was just wondering. Is it possible for a human to maneuver the ship anything like that?"

"Sure it is. Just like that. You just have to feel her motion, anticipate the right moments to kick in different thrusters, and not try to haul her around like a bag of bricks on the end of a rope. You don't look like you believe me."

"I'm sorry, but... the maneuvering system computers handle complex problems in a flash. How could any human do what they just did?"

"By feeling the ship. Look, you've been real straight with me, Paul, so I'll tell you a secret. If you promise not to tell anyone else." Paul nodded, frowning in puzzlement, as Jan tapped her display. "Here's the automatic ship's log for the maneuver we just completed. What's it say?"

"It says... it says the automated maneuver controls were disabled. The maneuver was controlled from—" Paul checked the words again in disbelief. "From the officer of the deck's watch station. You handled that maneuver? Manually?"

"Yeah. I disabled the automated controls beforehand. The maneuvering control relays are right here on the chair handles, so you can manipulate them easily while everyone else is staring at the displays."

"Geez. If Wakeman had found out—"

Tweed grinned nervously. "He won't. Not from you. Right?"

"I promised. But that's amazing. You're a great ship handler, Jan. That maneuver was perfect."

"Thanks. Now remember what I told you. It's a secret."

"But—"

"A secret. Nobody else hears a word of it."

"If they review the log—"

"Nobody looks at the log. They're too busy handling whatever's going on right now to worry about what happened five minutes ago. Don't tell anybody else what I showed you, Paul."

Tweed's face was firmer than Paul had ever seen it, so he nodded in assent. *I guess she just wants to prove to herself how good she can be at something. But why not let the others know? I don't understand. Good thing no one spotted her working those controls.* Paul frowned again, remember the XO's eyes on him when he snagged the tiny bit of flotsam. *Herdez doesn't miss anything. Does she know? She must know. That "Good job, Lieutenant Tweed" bit. Why would she say that about just activating an automated maneuvering sequence? But it's like she's keeping it a secret that she knows Tweed's secret because she knows Tweed needs it to be a secret for her own reasons.* Paul shook his head, slightly dizzy from following his last thought train. Jan flicked another nervous smile his way and he nodded back to her in reassurance.

"The SASAL ship is running." Paul glanced up in surprise at Lieutenant Sindh's calm statement. "They, or South Asian deep space sensors, must have spotted us when we maneuvered for intercept."

"They're going to get away?" Paul felt a mix of regret and relief.

"Maybe. We're calculating course options now, trying to see if we can still manage an intercept inside the US zone."

Lieutenant Bristol looked up from his meal. "What if they can't? Can we intercept them outside the zone?"

"We *can*. The question is, *may* we?" Sindh glanced at Paul. "What do the orders say, almost-a-JAG?"

Paul snorted at the nickname, then concentrated on remembering the twists and turns of their convoluted orders. "There's a lot of room in there for the captain's discretion. But, orders aside, we don't really have legal authority to stop another ship which isn't in an area we claim."

"Even if he used to be in our area?"

"That's right. If we don't catch him inside our zone, we're not supposed to haul him over outside of it. It's sort of a jurisdictional thing. Just chasing him out of our zone enforces our claim."

Jen Shen swung over to grab another tube of coffee. "Unambiguously?"

"Well, no. Not like actually catching him in our area."

Sindh looked around the wardroom as if evaluating her audience. "Chasing another ship out of the zone isn't going to generate lots of good visibility for the *Michaelson*. Or her captain."

Paul bit his tongue. *She's saying what we're all thinking. Wakeman isn't going to let a potential career boost like seizing that ship slip through his fingers.*

"If we do that, seize the SASAL ship outside our zone, won't it generate bad visibility?" Bristol asked. "Since it'd be illegal?"

Sindh made a face. "I don't think Paul said such a seizure would be illegal. He said we're not supposed to do it by international standards."

Paul nodded. "I'm no expert, but it seems to be really complicated. The XO has had me draft some point papers to try to explain it all to the captain—"

Jen snorted. "Explain complicated stuff to Cap'n Pete? Good luck. He's so dense he bends light."

Sindh suppressed a smile. "Jen..."

"Okay, okay. I'll watch my words. But the point's the same. Trust me, if there's room in our orders for our captain to figure he can grab the SASAL ship in or out of our claimed area, he'll try to do it."

On the heels of her statement, the bosun's pipe shrilled on the all-hands circuit. "All hands prepare for maneuvering in five minutes. Secure all objects and materials. Undertake no task that cannot be completed prior to maneuvering."

Sindh looked toward the speaker. "I suppose that means we've calculated a new intercept trajectory. We'd best get comfortable. If the captain is going to try to manage an intercept within our area, this might be a long burn to build up sufficient velocity."

Jen hoisted her coffee, then dropped the tube back into storage undrunk. "Yeah. 'Damn the torpedoes,' but since we don't know how long we might be pinned down I'm not drinking this."

"High-g acceleration is hell on a full bladder," Sindh agreed.

It felt strange. They were in a chase, heading at high speed toward a point where they should intercept the fleeing SASAL ship just inside the American area. But, as if in a dream, the huge distances to be covered caused the chase to play out in slow motion over days and weeks. On maneuvering displays, the vectors of the *Michaelson* and the other ship continued converging, but at an apparent snail's pace. Physically, the SASAL ship was off the *Michaelson*'s starboard bow and about ten degrees above the plane of the *Michaelson*. As the ships converged, that position never changed even though the distance to the other ship steadily decreased. Constant bearing and decreasing range had been the formula for intercept or collision for as long as ships had sailed, and it applied just as surely in space.

Inside the *Michaelson*, activity had the same hurry-up-and-wait feeling. Preparations, planning, and training for the impending encounter were run through and then run through again.

It's like they expect us to intercept the SASAL ship in a couple of hours, but then we come out of the training sessions and realize it's still a couple of weeks away. How's anybody supposed to keep their adrenalin pumped for that long?

Paul glumly went back to scanning the section of the Ship's Organization and Regulations Manual update he'd been assigned to review. Possible impending combat or not, the *Michaelson*'s command structure had no intention of letting routine paperwork slide, and there wasn't anything more tedious or routine than updating the SORM. *General quarters. Ship's company to battle stations. Highest state of alert and readiness. Blah, blah, blah. Station assignments. Assistant combat information center officer, which is me, posted in the combat information center. That'd make a lot more sense if I had a real job to do in CIC.*

During general quarters, Commander Garcia had posted Paul behind a multi-spectrum sensor tracking panel, ordering him to supervise the two enlisted operations specialists who crewed the panel. However, the two enlisted knew their jobs better than Paul ever would and didn't need supervision. They knew it, Paul knew it, and Garcia knew it. "The real reason you're here," Jan Tweed had confided to Paul, "is so that if I get disabled in action, or relieved for cause by Garcia, you can take over for me." Which truth had left Paul feeling like a cross between a spare tire and a vulture.

The decompression alarm located not far from Paul's right ear suddenly began whooping wildly. Paul flailed his arms, shocked from his near doze over the boring paperwork, then slapped the ensign locker's comm unit. "Engineering, I've got a decompression alarm in space—"

"Understand," the engineering watch stander broke in, her words barely audible over the clamor of the alarm. "We've already checked your stateroom's status. There's no decompression under way. False alarm."

"Thank you!" Paul yelled back over the alarm. "Now can you reset the alarm before it deafens me?"

"Uh, sorry, sir. Remote reset isn't working. Do you know how to do a local reset?"

"What?" Paul shook a fist at the alarm, then jerked in surprise as the hatch to the locker popped open and Jen Shen swung in.

"Real or false alarm? I assume false since the hatch opened for me."

"False, Jen. How the hell do I stop it?"

"Like this." She flipped up a panel next to the alarm, made a fist and punched the touch pad that rested under the panel. The alarm's wail finally shut off. "When the alarms stick you have to joggle the 'trons a little. Don't ask me why."

Paul rubbed his forehead, fighting down a headache inspired by the alarm's scream. "Why'd it go off in the first place?"

"Hell if I know. If you ask the crew, they'll tell you it was Petty Officer Davidas."

"Huh?"

"Yeah. You hadn't heard? If anything unusual happens now the crew says it's Davidas screwing with stuff."

"They think the ship's haunted?"

"Well, yes. But not in a bad way. Davidas was a good guy, so none of the crew think he'd do anything to hurt them. But they figure he is having fun at their expense." Jen grinned as Paul flinched again at a stab of pain in his head. "Or your expense, in this case."

"I don't believe it. We're a million miles away from civilization, and the crew thinks the ship's haunted, but they're not worried about it. I'll never figure out sailors."

"Yeah, you will. Let me tell you a secret." Jen Shen leaned so close to Paul that he could feel her breath against his cheek. "You're becoming a sailor yourself, Mr. Sinclair." Then she winked, laughed, and swung out of the compartment.

Paul rubbed his cheek, his senses overloaded by recent events, but with an odd feeling that seemed like pride stirring inside. *She really thinks I'm becoming a sailor?*

The South Asian Alliance ship had held a steady course as the *Michaelson* closed on it. As the kilometers between the ships dwindled, more and more details had become apparent, until the *Michaelson*'s combat intelligence systems had been able to identify the ship.

"He's a research ship?" Paul checked the display again.

"Yeah. Pavarti-Class." Jan Tweed pointed to the same data. "A crew of about twenty, plus another twenty scientists, if they're carrying a normal amount of people."

"No weapons."

"None to speak of, no."

"Then we don't have anything to worry about."

"Not if he's really a Pavarti, no. That is, if he really is a Pavarti and hasn't been modified to carry armament."

Paul checked the data again. "You know, this'd actually be simpler if we knew we were dealing with a warship up front."

"Yeah, it would be." Jan twitched as an alarm sounded, focused on the SASAL ship. "Damn. They're maneuvering." She hit her comm pad. "CIC, I want an estimate of what that ship's doing soonest. Captain, this is the officer of the deck. The SASAL ship is maneuvering."

"Captain's on the bridge!" Wakeman was there almost before Tweed finished speaking.

He swung into his chair, peering at the main display. "What's he doing? What's he doing?"

"We don't have an estimate, yet, captain." Tweed was chewing her lip, perspiration standing out on one cheek. "We have an aspect change, so he's changing heading, and a main drive burn." The display chirped, bringing a narrow probability cone to life. "It looks like he's altered course a bit and put on speed to try to clear the area before we can intercept."

Wakeman stared at the display. "Give me a new intercept course. Now!"

Tweed fumbled at her controls, sweating more heavily, as Wakeman reddened with impatience. Paul helped where he could, but the system would only accept input from one watch station at a time. Finally, the new course popped up on the display. "There, captain."

"That's no good! Look at it! That's outside our area! I want an intercept inside our area!"

Commander Herdez had appeared on the bridge, unnoticed in the tension, and was now leaning over Tweed's shoulder, studying her work. "Captain, ship's systems say this is the earliest possible intercept we can manage at this point."

"It's not good enough! Give me a better one!"

"Captain, I've confirmed Lieutenant Tweed's work. Due to the SASAL ship's speed increase and course change we cannot intercept inside our area. This display shows the earliest point at which we can intercept outside our area. If we put on any more speed, we'll be unable to brake quickly enough when we reach the SASAL ship and shoot past it."

Wakeman glared at the symbol representing the SASAL ship. "Why'd they wait until now? We're so close! It's like they're taunting us." His eyes fixed on Herdez. "That's what they're doing, isn't it?"

The XO crossed the bridge quickly, hanging close to Wakeman and whispering urgently as Paul strained to hear any of her words without success. Wakeman's face kept getting redder, until he waved a hand in angry dismissal. "I know all that. And I know our orders. If that's the best intercept we can manage, we'll damn well do it. Let's go!"

Lieutenant Tweed hesitated. "Captain? You mean execute the earliest intercept maneuver?"

"Yes! Is there something wrong with your hearing? Execute! Execute!"

Tweed froze for a second, then replied in a slightly ragged voice. "Aye, aye, sir. Bosun, warn the crew. Maneuvering in five min—"

"In one minute! We're not letting this bastard get away!"

"Maneuvering in one minute." Tweed, her face rigid, waited through the seconds, then punched in the command.

Paul, watching as covertly as he could, saw her hands gripping her arm rests, not inputting any further maneuvering commands. *She's too upset or too angry to do this maneuver manually. Not that I blame her.* His muscles tensed against the force of the main drive. *This is a hard burn. With only one minute's warning I hope nobody got caught in the middle of something they couldn't secure in time.* Vectors swung around once more, eventually steadying onto a new intercept point several thousand kilometers outside of the area claimed by the United States. *Four days. There's nothing else that ship can do to try to outrun us. We're faster. One way or the other, this chase is going to end in four more days.*

"Sinclair."

Paul jerked his head around at Commander Garcia's hail.

"The captain wants you on the bridge for this intercept."

"Sir?" Maybe Paul didn't have much to do in CIC, but he was Tweed's assistant, which meant his duty station was supposed to be here. Granted, with both Garcia and Tweed on hand as his immediate superiors, odds were Paul would never have anything to do except watch and learn, as Tweed had once advised him. Unless both Garcia and Tweed somehow died or were incapacitated, Paul wouldn't be giving any orders in CIC. Still, he had a job here. "My general quarters station—"

"Is wherever the captain tells you it is! Get your butt up there."

"Yes, sir." *Whatever the captain wants of me on the bridge, I guess it doesn't matter too much. I'm not going to be giving any orders here or there, not unless that SASAL ship somehow knocks out every other line officer on the ship.* Paul looked down at the two enlisted crewing the console he was supposed to superfluously supervise. "Sorry, guys. You'll have to handle this one without me."

One of the operations specialists grinned. "We'll do our best, sir."

Paul swung out past the other enlisted and officers at their stations, down the passageway leading to the bridge. At every bulkhead, he had to stop to open and then resecure airtight hatches sealed for general quarters. It made for a tedious journey, but Paul had no intention of attracting the wrath of the XO by failing to maintain airtight integrity on his route.

The bridge itself was far more crowded than usual already. Lieutenant Sindh, the general quarters officer of the deck, glanced over at Paul as he entered the bridge, a questioning and challenging look on her face. "The captain wanted me here," Paul answered the unspoken question. He felt awkward, not being part of the normal general quarters watch team, and fearing his presence might disrupt them somehow. But Sindh simply nodded and turned back to her console, the rest of the bridge watch continuing their functions as if Paul hadn't arrived.

Wakeman, sitting in his chair on the starboard side of the bridge, looked over and gestured sharply. "Sinclair. Make sure you're close enough to answer any questions I ask."

Paul wriggled through the watch standers, finally finding a clear spot aft and near the starboard side of the bridge. He fastened his tie-downs to the nearest securing stations, looked around to be sure he wasn't blocking anyone's view of any important display, then hung silently, his eyes on the main display.

This close, the SASAL ship was easily visible on the main display, its image magnified by the *Michaelson*'s visual sensors. Unlike the smooth surface of the warship, the research ship was blocky, studded with pods and apparently tacked-on compartments. Without air or water resistance to worry about, civilian spaceships often had such additions applied apparently haphazardly, though Paul had been told they were actually added with enough care to ensure the ship's center of mass and line of thrust stayed more-or-less aligned.

Paul looked forward, up, and to the right, as if there were a porthole there through which he could see the fleeing SASAL ship directly. If neither ship did anything else, the SASAL ship and the *Michaelson* would maintain the exact same bearings relative to each other right up to the moment their hulls bumped. Not that either the *Michaelson* nor the SASAL ship would actually let that happen.

"Okay, then." Wakeman actually rubbed his hands together, smiling in anticipation. "Let's ensure this wise guy sees us. Deactivate the visual bypass system."

"Deactivate visual bypass system, aye. Visual bypass system deactivated, sir." The lenses and the screens on the outside of the hull switched off, clearly revealing the *Michaelson* in all her menace to the nearby SASAL ship.

"Communications. Call that ship and tell them to heave to for boarding. I want them at dead-stop relative to us."

"Aye, aye, sir." Long moments passed, while Wakeman smiled confidently. "Sir, there's no response."

"Are they receiving your message?"

"Yes, sir. There's no doubt of that."

Commander Herdez, occupying her chair on the port side of the bridge, broke in. "What if their comm suite is down?"

Wakeman scowled. "Can't we tell them to stop anyway?"

"Yes, sir," communications replied. "We can display a visual signal on the bypass system screens. International coding. There's no way they could miss that."

"Then do it!" Minutes passed, while the distance between the ships shrank further.

"No response, sir."

"I can see that!" Wakeman pointed at the display. "He's not maneuvering at all! How can we get his attention?"

"Sir, we can pulse a low-power particle beam off his hull in the same international code. If there's anyone alive on that thing they'll have to hear that. It's like hitting the hull with a hammer."

"Yes! Good. Do it." Wakeman had lost his smile, his complexion slowly reddening.

"No response, sir."

"Damn him! Weapons!"

"Yes, sir."

"I want a shot across his bow. Make it powerful and make it close!"

"Captain?" Wakeman turned, scowling, at Herdez' voice. "We're outside the American-claimed area. Use of force at this point—"

"Is justified by our orders! Right, Sinclair?"

Paul spent a fraction of a second lamenting the fate which had placed him in the middle of a debate between the captain and the XO. "Sir, our orders allow you to take any action which you deem necessary and appropriate."

"Yes! You hear that, XO? Firing across their bow is necessary and damn well appropriate, I say. Weapons? Fire when ready."

"Aye, aye, sir." A moment later the *Michaelson* shuddered slightly as she fired a multi-second burst from a high-powered particle beam which ripped through the space only a few kilometers ahead of the SASAL ship.

"Now what?" somebody muttered.

"He's maneuvering, captain," Lieutenant Sindh called out. On the visual display, Paul watched the shape of the other ship alter as its thrusters pushed its bow around.

"What the hell's he doing?" Wakeman asked.

"Sir, I can't... he's lit off his main drive." Projected vectors leaped to life on the maneuvering display.

"He's coming straight at us! Is he trying to ram us?"

"Sir, it's too early to—" Sindh's voice was cut off by the wail of the collision alarm as it was automatically triggered by the ship's maneuvering systems. "Disable that alarm! Captain, he's turned toward us and pushed onto a faster intercept. It looks like he's aiming to pass close above us from starboard bow to port stern."

"Close aboard? How close aboard?"

"Between one and two kilometers, sir."

"Is he insane?" Wakeman looked around as if seeking confirmation. "Why would he take that kind of risk?"

As if in answer, Commander Garcia called up from CIC. "Captain, the SASAL ship's projected course will put it in perfect firing position as it passes close above us. We'd be sitting ducks."

"What?" Wakeman stared at the display. "But it's unarmed, right?"

"Captain, we can't confirm that. He's not *supposed* to be armed."

Everything seemed to be happening very fast. Paul, hanging silently now, tried to grasp the situation as the SASAL ship moved onto a near-collision course. *I never realized how all those months of doing practically no maneuvering made us so unprepared for something like this. All of a sudden we're dealing with another ship nearby and we have to react fast and nobody's used to it. Even Lieutenant Sindh must be seriously out of practice.* Paul found himself wishing that Jan Tweed was at the maneuvering controls.

"Weapons! I want you locked on that ship! Communications! Tell him to veer off! What's happening now? Somebody tell me what's happening now!"

"Ten minutes to closest point of approach," Lieutenant Sindh announced. After months of having the luxury of long periods to plan maneuvers, they were now faced with less than ten minutes to act. On the display, the SASAL ship seemed to be closing on them with shocking speed.

"I need options, people! What's he doing?"

Commander Herdez spoke firmly over the growing tension on the bridge. "So far, the SASAL ship has displayed a pattern of taunting us. It is reasonable to assume this is another attempt to discomfort us."

"Reasonable?" Wakeman switched his gaze rapidly from Herdez to the displays. "I don't—"

"Eight minutes to CPA, captain."

Garcia came back on. "Recommend maneuvering immediately to complicate his firing solution, captain."

"Firing solution? He's not armed. Is he armed?"

"Sir, we don't know. He's on a perfect firing approach."

"We can detect if he's charging weapons! Right? Right?"

"Yes, sir," Garcia answered. "But we haven't— Sir, my watch says they just detected a transient."

"A transient?"

"Yes, sir. It could have been caused by a power surge leaking past a well-shielded weapon—"

Herdez spoke again. "Is that the only possible explanation?"

"No, ma'am."

"What does the combat system evaluate the transient as?"

"Ma'am, it, uh, doesn't seem to—There's another one. I've got another watch stander reporting a transient detection."

Herdez looked at Wakeman across the bridge. "Captain, I don't trust—" The collision alarm wailed again. "Secure that alarm!"

"Five minutes to CPA, captain. Combat recommends immediate maneuvers."

Wakeman was staring at the display, then, like Paul had earlier, switched his gaze to look at the bulkhead in front of him and just above his head where the SASAL ship would be visible if there were a porthole there. "He's on a firing run."

"Captain?"

"The bastard's on a firing run. He's got concealed weapons. We detected them powering up. He lured us out of the American area and got us to fire that warning shot first so he could claim self-defense and now he's going to pass close above us and fire into us. Weapons."

"Aye, aye, sir."

"Are you locked on?"

"Every weapon that will bear on the target, sir."

Paul, watching the situation spin out of control but unable to imagine any way to intervene, wondered briefly at what point the SASAL spacecraft had changed from a ship to a target.

"Three minutes to CPA, captain."

"Too close! Too damn close already! Fire at will!"

"Captain?"

"Open fire, dammit! All weapons! Kill that bastard!"

"Open fire, aye."

The lights dimmed as the *Michaelson*'s battery of energy weapons discharged and recharged repeatedly. Material weapons created debris and shrapnel which in space would be an endless source of peril to other ships. Particle beams and lasers evaporated their points of impact, spearing through obstacles and creating holes in vital equipment of all kinds, as well as any humans unfortunate enough to be in the way. Paul imagined he could see the SASAL ship staggering as invisible demons ripped through it from stem to stern. Lacking the sort of water blanket the *Michaelson* boasted, which wasn't cost-effective on civilian ships, the SASAL ship was helpless before the onslaught. Atmosphere and vaporized fluids vented from dozens of places, causing the stricken ship to wobble in its course as the escaping jets pushed it erratically.

"Officer of the deck!" Herdez snapped. "Immediate evasive action. Get us down and clear."

"Aye, aye, ma'am." Sindh, who like everyone else but Herdez had been focused on the damage being done to the SASAL ship, frantically slapped the thruster controls, pushing the *Michaelson* down and away from the threat of collision as the other craft staggered past overhead.

Paul blinked in the sudden silence. Everyone was watching the display, where the riddled hulk that had once been a living ship continued on its course past the *Michaelson* and on into empty space. After literally weeks of preparation and hours of tension, the combat had taken only a couple of minutes.

"Officer of the deck." Herdez spoke now with her habitual calm and control. "Plot an intercept of that hulk." She looked toward Captain Wakeman, who was staring at the display as if uncomprehending. "We will need to board the wreckage."

Wakeman focused on her, his eyes wide. "Board it?"

"To determine if there are survivors. And to find evidence of the weapons they were carrying."

"Right. Evidence. OOD, get that course plotted."

"Aye, aye, captain."

Paul squinted at the display near his seat in the *Michaelson*'s gig. The hulk that had been a SASAL ship had long since ceased venting material, using up whatever had been onboard during the days the *Michaelson* spent bringing her mass around and accelerating on another vector to cautiously reintercept the wreck. Captain Wakeman had spent a good part of that period crafting and recrafting a message reporting on the incident and his certainty that he had saved the *Michaelson* from destruction by a ship which had planned its attack for months.

The final portion had been nerve-wracking to Paul, who had been on watch as the *Michaelson* matched course and speed precisely to the hulk so that the crafts hung motionless relative to each other even though they were hurtling through space at high velocity. "At least we know he's not going to pull any last-minute maneuvers this time," Lieutenant Tweed had observed dispassionately.

Now, as the gig drew closer, Paul could tell Lieutenant Tweed had been, if anything, understating things. There'd been no sign of life on the SASAL ship since it had been riddled by the *Michaelson*, and the amount of damage Paul could easily see explained that all too well.

Paul glanced over at Sheriff Sharpe. As the ship's legal team, they'd been tapped to assist in the boarding and inspection of the wreck. Sharpe looked back, then smiled grimly. "Sir, if I may offer a small bit of advice, when we get onboard that thing, I wouldn't look at stuff too close."

"Excuse me? That's why we're boarding it. Us and the rest of the boarding party. To look at stuff."

"Sir, I've assisted in some pretty unpleasant crime scene investigations in my time. I'm just suggesting not looking too close at certain things. That's all. You'll understand."

Soon enough, Paul did. While the chief engineer of the *Michaelson* led a group through the wreck searching for its concealed weaponry, Paul and Sharpe were ordered to find the captain's quarters and search it for records or orders which might provide further evidence of ill intent.

His progress through the wreck seemed dreamlike, floating through silence and darkness lit only by the areas his survival suit light fell upon or those spots where openings torn in the ship let through solid splashes of sunlight. The lack of atmosphere inside the wreck meant that none of the light spread in any way, so a location would be either brightly lit or totally dark. Paul set his suit light to its widest beam and moved cautiously, fearing jagged edges that might rip his spacesuit, but the energy weapons that had savaged the SASAL ship had left absurdly precise holes. Only where the ship's own equipment had flared or burst in its death throes did any torn surfaces exist.

They found the first body floating not far from their entry point. The wound on it caused from being nicked by one of the *Michaelson*'s powerful energy weapons was absurdly clean and smooth, instantly cauterized even as it was inflicted. The rest of the body, however, had nothing clean about it. "Oh, God." Paul looked away hastily. *I've never actually seen a human body subjected to explosive decompression before. Now I know what the Sheriff meant when he said not to look too close.* He couldn't throw up, not in a suit, so he gritted his teeth and closed his eyes, fighting down nausea.

"Sir?" Sheriff Sharpe had one hand on Paul's arm. "You're better off occupying your mind with something else, sir."

"Meaning exploring for records."

"That'd do, sir."

"Remind me to listen to you next time."

"Hey, sir, with that kind of learning curve you may make lieutenant junior grade, yet."

Even though he was grateful for the distraction posed by Sharpe's banter, Paul still glowered at him. "Let's head on down this way. The diagrams from our merchant shipping database say the captain's quarters and the bridge should be over there." Finding a hatch with a name embossed on it just off the bridge, Paul looked inside. The stateroom was empty, making it all the more likely this space belonged to the ship's captain, who must have been on the bridge while the SASAL ship was making its run on the *Michaelson*. "I'll check the desk area."

Paul had to pound on the desk and use one of his suit tools before he could yank open drawers that had already been frozen into place, hastily pocketing the data discs he found inside. Much of their content might have been damaged by vacuum and cold, but something might be recoverable. A picture fastened to the desk showed several people, doubtless the dead captain's relatives or family. Paul tried not to look at the picture as he rummaged for anything else that might constitute evidence. He added a few pages of printout in a foreign language, then turned to see Sharpe going through an open safe on another bulkhead. "That was lucky."

"What was lucky, sir?"

"That they left the safe open."

"They didn't leave the safe open, sir." Sharpe grinned conspiratorially. "Certain talents come in handy in my line of work."

"Good thing you're on our side, Sheriff. Anything good?"

"Your guess is as good as mine. Data discs, some foreign currency, and maybe a diary or personal log."

"Take it all." Paul swung slowly around, his light illuminating the bulkheads around him. "What's that?"

Sharpe moved close to the locked panel, examined the lock for a moment, then Paul could see his head nod. "Retinal-scan lock. Too hard to crack this one, sir. Request permission to pop it."

The captain told us to check everything. "Permission granted."

Sharpe yanked a round spool of material out of his suit's belt. He carefully unwound the cord making up the spool, revealing it to be about the thickness of a little finger, and pressed the cord against the outline of the door. When his work was complete, Sharpe brought out an object the size of his thumb, inserted it in one end of the cord, then twisted the end of the object. "I'd look away if I was you, sir."

Paul hastily averted his gaze. The bulkhead where he was looking danced with jagged reflections as the cord flared to life at the point where the fuse had been inserted. When the reflections stopped,

Paul looked back, seeing a gap edged by white-hot metal where the outline of the door had been. Sharpe waited while the metal rapidly cooled, then pulled the door free.

Inside, a small compartment about a meter on each side and less than a half meter deep held a half-dozen hand weapons. Boxes of ammunition were fastened near each weapon. Sharpe moved one suited hand carefully around inside the compartment, checking for other objects, then moved back. "Just the guns, sir."

"Why would a scientific research ship have pistols onboard?"

"Oh, lots of reasons, sir. But I'd bet the main reason was discipline. I don't know enough about crews on civilian ships to be sure, but it's not a wonderful life out here, sir. If somebody in the crew went off the deep end, you might need one of these to take him down. Or maybe suppress a mutiny."

"Yeah. That makes sense. There's also those recurring rumors of pirates. I guess this would be a cheap form of insurance against that, too."

"That it would, sir, though I think space pirates are a threat confined to the average bad movie."

"I agree. Do we need to take these?"

Sharpe moved his hand as if trying to scratch his head through the suit. "Well, sir, they are weapons. But the only way you could use one of these against us would be by suiting up and firing out an opened airlock. Even then, I can't see them penetrating our hull."

"Okay. Leave them for now. I'll ask the chief engineer later if we need to pick one up." Paul hesitated, steeling himself. "Let's get to the bridge."

He managed to handle it by pretending he was moving through a particularly detailed horror scene manufactured for Halloween.

Close to a dozen bodies in various states of damage were either strapped into chairs or hooked onto nearby tie-downs. Despite himself, Paul's gaze swept across one face, which despite the stresses of decompression still bore a visible expression of shock literally frozen into place. *I guess we surprised them.* "I'm not finding anything, Sheriff." Not surprising, really, that there was nothing loose to be found, since no one in their right mind wanted data discs or papers flying around a bridge when a ship maneuvered.

"Me neither, sir. Should I try tapping the central data system?"

"No. The chief engineer has some people with him who are responsible for that. Can you tell which one's the captain?"

Sharpe spread his hands. "I'm sure he or she's in here. But these guys aren't wearing any rank that I can see."

Paul tried to focus closely on the collars and sleeves of the corpses and avoid noticing any other details. "No. I don't see any, either. There's four chairs here, but they've got identical control consoles in front of them." He moved past the still-occupied chairs, nerving himself for brushing against the bodies, and peered closely at the consoles.

"Looking for something in particular, sir?"

"Yeah. Firing controls."

"See any?"

"No. Not any dedicated ones. But that doesn't mean anything. These displays could have held virtual weapons control panels. There's no way to tell that, now, though." Paul triggered a different communications circuit to talk to the chief engineer. "Sir, this is Ensign Sinclair. We've finished going over the captain's quarters and the bridge."

"Did you find any weapons?"

"Yes, si—"

"*You did?*"

"Uh, yes, sir. A half-dozen hand weapons."

"Hand weapons?" The chief engineer's elation of a moment before vanished. "You mean pistols?"

"Yes, sir. In the captain's quarters."

"That's all?"

"Yes, sir."

"What about the bridge? Any sign of weapons controls?"

"No, sir. No dedicated ones." The chief engineer's insistence had driven Paul's dread of his surroundings away, replacing it with a growing sense of another kind of unease.

"Damn."

"Sir?"

"We haven't found any, either."

"But..." The information couldn't seem to settle in, as if it were too unreal to be true. "You didn't find any weapons, sir?"

"That's right. No weapons. No extra energy capability to power weapons. No combat systems of any kind. No wiring for combat systems. Nothing. Just a lot of dead civilians on a ship that is apparently only outfitted to conduct scientific research."

"But... that means..."

"That means you'd better break out your legal books, Mr. Sinclair. We've got one hell of a problem to deal with."

Paul looked over at Petty Officer Sharpe, who was shaking his head. *We blew away a bunch of helpless civilians? Oh my God.* Paul was abruptly aware again of the dead bodies around him, but now their faces seemed to reflect not shock, but accusation.

7

Kris Denaldo entered the wardroom where the second shift was eating lunch, ran her eyes along the table, then pulled herself near Lieutenant Bristol. "Looks like you're senior officer present. Request permission to join the mess."

"Knock it off, Kris. Sit down."

"Hey, I'm just trying to maintain wardroom etiquette."

"Like you have to do that among junior officers." Bristol cocked an eyebrow at her. "You look pretty beat."

"I just came off watch." Kris looked around at the others, who were also watching her, then sighed. "Okay. I hate standing watches right now."

Carl Meadows tossed a meal pack to her. "Lunch is beefy green bean stew. Just like Mom used to make. Why do you hate standing watch now in particular?"

"Why now? Are you kidding? We're still holding formation on that thing. The wreck." She shivered. "I swear, sometimes I almost think I can see them, looking out at us, planning some way to get even."

"Kris, I've been over there. So has Paul. It's a dead ship."

"I *know* that."

"Do you happen to know why all the department heads got called to the captain's cabin a few minutes ago and left us unsupervised by older and allegedly wiser heads?"

"Oh, yeah." She gestured in the general direction of Earth. "We got a message in from fleet staff, ordering Wakeman to immediately transmit all available evidence of armament on the SASAL ship. Emphasis on *immediately*."

"There's no evidence to transmit. They've already sent us other messages asking for it."

"Right. Three others. And we've sent back replies that promise the evidence but don't provide any. Fleet staff's gotten more and more insistent, and I guess fourth time's the charm. This one ordered that the evidence be forwarded to fleet staff within one half-hour of transmission of the message."

Meadows laughed briefly. "Fleet staff is sort of pushing the light-speed limit, aren't they?"

"They never take the real world into account when planning stuff. Why start now? Anyhow, not long after that message came in, we got ordered to pass the word for the department heads to meet with the captain. I figure it's cause-and-effect."

"Good bet. Wakeman's spent a lot of time in his cabin. Does anybody know how he's doing?"

Lieutenant Bristol looked around the wardroom carefully, as if wanting to be certain of his audience, before answering Carl Meadows' question. "Sykes tells me Wakeman is in major denial. He's still insisting that SASAL ship was making a firing run on us."

"Major denial is right. We've already sent over two more search teams looking for evidence of weaponry, and both found nothing more than the first team did."

"And," Jen Shen added, "Cap'n Pete himself insisted on personally commanding the last search team. He's been there. He's seen there's nothing on that wreck."

Kris looked at Paul. "He wouldn't be the first to want to see something that wasn't there. Remember those weapon-charging transients that CIC reported? I heard a rumor there's no trace of any such detections in the combat system records."

Paul nodded reluctantly. "The rumor's right. The operations specialists swear they saw them, but the system records say the sensors never detected them and never displayed them."

Carl Meadows shook his head. "Funny what stress can do."

"Not so funny when you think about that dead ship out there."

"You know what I meant." Meadows fiddled with his drink for a moment. "There's going to be hell to pay for this. The intelligence summaries say the SASALs are screaming to everyone who'll listen, claiming we murdered the crew of that ship on purpose and demanding 'justice,' whatever that means in this case."

"How'd they find out what happened? That ship sure didn't send any messages out."

"Paul, you can't hide weapon discharges from deep-space sensors. The SASALs, and anybody else looking this way, would have seen both ships close on each other, then the weaponry discharging, and then their ship goes silent. Even an idiot could draw an accurate conclusion from those observations."

Jen slammed her hand onto the table. "Speaking of idiots, those idiots caused this as much as Wakeman did! What were they doing? Teasing and taunting us, refusing to communicate, then making a near-collision run at us? Did any of them stop to think the *Merry Mike* is a heavily armed warship? Stupid. They were stupid!"

"I'm not disagreeing with that. But how much of the rest of the human race is going to agree with what we did?"

"*We* did?" Jen questioned. "I don't remember Cap'n Pete asking for my input when he was leading us into this mess."

"Scapegoats don't necessarily have to be guilty. Paul, could they nail anyone besides Wakeman if they wanted to do it?"

Paul glanced around at all the faces watching him. "If they wanted to, sure. They could court-martial all of us, if they wanted to. Would it stick? That's a different question. Even what happens to Wakeman is going to depend upon what they want to do."

Jen frowned at him. "Surely they'll court-martial him."

"Maybe. Maybe not. This is an international incident. Our own national prestige is at stake. Do we care what the SASALs think? Do we need to accommodate them, or do we just thumb our nose at them? That's the difference between Wakeman getting a court-martial, or a slap on the wrist or less."

"I don't—"

Jen's next sentence was cut off by the shrill of the bosun's pipe over the all-hands circuit. "This is the executive officer. The *Michaelson* has just received orders to immediately terminate our patrol mission and return to Franklin Naval Station at best speed. We are currently calculating the necessary maneuver, which will require a sustained main-drive firing. All personnel should begin preparations. That is all."

The junior officers exchanged glances. Carl shook his head. "Hell to pay, and the bill just came in the mail. I never thought I'd be unhappy to hear we were going home early."

"Yeah," Bristol agreed. "Paul, you remember what you and Sykes said? Anything that got us sent home early might be real bad. You were right."

Paul nodded back mutely. Sometimes being right didn't feel very good at all.

Paul was swinging hastily toward the ensign locker so he could strap in prior to the main drive burn when he saw Ensign Jen Shen coming from the other direction. Jen gestured urgently to Paul, speaking in a low voice as soon as he drew near. "Hey. Don't ask me about my source, but I got some solid information on what happened during the department head meeting with the captain."

"Really? I thought there wasn't anyone in the cabin but the captain and the department heads."

"I told you not to ask me about my source."

"So what happened?"

"Wakeman showed the department heads a message that basically blamed them for the whole mess and asked them all to sign off on it."

Paul stared at her in disbelief. "You're kidding. Did they?"

"Are you nuts? Of course not. There was, apparently, much wailing and gnashing of teeth, but the department heads all refused to fall on their swords in order to save the career of Cap'n Pete."

"Boy, that must have been ugly. What did Herdez do?"

Jen shrugged. "She wasn't there."

"That's interesting."

"Yeah. I can't imagine the XO agreeing with Wakeman on that message. I don't like Herdez as a human being, but she's professional. She's surely not undermining the captain right now, but she wouldn't go along with trying to leave the department heads holding the bag, either."

"Then Wakeman is stuck with having to accept responsibility."

"Hah! Paul, you are so naïve it hurts sometimes. He can still try to blame the department heads, and both Wakeman and the department heads can still try to lay the blame on us dumb, incompetent junior officers and the dumb, incompetent enlisted."

"That'd never fly."

"You think? Want to make a little wager on them trying? As for it not working, I did a little quick research myself. There's been plenty of cases where senior officers screwed up, and then dumped the blame for it all in the laps of the most junior personnel they could pin it on."

Paul was still searching for a reply when the all-hands circuit came to life with the five-minutes-to-burn warning. "I guess we'll have to see what happens."

"I'm not going to be waiting to see what someone else does, and I don't recommend that you do, either. Get your story down, Paul. If you don't define what you did, someone else with more rank than you is going to do it for you."

"You're right. I'll do that. Right after the burn."

"Where you going to spend it?"

"Uh, in my bunk. That's a nice, secure place." Paul grinned as Jen smiled approvingly. "See. I am learning."

"So you are. Never pass up the chance for extra bunk time. Later, shipmate."

The only two bad things about the extended period confined to his bunk by the firing of the main drive were being tossed around by the maneuvering thrusters and the fact that the main drive burn ended while Paul was still trying to catch up on his sleep.

* * *

"Mister Sinclair, sir?" Sheriff Sharpe stuck his head into the ensign locker. "Just passing by to let you know captain's mast has been postponed."

Paul looked up from his work, then rubbed his eyes wearily. "When's it been rescheduled for?"

"To be determined, sir."

That's not good. Wakeman hardly leaves his cabin, and now he's putting off carrying out parts of his job. "Thanks, Sheriff. Say, mind having a seat while I ask you something?"

"No problem, sir." Sharpe pulled himself inside, then nodded toward Paul's desk. "Looks like you're working on a statement, sir."

"How'd you guess?"

"It seems to be a pretty popular hobby among the officers right now, sir, if you don't mind my saying so."

Paul smiled ruefully. "I can't very well object to you saying so when I want to ask you for some advice on it. I'm having a lot of trouble making it come out sounding right. No matter how I craft it, it sounds wrong."

"Ah." Sharpe nodded knowingly this time. "That's your problem, Mr. Sinclair."

"What is?"

"You're trying to *craft* your statement."

"I don't understand."

Sharpe folded his arms, looking upward as if dredging up memories. "I've been involved in a lot of criminal investigations in my time, sir, so I've seen and heard a lot of statements. Let me tell you, the worst ones are the statements that you can tell somebody *crafted*. They're so carefully phrased and they walk around important issues and they don't often say a helluva lot. You hear or read one of those, and it feels bad."

Paul rubbed his forehead this time. "Why?"

"Why? Look at it this way, sir. If all you're doing is writing down what happened and what you saw and what you heard, that's pretty straightforward, isn't it? No call for crafting anything, there. Just make sure the facts as you know them are laid out clear. But, if you're trying to craft something, what you're doing is one of two things. Either you're trying to make yourself look good, which makes you look bad, or you're trying to make somebody else look bad, which also makes you look bad."

Paul stared at Sharpe dubiously. "But how do I make sure I'm not, um, unfairly blamed for something?"

"You can't, sir. No matter what you write. Jesus Christ Himself could come down and dictate a statement and if He had anything in there nice about Himself somebody up the chain of command would say 'this guy's trying to make Himself look nice, so maybe He's guilty of something.' Sir, you're best off just laying out the facts. If you did okay, that'll be clear. If you screwed up, they'll find out anyway. Either way, you'll get credit for being up-front about what you did and for not trying to influence the opinions of the investigators."

Paul sat silent for a minute, thinking through Sharpe's advice. "You know, Sheriff, that's why I haven't been happy with anything I've written. Every time I expressed some sort of opinion, I thought it sounded like I was either covering my butt or trying to nail somebody else."

"Sir, with all due respect to your exalted status as an ensign, if they want your opinion on anything, they'll ask you for it."

Paul found himself laughing. "Sheriff, one of these days..."

Sam Yarrow edged into the ensign locker, eyeing Sharpe disdainfully. "Is there some sort of meeting underway or is this a social call?"

Sharpe, his face a professional mask, rendered a rigid salute to Ensign Yarrow. "Delivering a message to Mr. Sinclair, sir. I have completed that task and now request permission to continue with my other duties."

Yarrow glowered at Sharpe, but the master-at-arms had said nothing he could label insubordinate or improper. "Just go. I've got work to do."

"Yes, sir." Sharpe spun away, half-nodding at Paul as he turned, then was out the hatch.

Yarrow eyed the now-empty hatch entry sourly. "A word of advice, Paul. Don't get too familiar with any of the enlisted."

"Familiar? What the hell are you talking about?"

"Having a joke-fest with that guy in your stateroom, for one. He didn't belong in here."

Paul pondered a long list of possible replies, many of them profane, but decided to continue to follow Jen Shen's advice of refusing to confront Yarrow directly. "Thanks for the advice."

"I mean it. People are talking about you and that guy."

Yeah. I'm sure. We're heading home early to face what's certain to be a real nasty inquisition after blowing away a bunch of stupid but helpless civilians, everybody's worried about courts-martial and trying to justify whatever they personally did, and people are supposed to be talking about me being too chummy with Sharpe for proper officer–enlisted relations. Give me a break. I may not be perfect, but I know how to avoid crossing that line. "Thanks for telling me that."

"I don't want him in here again."

Paul counted to five slowly before answering this time. "Sam, this is my stateroom, too. If I need any enlisted to come in here to ask or answer a question for me so I can do my job, I'll do it."

"A good officer doesn't depend on enlisted to do his job."

"I guess that means I'm not a good officer."

Yarrow eyed Paul for a few seconds as if deciding how to respond, then finally smiled in a forced manner. "Funny. Just watch it. I'm trying to help you."

"Thanks."

"Sinclair!" Commander Garcia thrust his head into the stateroom. "Where's Tweed?"

Paul tried to fight down the automatic knot forming in his gut at the all-too familiar question. "I don't know, sir." Out of the corner of his eye, Paul could see Yarrow just barely failing to suppress a smug smile.

"Find her. Then both of you find Chief Imari. Then all three of you find me. We're going to review your divisional training and certification program, and it better be flawless, you hear me?"

"Yes, sir." *Training and certification? Why's he suddenly so hot on... oh. Any investigation is going to be looking into how well trained and qualified the operations specialists who reported those transients actually were. But Garcia can't just blame Tweed and me for any problems because he's signed off on the programs for all the divisions in his department. I guess trying to make sure there aren't any problems is part of him crafting his own defense.*

Garcia shifted his glare. "Yarrow."

Sam Yarrow looked up, unable to mask his surprise. "Yes, sir."

"You told me your division's qualification records were being maintained by Chief Herzog."

"That's right, sir."

"Chief Herzog says you transferred those records from him two months ago for your review and he's been locked out of them since.

Is that correct?"

Yarrow's face supplied the answer. Paul did his best not to let his own satisfaction show. *Forgot you'd done that, eh, Sam? And from what I hear of the way you treat Chief Herzog, I hope you weren't expecting him to help cover your butt. He probably loved the chance to drop a ton of bricks on you.*

Garcia's face darkened. "Is that correct?" he repeated.

"Uh, I, uh, think so, sir. I'll have to—"

"Get those records back to your chief so he can update them. I want them fixed immediately. Is that clear?" Commander Garcia focused back on Paul. "Why are you still here?"

"I... was just ensuring you were finished with me, sir."

"Find Tweed!" With that parting admonition, Garcia whipped his head out of the stateroom.

Paul closed out his work, making sure the personal encryption was active. He didn't think Yarrow would try to spy on him, but he also didn't put it past the other ensign. *I think I'll run down Chief Imari, first. She might have some good ideas where Tweed's latest hiding places are.* He swung out of the ensign locker without a backward glance at Yarrow.

Jan Tweed looked more haggard than usual on their next watch. "You okay?" Paul asked.

"I'll survive. It wasn't any fun having Garcia go through those qualification records."

"I was there, too, remember? At one point, I thought I'd start bouncing off the bulkheads if Garcia said 'I don't care if that entry isn't supposed to be filled in, do it anyway' one more time."

Jan managed a weak smile. "Paul, I've got about three months left on this tub before I transfer to shore duty. I had this weird idea those three months might not be too bad."

And you're running out of hiding places on the ship that Garcia, Imari or I don't know about. But Paul nodded in real sympathy. Despite the aggravation Tweed's avoidance behavior caused him, he'd grown to like her somewhat. He was still in awe of her ability to maneuver the ship by feel, and it was easy to empathize with the reasons she chose to hide. *And once Tweed transfers off, Garcia won't be able to ask me That Question anymore.*

A brief chirp from the watch panel announced the arrival of a high-priority message. Tweed visibly braced herself before calling it up, then read the message with a bleak expression. "The admiral's appointed an investigating officer to look into our encounter with the SASAL ship."

"That's no surprise. Why'd they tell us with a high priority message?"

"Because that officer is apparently hitting the deck running. We've got orders here to collect and forward statements from all officers onboard."

"We knew that was probably coming, too." Paul craned his neck to look at the message. "Wow. They want them back at Franklin within twenty-four hours of when this message was sent?"

"Like I said, our investigator is hitting the ground running." Tweed glanced at Paul. "Is your statement done?"

"Yeah. Yours?"

"Sort of. I've been working on some of the wording. I guess I'll finally have to decide how to say things now, though."

"I got some good advice on that, if you don't mind me passing it on to you once we get off watch." He decided not to tell her that Sheriff Sharpe had been the source, just in case that might bias Tweed against the advice. She kept so much of herself internalized that there was still a great deal Paul didn't know about Tweed, and probably never would.

"Sure, why not?" Tweed keyed in commands routing the message to the captain and executive officer, then punched the send command.

"Maybe the department heads should see it, now, too," Paul suggested, "so they have a heads-up."

"Maybe. At the moment I don't feel too charitable toward department heads, so I guess I didn't think of that, and now they'll have to scramble a little. Too bad."

Paul fought down a smile. Superiors could always make the lives of their subordinates miserable, but every so often the subordinates found ways to balance the scales a little.

Naturally, everyone ended up scrambling to get the statements collected and put into message format within the time limit. Paul and Jan were still on watch when Commander Garcia came onto the bridge. "You two make sure your statements are done no later than sixteen hundred. Is that clear?"

"Yes, sir," Paul answered for them both.

"You will transmit copies to both myself and the executive officer."

"Yes, si—Simultaneously, sir?"

"Isn't that what I said?"

The look on Garcia's face made it clear further questions would be a big mistake. "Yes, sir." Paul watched Garcia leave again, then looked at Tweed. "Jan, why are we sending these statements to both our department head and the XO at the same time?"

She smiled as if he'd told her a mildly amusing joke. "Why not?"

"Because we always do stuff like that by sending our input to the department head, who reviews it and makes sure he has everyone's input before forwarding it to the XO."

"So this time the XO wants the department heads to know everyone in their divisions has provided input, but doesn't want the department heads to review those inputs before they go to the XO. Maybe she figures some of those department heads might try to change some of those inputs, given the chance."

"Oh." *What was it Jen told me—something about Herdez' loyalty being to the Navy as an institution. The department heads, some of them anyway, are going to be looking out for their own welfare. But not Herdez. She's looking out for the Navy. I wonder how Wakeman will take that? Unless Herdez thinks defending Wakeman's actions is the same as sticking up for the Navy. I wonder what's going on in the XO's mind? Not long ago I was thinking I'd never know a lot about what went on inside Jan Tweed, but compared to Herdez, Tweed is transparent.*

Tweed smiled wryly at Paul. "I guess a lot of people are going to have trouble figuring out what to be thankful for tomorrow, huh?"

"Tomorrow? Why tomorrow?"

"Fourth Thursday of November. Also known as Thanksgiving. Remember?"

"Tomorrow's Thanksgiving?" Paul shook his head. "I don't believe it. You don't expect something like that to sneak up on you."

"We've been busy."

"I know. Like you said, there's not all that much to be thankful for right now, is there? Except for the fact that we're not Wakeman."

"Good point, but I've always been grateful for that."

Paul spent the afternoon reviewing his statement for completeness, fighting down repeated urges to add anything other than the bare facts to the narrative, then sent it to Commander Garcia, reveling in the knowledge that his department head wouldn't have any chance to demand that Paul make meaningless changes like altering every appearance of the word *happy* to the word *glad*. "Hey, Sam, you hear anything about holiday routine tomorrow?"

Yarrow, laboring over his own statement, which appeared to be much longer than Paul's, looked up with unconcealed annoyance. "No. Don't hold your breath waiting for it."

"But tomorrow's Thanksgiving."

"It's also an underway day." Yarrow bent back to his work, ostentatiously ignoring Paul.

Paul made a rude gesture, unseen by his fellow ensign, then left in search of better company. He found Jen Shen sitting in the wardroom, her face uncharacteristically bleak. "Hey, Jen. What's up?"

"Did you hear about Kris?"

Paul, jerked out of his absorption in the upcoming holiday by the question, looked at her in alarm. "No. What?"

"She's in sickbay."

"What happened? An accident?"

"Not exactly. More like a train wreck we've all seen coming." Jen closed her eyes. "This morning Kris started acting strange. Saying things that didn't make sense, starting to do something and then stopping, that kind of thing. This isn't for general dissemination, but the doc diagnosed Kris as suffering from exhaustion."

"Oh, man. She's in sickbay? Can I... I mean, are visitors okay?"

"No. The doc's got her sedated. I gather he's going to keep her out for about thirty-six hours to let her body catch up with her brain. Then another twelve hours' bed rest to evaluate her condition, and if everything seems to be clicking right at that point they'll certify her fit for duty again."

"What about the XO? What'd she do?"

Jen smiled bitterly. "Herdez has pulled two of Kris' collateral duties and reassigned them to other junior officers. You're looking at one of them. I think Carl got the other. Feel free to look relieved you didn't get picked. I would in your place. I guess Herdez wanted to see how far Kris could run before she hit the wall. Maybe that's being cynical, though. Herdez might not have realized Kris couldn't handle it indefinitely."

Paul nodded. "Yeah. Maybe it was a miscalculation. The XO's human, too."

"Sometimes I wonder about that."

"Geez, Jen. I'm sorry."

"It didn't happen to me, Paul. Not yet." She looked away. "You've taken materials courses. You know how they figure out how much pressure something will take. They just keep adding on, a little at a time, and eventually whatever is being stressed cracks or shatters or whatever. The Navy does the same thing to us. Maybe now that Kris has hit the limit they'll want to see how much I can take. Or you."

"No, Jen." Paul sat near her. "Kris wouldn't say no. She just kept pushing herself. But you're smart enough to know when it's getting to you."

"Since when do you know so much about me?"

"I... sorry. I guess I don't."

Jen unbent slightly at the look on Paul's face. "Hey. I know you were just trying to cheer me up. I didn't mean to bite your head off."

"That's okay. I understand. Really."

"No, you don't. You won't understand until you see that wall looming in front of you and you have no idea if you can put the brakes on yourself in time, or if the command structure will even let you put the brakes on. But that's okay. I'll still give you points for meaning well."

"There's nothing we can do for Kris?"

"Only one thing, if I know Kris. If she gets cleared by the doc, don't let on you know anything happened to her. Non-event. Cleared from memory. Deal?"

"Deal." *Thanksgiving, huh? I wonder what I'm going to be thankful for tomorrow? Right now there's not a lot on the list.*

Paul's dark reverie was interrupted as Commander Sykes swung into the wardroom, expertly propelling himself with a minimum of effort to his favored chair, into which he slid with a sigh of satisfaction. "Ensign Shen. I was hoping to encounter you."

Jen nodded wearily. "You found me. What do you need?"

"This isn't a work request, Ms. Shen. I've just come from sickbay, where I had a pleasant conversation with the ship's doctor regarding your roommate, Ensign Denaldo."

"What? The doc wouldn't tell me much of anything. Why'd he talk to you?"

Sykes smiled. "Professional courtesy. Limited-duty officers such as the doctor and myself must stand together against the disdain of line officers. In any event, I wanted to tell you that, after running such tests as he can onboard, it is the doctor's firm opinion that Ms. Denaldo is suffering only from physical exhaustion, with no underlying conditions, and once she has rested she will be, as the old chestnut goes, good as new."

Jen actually smiled, her relief plain. "That's wonderful. Thanks, Suppo."

Sykes waved his hand dismissively. "No thanks required. All in the line of duty. Hah. You heard that? I got to use the words *line* and *duty* while describing my work. Not bad for a supply officer." He eyed Jen as she failed to respond to the joke. "You don't seem as happy at the news as I expected. Are you concerned about yourself?"

"No, Suppo. I'm just a little tired."

Paul tried to keep from frowning at Jen's denial. It was her business whether she wanted to discuss her fears with Sykes, and he certainly didn't have the right to contradict Jen if she didn't feel like talking.

Judging from Sykes' expression, though, he didn't believe Jen anyway. "Young Ms. Shen, it isn't respectful to mislead your elders. You are concerned about yourself in the wake of Ms. Denaldo's misfortune, aren't you? Don't look so guilty. You have every right to be concerned. It's not as if you weren't thinking of Ensign Denaldo's well-being first."

Jen shook her head. "Suppo, you wouldn't understand."

"Because I don't work at least twenty-five hours a day like you line officer types? I'm wounded, Ms. Shen. At the very least, you should credit me with being a keen observer of the human condition."

Jen didn't rise to Sykes' last statement, so Paul intervened. "What do you think, Suppo?" Jen shot him an annoyed glance but didn't shut off the conversation.

Sykes rubbed his chin. "About what happened to Ensign Denaldo? It's a more common affliction than it should be. You line officers have to think of yourselves as runners. Yes, I said runners, and I don't just mean in the literal sense of dashing to and fro with your pants on fire trying to deal with the latest crisis, real or imagined. Your work requires you to be marathoners, maintaining a punishing pace for long periods. You have to keep running, but the goal is to reach the finish line without dropping out of the race." Jen was eyeing Sykes now, her face intent as the supply officer continued. "Sometimes, naturally, you have to sprint. A real crisis that involves a threat to human life or something like that. There's no helping pushing yourself too hard for a while under those circumstances.

But you have to ease up when you can. Sometimes, all other factors permitting, you might even slack off to a walking pace." Sykes cast a quizzical glance at Paul and Jen. "You line officers do slow down to a walk every once in a rare while, right? In any event, I hope you see why I use the analogy. You have to pace yourself over time so you can keep going. It's all much harder to do in practice than in theory, of course, but the alternative is at some point failing to be able to do your job at all. I don't know about you, but the idea of exhausted, totally strung-out officers making life-and-death decisions about matters in which I am involved does not give me a warm and fuzzy feeling."

Jen shook her head again. "Suppo, that's easy to say, but with my department head and the XO riding me, where's the time for easing up? What do you think would happen if I said, 'Sorry, can't do this, I'm taking a break?'"

Sykes shrugged. "And, as is well known, junior officers are always one hundred percent candid with their superiors. I can't tell you how to find the time, Jen, because I'm not running every second of your life. Neither is your department head, though I'm certain it seems like he's attempting to do just that at times."

"And if he isn't, then the XO is. How do I catch a breath when Commander Herdez is looking for the smallest sign I'm underemployed?"

"You think Commander Herdez would begrudge you some downtime?"

"I know she would!"

"Ah. Have you perhaps noticed that no critical engineering activity is routinely scheduled for Sunday mornings on this ship?"

Jen frowned, nodded with visible reluctance, then noticed Paul's questioning look. "Regulations say you're not supposed to schedule any work activity for Sunday mornings," she explained. "Day of rest, or at least morning of rest. But the regulations say that if something critical needs to be done in engineering, of course that can take place. So just about every ship always schedules critical engineering work for Sunday mornings, because they can." She gazed back at Sykes. "But, no, this ship doesn't. Are you trying to say that's the XO's policy?"

"Who else could cause it to happen, young lady? The ship's executive officer is in charge of scheduling events."

Jen gave Paul a puzzled look before focusing back on Commander Sykes. "Then... I guess Commander Herdez must be responsible. I never thought about that. Why'd she do that?"

Sykes raised both eyebrows at the question. "We were just discussing rest, I believe. What do you do on Sunday mornings? When you're not standing a watch, that is."

"I usually try to catch up on some work..." Jen's voice trailed off. "I should be resting?"

"An alien concept to the minds of ship drivers, isn't it? Ponder it long enough, and perhaps the idea will take root. It is officially endorsed, you know. The Navy has provided you with a bed on this ship. You should make use of it every once in a while." Sykes paused, frowning at the two ensigns. "Naturally, I mean individual use. I wouldn't want to be accused of urging two impressionable youngsters down the path to unauthorized social interactions."

Paul covered his face with one hand to cover up his embarrassed reaction to Sykes' joke, while Jen looked pained. "Suppo, I hope no one's trying to spread rumors."

"If they are, I haven't heard of them. But one never knows. I'm simply trying to be prudent." Sykes sighed theatrically. "Young people these days. Meeting, getting married, having children. Nothing at all like when I was young."

The absurdity of the statement, paired with Sykes' tone of apparently sincere nostalgic regret, finally forced another smile out of Jen. "Suppo, just how long ago were you young?"

"It's been a while. Back then you could walk from South America to Africa. Oh, occasionally the land-bridge would flood at high tide, but that just added to the excitement of the outing. The continents have drifted much farther apart now, of course, so that little walk is gone the way of the woolly mammoth. Speaking of which, did I ever tell you about my childhood pet? We called him Harry. Sort of a pun, you see."

Jen laughed this time. "Please. No more. Thank you for the advice, commander. Next time my department head finds me snoozing away, I'll send him to talk to you."

"My office is always open," Sykes assured her, waving his hand around the wardroom as if staking claim to the entire compartment. "Though tomorrow it will be dedicated to Thanksgiving dinner. See the decorations?"

Paul looked around curiously. "No, sir."

"Of course not. They're virtual decorations. When the display projector works. Which, at the moment, it does not."

Jen grinned. "And it's not going to be working soon. We're remanufacturing the control box to try to fix it. Maybe it'll be done in a few weeks."

"Take your time, Ensign Shen." This time Sykes shook his head. "The officially approved, nondenominational, interfaith decorations, guaranteed inoffensive to any human regardless of personal mindset, are truly horrible in their bland mediocrity. You may take a moment to give thanks tomorrow that the projector remains broken."

Paul smiled. *Okay. That's one thing to give thanks for. That and the fact that Commander Sykes cared enough about what happened to run Jen down and give her that talk. Like Jen told me, he's a good pork chop. And a better officer than I'd realized. I wonder what they're going to serve us for Thanksgiving? Something special?*

"Hey, Suppo." Jen held up her portion of turkey loaf, which had been so heavily processed and reprocessed that its texture resembled tofu. "The scuttlebutt was we'd have real turkey for Thanksgiving."

Sykes smiled. "Ensign Shen. Ensign Shen. Close your eyes, young lady. How many real turkeys do you see? That's how many we have on this ship."

"Is it too much to ask that this crap actually taste something like turkey?"

"Yes." Sykes smiled again. "When you joined, the Navy promised to feed you, Ensign Shen. But it didn't promise how often it'd feed you, nor how well."

Carl Meadows swallowed a portion of his turkey loaf with evident difficulty. "Just be grateful they served us this and not one of those lamb roasts."

Lieutenant Sindh choked momentarily. "Why did you have to mention that? Those so-called roasts taste so gamey they ought to be banned under the chemical weapons treaty."

"Where do they come from, anyway? I can't believe that meat is actually from a lamb."

"Well, technically maybe not." Everyone eyed Lieutenant Bristol suspiciously. "They've really improved the solid waste recycling end products and—" Bristol made a futile attempt to dodge the turkey loaf packets hurled at him. "It's a good thing there's no bones in that stuff."

"Oh, I bet there's bones," Jen groused. "Ground up along with damn all everything else."

"Maybe they use something like the turbines, Jen," Paul suggested. "You know, feed a turkey in one end—"

"Feathers and all?"

"Feathers and beaks and all, yeah. Grind it all down and package the end product."

Lieutenant Sindh choked again. "This food is disgusting enough without you guys making it worse. Serves me right for getting stuck eating with the junior officer shift."

Bristol smiled. "You'd prefer eating with the senior officers? Present company excepted, of course," he added, bowing slightly toward Commander Sykes.

"No. No way. Present company excepted, of course." Sindh mimicked Bristol's gesture to Sykes.

Sykes smiled in return, unbuckling his seat strap. "It's nice to receive proper obeisance, but I must leave prior to the dessert course."

"Why?"

"Discretion is the better part of valor. Please just keep in mind that I was not allowed any input to the menu. It was fixed by the gods of supply, loaded onboard in prepackaged lots, and I am merely the messenger who delivers it."

"Suppo." Jen snagged Sykes as he tried to pass her. "What's for dessert?"

"I wouldn't want to spoil the surprise."

"Spoil it. Please. Sir."

"I believe the dessert is commonly known as cannonballs."

"Cannonballs?" This time Paul choked. They were an infamous dessert at the Naval Academy. Officially an apple baked in pastry, cannonballs were actually small portions of apple locked deep within thick doughy shells. Anyone foolish enough to actually consume one ended up with their stomach feeling as if they had ingested a cannonball in truth.

"Get him!" Meadows howled, but Sykes had already slipped away from Jen and swung expertly out the hatch. "Never mind. We'll never catch him now. Suppo's pretty agile for an old guy. Is anybody going to eat their dessert?"

"Are you kidding?"

"No. I just figured we could sort of deliver any leftovers to Commander Sykes' stateroom." Carl looked inquiringly at Bristol. "Which we could do, if we could get the help of a certain assistant supply officer."

"Say no more." Bristol shook his head in mock horror. "Cannonballs. This is a crime against humanity." He turned to Paul. "Correct, ship's legal officer?"

"I'm sure it must be illegal under some provision of the Uniform Code of Military Justice. Or international law. Or something." Paul spent the next half-hour mostly listening and laughing as his fellow junior officers spun ever more fantastic plots to dispose of the cannonball desserts. *So. Happy Thanksgiving. And I am thankful for something. As bad as things can be, at least I've got some shipmates who are literally in the same boat, and together they make things not only endurable, but sometimes even fun.* At the moment, the investigation of the incident with the SASAL ship and the threat of whatever awaited them back at Franklin seemed very far away. And that was fine.

The next few weeks passed in the odd limbo of underway time.

The ship's interior lighting cycled on and off to mark the passage of human days, but Paul's life remained defined by the hours spent on watch and a ship's workday which seemed to cover most of the time not devoted to watch standing. Sleep fell where possible into the cracks of that schedule. With morale on the ship sinking lower with every kilometer covered on the way back to Franklin, holiday celebrations normally constrained by tight spaces and lack of materials for decoration received even less attention than usual.

One morning, Paul stared at his personal calendar for long minutes before realizing that December 25th ought to have a special significance beyond another processed turkey meal. *It's not like I could go out shopping for presents or anything.* Moments later his data link beeped, announcing the arrival of a sentimental e-card from one of the other officers. *Hey, that's cool.* Paul called up some of the card formats in the ship's database, hastily crafting his own card as other beeps announced the receipt of further holiday cards from other officers in the wardroom. Later, he spent a fairly happy half-hour, clicking through his collection of received cards several times as if they represented a pile of gifts under an elaborately decorated tree.

New Year's Eve didn't quite sneak up the same way. Paul, due to go on watch at 0400, decided not to stay up to mark the moment, instead choosing to grab a few precious hours of sleep. Unfortunately for Paul, Senior Chief Kowalski had other plans.

"Mr. Sinclair! On deck, sir!"

Paul hastily shrugged into his uniform, blearily checking the time. *Half an hour to midnight. What the hell does the senior chief need me for right now?* Poking his head out of the stateroom hatch, he saw Kowalski floating nearby, holding an object in one hand. "Is that a fruitcake? A real fruitcake?"

"Very good, sir!" Senior Chief Kowalski beamed happily at Paul, then pointed aft. "With your permission, I will lead the way, sir."

"The way to where?"

"Why, Mr. Sinclair, you've never heard of parading the holiday fruitcake? You are in for a treat, sir, a rare honor. Please come along, sir."

Baffled, Paul followed in Kowalski's wake as the senior chief pulled himself one-handed along the passageway, holding the fruitcake prominently in his other hand. A weird shriek behind him shocked Paul, who turned to see one of the *Michaelson*'s petty officers with a bagpipe strapped to her and two assistants towing her along with the small procession. Despite the difficulties of playing a bagpipe in zero gravity while being towed through the constricted spaces of a warship, the petty officer made a creditable effort at Scottish marching tunes and hymns, the wails and screeches of the music following Paul and Kowalski as they traversed the ship, with only occasional interruptions as the bagpipes or the petty officer banged into an obstruction. Everywhere, groups of sailors gathered to cheer them on and fall in behind the parade.

Eventually, the group reached the bridge, where an increasingly mystified Paul found Commander Herdez awaiting them despite the late hour. Senior Chief Kowalski stopped directly in front of the executive officer, proffering the fruitcake in one hand as he saluted rigidly with the other. "Commander Herdez, ma'am, it is my honor and privilege to present the holiday fruitcake."

Herdez returned the salute, her expression, like Kowalski's, absolutely serious. "I accept the honor of receiving the holiday fruitcake. Have you examined the holiday fruitcake to determine if it is fit for human consumption, Senior Chief Kowalski?"

"I have, ma'am."

"And your conclusion?"

"I regret to report that the holiday fruitcake is not fit for human consumption, ma'am."

"Then you and Ensign Sinclair are ordered to consign it to Davy Jones' Signal Shack in the depths of space, senior chief."

"Aye, aye, ma'am." Kowalski saluted the executive officer again, a gesture Paul hastily copied, then turned and led the procession off the bridge, the bagpiper starting her musical accompaniment again as they went.

This time the procession and its crowd of hangers-on proceeded outward toward the hull until they reached one of the launch tubes providing access to outer space. A gunner's mate stood at attention by the tube, waiting until Kowalski came to a halt before him. "Mr. Sinclair and I have orders to consign the holiday fruitcake to the depths of space."

The gunner's mate nodded, then popped the outer and inner seals of the launch tube, revealing the spring-loaded launch platform resting cocked at its base. "Davy Jones' Signal Shack is targeted and awaiting the arrival of the fruitcake, senior chief."

Kowalski offered the fruitcake to Paul. "Sir, if you would do the honors."

"Sure, senior chief." Paul placed the fruitcake on the launch platform, then moved back as the gunner's mate resealed the tube.

Kowalski indicated a chronometer on the bulkhead nearby, where the time was running down to midnight. "At exactly midnight, we will launch the fruitcake, Mr. Sinclair." The gunner's mate keyed open panels on either side of the launch tube, revealing the buttons for manual launch commands. Kowalski took up position at one, waving

Paul to the other. Then they waited as the final minutes ticked off, the bagpipes having mercifully fallen silent at last, even though the buzz from the observers crowding the passageway in both directions provided plentiful background noise. Paul took advantage of the relative quiet to lean close to Kowalski. "Senior chief, what the hell are we doing?"

Kowalski looked surprised. "Why, sir, you've never heard of the parading and launching of the holiday fruitcake? It's a naval tradition, sir."

"A tradition? This happens every year?"

"Every New Year's Eve, yes, sir. On every ship underway. It's been that way about as long as there's been a space Navy."

"And Commander Herdez is okay with this?"

"Sir, the executive officer understands the value of traditions. She also, if I may say so, understands the importance of keeping morale from sinking any lower, and even perhaps raising it a mite, with a harmless tradition such as this."

"Harmless? Isn't that thing going to be a hazard to navigation?"

"The fruitcake, sir? No, sir. The launch tube's oriented to fire the fruitcake up out of the plane of the solar system. Just like the launch tubes on every other US Navy ship underway right now. There's about a dozen ships out now, Chief Imari informed me. Think of it as humanity's holiday salute to the universe, sir."

"I see. Why am I helping with this?"

"The same reason I am, sir. Tradition says the most junior officer and the most senior enlisted on the ship will parade and then launch the fruitcake. That's you and me. Ah, almost midnight. Stand by, Mr. Sinclair."

Paul placed his thumb on the firing switch, watching as Senior

Chief Kowalski did the same on the other firing panel. The last seconds scrolled off, and as the time hit midnight, Paul and the senior chief both pressed their switches. The jolt of the launch was barely discernible, followed by a minuscule firing of maneuvering jets to compensate for the ejection of mass from the *Michaelson*. The gunner's mate checked his readings, then gave a thumbs-up to indicate the fruitcake had indeed been launched on its endless journey to Davy Jones' signal shack, the space Navy's equivalent to Davy Jones' locker at the bottom of Earth's seas.

Senior Chief Kowalski faced the crowd, his expression solemn. "We have consigned the holiday fruitcake to the depths of space, to serve as a warning to all the universe of the awful culinary weapons available to the human race. Yet our motives are also noble. Mayhap in the far future, billions of years from today, some other race of spacefarers in dire need of provision will find the holiday fruitcake and be able to feast upon its substance, as edible and tasty after an eternity in space as it is at this moment. All salute the holiday fruitcake!" Senior Kowalski saluted, a gesture copied by Paul and everyone else visible. "That is all."

Paul waited for a few moments to let the crowd disperse, graciously accepting the congratulations of a number of enlisted sailors for his role in the parade and the launch. By the time he made it back to his stateroom, the year was another thirty minutes older, that period referred to by military personnel as o-dark-thirty to signify the darkest and most wearying portion of the night. *What the hell. That still gives me two hours to sleep before I need to get up for my watch.* Paul swung gratefully into his bunk, his visions before sleep set in filled with images of volleys of fruitcakes soaring through space, eternal monuments to the human sense of the absurd.

* * *

Franklin Station again. As their course had taken the *Michaelson* back into more heavily traversed portions of the solar system, they'd encountered more and more shipping. The opportunity provided to relearn operating around lots of other spacecraft had been invaluable, Paul thought, staring at the clutter of ships and small craft buzzing around the massive orbital facility, but not nearly intensive enough to prepare them adequately for this. *Did we actually go through this kind of mess when we left?* He glanced over at Jan Tweed, who was visibly sweating. *Thank heavens we're under station piloting control this close in, because the rules mandate automated docking. But if anything goes wrong, we're still supposed to take charge of the helm and somehow weave through all those other craft. Please, don't let anything go wrong.*

"Captain's on the bridge."

Tweed and Paul, absorbed in watching the outside situation, jerked in surprise at the bosun's announcement. Tweed turned to the captain, licked her lips, then began a situation summary. "Captain, we are—"

Wakeman silenced her with a look and a gesture, belting himself into his chair with all the enthusiasm of a prisoner fastening the restraints on an electric chair. He sat silent, apparently staring at the main display, but with his eyes unfocused.

"Lieutenant Tweed." Jan spun around as Commander Herdez entered the bridge and made her way to her own chair. "Have all departments reported readiness for entering port?"

"Yes, ma'am."

"How long until we tie up?"

"Thirty-five minutes to berth contact, ma'am, according to Franklin's piloting system."

Paul felt himself hunching down and made an effort to sit normally, sparing a sympathetic glance toward Tweed, who was sweating more heavily now. *Wakeman's sitting over there like an unstable explosive. No telling what might make him blow up at us. And now Herdez is here watching us, too, like she knows Wakeman might not spot any screw-ups, or might order something stupid this close in to Franklin. I have a feeling this is going to be the longest thirty-five minutes of my life.*

Exactly thirty four minutes and twenty seconds later, the *Michaelson's* lines were shot out to waiting grapples as the ship came to a dead stop relative to Franklin. The grapples locked on, merging the *Michaelson's* mass to that of the station. The feeling of a steady one gravity's worth of acceleration settled on the ship as it joined with the station's rotation. Tweed signaled to the bosun, who shrilled his pipe before making the age-old announcement. "Moored. Shift colors."

Wakeman pulled himself out of his chair and out the hatch so quickly that the bosun barely had time to call out. "Captain's left the bridge."

Herdez unstrapped herself, nodding to Tweed and Paul. "Good job. Notify me when you stand-down the bridge watch."

"Aye, aye, ma'am." Tweed watched her leave, then slumped back, breathing heavily. "God. Last time. I hope."

Paul noticed her hand was shaking. "I don't understand, Jan. I know it wasn't fun having Wakeman and the XO up here, but you handled the ship great out in open space. Why do ops near Franklin freak you out?"

"Look at the display! How many ways can you screw up here? I can't even count them. No. I hate this part. I like driving the ship out where it's free and clear, but not in traffic like this. Last time, Paul.

I'll never have to do this again." She saddened abruptly. "I'll never get to maneuver her out in the big empty again, either. I'll miss that."

"I understand." Like so much else about Jan Tweed, her fears were easy enough to comprehend, even if they served mainly as a cautionary example for Paul. "Looks like the quarterdeck is sealing to Franklin."

"Good. When that's done, we're out of here." She triggered an internal communications circuit. "Quarterdeck, this is the bridge. Who's got the watch down there?"

"Ensign Denaldo. Seals are checked and cleared. Internal and external pressure readings are equalized. Request permission to pop the hatch." Since her rest in sickbay, Kris had apparently been none the worse for wear and had returned to full duty almost immediately. The only lingering effect had been a slightly slower working pace, interspersed with occasional down time. Kris had told Paul during one such period that Herdez had "strongly suggested" she relax once in a while. Officially, the exhaustion incident had apparently never happened, though Paul suspected Kris was on probation against over-working herself again.

Tweed checked her own read-outs before replying. "Permission granted."

"Seals released. Hatch opening." A pause while hydraulics moved tons of material in the hatch ponderously out of the way. "Hatch open and secured. Assuming the watch."

"Understood. Bridge watch standing down."

"No brass band."

Paul winced at Kris' last observation. Normally, a ship returning from months in space would have a joyful reception awaiting. A band, any family members and friends of the crew who could manage to be there, and assorted high-ranking officers from the staff on Franklin. But not this time. Paul called up a picture from the quarterdeck camera. No band and no brass of any kind. No well wishers, either, which would have required active discouragement of their presence by the command on Franklin. A lone captain stood there, with a single enlisted assistant. Paul zoomed in on the image, close enough to see the insignia which revealed the captain was a Judge Advocate General's officer. *A JAG. The only one to greet us back is a lawyer. No one else wants to be seen welcoming us, or was allowed to be seen welcoming us. That pretty much settles it. They're going to try to hang Wakeman. And maybe some of the rest of us as well.*

8

Paul tried to maintain his composure as he waited outside the wardroom. The JAG captain hadn't wasted any time in getting her investigation rolling. He knew she'd already talked to Captain Wakeman, Commander Herdez and all the department heads. Now the JAG had reached far enough down the food chain to snare Ensign Paul Sinclair.

Tweed left the wardroom, her shoulders hunched in a defensive slump, nodded briefly to Paul as she waved him in, then headed off on some unknown errand. Paul exhaled slowly to relax himself, then entered. The JAG, seated at the wardroom table, glanced up at his entry. "Ensign Sinclair?"

"Yes, ma'am."

"Have a seat." Paul took the indicated chair, on the other side of the table from the Navy lawyer, then waited with fraying nerves while she finished entering something into her data link. "Alright, then." The JAG favored him with a brief smile. "Ensign Sinclair. Ship's legal officer. Correct?"

"Yes, ma'am."

"You'll need to sign this." The data link displayed a standard form for attesting to sworn testimony. "It requires you to swear to the truth of your statement."

Paul signed. Command-level investigations didn't require witnesses to be sworn. JAG-level investigations did. It was just one more sign of how seriously the incident with the SASAL ship was being treated.

The JAG checked the signature, downloaded the form to her files, then faced Paul again. "Mr. Sinclair, I'll tell you frankly that your statement was a pleasure to read. Concise and to the point."

"Thank you, ma'am."

"Is there anything in that statement you wish to change?"

Paul looked away for a moment, concentrating. "No. No, ma'am."

"I want to be certain of one thing. Your statement indicates that prior to firing a shot across the bow of the SASAL ship, Captain Wakeman asked you for your opinion on whether his orders authorized such an action."

"Yes, ma'am."

"And you told him that, in your interpretation, they did."

"Y-yes, ma'am."

"Did Captain Wakeman ask you any other questions subsequent to that?"

"You mean while we were all still on the bridge? No, ma'am."

"Prior to actually firing on the SASAL ship, did he again ask you if you believed his orders authorized such an action?"

"No, ma'am."

"You're certain?"

"Absolutely."

The JAG smiled slightly, her lips pressed tightly together. "Thank you, Ensign Sinclair. Have you discussed your statement with anyone else on the ship in anything but general terms?'"

"Well, yes, ma'am."

"And who was that?'"

"The chief master-at-arms. Petty Officer First Class Sharpe."

"Ivan Sharpe? I know the man. What was the nature of your discussion with him?'"

"He advised me to write a, uh, concise and to-the-point statement, ma'am."

"Ah. Very good. Congratulations on taking Petty Officer Sharpe's advice. I know a few full-fledged lawyers who wish they'd done the same." She cocked a questioning eyebrow at Paul. "You appear to have done a good job as ship's legal officer. Are you at all interested in pursuing a legal degree and transfer into the JAG corps?'"

"Uh, no, ma'am. Not really." *She doesn't need to know my brother's a civilian lawyer and I've been butting heads with him since we were kids. Nor that my dad was happy I chose to be a line officer like he'd been. And being collateral duty legal officer on this ship hasn't exactly made my life happier. Three good reasons not to be a lawyer, and none I know of to become one!*

"That's all right, Mr. Sinclair. Not everyone wants to be a lawyer. Thank you. That's all. Please send in the next witness."

"Yes, ma'am." Paul fought down an impulse to grin with relief as he left, then frowned as he remembered one of the JAG's questions. *Why'd she want to know if I told Wakeman if our orders said it was okay to shoot at the SASAL ship? Where would... Wakeman. I'll bet Cap'n Pete claims I gave him that advice. Like Jen said he would, he's still trying to place the blame on everyone else. I guess it's sort of a compliment that he thinks I'm important enough to be a target for some of the blame.*

Later, comparing notes on their interviews with some of the others,

Paul repeated his suspicion. Lieutenant Sindh nodded knowingly as he did so. "That also explains a question I was asked, I believe. The JAG wanted to know if I'd told the captain the SASAL ship appeared to be trying to ram us."

"*Ram* us?" Carl Meadows stared at her. "Wakeman's trying to claim the SASALs were on some sort of suicide mission?"

"No. I think he's trying to claim all of us in a position to do so were giving him advice that made his actions seem correct at the time. In other words, that he acted properly based on the information and assessments we provided."

"What a sleezeball. I wonder what Wakeman's blaming me for? Using up some of the ship's oxygen so he didn't have enough to think straight with? Or the fact that my weapons worked when he told us to fire? Hey, if they'd all failed then we wouldn't be in this mess. It's too ridiculous."

"Be careful." Lieutenant Sindh looked at all present, a warning expression clear on her face. "This is the sort of thing which could easily drag down everyone involved in any way. Guilt by association. Even if Wakeman is found one hundred percent responsible, his accusations will find fertile ground if we act in a way that seems to support them."

"What do you mean?"

"I mean if we go around bad-mouthing Wakeman, calling him a fool and an idiot, it will cause those who hear us to believe we did fail to properly support him."

"He is a fool and an idiot!"

"I know that as well as you do. Everyone else doesn't. To them, he's a ship's captain who was depending upon his crew for the best possible support. We need to ensure people know that we gave him the best possible support, despite what we know to be Wakeman's many and manifest failures as a commanding officer. They won't believe we gave him good support if we're openly contemptuous of the man."

Meadows stared down at the deck as if unable to think of a rebuttal. "Okay. You're right. No sense in the rest of us sinking any deeper into this than we have to."

Sindh looked straight at Paul. "What could be the outcome of this investigation? Can you guess?"

"Sure I can guess. It's serious. A JAG-level investigation means the result could be a recommendation for a court-martial."

"*A* court-martial, or multiple courts-martial?"

"Possibly multiple ones. Yeah. Or maybe letters of reprimand. Or maybe nothing. It all depends."

Carl looked up again. "There's SASAL representatives on the station. They've been invited up as observers."

"How'd you find that out?"

"I know somebody who's involved with the care and feeding of them. They gave me a heads-up."

"Observers." Sindh ran the word around her mouth as if she didn't like the taste. "What will they be observing? Surely not the delivery of a letter of reprimand."

Paul shook his head. "The JAG-level investigation hasn't even been completed. How could they have already brought up a SASAL delegation to observe a court-martial when the investigation hasn't made any recommendations yet?"

"How? Sometimes, Paul, the results of investigations are foreordained. Not officially. Oh, no, never that. But it's understood. There's reports of a major oil discovery in SASAL territory. SASAL possession of such a resource makes them important friends for the US to have. The South Asian Alliance would not regard a pro forma wrist-slap or exoneration of Captain Wakeman as a friendly act."

"Even though their ship all but invited it? But the system isn't supposed to work that way."

"Paul, you've been in the Navy for a while now. How many systems work as they are advertised?"

Paul stared back at Lieutenant Sindh. Like Carl before him, he couldn't think of anything to say.

The next few days were an odd mix of routine and suppressed tension. Paul began seriously considering the temporary use of some of Tweed's hiding places as Commander Garcia became more incendiary than usual. Wakeman spent almost every hour of every day in his own cabin, rarely venturing out and then not speaking to anyone. The junior officers began referring to Wakeman as the Neutron Captain, since he passed through groups without interacting in any way. Paul found himself checking not only the calendar but also the clock, wondering how long it would take for a high-priority investigation to produce recommendations, and how long it would be before those recommendations were acted upon. If someone had really decided on the results beforehand, it might not take long at all.

"All officers assemble in the wardroom."

Paul responded as quickly as he could, finding the small space packed with most of the rest of the other officers already. "Hey, Carl. Where's the department heads?"

"Somebody told me Herdez already called them in separately."

"That doesn't sound good." Paul looked up with surprise as Jen

Shen squeezed into the wardroom. "Jen, aren't you on watch?"

"Yeah. Senior Chief Kowalski relieved me for a few minutes. He said the XO wanted every officer here."

Lieutenant Sindh, taking up station near the entrance, craned her head in an attempt to tally everyone's presence. "Ensign Shen. Are you here, yet?"

"Yeah, I'm here."

"Sinclair? Bristol? Okay, I see you both. Alright, that's everyone. Hold on." Sindh vanished for a few moments, then reappeared. "Attention on deck."

The officers straightened into the best semblance of attention they could manage while crowded so close. Paul eyed the hatch curiously. The attention on deck command was reserved on a ship for the captain or any visiting senior officer, and there weren't any visiting seniors present at the moment. *Wakeman's coming out at last? What's he got to say to us?*

But instead of Wakeman, Commander Herdez entered. "At ease." Her face a professional mask, Herdez surveyed the other officers for a long moment. "We have been notified by Commander, United States Naval Space Forces that Captain Wakeman has been relieved of command of the USS *Michaelson* effective immediately. I am to serve as acting commanding officer until Captain Wakeman's relief arrives. I expect you all to continue to exercise your duties to the best of your abilities and to ensure your personnel do the same."

"XO?" Lieutenant Sindh spoke in a subdued voice. "What's happening to the captain?"

Herdez didn't register any emotion as she replied. "Captain Wakeman is being referred to a court-martial which is to be constituted by order of Commander in Chief, US Space Forces. At this time, I do not know the exact nature of the charges."

"Only him?" Carl Meadows blurted, then reddened as Herdez eyed him. "I'm sorry, ma'am. But, Captain Wakeman's the only one being charged?"

"That's correct. I expect we will be notified as to which officers and enlisted will be required to function as witnesses at the court-martial. Until such time, we still have a ship to run. Are there any further questions?"

Kris Denaldo raised one hand tentatively. "Ma'am? If we see Captain Wakeman, what do we... um..."

"If you encounter Captain Wakeman, you will render him the military courtesies appropriate to an officer of his rank. He is no longer commanding officer of the *Michaelson*, however, and no longer entitled to anything that position entailed."

"Thank you, ma'am."

Herdez nodded to the group, then left. "Attention on deck," Sindh called out, quickly followed by "At ease," after Herdez had cleared the hatch. "Okay, boys and girls. Now we know. Let's get back to work."

Carl looked over at Paul. "I always imagined I'd be cheering the day Cap'n Pete Wakeman left this ship. Why don't I feel like cheering?"

"I don't know. Neither do I. He's getting what he deserves. Right?"

"I think so. You don't sound so certain."

"How could I not be certain?"

Carl shrugged. "I don't know. Hey, do you know where Jan Tweed is?"

Paul didn't try to disguise his automatic flinch at the question. "No. Now what?"

"Relax. Her orders came through. I just want to make sure she knows."

"That's great. If I see her I'll let her know."

"Thanks. Now I have to run down Sam Yarrow."

"Did he get orders, too?"

Carl smiled at Paul's hopeful expression. "No. Promotion list came through. Yarrow made JG."

"Whoopee." Popular belief was that the average officer would be promoted from ensign to lieutenant junior grade as long as he or she could hear thunder and see lightning. But the promotion still meant a great deal as an escape from the ghetto of being an ensign. "That means we'll get a new bull ensign, right?" Yarrow's reign as the most senior of the ensigns had been notable not for his support of his juniors but rather for their distrust of him. Now that he'd been promoted, some other ensign would be designated the bull. "Who's next in seniority?"

"Jen Shen."

"Jen? We'll have a female bull? She'll be great at the job, but isn't that sort of an oxymoron?"

"Are you going to tell Jen she's an oxymoron?"

"Hell, no. I value my life too much to do that."

"You're learning, Paul. Maybe you'll make JG, too, someday."

"Thanks." Paul followed Carl out, then hesitated in the passageway, unable to decide his next action.

Over the ship's all-hands circuit he heard two quick bongs of the ship's bell, followed by two more, then the announcement, "*Michaelson*, departing." The captain of the ship was referred to by the ship's name when he or she arrived or departed onboard, a tradition going back who knew how long. A few minutes ago he would have known the person leaving the ship was Wakeman. Now he knew it was Herdez, doubtless reporting in person to higher authority. Odd, how quickly a universe could change.

"Is something the matter, sir?"

Paul looked up as Senior Chief Kowalski came past. "Sorry, senior chief. I was sort of lost in thought."

"Not happy thoughts, if I'm any judge."

"Are you surprised? How's the crew taking all this, senior chief?"

Kowalski grimaced. "About as you'd expect. A few want to cheer."

"Only a few?"

"Yes, sir. Oh, Mr. Sinclair, you and I both know the captain wasn't too popular on the mess decks. But it's hard for most folks to be happy about someone else getting hammered, even if they think he deserved it. Meaning no disrespect to Captain Wakeman, of course, sir."

"I understand. What you say is true, senior chief."

Kowalski peered closely at Paul. "You worried, sir? About yourself?"

"About me? No. I don't think they'll try to pin anything on me. It looks like Wakeman is the only one being charged."

"That's not what I meant, sir."

Paul looked back at the senior chief, a man subject to his every legal order, yet also literally old enough to be his father. "Yeah, I'm worried. I'm not sure I'm doing as well as I should. At everything."

"Well, sir, I can't comment on everything. And there's nothing wrong with wondering if you can do better. But you're doing okay, sir. I think you're a good officer."

Paul stared back this time. "Really? Thanks, senior chief. That means a lot."

"No problem, sir. You earned it. Just don't rest on your laurels." Kowalski moved on down the passageway. "By your leave, sir."

"By all means, senior chief." Paul squeezed up against the bulkhead to let Kowalski past, then decided to go in search of Jan Tweed. Telling Tweed about her orders would be a rare opportunity to give her good news once he'd run her down.

Less than twenty-four hours later, Paul found a message on his data link from a Commander John Wilkes, Judge Advocate General's Corps. *"Commander Wilkes has been appointed trial counsel in the case of the United States versus Captain Peter Wakeman."* Trial counsel. That's the prosecutor. *"Contact Commander Wilkes as soon as possible to arrange an interview. Remain available at all times as a potential witness."* Okay, that means a convening order has been issued, right?

Paul called the ship's office, where administrative issues were handled and any incoming official mail was routed to the right officers. "Have you guys received a copy of the convening order for a court-martial against Captain Wakeman?"

"Uh, sir, that document was marked for delivery to the XO. I'm sorry, I mean acting-Captain Herdez."

"I'm the ship's legal officer. I have a need to see it, too."

"You weren't on distribution, sir."

Paul shook his head, annoyed. "Is it marked Eyes Only?" He knew it wouldn't be. Convening orders and charge sheets were matters of public record.

"No, sir. I guess there's no problem with you seeing it, then. We'll shoot a copy to your message queue."

"Thanks."

A moment later his data link chimed to indicate receipt of the document. Paul called up the convening order, scanning it first. *It's a general court-martial, alright. A military judge and five members.* He went back, reviewing the names of the members of the court-martial, then called up data on those officers, curious as to their service histories. *The military judge is Captain Olivia Holmes. Her service history is one hundred percent JAG, but what else would you expect? President of the court-martial is Rear Admiral Charles "Chip" Fowler. OSWO, of course. Commanded various ships, also of course. The usual service awards. Wow. His brother's an admiral, too. Talk about sibling rivalry. Okay, what about the other members? Captain Hailey Nguyen. She's also OSWO. Just came off command of the* Mahan. Mahan *was the ship we relieved in that patrol area. She's not likely to cut Wakeman any slack. Then Captain Jose Feres. OSWO, last command was the* Farragut. *That's three space warfare specialists, all with command experience. Then there's Captain Pedro Valdez, Supply Corps. I bet he'll feel like a fish out of water, but they had to dig up five officers who were at least captains to serve on this court-martial, and there can't be all that many candidates on Franklin. Finally, Captain Gail Bolton. Intelligence specialist? Oh, yeah, they pulled her off the fleet staff.*

Wakeman's certainly getting a jury of his peers. I wonder if he's happy about that or scared to death?

The convening order had an attachment. *The charge sheet. I guess we'll finally find out what charges they're going to try to use to hang Wakeman.* Paul stared as the attachment downloaded. *Why is it so long?* He waited impatiently, then began running down the charges. *Violation of Article 86? Leaving Place of Duty? Two specifications? Why are they bothering bringing in Article 86?* Next came Article 92... "Failure to Obey Order or Regulation... first specification... in that Captain Peter Wakeman did... fail to maintain his assigned duty within the patrol area designated by general order 245-95"...*that's the same as the reason for one of the Article 86 charges...* "second specification... failed to conform to operating instructions for his patrol... third specification... failed to conform to fleet guidance on encounters with third-party shipping... fourth specification... failed to conform to rules of engagement as promulgated in general order 267-97... fifth specification... failed to obey a lawful order from his immediate superior to keep said superior advised of all movements... sixth specification... derelict in the performance of his duties under fleet operational standards... seventh... derelict under requirements of Open Space Navigation Treaty... eighth... derelict in carrying out operational orders... ninth... derelict in exercising command functions during crisis as set forth in fleet instruction..."

Paul surfaced from his reading, blinking in amazement. *No wonder this charge sheet is so long. What else are they hitting Wakeman with?* He began scrolling through the charge sheet again. "Article 107. False Official Statement. In that Captain Peter Wakeman did... knowingly provide false information in a message sent to Commander, United States Naval Space Forces regarding his encounter with a ship of the South Asian Alliance"...*Three specifications... one for each message Wakeman sent.* "Article 110. Improper hazarding of a vessel." *Good Lord, that's potentially a death penalty offense.* "In that Captain Peter Wakeman did... wrongfully and willfully hazard the USS *Michaelson* by bringing said ship into proximity with another spacecraft without justification... second specification... wrongfully and willfully hazard the USS *Michaelson* by failing to maneuver his ship to remain clear of another spacecraft, thus risking collision... Article 111... Drunken or Reckless Operation of Vehicle, Aircraft or Vessel." *Give me a break!* "In that Captain Peter Wakeman, while serving as commanding officer of USS *Michaelson*, did suffer his vessel to be hazarded negligently by failing to order maneuvers to open the distance with another spacecraft when warned of a risk of collision... Article 119... Involuntary Manslaughter... in that Captain Peter Wakeman did, through culpable negligence, bring about the death of thirty-seven individuals manning a ship of the South Asian Alliance..."

Paul sat for a long time, staring at the charge sheet, a lump in his stomach. *They threw the book at him. Every charge they could come up with. I'm surprised they didn't try to toss in bigamy and burglary. Yet, the death of the SASAL crew almost sounds like an after-thought. What's the point of all that? To make sure Wakeman gets nailed? After all, the more he's charged with, the more guilty he must be, right?*

"Hey, Paul." Jen leaned into the stateroom. "My department head got a message from some JAG about maybe being a witness, so he's running around with his hair on fire. Does that mean a court-martial's going down?"

"Yeah." Paul indicated the document on his screen. "A general court-martial."

"That's the worst there is, right?" Jen came into the stateroom, peering at the display. "That thing's dated yesterday. Do you think Wakeman's seen it, yet?"

"I'd bet he saw it yesterday. I've been reading up on this stuff. They've got to give Wakeman a minimum of five days after being notified he's being court-martialed to get his defense together before they actual start his trial. The sooner they handed him a copy of this, the sooner that clock starts ticking."

"Wow. So you think they're going to do this as fast as they can, huh?" Jen looked away from the message, focusing on Paul, and frowned. "What's bothering you?"

"I read the charges."

"I can't imagine it's any fun to relive that mess. None of it was your fault, Paul."

"I know. It's just..."

She sat down. "What?"

"They're trying to hang Wakeman, Jen."

"Literally?"

"Uh, no. I don't think so, although some of the things they charged him with allow the death penalty."

Jen's eyebrows shot up. "You're kidding. I didn't expect that, even for Cap'n Pete."

"I guess I didn't either. Jen, I want the guy to be called to account for what he did, but I don't feel right about all these charges."

"Why? What's the big deal?"

"Jen, look at this charge sheet. They're piling on the charges."

"Piling on? What's that mean?"

"It means they're charging Wakeman with everything they conceivably could, regardless of whether or not it increases the potential penalty. They're officially called, um, lesser included offenses."

Jen shrugged. "Hey, if he did it, he did it. What kind of extra charges are you talking about?"

Paul pointed toward his display. "Well, look here for example. Right at the top. They're charging him with two counts of violating Article 86."

"Article 86?" Jen squinted at the charge sheet skeptically. "They're charging Wakeman with being AWOL?"

"No. It's not the Absent Without Official Leave component of Article 86, it's the Leaving Appointed Place of Duty component. They're charging Wakeman with Article 86 first for leaving our patrol area while we were chasing the SASAL ship, and then again for matching course with the wreck and accompanying it for a few days instead of heading back into our patrol area."

"You're kidding. We were in hot pursuit of the SASAL ship, and no one in their right mind would have just let the wreck zoom off into nowhere without going aboard."

"Then you see my point."

"Okay. I will, with great reluctance, agree that those two charges are over-the-top. But it isn't like Wakeman doesn't deserve to be hammered. He was a lousy commanding officer."

"I'm not debating that. I think he's also a lousy human being. But he's not on trial for his general performance as a commanding officer. No. He's being tried for the specific actions he took while pursuing and firing on the SASAL ship. And some of these charges are nailing him for doing things anybody would've done."

"Like shooting at an unarmed ship?"

"I said some of them! Why couldn't they have just charged him with involuntary manslaughter? And maybe the false official statement charge, because he knew those messages we sent didn't reflect what we'd found on the SASAL ship. Why all this other stuff? It's like in medieval times when they'd sentence someone to be hanged, then drawn and quartered, and then beheaded. It's overkill. And like I said, some of this stuff he's being charged with is the same sort of thing we'd have done in his place with the orders we had."

Jen leaned back, crossing her arms. "So, you don't think it's fair, huh? What are you going to do about it?"

"I don't know."

"Are you planning to somehow go to the mat defending Cap'n Pete's virtues as a commanding officer and leader because you don't think the system is being fair to him?"

"No! But... look, I just don't know."

"Will you at least promise me not to do anything stupid in the name of some personal concept of nobility?"

Paul frowned at her. "Why? What do you care what happens to me?"

"Who said I care?

"It sounds like you care."

"Ha! Don't get your hopes up, Sinclair. I'm just trying to keep your butt out of a bight so I don't get stuck trying to pry you loose and having to pick up all the pieces afterward."

Paul stared stubbornly at his display, unwilling to meet Jen's eyes. "Thanks for the vote of confidence."

"Oh, for heaven's sake. Don't get your ego up. I hate seeing my friends dig themselves into deep holes. Does that sound better?"

Paul sat silently for a minute, while Jen waited as if sensing he needed time to think. "Jen, did you ever see something happening that you thought was bad, and everything you'd ever been taught said it was wrong to do nothing, but you ended up doing nothing anyway?"

"Duh. That's life. Theory versus practice."

"But didn't it bother you? Doesn't it still bother you? I remember back at the Academy, seeing some guy doing stuff that should have gotten him kicked out, but getting away with it all because he had the right connections. Thinking I ought to raise a stink. But I didn't. Now that guy's an officer and probably well on his way to becoming another Peter Wakeman. Because I didn't do something when I knew I should. How many lives will he make miserable? How many people might *he* kill through his own incompetence?"

Jen exhaled heavily. "Paul, part of me wants to try to slap some sense into that brain of yours. And part of me is amazed that someone can still believe in ideals like that. This is the real world. You're not personally responsible for all the injustices that take place. You can't stop them, you can't fix them. If you'd made a fuss over that jerk at the Academy, maybe you would've been kicked out, too. Then you would've ruined your life, and that well-connected bozo would have gone on to live happily ever after anyway. Right?"

"That makes sense, but... it just doesn't seem right. Is my highest priority in life supposed to be looking out for my own best interests?"

Jen looked beseechingly upward. "Heaven help me. It's not that simple. You're worried about people doing bad things? Wakeman did a bad thing. Now, he's going to get hammered. What's the problem?"

"He didn't get us into that mess alone, Jen. Our orders gave him discretion to get us there, and the people writing those orders knew Wakeman."

"Okay. Even if you happened to be one hundred percent right about that, and I'm not conceding that fact except for the sake of argument, even then, I can't see risking your career for the sake of Cap'n Pete. People like him aren't worth it."

"Then who is? Only people I like?"

"That's one way of looking at it. If I was the one being hammered I'd be really happy to have you donning your righteous armor on my behalf."

Paul nodded. "And I would, Jen. For you. In a heartbeat."

She eyed him for a moment, then smiled. "I bet you say that to all the auxiliary engineering officers you meet. So, does that perspective resolve your moral dilemma?"

"No. Where's the morality in only acting right on behalf of those you like?"

Jen shook her head. "You, Paul Sinclair, obviously read all the wrong books when you were growing up. And believed them. Heroic knights and common folk dashing off on noble quests just because it was the right thing to do. Fighting impossible odds against evil. Making the world a better place by their efforts and example and sacrifice. Right?"

"It sounds like you read the same books."

"Yeah, but I stopped believing in them. Malory's book is called *The Death of Arthur*, remember? That's what the Round Table's idealism came down to: murder, adultery, war and a king and his son killing each other. Forget the noble causes, Paul. Look out for yourself. There's no sense in making your life any harder right now."

"I didn't think life could get any harder."

"That's probably what Kris Denaldo thought. She's picked herself up and learned the right lesson. I'd rather you didn't hit the same sort of wall before figuring out where you went wrong."

Jen's words made sense. He'd learned a long time ago that the world didn't work the way it should, and that trying to make a difference usually didn't seem to make any difference. *She's trying to keep me out of trouble. So why does her advice grate me the wrong way? She's right. Isn't she?* "Maybe."

"Instead of worrying about the fate of Cap'n Pete, shouldn't you be trying to catch up on some of your other duties?"

"Maybe."

"If they want to pile on the charges against Wakeman, they'll do it. It's not like you can make any real difference there. Right?"

"Maybe."

"And shouldn't you be agreeing with what I'm saying instead of repeating, 'Maybe?'"

Jen's last statement caught Paul off-guard, so that he found himself laughing. "Is that the key to happiness in life, Jen? Agreeing with you?"

"I certainly think it'd be a better world if everybody did that. My last advice to you right now is to get out of your stateroom and get to work, Paul."

"Okay. Thanks, Jen."

"So you're going to do what I said?"

"Uh... maybe."

Jen paused on her way out of the stateroom to glare back at him. "You're hopeless, Sinclair. I don't know why I bother."

Regardless of the truth of everything else Jen had said, she was right that Paul had plenty of other work to occupy his time and his mind. Paul located Chief Imari so they could review divisional training records, then sweated over the wording of a couple of fitness reports for enlisted personnel that Jan Tweed had asked him to take care of. After that, he pigeonholed Carl Meadows long enough to get a couple more of his OSWO qualifications signed off so that Garcia wouldn't flip out over Paul's lack of progress in that area.

All in all, it almost made him forget the upcoming court-martial, except that almost every task took him through a space or dealt with a document that brought Captain Wakeman to mind. The fact that he could neither shake his misgivings nor resolve them made Paul more and more restless, to the point where he headed aft as far he could go on the *Michaelson*, right back to the bulkhead unofficially labeled The End of the World, then turned and began working his way forward just to remain in motion.

Just past the crew's mess deck he found the chief master-at-arms, Petty Officer Sharpe, leaning against a bulkhead with arms crossed, checking out crew members who edged past him with assorted expressions of greeting, worry or hostility. "Hey, Sheriff."

"Hey, boss. Were you looking for me, sir?"

"No, not really. But I haven't seen you for a few days. How's the criminal element doing?"

Sharpe grinned. "Oh, they're being real good, sir. Or at least real careful. Nobody but nobody wants to end up restricted to the ship right after we get home from a patrol. So there's nothing legal to worry about. Except, well, you know."

"I know. Have you seen the charge sheet?"

"Have I seen the charge sheet? Sir, I haven't read a novel that long in ages. It's a doozy."

Paul shook his head angrily. "Sheriff, did you ever see someone hauled up on charges they didn't deserve? I mean, maybe they weren't great sailors or anything, but instead of being called to account for their real failures they ended being nailed on something they didn't necessarily do?"

"Why, sir, wherever could you have found that example?" Sharpe cocked his head to one side, regarding Paul intently. "Begging your pardon for the question, sir, but does this mean you're not happy with what's happening to Captain Wakeman?"

"You got it. I want him punished, but not the piling on, not the charges for doing things I might have done. Do you think I'm an idiot?"

"Sir, even if I did I wouldn't say so. Mama Sharpe didn't raise a fool. But justice is a funny thing, sir. Sometimes it happens in the wrong way but ends up doing the right thing."

"Then you never had a case where you felt somebody shouldn't be convicted on the charges against them, even if they were some kind of dirtball?"

"Dirtballs deserve whatever they get, sir."

Paul thought about that, then smiled wryly. "I forgot. You're a cop, Sheriff."

"Yes, sir."

"So you're going to see things in a pretty black-and-white way. A dirtball's got to be guilty of something, right?"

"You got it, sir."

"But I'm seeing a lot of shades of gray, Sheriff."

"Now, sir, don't you be turning into a lawyer on me."

Paul smiled again. "Surely there's a middle ground between lawyers and cops."

"I don't think so, sir. And if there is, you wouldn't want to be there because you'd be in the line of fire." Sharpe's own smile faded for a moment. "Mr. Sinclair, I think I understand what's bothering you. It doesn't bother me, but like you say, I'm a cop. And I'm not you. If there's something you think you ought to do, then that's up to you."

"Gee, Sheriff, I'd hate to let you down."

"Mr. Sinclair, as long as you're doing what you really believe is right, I can't very well think less of you. Not that you should necessarily care what I think. I might wonder why you did it, just like I'm wondering why anything about this is bothering you. But I'm just a cop. I catch dirtballs and let the justice system take it from there. You're the officer who has to worry about shades of gray."

Paul smiled again. "Yeah. You're right. I just wish I knew what was right for me to do. If anything."

"Seeing as I don't understand the problem, I can't help you there, sir."

"No, you can't. Thanks, Sheriff."

"For not helping you? This job gets easier every day."

"Go away, Sheriff."

"Aye, aye, sir."

Late afternoon found Paul in the office of Commander John Wilkes. Wilkes went over Paul's statement, asked for a few more details, told Paul he was on the list of witnesses to be called during the court-martial, then dismissed him. The brevity and coldness of the process left Paul feeling like a small cog in a steamroller aimed at Wakeman.

Dinners in the wardroom had been less than festive ever since the encounter with the SASAL ship, and since Wakeman's removal from command had become even more somber. Paul left fairly quickly, going back to his stateroom to dig further into his backlog of work. Sam Yarrow eventually came in as well, smiling with the same self-satisfied expression he seemed to have worn constantly since being promoted to lieutenant junior grade. "Working hard, Sinclair? Or hardly working?"

Paul glanced briefly toward Yarrow. "Working hard."

"Good idea. You'll need the best record you can get coming off this tour."

"What's that mean?"

"You know. Wakeman. What he did. Do you think any promotion board will look favorably on a fitness report signed by him?"

Paul took the time to glance at Yarrow again. "They did in your case."

"No. My promotion board met before Wakeman screwed up. But you guys..." Yarrow let his sentence trail off meaningfully. "Too bad."

Paul counted to five inside before speaking again. "I thought you liked Wakeman, Sam."

"Huh? No. No way. He's not half as good a leader as somebody like, say, Commander Garcia."

"Just to pick a name randomly, huh, Sam? Thanks for your sympathy, but I'm sure any promotion board will judge me on my merits."

Yarrow chuckled. "Boy, are you still clueless."

"Go to hell, Sam." Paul closed his work out and left the stateroom, standing in the passageway for a moment to cool off. At this time of day, in port and after the bustle of work had temporarily died down, the small stretch of passageway loomed empty in either direction. *Carl's on watch. I can't bug him. If Herdez caught us chewing the fat while he was standing the quarterdeck watch she'd rip us both up one side and down the other.* He glanced down toward the other ensign locker, thinking briefly of visiting there. *No. Jen and Kris don't need me moping around. Especially Jen. I wish she understood what was bothering me. Hell, I wish I understood what was bothering me.* He hesitated a moment longer, then headed for the wardroom for some coffee.

Paul swung into the wardroom and made a bee-line for the coffee. He nodded in greeting toward Commander Sykes, who occupied his habitual place in his informal wardroom office. "Good evening, sir."

"Good evening, Mr. Sinclair. Care to sit for a moment?"

"You want to talk to me, sir? Sure." Paul sat down, eyeing Sykes curiously. "Did my supply petty officer screw up?"

"Not at all. All is well in the world of supply. Which is as it should be. How are things in the world of ship's legal officers?"

"Not too bad. Pretty quiet, really, except for the, uh, court-martial."

"Ah, yes. The court-martial." Suppo took a drink from his own coffee. "My sources tell me that you have some misgivings on that count, Mr. Sinclair."

"Who told you that?"

"A good supply officer guards his sources, Mr. Sinclair. Care to talk about it?"

Paul took a long drink of his own, then shook his head. "What's to talk about? Captain Wakeman is being hammered. You've seen the charge sheet, right?"

"And a very long charge sheet it is."

"Yeah." Paul grimaced, staring at the table for a moment. "Damn it, Suppo, why couldn't they have just charged Wakeman for the big stuff he did wrong instead of piling on everything they possibly could?"

"This offends your sense of justice?"

The simple question crystallized the growing misgivings that Paul had been battling. "Yes. It does. Not that I can figure out why."

Sykes leaned back, placing his hands behind his head as he gazed upward. "Legally, as I'm sure you know, being legal officer, all of those charges can be justified in some way. But justice, well, that's another thing, isn't it, young Mr. Sinclair?"

"And this isn't about justice, is it, sir? They need a scapegoat. Wakeman's it."

"Not entirely correct. Scapegoats are often innocent of misdeed. I think we both agree that Captain Wakeman is far from innocent in this matter. But Wakeman is certainly to be made an example of for the purposes of satisfying those who wish to see someone pay for what happened to the SASAL ship."

"Is that why we should be court-martialing Wakeman, sir? Because someone needs to be satisfied? Even though a lot of other factors contributed to Wakeman doing the wrong thing?"

"What do you think?"

Paul sat silent for a few moments. "I think that's wrong."

"Ah. You've identified a wrong. Do you intend attempting to right it?"

"What? Suppo, I don't even know what 'right' is in this case."

"But you've said you do know what's wrong. So I'll ask my question a little differently. What do you intend doing about that wrong?"

"What can I do?"

Sykes raised his eyebrows as if surprised at the question. "You were on the bridge. You are the ship's legal officer. I assume you have been tapped as a prosecution witness?"

"Yes. I have."

"Where your testimony will serve to further what you have said you see as a wrong."

"What else can I do?"

Sykes smiled gently. "Your testimony is your own, Paul. What you do with it, what you say and how you say it, is yours to decide. If you so choose."

"Suppo, I'm just an ensign. An ensign who's still new enough to still be learning how to tie my figurative shoelaces right so I don't trip over my figurative feet every time I try to do something. The senior unrestricted line officers making up the majority of the court-martial members don't really care what I have to say one way or the other."

Commander Sykes shook his head. "There you're wrong, lad. They don't care what *I* have to say. I am a supply specialist, a limited-duty officer with restricted responsibilities. Unrestricted-duty officers such as the warfare specialists represented on that court-martial don't give a flying leap about whatever opinions I may have about the leadership or operational decisions of one of their fellow line officers like Captain Wakeman. But, you, Mr. Sinclair, are one of them. Don't interrupt one of your elders, son. It's a fact. You're unrestricted line. That one thing means that even though you are still a young and barely experienced ensign, you have taken on responsibilities that I will never face. Should we be in battle or other peril and every other officer on the ship dropped dead in an instant, I would still not be in command. I can't. The Navy says so. But you would be. Even now."

Sykes sighed, rubbing the back of his neck. "Trust me on this, young Mr. Sinclair. They'll listen to what you have to say, all right. They may decide after listening that you're an idiot and disregard your testimony, but until and if that happens, they *will* listen to you. You're one of them."

Paul stared back mutely for a moment. "What would I say, Suppo? And why? Why risk my career or my neck or whatever for the likes of Captain Wakeman?"

Commander Sykes shrugged. "What would you say? The truth as you saw it and know it. Whatever that may be. As for why... only you can answer that, Paul."

Paul spent a restless night, waking finally with a sense of having tossed and turned the entire time and with no feeling of rejuvenation. The morning passed with routine tasks, none of which seemed to engage his mind. When noon finally came, he had no appetite and simply went to his stateroom.

Paul found himself standing in front of the small acrylic mirror in the ensign locker, rubbing his face wearily. *What do I do? I keep feeling like I shouldn't let them railroad Wakeman, but the guy's a jerk. And he's a marked man. That's obvious from the charge sheet. What difference will anything I do make? If our positions were reversed I know he'd let me twist slowly in the wind. Hell, Wakeman would help put the rope around my neck if he thought it would make him look better. But if I act like Wakeman would, what right do I have to condemn him?* He looked up, meeting the reflection of his eyes in the mirror. *Damn mirrors. When you look in one you don't just see your face, you also see everything you've ever done written on your face. Maybe Eve didn't offer Adam an apple. Maybe she made a mirror, and Adam looked into it and saw himself and knew he could never hide from himself again. So, Paul Sinclair, what are you willing to see when you look in a mirror?*

"Lieutenant Commander Garrity?" The walk from the *Michaelson* to the lawyers' offices hadn't been all that far, but had felt longer with uncertainty dragging at his feet every step of the way.

Wakeman's defense counsel looked up from her work to see Paul standing in the doorway. "Yes. Ensign Sinclair, isn't it?"

"Yes, ma'am. I, uh, I'd like to talk to you."

"What about, Ensign Sinclair? You're listed as a witness for the prosecution."

"I... I think... my testimony might be more appropriate as a defense witness, ma'am."

Garrity couldn't hide her surprise, followed by interest. "You do?"

"I think so, ma'am."

Garrity smiled encouragingly. "Let's talk. Have a seat."

9

When Paul got back to the ship, Carl and Jen were sitting in the ensign locker idly bantering back and forth during the brief period left before ship's work resumed after the break for lunch. Jen took one look at Paul, then glowered at him. "You did it, didn't you?"

"Yeah."

Carl looked from Paul to Jen. "Did what?"

"Something noble. And stupid. Right, Paul?"

Carl laughed. "Oh, man. Did you change your statement or something?"

"No." Paul sat down, avoiding looking at either of the others. "I just went to Lieutenant Commander Garrity, she's Wakeman's defense counsel, and got added as a witness for the defense."

"The *defense*? Of what Wakeman did?"

"No!" Paul almost yelled it, wondering why even he felt frustrated with himself. "Not of what he did. Of what he's charged with. Of why he did it. Of why we found ourselves in that position in the first place."

Carl glanced at Jen. "Did you understand that?"

"Not entirely. Paul, you *did* think this through, right?"

"Yeah. I thought it through."

"And you did it anyway? Why?"

"Because I don't want to spend the rest of my life avoiding mirrors."

Carl stared back, his puzzlement obvious, but Jen slowly nodded in understanding. "Mirrors can be real difficult. So did this Garrity tell you what Wakeman's defense is going to be?"

"No. I gather she doesn't have much to work with."

"Duh."

"I just talked to Garrity about what I'd seen, what our orders were like, that kind of stuff. She's going to work that into her defense."

"How?"

"I don't know. It's not my place to know."

"Then what is it you're going to say as a defense witness?"

"I'm not sure."

"Paul Sinclair, you are the most exasperating human being I have ever met! What is this going to do to your career?"

"I'm not sure of that, either."

"Shouldn't you be?"

He stared at the deck, then back up at Jen. "No. No, I shouldn't. Because if I didn't do anything that I thought might hurt my career, I'd be Sam Yarrow. I don't want to be Sam Yarrow."

Carl looked over at Jen. "He's got a point."

"Yeah. On his head." Jen stood up, eyeing Paul sourly. "What am I going to do with you? I've got some work that's going to keep me busy all afternoon. If you want to talk after that, look me up." She swung out through the hatch, the sounds of her movement through the passageway fading rapidly.

Carl scratched his head. "Well, Paul, I'm not sure I'd have done what you did, but it took some guts. Do you think it'll matter?"

"I have no idea. But I guess I finally decided that whether it mattered or not to everybody else, it did matter to me."

"Another good point. Tell that to Jen when you talk to her tonight."

"I'm not sure I should talk to her tonight."

"She wouldn't have offered if she didn't want you to."

"But Jen seemed real unhappy with me."

"Nah. She's just a little aggravated. If Jen had been real unhappy with you, she would have ripped off your arm and then used it to beat you senseless. Oh, by the way, Commander Garcia was looking for you."

"Great."

"Where are you going?"

"To find Jan Tweed."

Paul discovered that word of his action was quickly circulating through the ship. He could track its progress by seeing how other members of the crew looked at him. Their questioning expressions and the wave of whispered conversations following him through the ship began to irritate Paul more and more. He finally found Jan Tweed, in a hiding place he'd have never imagined without a hint dropped by Chief Imari, then hauled her to see Garcia so they could both be chewed out at some length for the cleanliness of the spaces assigned to their division and the general appearance of their enlisted personnel. But after Garcia had finished his tirade he gave Paul a version of the look and hesitated before dismissing them. "Is there something else, sir?" Paul asked. *I've about had it. Go ahead with whatever you want to say.*

Almost as if sensing Paul's defiance, Garcia eyed him for a

long moment, then shook his head. "No. No, Sinclair. Don't embarrass me."

"Yes, sir." *Garcia didn't ask me anything, but he sure commented on the answer I didn't give.*

Jan Tweed stopped Paul before they separated. "What was that last thing about?"

"I guess you're probably the only one on the ship who hasn't heard. I've agreed to be a defense witness at Wakeman's court-martial."

Tweed seemed baffled. "Why?"

"Because I thought it was the right thing to do."

She stared at him a moment longer. "Why?"

"I thought Wakeman was being railroaded, and—"

"And whatever he gets, he deserves."

For the first time since he'd met her, Paul saw flat disapproval in Jan Tweed's eyes. "I want him to get what he deserves. I just don't want him to get more than that."

"Why not? It's the sort of thing he's been doing to us, isn't it? Doesn't Wakeman deserve the same sort of treatment he's given *us*?"

Paul looked away, unable to bear her anger. "I'm sorry, Jan. I know what guys like Wakeman have done. I just don't want to end up like them."

The silence following his last statement stretched so long that Paul looked back at her, finding Jan still watching him, her face working with emotion. "I didn't want to end up like *this*, Paul. Wakeman can go to hell. And if you help get him off you can go to hell, too."

"Jan, I don't want to help him get off scot-free. I want him called to account. There's no way anything I say can exonerate everything Wakeman did." Her face steadied, but remained unhappy. "Jan, you taught me a lot of good lessons. I mean it. I don't want you leaving the ship hating me."

"I don't hate you, Paul. I don't understand you. I'm worried that you're doing something that will let someone I do hate literally get away with murder. But what do you care what I think? I'm Jan Tweed, object lesson in failure for new officers."

"That's not true!" Paul shook his head, keeping his eyes fixed on hers even though she tried to evade them. "Jan, you taught me a lot of good lessons."

Her face softened, falling back into its familiar protective mask. "Thanks. But there's more to being a naval officer than that." Tweed's face closed down and her shoulders went into their defensive hunch as she turned away. "I don't hate you, but if you let Wakeman get off free you'll have hurt me."

"He won't get off free." *Can I really promise that? It seems impossible, but what if he did? I don't want to be responsible for that.* Paul watched Tweed leave. *Is there any way I could have been true to myself without hurting Jan Tweed, who's already taken enough hurt? Should I have done what I thought was right even if I knew it would hurt Jan some more?* Paul already knew the answer to the last question, but he didn't want to admit it to himself, not while he could still see Tweed making her dejected departure.

Commander Herdez faced the officers of the USS *Michaelson*, who stood in two ranks on the pier just outside the quarterdeck. "Some of you are designated as witnesses in the court-martial of Captain Wakeman which begins today. Those witnesses will be required to be present each day in the courtroom and are therefore excused from regular duty during the court-martial in order to ensure their presence. Since the court-martial is a public proceeding the rest of you are free to attend as spectators on your non-duty days. I expect every one of you to comport yourselves at all times in such a manner as to reflect credit upon the USS *Michaelson*. Are there any questions?"

Everyone stood silent, their expressions fixed with professional lack of emotion.

"Very well. Dismissed. Duty officers return to the ship."

Herdez turned and began walking toward the location where the court-martial would be held, a courtroom near fleet staff headquarters. The straight ranks of officers dissolved, the department heads following individually in Herdez' wake, while the junior officers clustered into a few small groups to give their seniors time to get out of easy earshot. "I'm sorry I'm going to miss this," Kris Denaldo remarked. "But duty calls."

Paul shrugged. "You won't miss all that much today. A lot of what happens today should be boilerplate legal procedure, the sort of stuff they do in every trial."

"How do you know that?"

"It's in the Manual for Courts-Martial."

Jen speared Paul with an intent look. "Have you changed your mind?"

"About testifying for the defense? No, I haven't changed my mind."

"Not worried, huh?"

"Right, Jen. I'm not worried. I'm terrified."

"But you're doing it anyway, huh? Well, good luck."

Paul stared at her, surprised. "Really? I thought you thought I was an idiot for doing this."

"I changed my mind. Listen, I may have to bail out of the court-martial early today because of a test being run on some of my gear. Make sure you look me up when you get back to the ship."

"Sure."

They all followed after the senior officers, catching up with them outside the entrance to the courtroom. The separate groups of officers stood around awkwardly until the court's bailiff cracked the door. "You may all enter now. Witnesses should sit in the front row of seats. All spectators must be seated behind them."

Paul found himself suddenly worried that the front row would be so narrow that he'd find himself shoe-horned between Garcia and Herdez, but there were enough seats that everyone was able to sit at least one seat away from anyone else.

He glanced around the room, trying to calm himself. *Relax. You aren't going to be doing anything for at least a day or two. They have to run through all the stuff they always do at the start of a court-martial, then the prosecution will call all its witnesses, and only then will I be called. No sense sitting on the edge of my seat the whole time.*

Front and center in the courtroom sat the judge's bench, elevated above the rest of the tables and seats. Two doors in the back of the room presumably led to the judge's chambers and to the room where the members of the court would wait and relax. On one side of the room, angled to face the area just before the judge's bench, a long table draped with a Navy blue tablecloth and equipped with five chairs was obviously intended for the senior officers who would serve as the members of the court. Facing the judge's bench on either side were the two tables where the trial counsel and the defense counsel would be seated, as well as Captain Wakeman himself at the defense table. A few meters behind those tables the ranks of witness and spectator chairs began, an aisle up the center left clear.

Somewhere, invisible in the gray uniformity of the walls around him, fiber optic lenses allowed cameras to not only record the entire trial, but also provide a means for remote observers to monitor the court-martial as well. *Carl says the SASAL observers weren't allowed in the courtroom because Admiral Fowler threatened to raise hell, so they ginned up the excuse that classified material might be discussed and made the SASALs watch from a remote site with a video feed that could be censored. Just as well. I sure don't want them in here making me feel even guiltier about what we did to that ship than I already am.*

Paul twisted around to see the rest of the room, seeing the other junior officers seated several rows behind him against the back wall of the courtroom. Carl Meadows caught his eye, then he, Mike Bristol and Jen each raised a hand to wave at him while they grinned inanely like merry vacationers on tour. Paul grinned back, shaking his head. *Thanks, guys. Glad to know you're with me, even though none of you seem to think I know what I'm doing.*

The main entry door opened again. Commander Wilkes, the trial counsel, strode rapidly up the aisle and to his table. A few moments later, Lieutenant Commander Garrity entered, with Captain Wakeman following close behind her. The courtroom, already quiet, seemed to lose every trace of sound as Wakeman walked stolidly up the aisle, his face fixed in stubborn determination. With a gesture, Garrity invited Wakeman to sit at the defense table, then seated herself. Looking back, she saw Paul and nodded in recognition. Paul almost felt afraid to breathe, fearing the sound would somehow shatter the silence engulfing the courtroom.

The bailiff walked to the front center of the room near the judge's bench, the eyes of everyone in the room on him, and cleared his throat as if he needed to do so to attract attention. The sudden sound came as a relief, and Paul inhaled deeply. The bailiff scanned the room to ensure he had everyone's attention. "When the military judge enters, I will announce 'All rise,' and everyone is to rise. The military judge will instruct everyone to be seated. When the judge directs me to summon the members of the court, everyone should rise once again. The military judge will once again instruct when you are to be seated. Are there any questions?"

After waiting a moment, the bailiff went to the side entrance, cracked the door, and spoke briefly in a low voice, then came back to stand near the judge's bench, looking toward the side entrance. As the door swung open wider, the bailiff faced forward. "All rise."

Everyone in the room stood, waiting as Captain Holmes strode to her bench and sat down before looking around. "This Article 39(a) session is called to order. You may be seated."

Commander Wilkes stood. "The court-martial is convened by general court-martial convening order 0312, Commander, United States Space Forces, copies of which have been furnished to the military judge, counsel, and the accused. The charges have been properly referred to the court-martial for trial and were served on the accused on 18 January 2099. The accused and the following persons detailed to the court-martial are present: Rear Admiral Fowler, Captain Nguyen, Captain Holmes, Captain Feres, Captain Valdez, Captain Bolton, Commander Wilkes, Lieutenant Commander Garrity."

"Very well. Bailiff, please ask the members of the court-martial to enter."

The bailiff went to another door, cracked it, nodded, then stood aside. "All rise."

Everyone stood again as Rear Admiral Fowler led the four captains into the courtroom and over to their table. Fowler took the center seat. Captain Nguyen and Captain Feres hesitated, then Nguyen sat to Fowler's right and Feres to his left. The supply captain, Valdez, took the outside seat to the right and Captain Bolton, the intelligence officer, took the outside seat to the left. Admiral Fowler looked to both sides. "Everybody in the right seats by seniority? Good." He nodded to Judge Holmes.

"You may be seated," the judge advised everyone else in the courtroom. "Continue, trial counsel."

Wilkes faced partway between the judge's bench and the members' table. "I have been detailed to this court-martial by order of the fleet Judge Advocate General's office. I am qualified and certified under Article 27(b) and sworn under Article 42(a). I have not acted in any manner which might tend to disqualify me in the court-martial."

Lieutenant Commander Garrity stood. "I have been detailed to this court-martial by order of the fleet Judge Advocate General's office. I am qualified and certified under Article 27(b) and sworn under Article 42(a). I have not acted in any manner which might tend to disqualify me in the court-martial."

Captain Holmes nodded to both the lawyers, then looked toward Captain Wakeman. "Captain Peter Wakeman, you have the right to be represented in this court-martial by Lieutenant Commander Garrity, your detailed defense counsel, or you may be represented by military counsel of your selection, if the counsel you request is reasonably available. If you are represented by military counsel of your own selection, you would lose the right to have Lieutenant Commander Garrity, your detailed counsel, continue to help in your defense. Do you understand?"

Wakeman licked his lips before replying. "Yes. I understand."

"In addition, you have the right to be represented by civilian counsel, at no expense to the United States. Civilian counsel may represent you alone or along with your military counsel. Do you understand?"

"Yes."

"Do you have any questions about your right to counsel?"

"No."

"Who do you want to represent you?"

"Commander Garrity."

"Very well. Counsel for the parties have the necessary qualifications, and have been sworn. I have been detailed to this court by order of the Judge Advocate General's office of the Commander, United States Space Forces."

Wilkes walked forward a few paces, then pivoted to once more face both the judge and the members of the court-martial. "The general nature of the charges in this case allege negligent and reckless behavior on the part of Captain Wakeman which resulted in loss of innocent life. The charges were preferred by Commander, United States Naval Space Forces, and forwarded with recommendations as to disposition to Commander, United States Space Forces." He looked directly at the judge. "Your Honor, are you aware of any matter which may be a ground for challenge against you?"

"I am aware of none."

"The government has no challenge for cause against the military judge."

Garrity stood again. "The defense has no challenge for cause against the military judge."

The judge looked at Wakeman once more. "Captain Wakeman, do you understand that you have the right to be tried by a court-martial composed of members and that, if you are found guilty of any offense, those members would determine a sentence?"

"Yes."

"Do you also understand that you may request in writing or orally here in the court-martial trial before me alone, and that if I approve such a request, there will be no members and I alone will decide whether you are guilty and, if I find you guilty, determine a sentence?"

"Yes, I understand that."

"Have you discussed these choices with your counsel?"

"I have."

"By which type of court-martial do you choose to be tried?"

From where Paul was sitting, he couldn't tell if Wakeman had glanced over at the members before answering. "By members."

"Very well." The judge gestured to Wilkes. "The accused will now be arraigned."

Wilkes indicated the data link he held in one hand. "All parties and the military judge have been furnished a copy of the charges and specifications. Does the accused want them read?"

Garrity didn't bother looking toward Wakeman before she replied. "The accused waives reading of the charges."

The judge nodded to Wilkes. "The reading may be omitted."

Wilkes nodded back. "The charges are signed by Commander, United States Naval Space Forces, a person subject to the code, as accuser; are properly sworn to before a commissioned officer of the armed forces authorized to administer oaths, and are properly referred to this court-martial for trial by Commander, United States Space Forces, the convening authority."

Judge Holmes focused on the defense table again. "Captain Wakeman, how do you plead? Before receiving your pleas, I advise you that any motions to dismiss any charge or grant other relief should be made at this time."

Garrity stood more slowly this time. "Your Honor, the defense moves that all charges be dismissed as being at variance with naval custom and regulations requiring commanding officers to execute their orders to the best of their ability and guard their ships against harm."

"The motion is denied. It has already been noted that the charges were properly brought by Captain Wakeman's operational commanders. Do you have any further motions?"

"No. Captain Wakeman pleads not guilty to all charges and specifications."

"Very well. Will the prosecution make an opening statement?"

Commander Wilkes nodded again. "Yes. The prosecution intends to demonstrate that Captain Wakeman disregarded his orders to patrol a designated area of space claimed by the United States, that he conducted an unauthorized intercept in unclaimed space territory of a ship belonging to another nation, and that this intercept was conducted in a reckless, negligent and aggressive manner which culminated with Captain Wakeman ordering his ship to fire on an unarmed ship, resulting in the deaths of thirty-seven civilians and the effective destruction of the other ship. Captain Wakeman had numerous opportunities to follow other courses of action, but he rejected every chance to conform to his orders and standing instructions, and to defuse a situation which became deadly as a result of his own carelessness. As such, Captain Wakeman should be found guilty on all charges and specifications, for each charge and specification is based upon his decisions, his actions, and his failures to properly command his ship."

Wilkes returned to stand by his table while Judge Holmes looked toward Lieutenant Commander Garrity. "Will the defense make an opening statement?"

"Yes, Your Honor. The defense intends to prove that Captain Wakeman was indeed following his orders as reasonably interpreted by himself and other members of his crew. Further, the defense contends that Captain Wakeman's encounter with the civilian ship of the South Asian Alliance was marked not by recklessness or carelessness, but by a compounding series of events which left Captain Wakeman perceiving only one course of action to ensure the safety of his own ship. As such, the defense intends to demonstrate that Captain Wakeman should be found not guilty on all charges and specifications."

Garrity sat again. Judge Holmes looked around the court, her gaze lingering on the officers from the *Michaelson*, then settling on Commander Wilkes. "Proceed."

"Thank you. The United States calls as its first witness Commander Allan Garcia."

Garcia stood and marched to the witness stand. He'd obviously made an effort to look immaculate, but the extra pounds of weight around his waist spoiled the effect somewhat. Wilkes came to stand before him. "Do you swear that the evidence you give in the case now in hearing shall be the truth, the whole truth, and nothing but the truth, so help you God?"

"I do."

"Are you Commander Allan Garcia, United States Navy, Operations Department head on the USS *Michaelson*?"

"I am."

"Do you know the accused?"

"Yes. Captain Wakeman has been my commanding officer for the past year."

"Now, Commander Garcia, as Operations Department head,

were you familiar with the orders issued to the USS *Michaelson* during the ship's last patrol?"

"Yes. Intimately familiar. That's part of my job."

"In general terms, what did those orders require of the USS *Michaelson*?"

"Well, in general, we were required to patrol through the American zone and challenge any third-party shipping which entered the zone without requesting and receiving permission."

"Did the orders indicate you should leave this patrol area at any time?"

"Not explicitly, no."

"When the USS *Michaelson* moved to intercept the vessel henceforth to be referred to as the SASAL ship, and the SASAL ship responded to this challenge by fleeing the area, did you regard your orders as having been satisfied?"

"Yes, I did. That's what they said. Challenge anyone entering the zone without permission, and that's what we did."

"But Captain Wakeman ordered the *Michaelson* to pursue the SASAL ship. Did he consult with you regarding this decision?"

"No."

"Did he seek your advice, as the department head responsible for operational matters?"

"No."

"After sustaining his pursuit for some time, Captain Wakeman brought the *Michaelson* close to the SASAL ship. Would you describe, in your own words, what happened?"

"Well, I was in combat. The combat information center, that is. Because we were at general quarters. Captain Wakeman tried to tell the SASAL ship to heave to so we could board it for inspection, but they didn't respond."

"Do you believe your orders authorized him to make this demand of the SASAL ship once it had left the American zone?"

"No. There wasn't anything in there about that."

"How did Captain Wakeman attempt to communicate his demands to the SASAL ship?"

"We tried a lot of ways. Radio first, of course, then visual signaling, and finally some particle beam taps on the SASAL's hull."

"Did the SASAL ship respond to any of these attempts to communicate?"

"No. Not a word."

"Commander Garcia, if you encounter another ship in international space which refuses to respond to your communications, what is standing policy for dealing with that situation?"

"Well, you make sure he's not in distress, and if he's not then there's not much you can do."

"What did Captain Wakeman do?"

"He ordered us to fire a warning shot across the SASAL ship's bow."

"A warning shot? Had he determined whether or not the SASAL ship was in distress?"

"Uh... no. We didn't take any steps to do that."

"So Captain Wakeman ordered you to use force in an attempt to compel the SASAL ship to comply with his instructions?"

"Yes."

"And what happened after you fired that shot across the bow?"

"The SASAL ship maneuvered. He turned his bow toward us and lit off his main drive so his course intersected ours."

"Intersected? You mean there was a risk of collision at that point?"

"Yes."

"And you recommended to Captain Wakeman that he maneuver the *Michaelson* to open the distance with the SASAL ship, didn't you?"

"Yes. More than once. That's standard procedure."

"And did Captain Wakeman do that? Did he follow standard procedure?"

"No. We maintained course and speed the entire time."

"And while the SASAL ship continued to close on the *Michaelson* as Captain Wakeman took no corrective action, what action did Captain Wakeman order?"

"He ordered us to lock weapons onto the SASAL ship, and about two minutes before the SASAL ship reached its closest point of approach he ordered us to fire on it."

Wilkes leaned forward, looking at Garcia intently, then faced the members of the court-martial as if addressing them instead of Garcia. "So, Captain Wakeman brought his ship close to the SASAL ship by leaving his ordered patrol area. Once close to that ship, he ordered it to comply with his instructions even though it had no legal obligation to do so. When it refused to respond to his commands, he ordered a shot fired near it, and when it reacted by turning to close on his ship Captain Wakeman ignored repeated advice to maneuver his own ship and instead ordered you to fire on the other ship. Is that correct, Commander Garcia?"

"Yes. That pretty much sums it up."

"Once the *Michaelson* had caught up with the wreck, which was all that remained of the SASAL ship, and sent boarding parties over to examine the SASAL ship, what did those boarding parties find?"

"Uh, nothing."

"Nothing?"

"Nothing out of the ordinary, I mean. I commanded the second boarding party. There wasn't anything on the SASAL ship that shouldn't have been there."

"Did the SASAL ship show any signs of having been prepared for any sort of combat situation?"

"No. They didn't have suits on, they didn't have interior airtight partitions sealed, nothing like that."

"Then the SASAL ship was unarmed and unprepared for any kind of combat when Captain Wakeman ordered that it be destroyed using the full firepower available to the USS *Michaelson*?"

"That's correct."

"No further questions."

Judge Holmes gestured to Garrity. "You may cross-examine."

Garcia sat stolidly while Wilkes returned to the prosecution's table and Lieutenant Commander Garrity came to the witness stand. "Commander Garcia, when Captain Wakeman ordered his ship to pursue the SASAL ship, did you advise him you believed this to be contrary to your orders?"

"Captain Wakeman had read the orders, just like me. He knew what they said."

"So you didn't say anything to him? You didn't indicate any belief that Captain Wakeman's actions might not be justified by your orders?"

Garcia bared his teeth in a humorless smile. "Captain Wakeman didn't take kindly to unsolicited advice. If he wanted your opinion, he'd ask you. If not, you were supposed to keep your mouth shut."

"Then you regarded it as your duty to keep Captain Wakeman happy instead of well supported?"

Wilkes was on his feet before the question ended. "Objection.

The question disparages the witness."

"I withdraw the question," Garrity stated, apparently oblivious to Garcia's reddening complexion. "Commander Garcia, during the actual intercept of the SASAL ship, what were your recommendations regarding communicating with the other vessel?'"

"I beg your pardon?'"

"You said attempts to communicate with the SASAL ship failed. What alternatives did you suggest?'"

"I... that wasn't my responsibility."

"Did you suggest Captain Wakeman ensure the SASAL ship was not in distress?'"

"I didn't have to. Captain Wakeman knows standard procedures as well as I do."

"So you simply assumed Captain Wakeman was aware of alternatives instead of advising him?"

"When the SASAL ship turned toward us, I advised Captain Wakeman to maneuver the *Michaelson*. I did that more than once!"

"Oh, yes." Garrity walked a few steps away from Garcia, then turned to face him again. "When the SASAL ship turned toward you. At what point did you first advise Captain Wakeman that the SASAL ship might be on a firing run?"

"I... I didn't..."

"Didn't you specifically state that the SASAL ship's course would place it in what you referred to as a 'perfect firing position'?'"

"I may have. That's all theoretical. You have to look at all possible alternatives. I didn't say the SASAL should was *going* to fire on us."

"Didn't a subsequent recommendation to maneuver from you make reference to confusing the SASAL ship's firing solution?'"

"Possibly. That's, again, a possible alternative. I didn't say that was what was happening. I said we needed to maneuver, and that was one possible reason."

"When Captain Wakeman asked you if the SASAL ship was armed, what did you reply?"

"I said we had no information to that effect."

"Didn't you actually say you could not confirm the SASAL ship was unarmed? Isn't that the same as telling Captain Wakeman the SASAL ship could have been armed?"

Garcia was reddening even more, just as Paul had seen him do so many times when his temper flared at his subordinates. "No. Different emphasis."

"Didn't you tell Captain Wakeman that the SASAL ship was on what you called a 'perfect firing approach'?"

"I may have. That's meaningless unless the ship is armed to fire upon you. And I didn't tell Captain Wakeman that the SASAL ship was armed."

Garrity shook her head. "No. You told him you couldn't confirm it was unarmed. What about the transients your watch standers reported and which you passed on to Captain Wakeman?"

"What about them? You pick up transients all the time. A lot of it's just noise from our own gear because the stuff's so sensitive."

"But you reported those transients to Captain Wakeman. According to the ship's log, you stated those transients could represent detection of charges leaking from shielded weapons. Isn't that correct?"

"Yes. Of course. It was my job to report that. And when Commander Herdez, she's the *Michaelson*'s executive officer, asked if they were definitely from weapons, I said no."

"Then, if I may summarize, during the approach of the SASAL ship, you made repeated references to firing runs and firing solutions, told Captain Wakeman you could not confirm the other ship was not armed, and reported the detection of what you said could be indications of weaponry being charged. Commander Garcia, what conclusions did you expect Captain Wakeman to draw from all that information?"

"It's not my job to second-guess what the captain will do with the information I give him."

"Would you agree that the information you provided would have led a reasonable person to conclude that the *Michaelson* was in imminent danger of being fired upon?"

"Objection." Wilkes waved toward Garcia. "The question requires that the witness speculate as to the state of mind of another person."

"I will rephrase the question. Commander Garcia, if you had received the information you in fact provided to Captain Wakeman, would you have concluded that the *Michaelson* was in imminent danger of being fired upon?"

Garcia stared back at Garrity, his face redder yet, his lower lip and jaw thrust forward. "No. I would have factored that information in with everything else."

Garrity met Garcia's gaze calmly, then turned away. "No further questions."

Judge Holmes looked toward Wilkes. "Does trial counsel wish to redirect?"

"I do. Thank you." Wilkes came forward again, smiling encouragingly at Garcia, who responded by visibly relaxing a bit. "Commander Garcia, how did Captain Wakeman respond to your reports on the SASAL ship? Did he ask for further information or assessments from you?"

"Uh, no. No. Captain Wakeman didn't."

"Did Captain Wakeman ever ask you for your assessment as to whether the SASAL ship was *actually* on a firing run or *actually* preparing to fire?"

"No. No, he didn't."

"Then he reached his own conclusions. The decision to fire, the assessment that the SASAL ship was a threat to the *Michaelson*, came entirely from Captain Wakeman?"

"Yes. That's right."

"No further questions."

"Commander Garrity?"

"No further questions."

The judge turned toward the members. "Admiral Fowler, do you or any of the other members have any questions for Commander Garcia?"

Fowler rubbed his chin with one hand. "I'm a little curious on one point, Commander Garcia. When you were talking about the *Michaelson*'s orders you said it wasn't your job to offer unsolicited advice to Captain Wakeman. Right? But you advised the captain to maneuver the ship. You did that repeatedly, you said. Wasn't that unsolicited advice?"

Garcia hesitated. "No, admiral. Sir, when we were talking about the orders I was talking about being the Operations head and offering advice on general operations, and then when we were encountering the SASAL ship we were at general quarters and I was in charge of CIC. So that was different, sir."

"How?"

"Well, it was a specific situation, sir."

Fowler glanced at the other members. "Anyone else? Captain Feres?"

"Yes, please, admiral. I have one question. Commander Garcia, wasn't all that talk about firing runs and positions also a form of unsolicited advice? Wasn't that intended to convey something to Captain Wakeman?"

"Sir, like I said before, I had to let Captain Wakeman know possible alternatives. I wouldn't have been doing my job if I hadn't told him these things were possible."

"But you yourself never believed the SASAL ship was on a firing run?"

"No, sir."

"Why didn't you convey that belief to Captain Wakeman?"

Garcia hesitated again, this time longer. "I... suppose... there wasn't sufficient time before Captain Wakeman reached his own determination."

Captain Feres tilted his head slightly, regarding Commander Garcia for several seconds in silence before speaking again. "Thank you, commander."

Paul glanced over at Lieutenant Sindh. *I wonder if she's remembering the way Garcia kept harping on firing runs and positions? He sure didn't sound so certain there wasn't any threat back then. But Feres certainly made Garcia look bad with that last question. Or I guess Garcia made himself look bad, and Feres just pointed that out.*

Fowler looked around again. "I guess that's it. No more questions from the members at this time."

"At this time? Very well." Judge Holmes focused on the witness stand. "Commander Garcia, you are temporarily excused. Please ensure you are present for the remainder of this court-martial in the event you need to be called again. As long as this trial continues, do not discuss your testimony or knowledge of the case with anyone except counsel. If anyone else tries to talk to you about the case, stop them and report the matter to one of the counsels."

Garcia stood stiffly, marching down to the back of the courtroom once again, his eyes scanning the rest of the audience in a challenging way as he went past each row of seats. Paul watched Garcia out of the corner of his eyes. *You certainly scored some hits on Wakeman, but I think you took some damage yourself, Commander Garcia.*

10

The next witness called by the prosecution was Commander Brilling, the chief engineer of the *Michaelson*. "Commander Brilling, you were in charge of the first inspection team sent over to the wreck of the SASAL ship from the *Michaelson*, were you not?"

Brilling seemed nervous, unhappy at interacting with people instead of his engineering plant. "That's correct."

"What was the purpose of that inspection?"

"Captain Wakeman told me we were to find and document all evidence of weaponry on the SASAL ship."

"And what weaponry did you find on the SASAL ship?"

Brilling seemed reluctant to reply. "None."

"None? There were no weapons?"

"Just some hand weapons that Ensign Sinclair found in the captain's cabin. Nothing besides that."

"So you found no means by which the SASAL ship could have presented a threat to the USS *Michaelson*?"

"No. No, there wasn't anything there."

"Did the interior of the SASAL ship show any signs of having been prepared for combat?"

"Uh, no. None of the airtight hatches had sealed. Uh, that is, a few had when atmosphere vented because of their automatic spring-loaded triggers, but the ship was pretty much wide open."

"Were the crew all suited up?"

Brilling grimaced in time to Paul's own internal flinch at the memory of the bodies they'd found. "No. They'd all... they were all dead. From decompression. Those that didn't get hit by our weapons."

"How much damage had the *Michaelson*'s weapons done to the SASAL ship?"

"Oh, it was effectively destroyed. We'd punched holes in him from one end to the other."

"Effectively destroyed." Wilkes walked away for a moment, then turned back to face Brilling. "Would you say the amount of force employed was excessive?"

"Objection." Garrity indicated the chief engineer. "The question calls for a subjective opinion."

"I will rephrase the question. Commander Brilling, could any threat from the SASAL ship to the USS *Michaelson*, even assuming the SASAL ship had been armed, been countered by using less force than was actually employed?"

"Uh, well, if we'd targeted the engineering spaces we could've taken them off line and eliminated his ability to power up weapons or maneuver."

"But you said the entire ship had been 'punched full of holes' or words to that effect. So the degree of force actually used was in excess of that needed to neutralize any threat from the SASAL ship?"

"Yes. You could say that."

"No further questions."

Lieutenant Commander Garrity stood before Brilling. "Commander, you said your search party was sent to the SASAL ship to, in your words, find and document evidence of weaponry on that ship. Did you expect to find weapons onboard?"

"Uh, I guess I did."

"Did Captain Wakeman expect you to find weapons onboard?"

"Yes. He sure did."

"So would you say there was an expectation of finding weapons onboard that ship?"

"I... well, if we knew weapons were there we wouldn't have had to send a search party to investigate."

"Were you personally surprised not to find any weapons?"

Brilling looked away, his mouth working, then nodded. "Yes, I was."

"Commander, if the SASAL ship had been armed, and if those weapons had been charged, would targeting the engineering spaces of the SASAL ship have eliminated its ability to fire on the *Michaelson*?"

"Well, not entirely. I mean, they still could've discharged whatever was in the weapons."

"So if the SASAL ship had been armed, then even if deprived of its engineering spaces, it could still have fired a volley into the *Michaelson* at point-blank range?"

"I... guess that's true."

"No further questions."

"Trial counsel will redirect." Wilkes took Garrity's place. "Commander Brilling, speaking for yourself, what evidence were you aware of regarding weapons on the SASAL ship prior to your leading a party aboard?"

"There wasn't any. That's why we went."

"There wasn't any. But you'd fired upon and destroyed that ship. Did you really *expect* to find weapons, or were you *hoping* to find weapons?"

Brilling flicked a glance toward Wakeman. "I... I... was hoping to find them."

"In order to justify the actions of Captain Wakeman?"

"It doesn't... I mean..."

Wilkes eyed Brilling with apparent sympathy. "Your ship had just destroyed another ship on orders of Captain Wakeman. Would it be fair to say you hoped that destruction had been justified?"

"Yes. Absolutely."

"And wasn't that hope what led you to 'expect' to find weapons onboard the SASAL ship?"

Brilling looked at the deck. "I think so. Yes."

"No further questions."

To Paul's surprise the prosecution next called Commander Sykes as a witness. *Why the supply officer next? I heard the weapons officer kept tripping over his tongue when he went over testimony with Wilkes. I guess Sykes is all that's left at that level, but what is Wilkes planning to get him to say about Wakeman?*

Sykes was sworn in and settled back in the witness stand as if he were holding court in the *Michaelson*'s wardroom. Wilkes came to stand before him. "Are you Commander Steven Sykes, United States Navy, currently assigned as supply officer to the USS *Michaelson*?"

"That is correct."

"And you have served on the USS *Michaelson* for fifteen months, and during that entire period Captain Wakeman has been in command."

"That is also correct."

"Commander Sykes, has Captain Wakeman ever given you reason to doubt his judgment?"

"Objection." Lieutenant Commander Garrity indicated Sykes. "This question is immaterial to the charges against Captain Wakeman, which concern his actions in several specific cases."

Judge Holmes looked at Wilkes. "Trial counsel?"

"Your Honor, I am seeking to establish a pattern of questionable judgment by Captain Wakeman during the last underway period for the USS *Michaelson*. Since this is the same period in which the actions in question took place, I believe it is material to determine if Captain Wakeman's record is consistent with the charges of later negligence and poor judgment."

Holmes pondered the matter for a moment. "Overruled, Commander Garrity. The question is judged material and is allowed."

Wilkes focused back on Sykes. "I'll repeat the question for you, Commander Sykes. Has Captain Wakeman ever given you reason to doubt his judgment?"

Sykes made a noncommittal face. "Everyone has bad days, Commander Wilkes."

"Perhaps I should be more specific." Wilkes leaned a little closer to Sykes. "During your last underway period, a captain's mast resulted in one of your petty officers being reduced in rate to a seaman. Do you know the case I'm speaking of?"

Sykes nodded. "That would be Petty Officer Arroyo."

"Did you think the decision reached by the captain in that case reflected good judgment?" A pause stretched while Sykes gazed imperturbably back at the prosecuting attorney. "Commander Sykes? Did you understand the question?"

"Certainly. No, I did not believe it reflected good judgment on Captain Wakeman's part."

"Captain Wakeman disregarded the testimony and character judgments rendered by both you and your assistant, Lieutenant Bristol, didn't he?"

"That's correct."

"Did Captain Wakeman give you any reasons for doing that?"

Sykes shrugged. "No, but then he wasn't under any obligation to do that."

Captain Nguyen interrupted whatever Wilkes had been planning to say next. "What exactly was this mast case about? What was it, uh..."

"Petty Officer Arroyo."

"Yes. What was it Petty Officer Arroyo did, or was accused of doing?"

"Captain Nguyen." Judge Holmes indicated Commander Wilkes and then Lieutenant Commander Garrity. "It is customary to allow both prosecution and defense to finish questioning a witness before the members ask questions."

"I'm sorry, Captain Holmes. Please continue, Commander Wilkes."

Wilkes smiled. "Thank you, ma'am. I have no objection to Commander Sykes answering your question at this time."

"The defense has no objection," Garrity stated.

"Very well," Judge Holmes replied. "Commander Sykes, what was it your petty officer was accused of?"

"He was accused of stealing a package of peaches, Your Honor."

Captain Nguyen let her surprise show. "A package... ? I see. Who brought the charge, Commander Sykes?"

"One of my chief petty officers, ma'am."

"But you yourself apparently didn't believe the charge should have been pursued?"

"No, ma'am. I believed it to be a matter of poor record keeping, not larceny."

Captain Nguyen smiled briefly at Sykes' last reply. "If we're supposed to condemn Captain Wakeman's judgment in this case, then I'd like to hear that chief's side of the story. Would anyone object to that? Is he to be called as a witness?"

Wilkes shook his head. "Unfortunately, Chief Mangala is no longer assigned to the USS *Michaelson*."

"He's been transferred?" Judge Holmes frowned at Wilkes. "Why was a potential witness allowed to transfer?"

Wilkes gestured toward Sykes as if seeking to deflect the judge's disapproval. "The transfer order was a high-priority personnel action, Your Honor. Since Chief Mangala did not seem to be a material witness to the charges against Captain Wakeman, I did not believe I had grounds for holding up that transfer."

"I see. Is the chief still available at all? Where'd he transfer to?"

Sykes smiled apologetically. "Ceres Station."

"Ceres? Good Lord, who'd he piss off?" Nguyen caught herself, looking around the room, embarrassed by her outburst. "I'd like my last statement stricken from the record, if that's alright, Your Honor."

Judge Holmes nodded obligingly. "Since I tend to agree with the sentiments expressed, I so order the statement stricken. Where is Chief Mangala at this moment?"

Sykes smiled again. "Chief Mangala is on the Ceres resupply mission which departed two days ago."

"Then I assume he's not going to be available for a few years, unless we set up virtual testimony by using communication relays. Do you want the court to pursue that, Captain Nguyen?"

Nguyen pursed her mouth, then shook her head. "No. This a minor issue. I don't want to devote too much time or resources to obtaining Chief Mangala's testimony. Thank you, Captain Holmes."

"Of course. You may continue, Commander Wilkes."

"Thank you, Your Honor." Wilkes turned back to Commander Sykes. "What is your personal assessment of Captain Wakeman's reliability and judgment?"

"Excuse me?"

"As one of his department heads, did you trust Captain Wakeman to make correct decisions?"

Sykes shrugged. "To be perfectly honest, Captain Wakeman rarely intervened in supply issues. As far as issues regarding the operations of the ship, I don't feel myself qualified to judge."

"You worked with Captain Wakeman every day. You are a commissioned naval officer."

"I am a limited-duty officer, Commander Wilkes. I do not have the experience to judge the actions of line officers."

"You're avoiding the question, Commander Sykes."

"No, I'm telling you it's a question I'm not qualified to answer."

"I ask the court to direct the witness to answer the question put to him."

Judge Holmes looked toward the members of the court-martial. "This matter appears to deal with line officer perceptions. I'd be interested in knowing the opinion of the line officer members."

Feres curled up one corner of his mouth in a half-smile. "Commander Sykes *is* answering the question. At least he is in my opinion."

Admiral Fowler nodded. "And mine. I think it is both proper and accurate for Commander Sykes not to express opinions on operational matters, just as it would be improper for me to pretend to be an expert on supply issues."

"Exactly so," Captain Nguyen agreed.

"Then the court rules that Commander Sykes has answered the question put to him. You may move on, Commander Wilkes."

"Thank you." Wilkes stared at Sykes for a moment, who met his look with a perfect display of nonchalance. "I have no further questions of this witness."

"Commander Garrity, you may cross-examine."

Lieutenant Commander Garrity eyed Sykes thoughtfully. "Commander Sykes, in your experience with Captain Wakeman, how often did he violate orders and instructions pertaining to supply issues?"

"Pertaining to supply issues? He didn't."

"Then you would say that in your experience Captain Wakeman took care to ensure you conformed to such orders and instructions?"

"That's correct. Captain Wakeman informed me that he had no wish to be embarrassed by any failures on my part to do my job properly."

"Thank you, Commander Sykes. No further questions."

Holmes looked to Wilkes. "Redirect?"

"Yes." Wilkes came close to Sykes again. "Commander Sykes, are you saying that you never failed to conform to all standing supply orders and instructions while serving on the USS *Michaelson*?"

"No. I didn't say that."

"If Captain Wakeman didn't direct you to, why did you deviate from those standing and instructions?"

"To get the job done, Commander Wilkes." Sykes smiled apologetically again. "I believe I'm what line officers refer to as a 'good' supply officer."

"What's that supposed to mean, Commander Sykes?"

Admiral Fowler interrupted whatever Sykes had been planning to say. "It means he bends the rules if he has to in order to get the supplies his ship needs. Right, Commander Sykes?"

"I prefer to describe it as being mission-oriented, admiral."

A low chuckle ran through the courtroom, drawing a warning look from the judge. Wilkes curled up both corners of his mouth in a pro forma smile. "No further questions."

After Sykes received the same temporary excusal as Garcia had, Judge Holmes looked around the courtroom. "Admiral Fowler informed me earlier today that he has an urgent personal matter to attend to later. Therefore we will only take one more witness's testimony today before closing. Call your next witness, Commander Wilkes."

"The United States calls Lieutenant Sindh."

A few minutes later, the swearing in and identification completed, Wilkes stood before Lieutenant Sindh, eyeing her intently. "Lieutenant, you were officer of the deck during the encounter with the SASAL ship. During that incident, was Captain Wakeman in control of himself and the situation?"

"Objection. The question calls for the witness to state an opinion."

"I'll rephrase the question. Lieutenant Sindh, did the actions of Captain Wakeman during the incident inspire confidence in you?"

"No, sir."

"Did you have the sense that Captain Wakeman was in control, or did you believe he was reacting to events?"

"At first he was in control of things, sir. Then it seemed to shift and nobody knew how to react."

"Nobody? Or just Captain Wakeman?"

"Objection. Opinion."

"I'll rephrase. During the period preceding firing upon the SASAL ship, that is during the last few hours prior to that, did Captain Wakeman express any misgivings or concerns that you are aware of?"

"Just about the SASAL ship maybe getting away, sir."

"Did he express any concern on the bridge about the SASAL ship being a potential threat to the *Michaelson*?"

"No, sir, not until after the ship changed course toward us."

"Lieutenant Sindh, as the officer of the deck during a general quarters situation, you are briefed on any plans to deal with enemy action or respond to any crisis. Isn't that correct?"

"Yes, sir."

"We're you briefed on any plans to react to movements of the SASAL ship?"

"No, sir."

"To the best of your knowledge, were there any plans for dealing with the SASAL ship if it did not cooperate with Captain Wakeman's instructions?"

"I wasn't told of any such plans, no, sir."

"Then, again to the best of your knowledge, would it be fair to say that Captain Wakeman had brought his ship into a confrontation with another vessel without any plans for handling that confrontation?"

"Yes, sir, I'd have to say that matches with what I know."

"And once that confrontation began proceeding in a manner Captain Wakeman did not anticipate, did he display any sign of having a plan of action prepared, of having thought through what might happen and how he would respond to it?"

"No, sir. My impression was that we were reacting to the actions of the SASAL ship."

"You were reacting to the actions of the other ship without any plan for dealing with those actions. Would you say then that the captain was in control of the situation, or not?"

"He wasn't in control of the situation, sir. We were reacting. Since the SASAL ship wouldn't—"

"Did you receive any orders from Captain Wakeman to maneuver the USS *Michaelson* during the incident?"

"No, sir."

Did you hear Commander Garcia recommending such maneuvers?"

"Yes, sir."

"In your experience, what is the proper course of action to take if another ship is on a course which threatens a collision with your own?"

Lieutenant Sindh took a moment to reply, apparently organizing her thoughts. "Well, the first thing you do is try to talk to the other ship."

"Why, Lieutenant?"

"To make sure that any actions you take, any maneuvers, are coordinated. Otherwise you might both turn away onto the same vector and end up still colliding."

"Did Captain Wakeman attempt to coordinate maneuvers with the SASAL ship?"

"He told our own communications people to tell the SASAL ship to veer off, sir."

"He told the SASAL ship? The same ship that hadn't responded to any earlier communications?"

"Uh, yes, sir."

"Is telling another ship what to do, a ship you can't be sure is receiving your communications, the same as what you called coordinating maneuvers?"

"No, sir."

"As an experienced officer of the deck, what course of action would you normally follow if another ship was on a near-collision course and had not communicated with you in any way?"

"I'd maneuver to open my CPA, sir."

"CPA?"

"I'm sorry, sir. Closest point of approach. I'd maneuver to try to put more distance between my ship and the path of the other ship."

"But Captain Wakeman didn't order that, did he?"

"No, sir."

"What would you expect to happen to you, as an officer of the deck, if you were in such a situation and failed to maneuver? If you simply maintained your own course and speed while the other ship came closer and closer?"

Lieutenant Sindh looked at Wilkes for a moment before replying. "I'd expect to be relieved, sir. Removed from my station as officer of the deck."

"Because you'd failed in your duties?"

"Yes, sir."

"But Captain Wakeman, who had control of the bridge at that point, never ordered any maneuvers."

"No, sir."

"Thank you, Lieutenant. No further questions."

Lieutenant Commander Garrity took Wilkes' place before the witness stand. "Lieutenant Sindh, in response to a question from the trial counsel on being in control of the situation, you were saying something about what the SASAL ship wouldn't do, and didn't get to finish. Would you like to finish what you were saying a moment ago?"

"Yes, ma'am. I was saying that since the SASAL ship refused to respond to any communications and was maneuvering around us, we didn't have any choice but to react to its actions."

"Did you anticipate the SASAL ship behaving in that fashion? Had you formed any plans yourself about what to do if the other ship refused to communicate and maneuvered aggressively?"

"Objection. It has not been established that the maneuvers of the other ship were 'aggressive.'"

"I will rephrase. Had you conceived of the SASAL ship behaving in the manner it did, and for dealing with that behavior?"

"No, ma'am. Nobody expected them to act that way."

"Would you characterize their behavior as unpredictable?"

"Objection. Opinion."

Judge Holmes looked toward the members. "Is this a reasonable judgment to demand from the witness?"

Fowler twisted his mouth while he considered the question, then nodded. "Yes. As a fleet officer of the deck, Lieutenant Sindh is qualified to make a judgment of that nature."

"Objection overruled. The witness will answer the question."

"Yes, ma'am. I would say the SASAL ship's behavior was unpredictable."

"Do you believe it is reasonable to expect someone to plan for the unpredictable?"

Lieutenant Sindh managed a small smile. "Uh, ma'am, it may not be reasonable, but in the fleet we're asked to do it all the time."

Garrity rubbed her mouth for a moment, apparently unhappy with the last reply but unable to retract what had been said. "Lieutenant Sindh, did you believe the *Michaelson* to be in danger when the SASAL ship came to a near-collision course?"

"There's always some danger when that happens."

"After the SASAL ship changed course and headed toward the *Michaelson*, didn't the *Michaelson*'s collision warning alarm sound?"

"Yes, it did. Twice, if I remember right."

"And isn't that system set to warn of situations in which the ship's tracking equipment assesses a danger of collision? That is, actual physical contact between two ships?"

"Yes, ma'am."

"Do you recall what the estimated closest point of approach was for the SASAL ship?"

"Yes, ma'am. It was about two kilometers. Maybe a little less."

"Two kilometers? At the velocities your ships were traveling? How dangerous is that?"

"Extremely dangerous."

Paul listened with growing curiosity. Garrity's questions seemed to be simply reinforcing Wilkes' point that Wakeman had failed to maneuver when he should have.

Lieutenant Commander Garrity looked over at the members before asking her next question. "Now, Lieutenant Sindh. The SASAL ship had refused to communicate with you."

"Objection. The reason for the failure to communicate remains unknown."

"I will rephrase. The SASAL ship had failed to communicate with you. It had changed course, coming to a vector which created the risk of collision between your two ships. Did you have any way of knowing how the SASAL ship would react if you maneuvered the *Michaelson*?"

"I don't understand the question, ma'am."

"If you had maneuvered the *Michaelson*, couldn't the SASAL ship have altered its vector to counteract that maneuver and maintain a situation in which your own ship's tracking systems had declared an imminent risk of collision?"

"Yes... I suppose that's true, ma'am."

"The SASAL ship had deliberately come to a course risking collision. Did you have any way of knowing whether or not it would do so again even if you maneuvered?"

"No. It could've done that."

"And you had no means of determining its intentions, did you, Lieutenant Sindh? Because the SASAL ship hadn't communicated with you, you had no way of knowing how it would react to an attempt to maneuver on your part."

"That's true, ma'am."

"Assuming the SASAL ship did maneuver in response to any evasive action you took, could that have actually brought about a collision even earlier than predicted by your own ship's tracking systems? Too quickly for the *Michaelson* to react again?"

"Objection. The defense counsel is asking the witness to speculate about events which did not occur."

"I withdraw the question."

Paul nodded to himself. *But you got your point out to the members of the court-martial, didn't you?*

Garrity came close to Sindh, looking at her intently. "Lieutenant Sindh, when the SASAL ship came to a near-collision course with the *Michaelson*, did you, as a qualified officer of the deck, feel your ship to be in danger?"

"Yes, ma'am."

"And is that assessment based upon your professional experience?"

"Yes, ma'am."

"Then would you regard it as reasonable for another professional officer to feel the same or greater degree of concern for the safety of the ship?"

Sindh paused before replying. "I... yes, ma'am."

"You wouldn't regard such a concern as unreasonable?"

"No, ma'am."

"Did you feel in danger? Did you think the ship was threatened by the actions of the SASAL ship?"

"Yes, ma'am. I did."

"Thank you, Lieutenant. No further questions."

Wilkes stood quickly. "I have a few more questions, if it please the court. Lieutenant Sindh, as the officer of the deck during this incident, did any action by the SASAL ship strike you as hostile? Not reckless, but hostile."

"No, sir. I can't honestly say the SASALs did anything I could definitely classify as hostile."

"Have you encountered situations before where civilian spacecraft maneuvered in a reckless fashion near your ship?"

Sindh couldn't help smiling bitterly. "Every officer has encountered such situations, sir. None of us are really comfortable with civilian spacecraft nearby."

"But Captain Wakeman brought his ship close to a civilian spacecraft."

"Yes, sir, he did."

"Even though civilian spacecraft sometimes maneuver recklessly."

"Yes, sir."

"Again, as a qualified officer of the deck, do you believe there is any circumstance in which you are authorized to fire upon another ship just because it is behaving recklessly?"

"I'm not aware of such a circumstance. No, sir."

"Do the standing rules of engagement, which you are required to be familiar with as a fleet watch officer, authorize you to fire upon a ship simply because it is acting recklessly?"

"No, sir."

"What would do if a ship was behaving in a reckless manner?"

"As I said before, I would attempt to steer clear of it, sir."

"But Captain Wakeman didn't even attempt to steer clear of the SASAL ship. He didn't even try such a maneuver."

"Uh, no, sir."

"Didn't Captain Wakeman in fact order you to close on the SASAL ship?"

"Objection." Lieutenant Commander Garrity stood as well. "It has already been established that Captain Wakeman's decisions to close on the SASAL ship occurred prior to the SASAL ship's own maneuvers. He did not order any closer approach after the SASAL ship itself began maneuvering."

"I withdraw the question. No further questions."

"Do the members wish to question the witness?"

Admiral Fowler looked to either side. "Apparently not."

Paul took a deep breath as Lieutenant Sindh stood and walked down off the witness stand. *I wonder if I'll do half as good as Sindh did? Sindh's a lot more experienced with handling pressure than I am, and Wilkes will be gnawing on me during cross-examination, not Garrity. The members were impressed enough by Sindh not to even ask her anything. What'll they do to me?*

Judge Holmes looked out over the courtroom. "The court-martial is closed. It will reconvene at ten hundred tomorrow morning in this courtroom."

Paul looked toward the back of the room as he stood. As she'd predicted, Jen wasn't there.

Carl spotted Paul looking his way and mimed a flat hand across his throat as he shook his head. The message *You're going to have a rough time* was unmistakable.

Thanks, Carl. Like I needed you to tell me that. I hope Jen has something pleasant to talk about.

Paul rapped a couple of times on the bulkhead next to the port ensign locker, then stuck his head inside. Jen Shen and Kris Denaldo were both in the stateroom, seated at their desks, Kris as usual absorbed in her work even though it was after normal working hours. "Hey, Jen. You asked me to look you up after the trial."

Jen leaned back in her chair, grinning at Paul. "Yeah, I did. I got some really good news, Paul."

"Really good news? What's that?"

"I got orders."

"Huh?" Paul felt a sinking feeling in his gut. *How can Jen have orders? A normal tour of duty for a junior officer on a ship lasts three years.* "Transfer orders?"

Jen fingered the gold bar on her collar and nodded. "Yeah. I got split-toured."

"Split-toured?"

"Instead of three years on the *Michaelson*, I get about a year and a half on this tub, and then a year and a half on another ship. It wasn't going to happen, because we were supposed to be out on patrol a few more months and that would have screwed up the timing, but since we got back early they were happy to use me to fill an upcoming vacancy on another ship. Cool, huh?"

Paul tried to absorb the news, and not let show how he felt inside. "When's your transfer?"

"About two weeks."

"What?" *Jen's leaving? So soon? She's my best friend on this ship. Maybe my best friend ever. Oh, hell.* "How... how can you do that? I thought transfers were frozen until the end of the court-martial, and we don't know when that'll be, yet."

"I'm transferring to the *Maury*. She's in long-term refit, so I guess they're not worried about me going anywhere even if the court-martial does drag on that long. So, yahoo! I'm getting off the *Merry Mike*! Aren't you happy for me, Paul?"

"Sure. Sure I'm happy. That's great, Jen."

"Why, Paul. You look a little down. Doesn't he look down, Kris?" Denaldo glanced at Paul. "Definitely."

"Are you going to miss me, Paul?"

"Sure I'm going to miss you."

"That's sweet. Isn't that sweet, Kris?"

"Definitely."

"I've got an unofficial farewell party at Fogarty's tomorrow night. All the best junior officers will be there. You're coming, right?"

"Sure. Wouldn't miss it for the world."

"Good. It wouldn't be the same without you. Can you make sure Paul gets to it, Kris?"

"Definitely."

Paul looked from Kris to Jen. *Kris isn't upset. Jen's happy. Why shouldn't she be? Why shouldn't I be? Jen's getting off this ship, and more power to her. We don't know what the new captain will be like, Jen and the XO don't get along, and her department head isn't any prize. It's pretty selfish of me not to be happy for her.* "Is that all you wanted to talk about, Jen?"

She smiled up at him. "Yup."

"Okay. Well, I need to catch up on the work I missed today, so I guess I'll see you tomorrow night."

"Oh, I'm sure I'll see you at the court-martial, too. We'll wave."

"Uh, yeah. Well, see you then." Paul headed slowly for the starboard ensign locker. *Home sweet home. A little confined space on a ship full of little confined spaces, where I spend every day working my butt off and getting yelled at. And just to make life even more pleasant I had to go and decide to be both noble and stupid like Jen said and stand on principle when it's not going to matter to anyone and is likely to get me shredded into hamburger on that witness stand. Then just to top it all off the one person I can always talk to about things is leaving. Man, life sucks. And there's nobody to blame but myself.*

Much of the morning of the next day was spent introducing exhibits, the trial counsel and the defense counsel haggling over which should be introduced and what, if anything, they meant. After an extended period devoted to that, Wilkes brought up a display in which a simulation of the *Michaelson*'s encounter with the SASAL ship played out. At decisive points, Wilkes cited the testimony of Garcia and Sindh to point out Wakeman's decisions and alleged failures. Paul found himself wincing, sick inside, as simulated weaponry flayed the simulated SASAL ship. Real people had died in the event portrayed there. Every once in a while he still saw the shocked face of the dead SASAL sailor in his dreams.

More witnesses were called, personnel from fleet staff who testified to the content and meaning of standing orders and instructions. A chorus of witnesses all joining in the same refrain: that Captain Wakeman had failed to follow the guidance contained in those documents. Garrity, like a desperate soldier fighting a hopeless rearguard battle, failed to halt the prosecution onslaught created by matching Wakeman's acts to the written words which were supposed to govern his actions.

Paul sat in his seat through lunch, not hungry and not feeling social. Carl Meadows came by as lunch was ending, looking at Paul with concern. "Where were you?"

"I'm okay."

"I didn't ask that. Jen, Kris and I are seated in the back if you need distant moral support."

"I know. Thanks."

"You sure you're okay?"

"Just a little wired, that's all."

"Kris says she has orders from Jen to personally escort you to Jen's farewell tonight and that she'll do it if she has to drag you every step of the way."

Paul managed a smile. "I'll be there."

The trial counsel only had one witness left who'd been scheduled but not yet called. Paul didn't think he'd ever concentrated so carefully on anything as much as he did now when she took her place on the witness stand. Commander Wilkes was culminating the second day of the court-martial with the witness who could be the most damaging to Wakeman. If she chose to be.

"Commander Herdez. How long have you served as executive officer of the USS *Michaelson*?"

"Approximately one year." Nothing about Herdez, her face, her voice, the way she sat straight-backed in the witness chair, gave a clue to her thoughts or feelings.

"And Captain Wakeman has commanded the *Michaelson* during that entire period?"

"Yes."

"What is your professional degree of confidence in Captain Wakeman's judgment?"

"Captain Wakeman was the captain of my ship."

Wilkes waited a moment, as if expecting Herdez to say more. "Meaning?" he finally prodded.

"Meaning that it was my duty to implement his orders to the best of my ability."

"I'm sorry, Commander Herdez, but I'm asking about your confidence in Captain Wakeman."

"And I am telling you he was the captain of the USS *Michaelson*. It was my duty to follow the captain's orders. It was not my duty to make evaluations of the captain's judgment."

Wilkes stared at her silently for a moment. "Very well, commander. It was also your duty to offer advice to the captain of your ship when circumstances warranted, correct?"

"Yes."

"What was your advice concerning pursuing the SASAL ship outside of your patrol area?"

"I believe that advice was offered in confidence."

"Would the court direct the witness to answer?"

Judge Holmes nodded. "So directed. Commander Herdez, you will answer questions regarding any advice given by you to Captain Wakeman concerning the incident in question."

"Yes, ma'am." Herdez didn't seem fazed by the rebuke. "I told Captain Wakeman that in my opinion we had carried out our responsibilities by chasing the SASAL ship from our patrol area."

"Then you told him you did not recommend pursuing the SASAL ship outside of your patrol area?"

"Yes."

"What was Captain Wakeman's response?"

"He disagreed."

Captain Feres coughed to cover up a laugh.

"What did Captain Wakeman say?" Wilkes pressed.

"He said he believed we should pursue and intercept the SASAL ship."

"Did he say why?"

"He felt our orders required such action."

"Is that the only reason he gave?" Herdez paused before replying. "I'll remind the witness she is under oath."

For the first time, emotion flashed across Herdez' face. "I did not need to be reminded of that fact," she stated icily. "Captain Wakeman stated that seizing the SASAL ship would generate a favorable reaction toward the ship from our fleet staff."

"A favorable reaction toward the ship? Or toward Captain Wakeman personally?"

"Captain Wakeman did not specify."

"He said nothing about believing intercepting the SASAL ship would be a feather in his personal cap?"

"I don't recall his exact words."

"But he did express the hope that he personally would gain favorable recognition as a result of his actions?"

"Yes."

"I see." Wilkes paced back and forth a few steps. "What about when you were closing on the SASAL ship? Did Captain Wakeman ask your advice during that period?"

"No."

"Not at all?"

"No."

"Don't you regard that as unusual? Negligent, even?"

"The captain of a ship is not required to ask advice of his or her subordinates."

"But doesn't a wise captain do so?"

"Some do and some don't, Commander Wilkes. I'm not in a position to comment on their professional judgment, either."

This time Feres just cleared his throat.

Wilkes stood directly in front of Herdez. "Isn't it a fact that prior to Captain Wakeman firing the shot across the bow of the SASAL ship, you publicly questioned the wisdom of that act?"

"No, it is not."

"You called to the captain across the bridge, pointed out that you were outside of the American territorial area, and raised the question of whether use of force under those circumstances was covered by your orders, did you not?"

"Yes. But those actions do not add up to publicly questioning the wisdom of the captain's actions."

Wilkes smiled. "Would you then characterize your questions as attempting to alter a course of action which Captain Wakeman seemed intent on pursuing?" Herdez hesitated again. "Commander?"

"Yes."

"Yes, you were attempting to dissuade the captain from firing that shot?"

"Yes."

"And what was Captain Wakeman's response?"

"He asked Ensign Sinclair, the ship's legal officer, if our orders could be interpreted as justifying his action."

"So he turned aside your concerns. He ignored the obvious intent of your question and instead turned to the most junior officer on the ship for some form of justification for the course of action Captain Wakeman had already decided upon. Isn't that correct?" Herdez sat silent, her face revealing nothing. "I asked you if that is correct, commander."

"That is one possible way of describing events."

"And once the SASAL ship had altered course, once it had begun closing on the *Michaelson*, did Captain Wakeman follow the advice of anyone else?"

"I don't recall—"

"The ship's log indicates Commander Garcia more than once recommended that Captain Wakeman maneuver the *Michaelson* to open this distance between the ships. Did Captain Wakeman order his ship to maneuver?"

"No."

"Several individuals heard you caution Captain Wakeman that the SASAL ship could be continuing its pattern of perceived harassment. Do you recall doing that?"

"Yes."

"Did Captain Wakeman acknowledge your advice?"

"No."

"Did Captain Wakeman begin to panic as the SASAL ship closed on the *Michaelson*?"

"Objection." Lieutenant Commander Garrity motioned toward Herdez. "Trial counsel is asking Commander Herdez to comment on Captain Wakeman's state of mind."

"I will rephrase. Did Captain Wakeman appear to panic as the SASAL ship closed on the *Michaelson*? Commander Herdez?"

"Captain Wakeman appeared agitated."

"Agitated? Did he appear to be in control of the situation?"

"There was no way for Captain Wakeman to control the actions of the SASAL ship."

"Did Captain Wakeman appear to be in control of the situation on the bridge of his own ship? Or was he simply reacting to events which he had allowed to get totally out of hand?"

"Objection."

"I withdraw the question. Commander Herdez, whose decision was it to pursue the SASAL ship?"

"Captain Wakeman's."

"Whose decision was it to fire a warning shot at the SASAL ship?"

"Captain Wakeman's."

"And whose decision was it to fire on the SASAL ship itself, killing its entire crew and crippling the vessel?"

"Captain Wakeman."

"You're an experienced fleet officer with an impeccable record, Commander Herdez. Would you have done any of those things? Would you have made any of those same decisions? Would you have ignored the advice of everyone around you?"

Herdez took a long moment to reply. "I was not the commanding officer. The ultimate responsibility for the safety of our ship, for executing our orders and carrying out our mission, did not rest with me."

"You're saying you would have done all those things, commander? Exactly as Captain Wakeman did?"

"I am saying I cannot claim to know what I would have done had the burden of command rested upon me."

Wilkes smiled slightly. "I have no further questions at this time."

Lieutenant Commander Garrity walked slowly toward Commander Herdez. "Commander, how long had the *Michaelson* been on patrol before the encounter with the SASAL ship?"

"Approximately ten weeks."

"And during that ten-week period, how many ships had come anywhere near the *Michaelson*?"

"Once we left the vicinity of Franklin Station we had very few encounters with other shipping."

"And most of those encounters were at great distances, weren't they? Yet, during the incident with the SASAL ship, you suddenly found yourselves in a very fast-moving situation. Do you think any crew could have performed optimally under those circumstances?"

"I kept the crew well trained, Commander Garrity."

"I don't doubt that, ma'am. But there's no substitute for actual practice, is there? Would you agree the crew was unpracticed in dealing with such a fast-moving situation?"

"Yes."

"Could this have affected the support they provided to Captain Wakeman?"

A pause. "Yes."

"Commander Herdez, your loyalty to your commanding officer is obvious and commendable. But Captain Wakeman is no longer your commanding officer. Why are you clearly unwilling to condemn his actions?"

Herdez gazed back at Garrity. "My duty as the executive officer is to support my ship's captain to the best of my ability. The moment I lose the confidence of my ship's captain I am no longer able to carry out that duty."

"And that is why you refuse to second-guess the decisions Captain Wakeman made during a fast-moving situation in which he believed his ship to be in danger?"

"That is why I refuse to second-guess any decision by my ship's captain."

"Thank you, Commander Herdez. No more questions."

Wilkes stood. "I'd like to redirect. Commander Herdez, you said your crew was well trained. Do you believe they were incapable of providing effective support to Captain Wakeman during the encounter with the SASAL ship?"

Paul gritted his teeth. *He's got her there. Herdez either says she failed to train the crew properly, or admits she did and that Wakeman didn't listen to them.*

Herdez shook her head. "No."

"So the crew was capable of providing effective support to Captain Wakeman?"

"Yes."

"Commander Herdez, if Captain Wakeman ordered his ship to ram Franklin Station, would you regard it as your duty to support his actions?"

Herdez almost seemed to smile for an instant before responding. "That situation has never arisen, Commander Wilkes, so I am unable to evaluate whatever factors might have led Captain Wakeman to make such a decision."

"You think there are circumstances under which such a decision would be supportable?" Wilkes let his voice rise with incredulity.

"Yes."

"Such as?"

"Occupancy of Franklin by hostile forces intent upon using its resources against us. Emergency destruction of the station following its evacuation. Maintaining a collision course with the station rather than undertaking avoidance maneuvers which would cause the loss of more critical assets. Emergency destruction of the *Michaelson* to neutralize an onboard threat to humanity. Orders directing—"

"Thank you, Commander Herdez." Wilkes shook his head as he returned to his seat. "No further questions."

"Do the members have any questions for Commander Herdez?"

Admiral Fowler regarded Herdez carefully, as if she represented an intriguing puzzle. "Commander Herdez, throughout the sequence of events leading up to the destruction of the SASAL ship by the USS *Michaelson*, did you ever question the correctness of Captain Wakeman's decisions?"

"Sir, I provided Captain Wakeman with my input to his decision process whenever I deemed it appropriate."

"But Captain Wakeman didn't pay a lot of attention to your input, did he?"

"He wasn't required to, sir."

"Did you agree with his decisions?"

"It wasn't my duty to agree or disagree with the captain's decisions, sir. My duty was to implement his decisions."

"Even if they violated standing orders?"

"The decision on whether actions violate standing orders rests ultimately with the captain, sir."

"Then you're not willing to state that Captain Wakeman's decisions in that regard were wrong?"

"I did not have the responsibilities of command. It's impossible now for me to say that the individual carrying those responsibilities at the time of those decisions was mistaken."

Fowler leaned back, smiling crookedly. "Correct me if I'm wrong, Commander Herdez, but we could ask you variations on those questions from now until the sun burns out and you'd keep giving us the same sort of replies, wouldn't you?"

Herdez' reply was, to all appearances, totally serious. "Yes, sir."

Fowler looked around at the other members. "Anyone else want a crack at her? No? I don't blame you. That's all for us, then."

After Judge Holmes dismissed Herdez, Wilkes came forward once again. "The prosecution rests."

"Very well. Commander Garrity, do you wish to make any motions?"

"Yes, Your Honor. I would ask that the members of the court-martial be excused prior to making my motion."

"Granted. The members are excused." Admiral Fowler nodded in acknowledgement, stood, and led the four captains out the back door. "You may continue, Commander Garrity."

"The defense moves for a finding of not guilty as to all charges and specifications based on a failure of the prosecution to prove essential elements in every case."

"The motion is denied. The prosecution has provided sufficient basis for deliberation by the members of the court-martial as to guilt or innocence for each charge and specification. Does the defense have further motions?"

"No, Your Honor."

"This court-martial is closed. It will reconvene at ten hundred tomorrow morning in this same courtroom for the presentation of evidence by the defense."

Paul stood along with everyone else, abruptly aware of muscles stiff from being held tense while Herdez testified and was cross-examined. Tomorrow, he'd be up there on the witness stand, like a silhouette in a shooting gallery. Tonight, all he had to do was say goodbye to Jen. Variations on being alone against the world. *I just have to make it through a few more days. Then it'll be bearable again. No sweat. Maybe if I repeat that enough I'll start believing it.*

11

Paul sat, nursing his drink at Fogarty's, watching Jen go from person to person and group to group. Farewells for people you liked were always bitter-sweet affairs at best. You couldn't help but be happy that they were leaving the pressure-cooker of being part of a ship's crew, but you also knew you'd miss them. He already felt as if Jen were separating from the wardroom of the *Michaelson*, and from him, and that fact contributed to the melancholy he already felt. Paul checked the time. *It's been almost three hours? I didn't realize. Maybe it's time to go.*

A moment later Jen came and flopped down in the seat next to him. "Hello, Mr. Sinclair."

"Shouldn't that be goodbye?"

"Not yet. You're sitting here all alone and quiet. What's on your mind?"

"You don't need my problems tonight, Jen."

"Who are you to say what I need? Feeling possessive?"

"No!" Paul looked away, suddenly annoyed with both Jen and himself.

"Hey, lighten up. How many drinks have you had?"

"Less than you, I'm sure."

"Guess again. This is number two."

"Really?" Paul looked at her, startled. "I know we have to work tomorrow, but don't the honorees at farewells usually get wasted?"

"I'm not much for traditions. What's bugging you, Paul?"

"Nothing."

"Bull. Talk to me."

"Okay. I'm worried about tomorrow. My testimony. What's going to happen."

"That's all?" Jen leaned to catch his eyes. "You're hiding something."

"Oh, hell, Jen. I'm sorry you're leaving. I don't want you to leave the ship."

"Really? Why?"

Paul gave her a skeptical look. "You're... my friend."

"You've got lots of friends, Paul."

"No, I don't. And even if I did, there'd only be one Jen." He raised his glass to hide his face behind the drink, trying to cover a sudden flush of embarrassment.

"Ah, what a sweet thing to say. Want to go for a walk?"

"Jen, your party—"

"Is over. I've talked to everybody. I saved you for last. Come on."

Paul followed, out of the bar and along the wide corridor lined with similar bars. Not speaking, Jen led the way in the general direction of the ship, then veered off into another area. After several minutes, she stopped near a doorway with a credit card slot affixed next to the lock. Similar doorways occurred at regular intervals for some ways down the length of the bulkhead. "Got me a rent-a-shack tonight, Paul. I didn't want to sleep onboard. Just a way of marking the fact I'll be leaving soon."

"Oh." Paul eyed the door curiously. He'd never actually been in a rent-a-shack on Franklin, though he was familiar with their counterparts elsewhere. A small room with barely enough space for a bed, a tiny lavatory and an entertainment console, rent-a-shacks were found everywhere people needed a few hours of privacy.

"You don't have to sound so impressed."

"Sorry. That's nice, Jen. I bet you'll be real comfortable."

"Maybe."

He glanced at her curiously, but Jen stood silent nearby for a little while. Paul waited, guessing she wanted the time with her own thoughts.

Finally, Jen looked over at him, a small smile on her lips. "So, you're going to miss me, huh?"

"Yeah. I already told you that."

"Are you going to miss me a little or a lot?"

"A lot, I guess."

"You guess?"

"Okay, I know. I will miss you a lot. Okay? I like you."

"A lot?"

"Yes, I like you a lot."

"I like you, too, Mr. Sinclair. I like you a lot, too."

"You do?"

"Why do you think we talk so much?"

"I never really thought about it, I guess. And since I found out you were leaving and we wouldn't get to talk anymore I haven't wanted to think about it. I don't want to say goodbye, Jen."

"I don't want to say goodbye, either. Matter of fact, it's a shame to say goodnight, isn't it?"

"Yeah, but I need to get back to the ship—"

"No, you don't." Jen hooked a thumb toward the door of the rent-a-shack. "There's a bed in there. It's no king size, but it's big enough for two."

Paul's next words froze in his throat. He stared at her for a long moment. "What?"

Jen pulled herself close to him, her smile growing. "Hey, sailor. New in town?"

"Jen, I, I..."

"Oh, he's shocked. He's stunned. Paul, you can be such an idiot. Kiss me."

"Uh, Jen, I, uh..."

"Relax, almost-a-JAG. We're not going to violate any regulations. Neither of us is in the other's chain of command, and in less than two weeks we won't even be on the same ship."

"Yeah, but regulations say people still assigned to the same command—"

"Shut up, Paul." Then Jen's mouth was on his, and her hands were touching him, and Paul suddenly realized that particular regulation probably wasn't all that important in this case anyway.

Paul awoke with a mild headache at odds with an overall sense of well-being. He turned his head, seeing Jen's eyes fixed on him. "Good morning."

She smiled. "I think so. How about you?"

"Oh, yeah."

"Good. Listen, Paul, I don't do one-night stands. We already know we like each other. I'd like a relationship now. A serious one. See how well we go together. Interested?"

"Very interested. And very surprised. I never thought you'd want to get serious with me."

"Yeah, well, you grew on me. I've been thinking about it for a while, but I wasn't going to do anything about it while we were living and working a few meters away from each other. When my orders came through I realized it was time to decide whether to walk away from you or not."

"You'd already decided when you told me about your orders, hadn't you? And told Kris to make sure I was at your farewell?"

"Yup. Planned the whole thing. Right up until we got in here, anyway. From that point on I improvised, but you didn't seem to mind."

"Darn right I didn't. But I've spent the last few days feeling so bad, thinking you'd be gone from my life!"

"That was obvious. It was *so* funny watching you slouch around all depressed."

"You are such a bitch."

"I know."

"I'm still glad you decided not to walk away. But, like you said, you're leaving the ship. We won't see nearly as much of each other."

"That's the reason I made my move. I want our personal stuff to stay personal, and off the ship or any other job. In a couple of weeks I'll be assigned to the *Maury*, and we can see each other openly and not break any regulations."

"So why didn't you wait until you'd actually transferred? I seem to recall a certain Jen Shen once advising me not to mess around with anybody else in the crew until I was walking off the ship for the last time."

She grinned. "And I meant it. But we're not in each other's chain of command, and I'm on my way gone. Close enough."

"Not that I'm complaining, but we wouldn't have to hide it at all if you'd waited a few more weeks."

"Okay, the truth is I figured you could really use something positive going on in your life right now."

"I sure could."

"That seemed really important. So I evaluated my options, weighed the risks and acted appropriately, like a good officer should. Happy?"

"Very. So you did it because you thought I needed it? You're really a very sweet person, Jen."

"I am not. You take that back." Jen glanced away. "To be perfectly honest, there was another reason. There's no telling when I could have gotten together with you again after I left the *Michaelson*. What orders our ships might have gotten right after I left. Where you might have gone, for how long, who you might have met. I might have lost my chance to do anything, and maybe lost you. I didn't want to risk that."

"Thanks. I'm glad you didn't."

"Now we just have to keep a lid on it until I leave the *Michaelson*. God help us if somebody like Herdez finds out. So don't go making goopy-eyes at me when we get back to the *Michaelson* or I'll deck you."

"Yes, ma'am, Ensign Shen."

"Good. Now, I've got another question." She sat up, turning toward him and leaning forward. "This testimony you're supposed to give today. Do you know what you're planning on saying, yet?"

"Huh? What?" Distracted by the sight of her breasts hanging not far from his face, Paul had totally missed the question.

Jen saw where his eyes were focused and grinned. "Oh, you like these, huh?"

"Well, yeah."

"Then never mind about the question. I'll ask it again later. Come here."

Paul didn't get a chance to find out what her question had been before they had to hastily leave to take separate paths back to the ship, but that didn't bother him a great deal.

If there'd actually been windows in Franklin Station, and if any of those windows had illuminated the route from the *Michaelson* to the courtroom, Paul would have said the sun was shining on his walk. *Funny. I'm still worried about my testimony. I'm still tense about what might happen. My guts twist every time I think about being questioned up there. But I feel good. Jen wants to be serious with me. Who would've guessed? Anybody but a dope like me, probably.*

Perhaps because of his mood he walked quickly and arrived first at the courtroom. He took a seat, trying to look calm despite his internal turmoil. Paul turned slightly in his chair so he could glance at others as they entered the courtroom, hoping to catch a quick glimpse of Jen. He saw all the department heads file in, most of them sitting in a pack, but Sykes slightly separated. Herdez came in, striding to her seat like a warship steaming past small sailboats, and also took a seat away from anyone else.

The junior officers began trickling in. Jen Shen arrived at last, walking briskly to take a seat in the back as usual, then glanced toward Paul and gave a brief nod and small smile in greeting. Paul returned the gesture. *Right. Just friends saying hi. No goopy-eyes. Whatever those are.*

Kris Denaldo entered as well, but instead of going with Jen she came up front and took a seat in the row just behind Paul, then she leaned forward and whispered in his ear. "Have you and Jen started picking out curtains, yet?"

"What? How did you—?" Paul looked down at his clothes as if something there had betrayed the events of last night.

"Relax. It doesn't show. Jen and I are girlfriends. We talk about stuff. Nobody else knows."

"Uh, thanks."

"She's worried about what you're going to say up there today."

Paul bit his lip. *Jen's got a right to be worried. Even before last night. She's a good friend.* "I'm not entirely sure. I've gone over stuff with Commander Garrity, but she wanted me to sound unrehearsed when she questioned me."

"You going to fall on your sword for Wakeman?"

"No. What happened wasn't my fault. I'm just not so sure it was his fault. Not on a criminal level, anyway."

"Okay. Jen told me she was attracted to your idealism. That's funny, huh? Ms. Cynic and Mr. Idealism. So, do what you think is right. Jen'll be there."

"Thanks. Thanks a lot."

"No problem." Kris got up again, moving back to sit next to Jen, where the two ensigns bent their heads together in conversation. Paul stole glances their way, afraid to let his eyes linger on Jen too long, and finally saw her looking up at him again. She shook her head as if exasperated, then one eyelid flicked in a wink almost too quick to see.

At precisely 1000 the bailiff made his "All rise" announcement and the legal ceremonies and procedures marking the entry of the judge and the members began. Paul took a close look at Wakeman, whose stubborn determination seemed to have slowly eroded into despair. Perhaps it was the way Wakeman was sitting this morning, but over the course of the prosecution's presentation Wakeman seemed to have collapsed in on himself like an inflatable doll with a slow leak.

Lieutenant Commander Garrity stood. "The defense calls as its first witness Operations Specialist First Class Yolanda Daniels."

Daniels walked to the witness stand, her uniform and military bearing immaculate. If she felt any qualms at being surrounded by officers it wasn't apparent from her squared shoulders and calm demeanor.

After the swearing in, Garrity stood before Daniels. "Are you Operations Specialist First Class Yolanda Daniels, assigned to the Operations Specialists Division in the Operations Department on the USS *Michaelson*?"

"Yes, ma'am."

"And is your duty station during general quarters at one of the consoles in the *Michaelson*'s combat information center from which primary combat system sensor results are displayed for warning and analysis?"

"Yes, ma'am."

"Petty Officer Daniels, what exactly does that job entail?"

Daniels looked around slightly, as if trying to gauge the ability of her audience to understand a technical explanation. "Ma'am, I occupy the console's primary monitoring station. That's the one on the right. Petty Officer Li occupies the back-up station on the left. When the combat system sensors detect anything they think might indicate a threat, we get an alert on the console and the raw data gets displayed along with the system's assessment of what it means."

"What sort of data are you talking about, Petty Officer Daniels?"

"Anything the sensors might pick up, ma'am. Visual, IR... excuse me, that's infra-red, ultra-violet, radio spectrum emissions, any kind of energy or visual detection that stands out from the background environment."

"How sensitive are these sensors?"

"Objection." Commander Wilkes spoke for the first time that morning. "That information is classified."

"Sustained." Judge Holmes addressed Garrity. "If the defense wishes to go into detail on that issue the court-martial will have to go into closed session."

"I understand, Your Honor. That won't be necessary. Petty Officer Daniels, can the sensors you help monitor detect energy weapons being charged on another ship?" Instead of answering, Daniels looked concerned. "That's all right, Petty Officer Daniels. I'm not asking for precise information or detailed capabilities. Just in general. Can your sensors do that?"

"Yes, ma'am. They can do that."

"What exactly is involved there?"

"Well, ma'am, when a weapon charges, an awful lot of energy has to be pumped into whatever's being used as a ready-storage source."

"A ready-storage source?"

"Yes, ma'am. That's what slams energy into the weapon when it needs to fire. But when you're pushing all the energy into the ready-storage source, you get leakage."

"Energy leaks out?"

"Yes, ma'am. Any place there's a gap in the shielding. Just like if there's a light under a blanket it'll shine through any holes."

"And under the right conditions you can detect that happening?"

"That's right, ma'am."

Garrity strode several steps to one side, looking away from Daniels now. "Petty Officer Daniels, I want you to tell us about the incident with the SASAL ship. You were in the *Michaelson*'s combat information center and occupying your duty station?"

"Yes, ma'am."

"What happened as the SASAL ship closed on the *Michaelson*?"

"I spotted a transient energy detection on my console, ma'am."

"The same sort of transient energy detection which could indicate weapons were being powered up on the SASAL ship?"

"Objection. It has already been established that the SASAL ship was unarmed. There were no weapons to power up."

Judge Holmes looked toward Garrity. "Well?"

"Your Honor, we're dealing here with events on the *Michaelson* prior to confirming that the SASAL ship was unarmed. Decisions made on the *Michaelson*, decisions made by Captain Wakeman, were based on the information available to him at that time. Ex post facto determinations of evidence found after that time do not bear on whether or not Captain Wakeman's decisions were correct based upon what he knew when he acted."

Holmes nodded. "Very well. Overruled. Continue, Commander Garrity."

"Petty Officer Daniels, did the transient you saw correspond to the sort of detection you would expect to see from weapons powering up?"

"Yes, ma'am. Exactly that kind of transient."

"And you reported that detection to your superiors?"

"Yes, ma'am. I passed it immediately to Commander Garcia, and I heard him pass it to the bridge."

"Commander Garcia didn't question your detection?"

"No, ma'am."

"He informed the bridge that the *Michaelson*'s combat system sensors had detected a transient which could indicate weapons were being powered up on the SASAL ship."

"Yes, ma'am."

"Has Commander Garcia or Captain Wakeman or any other officer ever questioned your qualifications to occupy your duty station at that console? Do you have their confidence?"

"No, ma'am, no one's ever questioned my qualifications. I know my job, ma'am. And Commander Garcia and Captain Wakeman, they know I know it."

"Thank you, Petty Officer Daniels. No further questions."

Commander Wilkes came forward, eyeing Daniels sternly. "Petty Officer Daniels, isn't it a fact that the combat systems on the USS *Michaelson* automatically maintain a record of all activity, including any detections by the sensors?"

"Yes, sir. It's usually on a seventy-two-hour loop, but we can permanently save anything we need to retain."

"And you did permanently save the combat system recordings of the encounter with the SASAL ship, correct?"

"Yes, sir."

"Do those recordings indicate your console ever displayed a transient detection such as you just described?"

Daniels hesitated, then her face hardened and she stared defiantly back at Wilkes. "No, sir."

"No? The combat system records indicate there was no transient detected when you say there was? That you never saw such a detection?"

"I saw a transient detection, sir."

"How do you explain the fact that such a detection isn't in the combat system records?"

"I can't, sir. But I saw it. It was plain as day. I know my job."

"I'm sure you do, Petty Officer Daniels." Wilkes held up his data link. "Trial counsel would like to introduce into the trial record this exhibit, which is an excerpt from a standard, definitive text on psychological wish fulfillment. In summary, it states that in periods of crisis or other intense emotion, individuals are capable of seeing things they expect to see, rather than what is actually there. Examples are provided herein from past military engagements in which combatants 'saw' nonexistent threat information."

The judge nodded. "The excerpt is accepted as Appellate Exhibit Six."

Wilkes turned back to the witness stand. "Petty Officer Daniels, isn't that possible? That you saw something that wasn't there because of the tense atmosphere inside the combat information center?"

Daniels stared steadily back at Wilkes. "Sir, I didn't imagine anything. I saw it."

"I'm sure you believe that, Petty Officer Daniels. I wouldn't suggest otherwise. But you were tense, weren't you?"

"Yes, sir."

"Everyone in Combat was tense, weren't they?"

"I'd say so, sir."

"Why?"

"Because of the situation, sir. Because that SASAL ship was coming right at us and not saying a word."

"How did you get into that situation, Petty Officer Daniels?"

"Sir?"

"How did the *Michaelson* come to be so close to the SASAL ship despite the other ship's failure to communicate?"

"We intercepted that ship, sir."

"So you wouldn't have been as tense if the *Michaelson* hadn't been in that position? If your commanding officer hadn't created a situation in which you were so fearful you imagined you saw weapons being powered up on the other ship?"

"Objection!"

"I withdraw the question. No further questions."

Garrity was looking down at the surface of the defense table, her mouth a thin line. Paul felt a stab of sympathy for both her and for Petty Officer Daniels, who was trying to maintain a cool military bearing despite Wilkes' attack on her testimony. Finally, Garrity looked up. "No further questions."

The next witness was Petty Officer Li, whose testimony went much like Daniels' had. Yes, he'd seen a transient, too. Yes, he was absolutely certain. No, he couldn't explain why the combat systems had no record of having displayed such a detection. When Li left the witness stand, Paul felt the testimony of the two operations specialists had resulted in a draw between the trial counsel and the defense with no gain for either side. Which would make what he had to say more important than ever.

I'm the last witness. Paul stole another look backward to where the junior officers sat. Jen and Kris gave him twin thumbs up. Carl Meadows made a gesture of squeezing something between his palms, then grinned reassuringly. *Right. No pressure. Hah. I feel like I'm under three g's of acceleration.*

"The defense calls as its next witness Ensign Paul Sinclair."

He walked up to the witness chair, no longer aware of anyone else in the courtroom. Commander Wilkes came into his line of vision. Whatever Wilkes thought or felt about Paul wasn't betrayed by his fixed expression as he administered the oath. "Do you swear that the evidence you give in the case now in hearing shall be the truth, the whole truth, and nothing but the truth, so help you God?"

Paul's mouth and throat suddenly felt dry. "I do."

Wilkes left and Lieutenant Commander Garrity came before him. "Are you Ensign Paul Sinclair, assigned as primary duty assistant combat information center officer and collateral duty ship's legal officer to the USS *Michaelson*?"

"Yes, ma'am."

"And in your capacity as ship's legal officer, did the ship's executive officer, Commander Herdez, ask for your interpretation and assessment of the operational orders issued to the USS *Michaelson* governing its last patrol?"

"Yes, ma'am."

"And did you provide such an assessment?"

"Yes, ma'am."

"Please summarize that assessment."

"Yes, ma'am." Paul took a deep breath before he started speaking. "Basically, I told the XO, Commander Herdez that is, that the orders seemed to be very broad in a number of critical areas, and also vague on a number of very important points."

"What made them very broad?"

"The wording, ma'am. The orders kept using terms like 'appropriate' and 'necessary' to describe what the captain should do instead of setting parameters, but then they'd turn around and say he shouldn't do anything that'd be wrong, but they didn't specify what that might be. You ended being confused after reading them as to what was and was not mandated, what was and was not prohibited."

"Shouldn't the captain have known what would be wrong, Ensign Sinclair? What was mandated and what was prohibited?"

"No, ma'am. The orders said we, our ship, needed to do anything necessary and appropriate to carry out our primary mission. It said the captain 'shall' do anything needed to counter attempts to violate our sovereign claim to that area of space. The kind of wording pretty much leaves it up to the captain to decide what methods are, uh, necessary and appropriate."

"Ensign Sinclair, this court has heard extensive testimony that Captain Wakeman's actions and decisions violated numerous standing orders and instructions. Do these orders which you have characterized as broad and vague have any bearing on those charges?"

"Yes, ma'am. Specific orders always take precedence over standing orders."

"Give an example of that, Ensign Sinclair."

"Well, take the standing order that ships remain within their assigned patrol areas for the duration of their mission. If you received an order from fleet staff telling you to leave your patrol area, you'd have to obey it regardless of what the standing orders say. Otherwise the fleet staff wouldn't be in charge, the standing orders would be."

Garrity looked toward the members' table, then back at Paul. "Where did you learn that, Ensign Sinclair?"

"At the Academy, ma'am, and again in space warfare specialty training."

"So it's taught to new officers as a pretty basic guiding principle?"

"Yes, ma'am."

"What did his orders say Captain Wakeman was to do in the event a foreign ship challenged United States sovereignty of the area you were patrolling?"

"They said he had to, uh, counter any such challenges."

"He had to? No vague wording?"

"The orders said 'shall,' ma'am, and I was taught 'shall' and 'will' means you have to do something."

"Captain Wakeman had to do something. What?"

"The orders didn't specify, ma'am. They said he should do what was necessary and appropriate."

"Did they say what he shouldn't do?"

"Sort of. That's the word they used. Should. Captain Wakeman 'should' refrain from doing anything which would, uh, cause adverse effects on, uh, US foreign policy." Paul fought to keep his voice steady as his memory faltered. He'd gone over those orders a hundred times in recent days, trying to memorize the critical passages, and had intended doing so again last night. Jen's surprise had altered those intentions, not that Paul regretted that fact even as he desperately tried to dredge up the right phrasing from his memory.

"And what does 'should' mean?"

"It means you ought to, ma'am."

"Ought to? Not have to?"

"That's right, ma'am."

Garrity began pacing slowly back and forth. "Let me see if I understand your testimony, Ensign Sinclair. You were asked by Commander Herdez to provide an analysis of your operating orders for the USS *Michaelson*'s last patrol. You did so, stating that the orders were broad, vague and unclear."

"Objection. Ensign Sinclair never characterized the orders as 'unclear'."

"I will rephrase. Ensign Sinclair stated the orders were broad and vague. The orders left considerable room for the captain's judgment as to what actions would be necessary and appropriate in carrying out the ship's primary mission, while cautioning the captain in less forceful language not to undertake other unspecified actions. Those orders took precedence over standing orders and instructions according to what the United States Navy teaches even its most junior officers. Is that an accurate summation?"

Paul had no idea how his words were being received by the members of the court-martial or any of the spectators or even Wakeman himself. He kept his eyes locked on Lieutenant Commander Garrity, afraid his composure might be rattled beyond repair if he saw negative reactions too clearly displayed. "Yes, ma'am. That's what I said."

"Given that interpretation, did Captain Wakeman's actions fall within the parameters set by his orders?"

"Yes, ma'am, I would argue that they did in most cases." There was a rustling sound, as of people whispering and moving, but Paul stayed fixed on Garrity.

"You think Captain Wakeman did the right thing in every instance cited by the prosecution?"

Paul licked his lips, trying to wet his dry mouth and throat before answering. *This one question could make or break my credibility. Careful. Careful.* "No, ma'am. I do not think he did what I would personally consider the right thing in every instance."

"Then why are you defending the fact that he took such actions, Ensign Sinclair?"

"I'm not defending Captain Wakeman's actions. I'm not saying they were right. I'm saying that his orders could be interpreted by a reasonable person to have authorized Captain Wakeman to do much of what he did."

"You're saying he acted according to his orders."

"In most cases, yes, ma'am."

"Because those orders were worded broadly enough, vaguely enough, that they authorized Captain Wakeman tremendous freedom to act in carrying out a mission he was required to carry out."

"Yes, ma'am."

"Don't you believe Captain Wakeman should be held accountable for the errors in judgment he made as a result?"

Paul stared at her, perplexed. *Why is she arguing against Wakeman? Or is she just trying to bring out stuff Wilkes is sure to bring out when he gets a shot at me?* "Yes, ma'am. We all have to be held accountable when we make mistakes. But if you give me an order, and word it so vaguely that I'm not sure what it is I'm supposed to do or how, and I guess wrong, then I'm not the only one responsible for whatever happens. Whoever issued the orders shares responsibility."

"You're saying Captain Wakeman's errors occurred as a result of the orders he was operating under? That therefore holding him solely accountable for those errors would be... what?"

"Unjust, ma'am." Another rustle of sound. Paul hoped he wasn't sweating, at least not so anyone could tell.

Garrity came to stand directly before Paul, her face stern. "Let's establish something for the record, Ensign Sinclair. Do you like Captain Wakeman?"

"Ma'am?"

"Captain Wakeman. Do you like him? As an individual?"

"No, ma'am."

"Do you respect him? Do you think he was a good commanding officer?"

Paul licked his lips again. "No, ma'am."

"A good leader?"

"No, ma'am."

"Did you personally agree with most of the decisions made by Captain Wakeman during the period leading up and including the encounter with the SASAL ship?"

"No, ma'am."

"Then why are you here, Ensign Sinclair? Why did you volunteer to testify in his defense? For a man you neither like nor respect as a commanding officer?"

"Because... I thought it was my duty to do so."

"Your duty? To strive for what result?"

"A just result, ma'am."

"Thank you, Ensign Sinclair. No further questions."

Paul took several deep breaths as Garrity walked back to the defense table, then stopped, afraid of hyperventilating. He kept his eyes lowered and unfocused, not willing to scan the crowd of spectators.

"Trial counsel, you may cross-examine."

Commander Wilkes walked briskly up to the witness stand, then eyed Paul with just a trace of disdain apparent. "Ensign Sinclair, how long have you been a naval officer?"

Paul had expected a question along those lines. "Almost five years, sir."

Wilkes raised one skeptical eyebrow. "Five years? I'm not talking about time at the Academy, Ensign. I'm asking how long you've been a commissioned naval officer."

"Almost five years, sir."

Captain Nguyen broke into whatever Wilkes had been planning to say next. "Excuse me, Commander Wilkes, Captain Holmes. Midshipmen at the US Naval Academy are commissioned naval officers. Ensign Sinclair's answer is accurate."

Wilkes nodded, recovering quickly. "Thank you, captain. Let me put it this way, Ensign Sinclair. Aside from periods spent in school or training, how much time have you spent in actual fleet operations?"

The question stung coming from Wilkes, someone Paul was certain had never spent a day in the fleet, but Paul kept his voice from betraying that emotion. "About six months, sir."

"Six months? That's all?"

"Yes, sir."

"Whereas Commander Garcia has over sixteen years of fleet experience?"

"Yes, sir."

"And whereas Lieutenant Sindh has six years of fleet experience? But you only have six months?"

Lieutenant Commander Garrity stood. "If it please the court, trial counsel is badgering the witness. The defense is prepared to stipulate that Ensign Sinclair has relatively less fleet experience than the other officers who have testified."

Judge Holmes nodded. "Very well. Let the record so stipulate. Move on, Commander Wilkes."

"Yes, Your Honor. Ensign Sinclair, how would you characterize your performance as a fleet officer?"

"Objection."

"Sustained. Commander Wilkes, copies of Ensign Sinclair's fitness evaluations to date have been entered in the court records. We don't need to go over that ground in your questioning."

"Yes, Your Honor. Ensign Sinclair, your legal experience is limited to four weeks, isn't that correct?"

"No, sir. My legal *training* is limited to four weeks. Since reporting to the *Michaelson* and being designated the ship's legal officer, I have been involved in legal issues on almost a daily basis."

"I see. Do you think this qualifies you as a lawyer?"

"No, sir."

"Do you aspire to be a lawyer?"

"*No*, sir."

Wilkes indicated his data link. "I have a supplemental statement from Commander Garcia which I'd like to enter into the record. Commander Garcia states in it that Ensign Sinclair used his legal duties as an excuse to avoid carrying out his line officer duties."

Judge Holmes looked over at Garrity. "You're not objecting?"

Garrity stood and smiled. "No, Your Honor. The defense would also like to enter a supplemental statement into the record. A statement from Commander Herdez, Commander Garcia's superior officer, to the effect that Ensign Sinclair spent time on ship's legal officer duties only in direct response to tasking from her and Captain Wakeman."

"I see. This appears to come down to a personnel management issue. What would the members recommend?"

Admiral Fowler grinned. "Let's junk both of them."

Wilkes actually looked rattled for a moment. "Admiral?"

"You heard me. I don't see where entering these statements into the record will prove anything. I'm sympathetic to the feelings of a department head that one of his subordinates is being diverted from his primary duties by a collateral duty. But I am also sympathetic to the demands made upon the time of a junior officer and the need to devote time to responding to appropriate collateral duty tasking from his superiors. Unless Commander Garcia's statement contains an itemized list of incidents and times where Ensign Sinclair failed to carry out his primary duties as a result of lower-priority tasks related to his job as ship's legal officer, I don't regard it as proving anything. Captain Nguyen? Captain Feres?"

Nguyen nodded. "I agree, admiral."

Feres frowned, then nodded as well. "I can see grounds for complaint on Garcia's part but... yes, admiral. There's no point in introducing these statements."

"Captain Valdez? Captain Bolton? Do you also agree? It's unanimous, Captain Holmes."

Wilkes seemed ready to continue to his argument, but Judge Holmes forestalled him with one hand held up in a stop gesture. "It's decided, Commander Wilkes. The members make a persuasive case. Neither supplemental statement will be entered into the court record. Please continue with your questioning of Ensign Sinclair."

"Yes, Your Honor. Ensign Sinclair, when Captain Wakeman prepared to fire a warning shot at the SASAL ship, did he ask you for advice on his authority to do so?"

"Yes, sir."

"And what did you tell him regarding his use of force at that point?"

"I told him that my interpretation of our orders was that they authorized him to fire the warning shot."

"You told the captain he could fire on the SASAL ship?"

"*No*. Sir. I told the captain our orders said he had discretion to act as he deemed necessary and appropriate. That was about firing a warning shot across the bow. The issue of actually firing on the ship was never addressed to me."

"Didn't Commander Herdez, the ship's executive officer, question the captain openly about the wisdom of firing that warning shot?"

"Yes, sir, she did. That's why the captain asked for my opinion on whether our orders authorized him to do it."

"So, in the face of obvious concern by the ship's executive officer, you told Captain Wakeman that he pretty much had a free ticket to do whatever he wanted?"

Paul took a moment to answer, trying to ensure his voice remained steady. Experience in reporting to, and being chewed out by, seniors like Garcia and Wakeman gave him the confidence to do so. "No, sir. The captain asked me about whether our orders authorized him to fire a warning shot. I told him I thought they could be interpreted to do so."

"Didn't that warning shot cause the SASAL ship to change course and precipitate the events which led to Captain Wakeman destroying that ship?"

"Objection. We cannot determine the cause of the SASAL ship's actions."

"I'll rephrase the question. Didn't the SASAL ship immediately change course after the *Michaelson* fired that warning shot, a course change which led to Captain Wakeman's decision to fire on the ship?"

"Yes, sir."

"Then you bear some of the responsibility for this tragedy as well, don't you?"

"Objection. The preliminary investigation of these events did not implicate Ensign Sinclair as being in any way responsible."

Wilkes shook his head. "Perhaps that conclusion should be revisited. If Ensign Sinclair's advice led Captain Wakeman to take a decisive action, his role in this should be closely examined."

Garrity faced the judge even though she addressed her question to Wilkes. "Are you claiming Ensign Sinclair's advice was inaccurate or incorrect to the best of his knowledge at the time?"

"I don't have to claim that. If he told his captain something that helped precipitate the chain of events which led to the destruction of another ship, then that taints his testimony."

"Wait a minute," Admiral Fowler interrupted the lawyers' verbal sparring. "Captain Holmes, may I?"

"Certainly, admiral."

"Commander Wilkes, you seem to be asking Ensign Sinclair why he answered to the best of his ability a question put to him by his commanding officer. Captain Wakeman asked Sinclair what their orders said regarding his discretion to act. In response, Sinclair provided the information his commanding officer asked for. As my mother always says, 'what're you gonna do?'"

"That's right," Captain Feres agreed. "What was Ensign Sinclair's alternative? Are you suggesting Sinclair should have refused to answer, or provided information he believed to be incorrect?"

Commander Wilkes smiled briefly. "No, sir. Of course not. But if Ensign Sinclair's advice contributed to the course of action followed by Captain Wakeman, then that would motivate Ensign Sinclair to attempt to exonerate Captain Wakeman and, by extension, himself."

Fowler frowned, looking at his fellow officers to either side. "That seems like a real Catch-22 to me, commander. If he gave his captain bad advice, then he's indeed guilty of contributing to these unfortunate events. But you're saying if he gave his captain good advice, or simply advice which to the best of his knowledge accurately reflected a portion of the orders under which they were operating, then he's still guilty because he'd be motivated by a desire to exonerate himself. Your line of questioning doesn't seem to leave Ensign Sinclair any proper course of action to follow. I repeat, what're you gonna do?"

Lieutenant Commander Garrity turned to face the judge. "If it please the court, I'd like to stipulate that during the verbal exchange in question Ensign Sinclair gave Captain Wakeman a response which to the best of his knowledge accurately reflected the information in the relevant portion of their operating instructions."

Commander Wilkes shook his head. "I would object to such a stipulation, sir."

Holmes twisted one corner of her mouth, looking toward the members to gauge their feelings. "I'm not willing to declare that Ensign Sinclair's advice was necessarily correct, but there's a presumption it reflected a reasonable interpretation of the *Michaelson*'s orders unless the trial counsel is willing to provide evidence to the contrary. Do you intend to present such evidence, Commander Wilkes?"

"No, Your Honor. I am not prepared to do that."

"Very well. Objection sustained. Commander Garrity's objection, that is. You may continue your questioning, Commander Wilkes."

Wilkes eyed Paul for a moment, his face hardening. "Ensign Sinclair. You've indicated you have little legal training and little fleet experience. You earlier stated you dislike your captain personally and professionally. Your department head expressed dissatisfaction with your performance as one of his subordinates. Are you prepared to state why you believe your testimony has any value compared to the other witnesses who have appeared before this court?"

"Objection. Trial counsel is harassing the witness."

The judge looked to the members once more. "Do the members of the court-martial believe the witness should be compelled to answer this question?"

Admiral Fowler nodded. "I'd certainly like to hear Ensign Sinclair's reply."

"Overruled. The witness is directed to answer the question."

Paul hesitated. *And it's a real good question, isn't it? Why should anyone care what I have to say? Not enough experience and a lot of screw-ups in the little experience I have had.* He still didn't look around, still afraid of what he might see on the faces of the others in the courtroom. *Jen believes in me. I hope. Does anyone else. Do I? Ever since I reported to the* Michaelson *I've been wondering whether I can handle this. Whether I'm good enough. Whether in a couple of more years I'll be another Jan Tweed, hiding from my bosses and from myself.*

Reporting to the *Michaelson*. Worried. All too aware of his inexperience. The first member of the crew he'd encountered, the man who'd brought him across the gangplank to the quarterdeck for the first time. Senior Chief Kowalski. *"You're doin' okay, sir. I think you're a good officer."* Even as he recalled that brief bit of praise, Paul knew it held the answer he wanted. Paul looked straight at Commander Wilkes. "I believe my testimony has value because I am an officer in the United States Navy, sir."

Wilkes stared back for a long moment, then turned away. "No further questions."

Judge Holmes looked to Lieutenant Commander Garrity. "Do you wish to redirect?"

"No, Your Honor. No further questions."

"Do the members of the court-martial wish to question Ensign Sinclair?"

"I do." Admiral Fowler regarded Paul for a moment, while Paul tried to fight down dizziness born of mixed tension and relief that the bout with the lawyers was over. "Ensign Sinclair, what was your major at the Academy?"

"International relations, sir."

"A bull major, huh?" Non-technical majors at the Academy were always labeled bull majors on the assumption that unlike hard science they primarily involved something similar to the end product of a bull's digestive process. "I guess you did a lot of reading."

"Yes, sir."

"Do you figure you're an expert on language as a result?"

"No, sir."

"What about legal language? Do you understand that real well?"

Paul swallowed before answering. "No, sir. Not real well. Enough to get by."

"You seem to have some pretty firm opinions about what those orders meant. How do you square that with what you say is your lack of expert language abilities?"

For some reason, that question caused defiance to flare briefly in Paul. "Sir, I didn't think operational orders were supposed to require experts in legal language in order to understand them."

Fowler's eyebrows rose for a moment. "Do you get along well with your superiors, Ensign Sinclair?"

"I... try to do my job, sir."

"What about Commander Garcia? He's your department head, right? Has he ever chewed you out?"

That had to be the easiest question he'd been asked. "Yes, sir."

"Did you deserve it?"

"Often enough, yes, sir."

"But not always."

"No, sir. I don't think so."

"Do you have trouble understanding orders given to you in the course of a normal work day?"

"No, sir."

"What would Commander Garcia say?"

"Sir... Commander Garcia has... expressed a different opinion on occasion."

"But not always."

"No, sir."

"You're ship's legal officer, so you also work for Commander Herdez. If I hauled her back onto the witness stand, would she say you can understand and execute orders?"

"Yes, sir, I believe she would."

"What about your own enlisted? If I brought them in here and asked them, would they say you know how to issue clear and understandable orders?"

"Yes, sir."

"Do they respect you?"

"I believe so, sir."

"Do they like you?"

"My enlisted, sir? I... have no idea."

"You've never asked them?"

"No, sir!" Fowler settled back, a small smile briefly forming. *You tried to trap me, didn't you, admiral? See if I was being professional with my enlisted, maybe if I'm really professional at all. I'm glad I didn't have to think about my response. But was Fowler impressed or just amused? Was he just playing with an ensign who stuck his neck out?*

Admiral Fowler looked around. "That's all for me. Anybody else have questions for Ensign Sinclair?"

Captain Nguyen leaned forward. "Ensign Sinclair, have you ever made any mistakes?"

That one was easy, too. "I've made a lot of mistakes, ma'am."

"What about this decision? To testify as part of Captain Wakeman's defense? Suppose Captain Wakeman is found guilty of all charges regardless of what you testified, and suppose as a result you are tarred with the same brush and find your naval career effectively terminated before it had barely begun. Will you regard this as a mistake?"

Paul stared silently at Captain Nguyen for a moment before replying, trying to fight off the sick feeling her question had brought back to full life. "No, ma'am."

"You wouldn't be unhappy?"

"Ma'am, I'm already unhappy." It wasn't until the members of the court all reacted that Paul realized his blurted reply could be construed as humorous.

Captain Nguyen smiled briefly, then turned serious again. "Ensign Sinclair, do you hope to ever serve under Captain Wakeman again?"

"No, ma'am."

"Not in any capacity whatsoever?"

"No, ma'am."

"Suppose Captain Wakeman is exonerated as a result of your testimony and returned to duty, and you received orders to serve under Captain Wakeman again. What would you do?"

Paul hesitated again, then suddenly knew without looking that Commander Herdez' eyes were locked onto him, awaiting his reply. *Herdez is a good officer. Hard as hell, but good. What would someone like Herdez, a good officer, say?* "I would serve under him and attempt to carry out my duties to the best of my ability, ma'am."

"Even though you've testified that you neither like nor respect Captain Wakeman? Why would you do that, Ensign Sinclair?"

"Because... because my duty isn't to Captain Wakeman as an individual. My duty is to the United States Navy, ma'am."

"I see." Nguyen looked toward Admiral Fowler. "I'm done."

Judge Holmes thanked Paul, then excused him as a witness. Paul stood carefully, worried that his legs might wobble, and made his way back to his seat.

Garrity stood as Paul sat down. "The defense rests."

"Lieutenant Commander Garrity, will Captain Wakeman be availing himself of pre- or post-Gadsden trial procedure?"

"Post-Gadsden, Your Honor."

"Very well. The court-martial is closed, and will reconvene at thirteen hundred in this courtroom for Captain Wakeman's statement, followed by closing arguments."

12

Paul waited, listening to others leaving, before he stood and made his way out of the courtroom. He was vaguely aware of some of the senior officers still standing in the room, and as he turned into the central aisle found his path blocked by Commander Herdez, who was talking to Commander Sykes. "By your leave, ma'am."

Herdez turned her head, saw Paul, and stepped aside so he could pass, her expression still revealing nothing. "Certainly, Ensign Sinclair."

Paul went out the door, took two steps to the side to clear the entrance, then fell back against the bulkhead behind him. *It's over. For me. One way or the other. I hope.*

"Where have you been?" Jen was there, eyeing him with an enigmatic expression. "How long was I supposed to wait out here?"

"I didn't know you were waiting."

"You think I'm going to let you wander around alone in the state you're in? You're a wreck, Paul."

"Is it that obvious?"

"It is to me. You probably fooled everyone else."

"I just hope it accomplished something."

"I'd be willing to bet it did, but regardless, you did what you wanted to do." Jen leaned close enough to whisper to him. "You're good, Paul. And I'm not just talking about last night."

"Really? You think I did okay?"

"Last night or just now?"

"Jen! Just now."

"You're not supposed to discuss your testimony with anyone, Ensign Sinclair." But Jen smiled approvingly, then moved away a little before speaking in a normal voice. "You got any lunch plans? Or are you going to sit in the courtroom through lunch again?"

"I think I feel like eating today."

"Good. Some of us are heading for Fogarty's. You in?"

"Sure."

In addition to Paul and Jen, "some of us" turned out to be Bristol, Meadows, and Denaldo. Jen took a seat across from Paul, then waved dramatically toward him. "Our hero."

Meadows grinned. "So, Paul, how much fun was that?"

"My fun meter is pegged, Carl. Right off the scale."

"I know you can't talk about what you said, but how'd it feel up there on the witness stand?"

Paul smiled and shook his head. "I wouldn't recommend it unless you wanted to know how it feels to face a firing squad."

"Yeah. I bet. They could have at least offered you a blindfold. I'm glad no lawyer asked me what my department head thinks of my work. Or what I think about my department head, for that matter. What was that bit about Wakeman having a choice of pre- or post-Gadsden trial procedure? What's that mean?"

"It's the way the next phase of the trial is handled. Used to be military trials would finish with the defense and prosecution making their final arguments, and the defendant wouldn't make a statement of any kind until after the court-martial members announced a verdict."

"Huh? What's the point of the defendant not making a statement until after he's found guilty? What good does it do then?"

"It was just supposed to affect his punishment. You know, stuff like I'm an orphan and I didn't really do it and even if I did do it I didn't mean to do it. The punishment he'd be sentenced to wouldn't be determined until after the defendant made a statement."

"That still sounds lame," Carl observed.

"Yeah. That's what Gadsden was about, I guess, whether or not a defendant could make his statement before the verdict was reached. They ended up doing the Solomon thing and sort of splitting the difference. The defendant gets to decide. That way he or she can't complain if their statement goes over the wrong way."

"So Wakeman's going to swear he's innocent of all charges, huh? That ought to be interesting to watch."

"Maybe. Maybe not. I really don't know what he's planning on saying. Garrity may not either. And Wakeman doesn't have to make a sworn statement. He can also make an unsworn statement. That is, he'd be giving his side of things but not swearing that what he's saying is true."

Bristol looked puzzled. "Why would anyone do that?"

"Because if they make a sworn statement they can be cross-examined on it. You can't be questioned about anything you say in an unsworn statement. It's a Fifth Amendment thing. You know, the right against self-incrimination."

"Oh. You can't make someone testify against themselves. Right?

And I can see where certain defendants wouldn't want to be asked questions about whatever they planned to say."

Paul grinned. "Exactly. Now you tell me something. How'd Suppo manage to get Mangala sent to Ceres Station?"

Bristol gazed back in apparent shock. "Commander Sykes? Are you implying he had something to do with Mangala's orders?"

"Perish the thought. How'd he do it?"

"Trade secret." Bristol grinned around his sandwich. "Don't mess with the supply officer."

"After that? No way. He might serve us cannonballs again."

"Won't bother me if he does," Jen declared. "I'll be on the USS *Maury*, living easy."

Carl shook his head. "Why do you think the *Miserable Maury* will be so easy? She's just another ship."

"That's what you think. She's a ship in long-term refit, and word is something critical on her breaks every time you look cross-eyed at her. I can't imagine how many times I'll get to wave goodbye to you guys while the *Merry Mike* sails off to cruise the sea of stars." Jen pretended to wipe away a tear. "I'm getting all emotional just thinking about it."

"Me, too," Kris agreed. "Don't forget you're still close enough for me to kick. And don't forget you'll probably be given a job trying to fix all that stuff that breaks at the drop of a hat."

"I'm stuck doing that now. At least if my ship is broken in port I can head out for a beer after work instead of standing a watch in the middle of the night in case the evil Virgins of Vega attack."

"Speaking of which, I hear there's a sequel to that movie coming out."

"Really? Is it going to be as bad as the first one?"

Kris grinned. "I hope so. I'd thought the first batch of Vegan Virgins used up all the silicone on their planet for their boob jobs, but apparently they found a fresh supply to, um, equip another invasion force."

"Maybe that's why they're trying to invade Earth again," Bristol suggested. "Mars needs women, Vega needs silicone."

Paul chuckled. "Maybe Mars should be invading Vega."

"Or Vega should be invading Franklin Station," Carl sighed. "We could use a few of those Virgins around here." He paused as Kris and Jen glared at him. "Sorry. I could use a few of them, I mean. Not to imply there's any shortage of virgins here. Or of exceptional women of any kind."

"Better quit before you dig it any deeper, Carl," Bristol laughed. "Save me a couple of those Vegan Virgins, though. You want a few, too, Paul?"

Paul kept himself from looking toward Jen but felt his face warming. "Uh, no. None for me, thanks."

Carl faked astonishment. "You're turning down Vegan Virgins?"

Kris sniffed disdainfully. "Paul simply has too much class to be interested in sluts like that."

"How can a virgin be a slut?"

"It's possible. Believe me. Maybe Paul's also allergic to silicone. What do you think, Jen?"

"Am I supposed to care what other people think about Paul Sinclair?"

"Well, he is your friend."

"Oh. In that case, Paul's obviously high-class and also possesses excellent taste in friends." Jen smiled at Paul while the others laughed.

Paul laughed as well, though partly in relief that an awkward moment had passed. *Yesterday at this time I was dreading the day Jen left the Michaelson. Today I'm looking forward to it because it'll mean we won't have to pretend to be uninvolved. Talk about things changing fast.*

By the time they finished eating Paul felt mostly recovered. The small group ambled back to the courtroom, finding the rest of the officers from the *Michaelson* were already there. Most of the department heads formed their usual cluster, with Lieutenant Junior Grade Yarrow hanging around the fringe like an adoring puppy. Off to one side, Commander Sykes and Commander Herdez stood talking to each other. Paul watched the last two for a moment. "That's kind of a funny pair, isn't it? I can see why Sykes doesn't want to hang with the other department heads. But why with Herdez?"

Bristol looked surprised at the question. "You really don't understand? Sykes and Herdez have a lot in common."

"You're kidding. Suppo's a major slacker, and Herdez is tighter than the atoms in a black hole."

"So? You're missing the fact that they both get the job done, and done right, and don't worry about blowing their own horns. Professionally, they're two of a kind."

"I'd never thought of that." Paul glanced at Sykes and Herdez again. *It's true. I'd happily entrust myself to the leadership of either of those two. Their leadership styles couldn't be farther apart, but like Bristol says, they get the job done.* "I guess you're right. They still seem like an odd couple, though."

"There's been odder couples," Kris Denaldo observed. Jen shot her a look under lowered brows, but Paul thought no one else noticed the by-play.

"It only looks odd," Bristol insisted. "It may seem weird, but those two are soul-mates in a way. Not that I ever expect them to end up in bed together."

Kris opened her mouth again, but whatever she'd been planning to say was interrupted by Jen's elbow jabbing into her side. "Ow."

"Are you okay, Kris?"

"Yes. Just a sudden pain in my side."

"Maybe it's something you ate," Jen suggested.

"I don't think so. It looks like everyone's heading in. Time for the big finale."

No longer in stand-by as a witness, Paul didn't have to sit in the front row anymore, so he stuck with the other junior officers as they entered the courtroom. Jen, towing Kris Denaldo with her, made a point of moving several seats over from where Paul, Carl and Mike Bristol sat down. The department heads scattered through the room, as if fearing being hit by the same bolt of rhetoric Wakeman might aim at another of their number. Lieutenant Sindh, a few seats down from Paul, stared grimly ahead. But Commander Herdez walked steadily to the front row, taking a seat near the center.

"The court-martial will come to order." Judge Holmes looked toward the defense table. "Commander Garrity, does Captain Wakeman still desire to make a statement prior to the final arguments?"

"He does, Your Honor."

"Very well. Captain Wakeman, you have the right to make a statement. Included in your right to present evidence are the rights you have to testify under oath, to make an unsworn statement, or to remain silent. If you testify, you may be cross-examined by the trial counsel or questioned by me and the members. If you decide to make an unsworn statement you may not be cross-examined by trial counsel or questioned by me or the members. You may make an unsworn statement orally or in writing, personally, or through your counsel, or you may use a combination of these ways. If you decide to exercise your right to remain silent, that cannot be held against you in any way. Do you understand your rights?"

Wakeman stood. Paul suddenly realized that Wakeman hadn't spoken out loud for the last few days, his only communications being whispered discussions at the defense table. Now, Wakeman's voice sounded almost rusty as he replied. "Yes."

"Which of these rights do you want to exercise?"

"To make an unsworn statement, orally, in person."

"Very well. You may take the witness stand and proceed." Despite the controlled temperature in the courtroom, Wakeman seemed to be perspiring as he mounted the steps to the witness stand. He paused for a moment after seating himself, as if he'd forgotten he wouldn't be sworn in before making his statement, then swallowed, cleared his throat and glanced down at his data link before speaking.

"The captain of a ship has many responsibilities. Many duties. I have done my best, my very best, to carry out all those duties. I have done my very best to execute the orders I have been given. Because I took my responsibilities so seriously, because I was so concerned with following the orders I had been given, I now find myself facing a court-martial."

Carl tapped Paul's elbow to attract his attention, then rolled his eyes dramatically. Paul smiled to indicate he understood Carl's message. *Poor Cap'n Pete. I may not like the things he was charged with, but this devoted-to-duty martyr routine is too ridiculous. To us, anyway. I wonder what the court-martial members think about it after all they've heard about him so far?*

Neither the admiral nor any of the captains gave any clue as to their thoughts as Wakeman continued. "At every point in the pursuit and encounter with the SASAL ship I made what I thought were the best decisions based on the information and advice I was given. That is surely what is expected of a ship's commanding officer. Indeed, if I hadn't made those decisions, I might well be facing charges for shirking my duty."

"But what I could not anticipate, what I could not overcome, was the failure of my own subordinates to adequately or properly support me. They gave me bad information, they gave me false information, they gave me recommendations which led to tragedy. I don't know what motivations were involved. I don't know why they failed to support me as well as I had supported them so often in the past."

Paul tried to keep his face as emotionless as he'd seen Herdez manage. *I can't believe Wakeman has the gall to be saying this. It's enough to make me wish I'd let him hang.*

Beads of sweat were visible on Wakeman's forehead. "I am guilty of nothing but attempting to carry out my orders. Nor am I fully convinced that all the facts have been brought out here, that the real mission and intentions of the SASAL ship have been accurately determined. Its actions clearly demonstrated a threat to my ship. Was I to allow my ship to be destroyed through failure to act? If so, I would surely deserve this court-martial. But I did not. I acted."

Paul stole a glance at Lieutenant Commander Garrity, sitting at the defense table with her elbows on the arms of her chair, her mouth resting against her hands where they were clasped together so that her expression could not be read. *Surely Garrity didn't advise Wakeman to make this kind of statement. Surely she's not happy that Wakeman's still trying to blame everyone else for Wakeman's own bad decisions, still trying to claim the SASALs were doing anything but playing a stupid and dangerous game. But she's a JAG. How is this "my subordinates let me down" stuff, and this "my ship was in peril" stuff, playing with the line officers among the court-martial members, all of whom have commanded ships themselves?*

Wakeman wiped one hand across his forehead. "I ask you to support me as the commanding officer of a ship, support me in a way my own subordinates did not. In a crisis, they failed me. I ask you not to fail a fellow officer. Do not condemn me because I cared too much, tried too hard, as commanding officer. My record prior to this... this tragedy speaks for itself. I cared about my ship and her crew! If I am convicted, some future captain will stay his hand when he should act in self-defense for fear of a similar fate. I'm sure such distinguished officers would never permit such a precedent to be set. Thank you."

Admiral Fowler raised a hand, stopping Captain Wakeman in mid-rise to leave the witness stand. "Captain Wakeman, I know you're not required to answer any questions about your statement, but I'd like to ask one anyway."

Lieutenant Commander Garrity was on her feet. "Admiral—"

Garrity was herself interrupted by Judge Holmes. "Admiral Fowler, we are legally prohibited from questioning Captain Wakeman regarding his statement."

"Even if he agrees to answer voluntarily?"

"Captain Wakeman is on trial. Nothing the court asks of him can be viewed as entirely voluntary."

Fowler nodded brusquely. "All right."

"Thank you, admiral. Commander Wilkes, is trial counsel prepared for closing argument?"

"Yes, Your Honor."

"Please proceed."

Wilkes faced the members. "Captain Wakeman has been charged

with many violations of military law, but all of those charges come down to one common element: the culpably negligent and derelict behavior of Captain Peter Wakeman in carrying out his duties as the commanding officer of the USS *Michaelson*. Nothing the defense has presented has refuted the basic facts of the case, that Captain Wakeman failed to maintain his assigned patrol duties, recklessly closed on another ship, and fired a shot at that ship without sufficient justification, after which Captain Wakeman failed to maneuver to avoid the possibility of collision, instead choosing to fire directly upon and destroy the other ship. It wasn't simply careless, it wasn't simply a misinterpretation of his orders. It represented culpable negligence. It represented dereliction of duty in failing to conform to orders and instructions with which Captain Wakeman was required to be familiar. I ask you to find Captain Wakeman guilty on all charges and counts, for he has failed in the most basic elements of his responsibilities as a commanding officer of a US naval warship, with tragic results."

Wilkes returned to his seat and Lieutenant Commander Garrity rose, also facing the members. "Captain Peter Wakeman was placed in an impossible position by orders which provided little guidance and broad responsibilities. Captain Wakeman's orders specifically called upon him to use his own judgment to determine which actions were necessary and appropriate to carry out a mission which had to be fulfilled. The decisions he made in attempting to carry out the mission were arguably misguided and even improper, but they were not criminally negligent or culpable. When suddenly embroiled in a crisis situation, a situation no one had anticipated, he was repeatedly warned of firing solutions and detections of possible weapon preparations. It doesn't matter that in hindsight we know the other ship was unarmed, what matters is that Captain Wakeman had to make a decision at that moment based on what he knew and what he was being told. I ask you to find Captain Wakeman innocent of all charges and specifications on the grounds that his actions were legitimate, even if flawed, attempts to carry out the letter and spirit of the orders he was operating under."

Garrity sat down again. Judge Holmes looked from the trial counsel to the defense counsel, then to the members. "Admiral Fowler, do you anticipate being able to render judgment tomorrow?"

"I can't promise that, Captain Holmes, but I think it's very likely. We still have the bulk of the afternoon and all evening to deliberate on this."

"Will ten hundred be an appropriate time to convene tomorrow?"

"I'd prefer oh-nine hundred, Captain Holmes. We ship-drivers start to go a little stir crazy if we can't start work until ten hundred."

"Very well. The court-martial is closed, and will reconvene tomorrow morning at oh-nine hundred in this courtroom."

Kris Denaldo gazed back at the door to the courtroom. "Well, tomorrow the wait is over. We find out what happens to Wakeman. It's going to be a long night for some people." She shifted her eyes to look at Paul and Jen. "I'm sure it'll pass quickly for you two, though."

Jen made a face. "Very funny. I've got duty tomorrow. First watch. I can't risk being late for that, so I'm sleeping onboard tonight."

"Oh? Well, I guess I could get a rent-a-shack if you need privacy."

"I am *not* going to be in need of privacy, thank you, Miss Denaldo. You know that sort of thing isn't allowed on a ship."

"You think you'll get caught?"

"Even if we don't, the crew has a way of finding out about that sort of thing. Which I don't need. And if we did get caught, I'd end up in Herdez' stateroom getting a lecture on keeping my raging hormones under control. Which I need even less."

"Oh, okay." Kris grinned mischievously. "In that case, Paul, I'm available if you need any company tonight."

"Back off, Denaldo! He's mine." Jen glared at Paul. "You'd better not even be thinking about it."

"I'm not. I'm too nervous to think about anything much but that verdict tomorrow. I guess I'll stay on the ship, too."

"Don't get any ideas. I meant what I said."

"I never doubted it. But we've watched a lot of movies on duty nights, right?"

"Okay. As long as you don't try to hold my hand."

"Can I do the yawn and stretch bit where my arm comes down around your shoulders?"

"You can if you want to lose your arm," Jen answered with a grin. "Any other questions?"

"No goopy-eyes?"

"Definitely no goopy-eyes. See ya, Kris."

They headed back toward the ship, quiet for a few moments. Paul, despite his worries, savored the sensation of Jen being near. "Jen, can I ask you something?"

"Maybe. What?"

"What's 'Jen' short for?"

She gave him a flat look. "Jenevieve."

"Jenevieve?"

"Is something funny?"

"No, no. It's just... you don't seem like a Jenevieve."

"Which is why everyone calls me Jen. And everyone will continue calling me Jen. Right?"

"Right."

"Good. Don't walk so close."

Paul edged out about a foot. "This isn't going to be easy."

"I never said it would be. Am I worth it?"

"Absolutely."

"Then stop complaining." But she grinned to take any sting out of the words. "What kind of movie are you interested in?"

"I don't know. Something mindless."

"With or without explosions?"

"Uh... doesn't matter."

"Mindless and with or without explosions? I think we have a few hundred movies in the ship's database that fit that description. Maybe we'll just do a random pull and see what pops up."

"Sounds like a plan."

"Admiral Fowler, have the members reached findings?"

"They have."

Paul was seated in the back, with Carl and Kris. Jen had been the officer of the deck on the quarterdeck when he left, waving a brief hello before returning his salute and granting permission to leave the ship. She'd miss the climax of the whole proceeding, but there really wasn't any way to justify asking that Jen be excused from duty just to watch a result which most of the other officers from the *Michaelson* were present for.

"Are the findings on Appellate Exhibit Seven?"

"Yes."

"Would the trial counsel, without examining it, please bring me

Appellate Exhibit Seven?" A long minute passed while Judge Holmes studied the exhibit, her expression providing no clue as its content. "I have examined Appellate Exhibit Seven. It appears to be in proper form. Please return it to the president." Holmes looked directly at Wakeman. "Captain Wakeman, would you and your counsel stand up please. Admiral Fowler, announce the findings, please."

Fowler looked around the room, his eyes lingering for just a moment on most of those present before returning to the document he held. "Captain Peter Wakeman, this court-martial finds you guilty of one count of violating Article 92, Failure to Obey Order or Regulation, as to the ninth specification, derelict in exercising command functions during crisis, and one count of violating Article 111, Drunken or Reckless Operation of Vehicle, Aircraft or Vessel, by failing to order necessary maneuvers to open the projected closest point of approach for another ship on a near-collision course. This court-martial finds you not guilty of all other charges and specifications."

"Does defense counsel wish to present any matters in extenuation or mitigation?"

Garrity glanced at Wakeman, who was sitting rigid next to her. "No, Your Honor."

"Admiral Fowler, have the members reached a sentence, or do you require further time for deliberations?"

"The members have reached a sentence."

"Admiral Fowler, would you announce the sentence please."

"Captain Wakeman, this court-martial sentences you to receive a letter of reprimand, to be placed in your permanent service record, for your failure to exercise command functions and your reckless operation of the spacecraft entrusted to your command by the United States Navy. It is also the unanimous recommendation of this court-martial that your qualifications to command units of the United States Navy or other portions of the Armed Forces of the United States be reviewed to determine whether sufficient grounds exist for their being revoked for cause."

Paul blew out a long, slow breath. *They didn't convict him of very much, but they're still hanging Wakeman in a way. His career is dead from this point forward, and everything he may have accomplished in the past is now overshadowed by this verdict and sentence. He'll never be promoted again, and if he's smart he'll retire as fast as he can put his papers in. I guess that's the bone being thrown to the SASALs. We're not saying we're at fault, but we're not letting the individual directly responsible off, either. Is that just? I think so. Wakeman is getting what he deserves and no more than that.*

But, then, I didn't have relatives among that SASAL crew. Nothing we could have done to Wakeman would have brought them back, though.

Fowler looked around the courtroom, then nodded to Judge Holmes. "That's all."

"Thank you, admiral." Holmes called Wakeman to his feet again and began reciting a long statement regarding Wakeman's right to appeal and the judicial review process which the court-martial's record would undergo. Paul let his attention wander from the legal boilerplate, really relaxing for the first time in he didn't know how long. A momentary silence caught his attention again, and he saw Judge Holmes scanning the courtroom. "The court-martial is adjourned."

Paul sat still while everyone filed out of the courtroom, waiting until almost all the others had left before approaching Lieutenant Commander Garrity at the defense table. "Ma'am, is there anything else I need to do?"

She smiled at him. "No, Ensign Sinclair. You did everything you needed to do."

Captain Wakeman, who'd been sitting silently since the court-martial adjourned, stood up abruptly. Wakeman faced Paul, his expression stern yet also indecisive, then shook his head and walked away without a word.

For some reason, despite everything which had happened, Wakeman's reaction still stung Paul. "I don't suppose I should have expected Captain Wakeman to thank me."

Garrity looked at Wakeman's back as he left the courtroom. "I don't think I'm abusing attorney-client privilege if I tell you that Captain Wakeman probably didn't thank you because he genuinely has no idea why you testified in his defense. His universe doesn't have much room in it for the concept of altruism."

"I should know him well enough to understand that without your telling me. But..."

"He's probably also still trying to figure out what you hoped to gain by doing it."

"Ma'am, I'm still not sure of that myself." Paul caught a glimpse of Kris Denaldo standing for a moment just outside the door, and felt a sudden chill as the conversation and the sight of her brought to his mind something which hadn't occurred to him before. *Kris told me Jen admired my idealism. But Jen doesn't like people who have weak characters. If Jen had known I was unhappy with what was being done to Wakeman but that I didn't have enough guts to do anything about it, would she have reached the same decision about us? Was it just her orders to the* Maury *that made up her mind, or did my decision play a part, too? She'll probably never tell me, but if I know Jen, I also know it mattered to her, perhaps enough to make all the difference.* "Maybe I did gain something very important.

Something I had no idea was on the line."

"Besides your self-respect, and the knowledge you have the resolve to act upon what you believe in? Those aren't small things."

"No, they aren't. But the other thing's really important. To me, anyway. At least, I hope it turns out to be. Thank you, Commander Garrity."

"Don't you be thanking me, Ensign Sinclair." She offered Paul a handshake. "Thank *you*. I can honestly say that your testimony is most likely the only thing that kept Captain Wakeman from being convicted on at least a few more of the most serious charges, and suffering a much more severe sentence. The prosecution clearly established that Captain Wakeman failed in many respects to live up to the leadership responsibilities of a ship's commanding officer. As captain of the USS *Michaelson*, he would have been responsible for what he described as the failure of his crew to be able to carry out their duties. But even in his defense I couldn't find much evidence of such a failure."

"Then why didn't the court-martial hammer Wakeman? If they thought the crew wasn't responsible, then Wakeman would've had to be the one who failed."

Garrity nodded. "There's no question that had Captain Wakeman paid more attention to the support some of his crew offered, he would not have found himself and his ship confronting the situation they did. I'm only guessing, but I believe the members concluded that Captain Wakeman's failure to listen to his officers and subsequent flawed decisions didn't rise to the necessary levels of culpable negligence or dereliction of duty needed to convict Wakeman on those charges. I've no doubt the members disapproved of Wakeman's decisions, but it's a fact of naval service that when Captain Wakeman was placed in command of the USS *Michaelson* he was granted the authority to use his own discretion for better or worse. And your testimony established that his orders left reasonable room for arguing that Wakeman's decisions fell within the wide discretionary boundaries established by those orders. Thanks for playing such a critical role in the case, although I admit neither I nor anyone else expected that of you when all this started."

Paul took the offered hand, shaking his head as he did so. "My testimony couldn't have been that important. Commander Herdez—"

"Commander Herdez is obviously an excellent officer, and equally obviously an officer who believes it is her duty to support her commanding officer. That loyalty is commendable but since it left Commander Herdez little room to testify in any other way than she did, her testimony didn't carry nearly as much weight as it otherwise would have. You, on the other hand, had no obvious motive for your testimony. You're clearly not stupid, so you couldn't have believed that hitching your wagon to Wakeman would be a good career move. You didn't like the man and you didn't like what he'd done. But you still felt obligated by a higher sense of duty to testify in his favor. I guarantee you the members of court-martial were impressed by that."

"Well... thank you, ma'am."

"Are you sure you're not interested in becoming a lawyer?"

"No, ma'am! No offense."

"That's okay, Mr. Sinclair. Goodbye and good luck."

Paul headed for the door, seeing that everyone else from the *Michaelson* had now left. He was almost there when Commander Herdez appeared in the opening. "Ensign Sinclair."

"Yes, ma'am."

"Would you care to accompany me to the officers' club bar?"

"Ma'am?" Paul looked around, expecting to see other officers who'd been invited to the same location. *They must already be on the way there.* "Certainly, ma'am."

But when they reached the bar it was empty but for one table where Admiral Fowler and Captain Nguyen were already kicking back and swapping sea stories. Herdez stopped briefly to pay them her respects, then led Paul to the far side of the bar. "What are you drinking, Mr. Sinclair?"

"Rum and Coke, ma'am."

"A good choice. I'll have the same." Herdez sat silently until their drinks came, then for a few moments longer, taking an occasional sip of her drink. "They serve good rum here. Barbados. Martinique. Saint Croix. Have you been to the Caribbean, Mr. Sinclair?"

"Just on training cruises, ma'am."

"A lot of fine sailors left their bones in those waters, Mr. Sinclair. We carry a considerable burden when we don these uniforms. We need to live up to those sailors' finest moments, and avoid their worst failures. Both as officers and as individuals." Paul, uncertain as to what if anything to say, waited until Herdez spoke again. "Captain Wakeman is not the finest officer I ever served under. I know you're well aware of his shortcomings. It's easy to follow great leaders, Mr. Sinclair. They make it easy. You accomplish great things because they make it easy. The challenge for all of us is to succeed when we do not benefit from a great leader."

"I never thought about that before, ma'am. But that's true."

"I know how the junior officers think, Mr. Sinclair. I was actually an ensign once, myself." Herdez smiled sardonically as she took another drink. "They wondered why I backed Captain Wakeman the way I did, even when the captain's actions were clearly unprofessional or mistaken. You've wondered that, haven't you?"

"Yes, ma'am."

Herdez seemed to be looking through the far wall of the bar, out through the intervening bulkheads and out into empty space. "Duty is a very stern mistress, Mr. Sinclair. It left me no alternative. Ultimately, the decision on how to interpret and act upon our orders rested with Captain Wakeman. As your testimony made clear, Captain Wakeman was put in a very difficult position by the wording of his orders and his mission assignment."

"Lieutenant Commander Garrity said the same thing, ma'am, but I thought the members of the court-martial didn't seem all that impressed by the fact that I thought the orders were hard to understand."

"They were impressed, Mr. Sinclair. They wanted to be sure you could reason well, but I have worked with officers such as Admiral Fowler and Captain Nguyen in the past. I know they believe it is our responsibility to draft our orders in such a fashion that they can even be understood by an ensign. I hope you don't take that statement adversely."

Paul couldn't help smiling. "No, ma'am."

"Good. You, personally, revealed during your testimony and the cross-examination that you can understand and interpret orders. But if the orders received by you or any other officer favor confusion and convoluted sentences over clarity and conciseness, it is little wonder if those officers are left uncertain as to the proper course of action either before or during a crisis. It is also little wonder if such an officer takes steps of which we disapprove after we have provided so little clear guidance as to proper courses of action, even if the officer is already a paragon of good judgment."

Paul nodded, not saying what both Herdez and he knew, that Wakeman had been far from a paragon of good judgment.

Herdez looked back at her drink. "The orders issued to Captain Wakeman in this case only exacerbated the challenge to his personal judgment. He did not rise to the necessary levels of performance, but that is not a criminal offense. The members of the court, by their recommendation that Captain Wakeman's qualifications for command be reviewed with an eye to revocation, obviously believed that failure does indicate Captain Wakeman is unsuitable for further command-level assignments."

"Ma'am, even with those orders, wasn't there something else we could have done? Before something like destroying that SASAL ship happened?"

Herdez glanced at him. "What you're really asking is if *I* could have done something else. Correct? Because I was the officer in the best position to do so. But, as I said before, duty left me no alternative but to support Captain Wakeman's decisions."

"You could talk to the captain in private, couldn't you?"

"Mr. Sinclair, you heard my testimony. You know I did that. But that's as far as it can go. Publicly, I must back the captain's decisions. All of them. And the captain must trust me to do so. Do you understand why?"

Paul stared down at the surface of the bar. "Not entirely."

"You will. Someday. For now, let me ask you. Suppose I overruled one thing the captain ordered. Just one thing. What would happen forever after when the captain issued an order?"

"We'd all look to see if you were going to overrule it. Is that why you needed to back Captain Wakeman, ma'am? Because otherwise he wouldn't really be captain?"

She took another drink. "A good leader doesn't need unquestioning obedience. People follow that leader because they choose to, because that leader has their trust. A poor leader requires unquestioning obedience, because without that a poor leader will lose all meaningful ability to exercise command. Would I have been fulfilling my duty to the Navy if I had caused Captain Wakeman to lose his ability to command the ship?"

"I guess not. Then you're saying the worse a commander is, the better his or her subordinates have to be?"

"In a nutshell, yes. Captain Wakeman's weakness as a commanding officer required corresponding strength from his subordinates. You do understand why?"

The question could have stung, but Herdez' tone was that of a teacher, not a superior annoyed by the lack of understanding displayed by a junior. Paul nodded. "Yes. It makes sense. I mean, I can imagine if every officer on a ship was messed up, that ship would be a disaster."

"Exactly."

"But, commander, what happens when something like that ship encounter occurs? If we're backing the captain for all we're worth, and he's ordering something stupid anyway, what can we do?"

"What we did, Mr. Sinclair. Follow the orders, then accept the consequences and work toward a just determination of fault."

"There's no other alternative?"

"I don't know of one." Another uncharacteristic smile from Herdez. "Perhaps you'll find one, someday. One that works for you. It's not impossible. I've just never found one."

"Ma'am, if you've never found an alternative, I don't see how I could." Perhaps because of the rum, Paul let the words slip out, then flinched inside. *Buttering up the XO to her face? Who am I, Sam Yarrow? Yeah, I really meant it, but what a stupid thing to do.*

Instead of upbraiding him for the implied flattery, Herdez shook her head. "Don't underestimate yourself, Mr. Sinclair. You have a great deal of potential. Yes, you require a lot of learning, a lot of guidance. To be truly effective, such guidance shouldn't simply direct you to whatever goal a superior thinks is best. It has to let someone such as yourself realize on their own what they should do, and then give them free rein to do it. As you did. And when a subordinate does that, it gives great satisfaction to those who are endeavoring to lead them."

Paul took a long, slow drink to give himself time to think. *She wanted me to testify like I did. Why didn't she just tell me to do it, or tell me she wanted me to do it? But then I wouldn't have learned anything about myself, would I? And Jen sure as hell wouldn't have been impressed if all I was doing was following the XO's orders. So, thank God Herdez did it her way. But how did she guide me? Sykes. That talk Commander Sykes had with me. Herdez and Sykes are soul-mates, Mike Bristol said. Did she ask Sykes to give me that talk? Or did Sykes just understand she wanted him to do that, because they're on the same wavelength for things they think that matter? Sykes didn't shoot down Wakeman on the witness stand, either, come to think of it.* "Commander Sykes did a good job of that," Paul finally offered, curious to see how Herdez would react.

"Did he?" If Herdez had known of Sykes' talk before this, she didn't betray the fact in any way. "It's a shame Commander Sykes is a limited-duty officer. Despite his somewhat relaxed attitude toward some matters, he would have made an excellent line officer. You'd do well to continue listening to him."

I wonder if that's why Sykes eats meals with the junior officers? Any of the department heads could have been assigned that duty, but it's Sykes. I never realized how subtle the XO can be. "I will, ma'am."

"Good. Now, as to another matter." Herdez bent a hard look toward Paul. "I see that you and Ensign Shen are getting along very well together. *Extremely* well."

"Uh..." *Oh, God. She knows. The XO knows.* Paul wondered if the blood was actually draining from his face or if it just felt that way. *How'd she find out? What's she going to do to us?*

Herdez was looking at her drink now, as if unaware of Paul's pallor. "I believe I can trust both you and Ensign Shen to act with all due discretion and restraint as long as you are both assigned to the *Michaelson*."

"Yes, ma'am. Absolutely, ma'am."

"Make no mistake, if I had any doubts about either your or Ensign Shen's ability to act appropriately you'd be getting a different type of guidance, Mr. Sinclair, despite the very short time remaining in which both of you will be assigned to the same command. After Ensign Shen transfers to the *Maury*, you may make the relationship public, of course. But even then it is best not to flaunt it."

"We will act appropriately, ma'am. And I don't believe Ensign Shen has any intention of ever flaunting it, ma'am."

"I wouldn't have expected anything less from Ensign Shen. Or from you." Herdez looked at Paul again, a ghost of a smile on her lips. "Good luck to you two."

"Th-thank you, ma'am."

"I only have another six months left on the *Michaelson*, Mr. Sinclair. After that, I don't know what my follow-on assignment may be. But I will be keeping an eye on you. You've shown an uncommon measure of character."

"Thank you, ma'am."

"I'm sure you need to get back to the ship. Thank you for your time."

Paul had no trouble recognizing the polite but unmistakable dismissal. "Certainly, ma'am. Thank you." He left, blinking a little in the brighter light outside the bar.

Jen was still on watch, manning the quarterdeck, the bright brass of the ceremonial long glass gleaming from where it was tucked beneath one arm, her uniform a vivid splash of color against the grays of the surfaces around her. Both her enlisted watch standers appeared to be off running errands, leaving her temporarily alone on the quarterdeck. Paul rendered his salute to the national flag aft, then to Jen. "Request permission to come aboard."

She flipped a quick salute of her own in response. "Permission granted. Everybody else got back a while ago, so I already know what happened to Wakeman. Congratulations, I guess. Where have you been?"

"Having a drink with the XO." Paul barely stifled a laugh at Jen's reaction. "I'm serious. She invited me to a bar and we had a drink and a talk."

She leaned in to smell his breath. "You've had a drink, alright. What did Herdez want to talk about?"

"Leadership stuff. Why she backed Wakeman the way she did, what you have to do sometimes to carry out your duties, how to guide juniors to carry out their duty. Stuff like that."

"Wow. She gave you a one-on-one leadership talk? You got yourself a mentor, Paul. Herdez could be one hell of a sugar-daddy.

Assuming you survive having her as a mentor."

"Maybe. I think she was happy with the way I testified."

"How can you tell with Herdez? The woman's as emotive as a rock. Did you talk about anything else?"

"Uh... one other thing. Herdez also knows about, uh..."

"About what?"

"You. And me."

"*You told her*?!"

"No! She knew! I have no idea how."

Jen sighed and shook her head. "Okay. So we're dead meat. Are we ordered to stay a minimum of two meters away from each other until hell freezes over? Or are we just confined to quarters until I transfer off the ship?"

Paul grinned. "Neither. She told us to be discreet, with no inappropriate behavior while you're still assigned to the *Michaelson*, and wished us luck."

"Wait a minute. This was Commander Herdez? Was she drunk?"

"Uh-uh. I don't know, Jen, but for a moment there she seemed almost maternal."

"*Maternal*? Herdez? Are you listening to yourself?"

"Yes. I can't explain it. I think she likes you, Jen."

"Heaven help me. He thinks one of the primary banes of my existence likes me, and he thinks our XO is acting maternal, of all things. Are you going to tell anyone else about this little chat you had with Herdez?"

"I'm sure not planning on it."

"Good. I'd like my last days on the *Merry Mike* to be free of accusations of hitching my cart to a lunatic. After all we've been through, I don't need a personal crisis now to top it off." Jen favored

Paul with a half-stern, half-pleading look. "Do me a favor, Paul. Try not to get into another mess like this Wakeman thing again."

"I'll try. It's not like I asked to be in the last one."

"No, but people who are willing to tilt at windmills tend to find themselves doing it again and again." She smiled. "But what am I complaining about? I knew what I was getting into."

"So did I." Paul smiled back at her. "After a few months of pure hell, I'm looking forward to whatever the future brings again."

"Hell ain't over yet. In a few weeks you could be ordered out for another long patrol and I'll be left on the pier doing the teary-eyed girlfriend waving goodbye bit."

"Really? You'd do that?"

"No. Not the tears, anyway. But you're still part of the crew of a warship. I'm going to be on the *Maury*, so when you're underway I can't help bail you out of whatever your latest screw-up happens to be. At least you'll still have people like Carl and Kris to depend on, but they'll also be depending on you. Because, Mr. Paul Sinclair, your actions have branded you a leader of men and women, a leader who will be looked to for inspiration and guidance by the poor, benighted junior officers of the world."

"Yeah, I'm sure."

"You don't believe me? Just wait. They'll look to Paul, because Paul has shown he has the guts to make tough decisions and stick to them. Things'll get tough and they'll turn to you and say, 'Paul, what should we do?' Don't blame me when that happens. You brought that little extra responsibility on yourself."

Paul shook his head. "I have a lot of trouble believing that. I'm still the most junior ensign on the ship. They're going to look to me for leadership? I don't think so. All they'll be asking me is how

I convinced Jen Shen to be my girlfriend."

"Since the world hasn't exactly been beating down my door for that privilege, people may not be nearly as impressed by that status as you think. But if you want to believe anyone'll be envious, more power to you. Just remember what I said, Paul. They're going to expect you to keep showing leadership. That's going to make things harder. What else do you have to worry about? Herdez. She's still the XO, and assuming she likes you, that means she'll be riding you harder than ever. Then there's the new captain. Nobody knows what she's like. She's meeting with all the officers at fourteen hundred, by the way, so you probably get some clues then. Maybe she's another Wakeman or just a Captain Bligh. Maybe you'll get lucky and have a real leader for a captain, but you can't count on it."

"So it won't be any worse than it's already been. Okay, maybe it'll be a little worse. I'll survive, and I'll learn. I know that now. And I'll come back to that not-teary-eyed girlfriend."

"You'd better, mister. Because I'll be waiting. Unless my ship's underway, too. Are you still sure you want to date another sailor?"

"As long as you're that sailor, Jen." Paul drew himself up to attention, rendering a precise salute. "Request permission to proceed on duties assigned, Ensign Shen."

She shook her head at the professionally rendered but facetious request, then grinned. "As if *you* need permission from me, or anyone else, to go where your duty leads you. But thanks for asking anyway." Jen returned the salute. "Permission granted, Ensign Sinclair."

ABOUT THE AUTHOR

John G. Hemry is a retired US Navy officer and the author, under the pen name Jack Campbell, of the *New York Times* national bestselling *The Lost Fleet* series (*Dauntless, Fearless, Courageous, Valiant, Relentless,* and *Victorious*). Next up are two new follow-on series. *The Lost Fleet: Beyond the Frontier* continues to follow Geary and his companions. The other series, *The Lost Stars*, is set on a former enemy world in that universe. Under his own name, John is also the author of the *JAG in Space* series and the *Stark's War* series. His short fiction has appeared in places as varied as the last Chicks in Chainmail anthology (*Turn the Other Chick*) and *Analog* magazine (which published his Nebula Award-nominated story 'Small Moments in Time' as well as most recently 'The Rift' in the October 2010 issue). His humorous short story 'As You Know Bob' was selected for *Year's Best SF 13*. John's nonfiction has appeared in *Analog* and *Artemis* magazines as well as BenBella books on *Charmed, Star Wars,* and *Superman,* and in the *Legion of Superheroes* anthology *Teenagers from the Future*.

John had the opportunity to live on Midway Island for a while during the 1960s, graduated from high school in Lyons, Kansas, then later attended the US Naval Academy. He served in a variety of jobs including gunnery officer and navigator on a destroyer, with an amphibious squadron, and at the Navy's anti-terrorism centre. After retiring from the US Navy and settling in Maryland, John began writing. He lives with his long-suffering wife (the incomparable S) and three great kids. His daughter and two sons are diagnosed on the autistic spectrum.

RULE OF EVIDENCE
JACK CAMPBELL
(writing as John G. Hemry)

PAUL SINCLAIR RETURNS IN A THIRD THRILLING VOLUME

When the USS *Michaelson*'s sister ship, the USS *Maury*, is wracked by devastating explosions that destroy its engineering section, Paul Sinclair must find out what really caused the explosions. But the more he learns, the more he faces the terrible possibility that the woman he loves may be guilty of sabotage and murder.

"One hell of a series. A humdinger. The Paul Sinclair series remains at the top of my list of Great SF Books."
SF REVIEWS

TITANBOOKS.COM

AGAINST ALL ENEMIES
JACK CAMPBELL
(writing as John G. Hemry)

THE GRIPPING FINAL CASE FOR LIEUTENANT PAUL SINCLAIR

Someone onboard the USS *Michaelson* is selling secrets, and to uncover the traitor, legal officer Lieutenant Paul Sinclair must walk the dangerous line between duty and honor.

"Hemry's real-world experience gives the investigation and subsequent courtroom scenes a convincing feel. If you crave a legalistic space-*Hornblower*, you'll enjoy this one and you'll look forward to what he gets into next."

ANALOG

"Hemry concludes an exceptionally thoughtful and intelligent series on a strong note."

SF REVIEWS

TITANBOOKS.COM

THE STARK'S WAR SERIES
JACK CAMPBELL
(writing as John G. Hemry)

STARK'S WAR
STARK'S COMMAND
STARK'S CRUSADE

The USA reigns over Earth as the last surviving superpower. To build a society free of American influence, foreign countries have inhabited the moon. Now the US military have been ordered to wrest control of the moon.

Sergeant Ethan Stark must train his squadron to fight a desperate enemy in an airless atmosphere at one-sixth of normal gravity. Ensuring his team's survival means choosing which orders to obey and which to ignore...

"Gripping. Sergeant Stark is an unforgettable character. *Stark's War* reads as if Hemry has been there."
JACK MCDEVITT

"When it comes to combat, Hemry delivers."
WILLIAM C. DIETZ

"Hemry has combined a keen sense of action with a fine look at the morality of following orders, and produced a groundbreaking story in the same vein as *The Forever War* or *Starship Troopers*."
ABSOLUTE MAGNITUDE

TITANBOOKS.COM

THE LOST FLEET SERIES
JACK CAMPBELL

DAUNTLESS
FEARLESS
COURAGEOUS
VALIANT
RELENTLESS
VICTORIOUS

After a hundred years of brutal war against the Syndics, the Alliance fleet is marooned deep in enemy territory, weakened and demoralized and desperate to make it home.

Their fate rests in the hands of Captain "Black Jack" Geary, a man who had been presumed dead but then emerged from a century of survival hibernation to find his name had become legend. Forced by a cruel twist of fate into taking command of the fleet, Geary must find a way to inspire the battle-hardened and exhausted men and women of the fleet or face certain annihilation by their enemies.

Brand-new editions of the bestselling novels containing unique bonus material from the author.

THE LOST FLEET

"Black Jack is an excellent character, and this series is the best
military SF I've read in some time."
WIRED

"Fascinating stuff… this is military SF where the military
and SF parts are both done right."
SFX MAGAZINE

"*The Lost Fleet* is some of the best military science fiction
on the shelves today."
SF SITE

TITANBOOKS.COM

THE LOST FLEET
BEYOND THE FRONTIER: DREADNAUGHT
JACK CAMPBELL

THE FIRST VOLUME IN THE BRAND NEW
FOLLOW-ON SERIES

Captain John "Black Jack" Geary woke from a century of survival hibernation to take command of the Alliance fleet in the final throes of its long and bitter conflict against the Syndicate Worlds. Now Fleet Admiral Geary's victory has earned him the adoration of the people and enmity of politicians convinced that a living hero can be a very dangerous thing.

Geary is charged with command of the newly christened First Fleet. Its first mission: to probe deep into the territory of the mysterious alien race. Geary knows that members of the military high command and the government fear his staging a coup, so he can't help but wonder if the fleet is being deliberately sent to the far side of space on a suicide mission.

"Campbell combines the best parts of military SF and grand space opera... plenty of exciting discoveries and escapades."
PUBLISHERS WEEKLY

"Another excellent addition to one of the best military science-fiction series on the market."
MONSTERS & CRITICS

TITANBOOKS.COM